Amicus Humani Generis

Amicus Humani Generis

SB Zarben

P.D. Publishing, Inc.
Clayton, North Carolina

Copyright © 2005 by SB Zarben

All rights reserved. No part of this publication may be reproduced, transmitted in any form or by any means, electronic or mechanical, including photocopy, recording, or any information storage and retrieval system, without permission in writing from the publisher. The characters herein are fictional and any resemblance to a real person, living or dead, is purely coincidental.

ISBN-13: 978-0-9754366-5-3
ISBN-10: 0-9754366-5-1

First Printing 2005

9 8 7 6 5 4 3 2 1

Cover art and design by Cal
Edited by Day Petersen/Lisa Keeter

Published by:

P.D. Publishing, Inc.
P.O. Box 70
Clayton, NC 27528

http://www.pdpublishing.com

Acknowledgements:

I began writing *Amicus* in 2002 and would like to thank all the people who read and commented on the on-line version of the story. They were instrumental in providing the motivation to complete this novel, the longest piece of writing I have done to date. I unfortunately cannot mention anyone by name but I believe anyone reading this book will know if they fall into that category. My heartfelt thanks to you all.

I'd also like to extend my gratitude to the two editors, Day and Lisa, as well as the graphic artist, Cal. All of them played a huge part in making this novel what it is while displaying infinite patience with my numerous questions and requests. Thank you for your hard work and dedicaiton.

For my sister. My best friend, confidante, and occassional cohort who I will miss dearly while she's at grad school. I will learn to pronounce Massachusetts before she graduates!

Prologue

Deep in the bowels of the nothingness of space it sat, squatting like a sentinel over its domain. Its dark presence served as an admonition, a warning for any unfortunate enough to find themselves in the void.

Danger.
Death.
Go no further.

But this day, chaos had erupted within the controlled order – retaliation, a riot. It was inconceivable, unimaginable, but it had happened.

The wardens found themselves the immediate targets; they were eradicated quickly and without fuss. Barriers between species were forgotten as the escapees worked methodically through all the decks, freeing all allies and disposing of foes. Finally, they reached the airlock and the ships were launched, leaving Marson Alpha IV floating dejectedly in space, its broken hulk no longer capable of inspiring fear. It had been overrun by the very people it had held for all eternity, and it had been destroyed.

The escapees never once looked back. They were free.

Chapter 1

"Attention, passengers, we are now within viewing range of the Marson prison. You may proceed to Viewing Decks One through Four. We will remain in the vicinity for two hours. Please direct any questions to the personnel on your deck. Thank you."

Ensign Connie Barker sighed as the ship-wide announcement ended. She loved her job on the *USC Avenger*, but after almost six years of service, certain things were starting to get on her nerves. This particular run and that particular message were featured at the top of her list.

Barker was an archeologist. To the rest of the world she would only ever be known as a Doctor of Ancient and Extinct Civilizations of Earth, but she called herself an archeologist; it was much simpler. She had made a study of the humans of Earth through the 20th century and all the way up to the 24th, and was considered the leading expert on the cultures of that time period. When she first got her job on the ship, she had been just as enthusiastic as any passenger to be visiting the notorious Marson. She had known that it would take several trips to the abandoned prison to learn everything about it, and she had been right. Her historic interest had lasted for about six trips, and then the novelty had worn off. Now it was nothing more than a boring routine.

She sighed as she turned the corner and jumped onto the lift. She was assigned to Deck Four this trip. For the sake of appearance, she was there to answer questions and she often did. But in actuality, she was there to keep the peace. When Marson prison was included on one of the tour runs, people always reacted in strange, unpredictable ways. Barker supposed that it was justified, in a way. Marson had been one of the cruelest prisons in history, locking up thousands of people of different species for the totality of their lives, most of whom hadn't deserved it.

Barker cringed as she stepped onto her assigned deck and took up a position in the front against the viewing window. As the automated spiel about the prison droned on, a fuming Barker just barely kept herself from running out of the room. She knew everything there was to know about the prison, and it infuriated her that the things that would have shown the Coalition in a less than favourable light were omitted from the recording, or glossed over, or denied completely. Nine out of ten people who took the tours did so to learn the truth about the infamous prison. Barker felt that it was their duty to supply that truth in its entirety. If they didn't, what was the point of supplying it at all?

She ran a hand through her short-cropped blonde hair and shook her head. The inaccuracy of the information was something that had been bothering her for a long time, but Barker had quickly realized that fretting about it didn't do anything except give her a headache.

Finally, the recording ended, and she was relieved that she at least didn't have to deal with that annoyance any longer. She scanned the crowd for potential troublemakers. Finding no one that looked overtly hostile, Barker sighed and leaned back against the viewing window, hoping it would be a nice, calm shift.

~~*~*~*

"Captain Harrison?"

The captain turned and looked at her man on Ops. "Yes?"

"There appears to be a ship about four minutes out."

"Appears?"

"Yes, ma'am. The reading is erratic, but it appears to be dead in the water. I'm not picking up any energy output and it..." Lieutenant Thorp trailed off in uncertainty.

The captain walked over to the Ops console. "Lieutenant? And it what?"

He looked up into the intelligent brown eyes peering down at him. "It doesn't match any ship in our database."

"What?" Captain Harrison directed her attention to the console displays, taking in the minimal readings. She verified that their computers could not identify the vessel. "Someone get Barker up here...I want her opinion."

She walked back to her chair and sat, her mind churning with visions of lost ships or, even better, a new race of beings. No matter what it turned out to be, it was her duty as a Captain of the Coalition to either provide assistance to the passengers on the vessel or make first contact. "Send a message to the ship."

"Yes, ma'am." The Ops Lieutenant keyed in a greeting on standard hailing frequencies.

Barker arrived on the bridge just as the message was sent. She sent a questioning look toward the captain, who motioned her to look at the Ops console. Barker took a look at the configuration and could not see any resemblance to any Earth vessel, nor to any ship that belonged to the allied planets. Ever.

The view screen crackled to life seconds later, showing a picture of a dirty metal floor covered with debris. The crackling sounds of electrical fires could be heard amidst the tearing of bulkheads. Suddenly, the view screen tilted upwards, providing a picture of a battle-scarred man, humanoid in appearance.

He blinked owlishly into the screen for several long moments, not sure if what he was seeing was real. Finally, he spoke, "Hello?"

Captain Harrison stood and moved closer. The man on the screen was filthy, with all manner of cuts covering his strained face. "Hello, my name is Captain Harrison. Are you in trouble?"

The man blinked bloodshot hazel eyes at the image of the captain and then started to laugh. "Trouble? Hahahaha!"

His cackle was insane, the pitch of it rising and hurting Barker's ears.

"Trouble? Oh no, dear Captain. I'm not in trouble." He shook his head violently and grinned madly. "I was in trouble four weeks ago. I'm waaayy past trouble; I'm already dead. And you will be too, if you aren't careful." At the conclusion of his cryptic statement, the mad cackling started again.

Harrison pulled back a little, not sure if the man was truly mad or just appeared so after a long stint in hell. "Please, sir, I want to help you; we all do. Can you tell me what happened? Is anyone else alive?"

The laughing stopped abruptly as the man gathered his wits about him. "What happened? We were attacked by the spawn of Satan, that's what happened." His eyes cleared as a resounding screech ripped through his ship. He shook his head and refocused on the monitor. "Listen to me, Captain. The only way you can help is to leave, as quickly as possible. We'll take these monsters down with us. No use giving them a new target. Just fly, fly as far away as you can before they get you too!"

"We? Is there anyone alive besides you."

He shook his head. "I don't know. Last person I saw alive was Janus, but that was..." his voice trailed off as he thought for a moment, "...five days ago, I think. Janus went down to the decks flooded with radiation. I don't know what she hoped to do. Just run, Captain, for your own good. Like I said, I'm already dead."

"Running is not in my nature. It is my duty to help you."

The ragged warrior turned violently back to the screen, his face an angry sneer. "Listen to me, *Captain*." He spat the word like a curse. "Don't be stupid. You have no idea what you're dealing with here. The second you even attempt to save whoever is left here, they'll get onto you, and then what will you do? Huh? You'll die, that's what. Nice and slow. We couldn't do anything for four weeks; what makes you think you can just come in and save the day? You don't want to go fall into the hell we did."

Barker stepped forward and opened her mouth before she considered her words. "Excuse me, sir? But why don't you want our help?"

He focused on the new person, his upper lip twitching in annoyance. "Don't you get it? You can't help me; I'm gone! Don't risk yourself in a fight you can't win." He reached forward for the control panel as if to end the transmission.

"Wait! Please. You said you've been fighting this menace for four weeks. Surely you discovered some weakness, something we can use to get you out of there."

He paused for a moment, considering. "Do you have any plasma guns?"

"Yes."

"How about pesticide?"

"Pesticide?"

"Yeah, to kill bugs."

"Um, yeah."

"Okay. If you insist on risking your lives, I can't stop you. Mix the pesticide in the plasma guns. Come with lots of first aid gear and people who aren't squeamish. Oh, and avoid Decks Two through Seven, Nine, and Thirteen. Last time I checked, they were flooded with radiation. Probably more of them are by now. You can use our computer; most of the sensors are still working. Address it as Sandra."

"Sandra?"

"Do you have a problem with that?"

"Um, no."

"Good," he growled.

Harrison took over the conversation again. "What's your name?"

"Everson Patrik."

A high pitched screech filled the damaged ship, followed by the sound of tearing metal. Patrik ducked wildly, knocking into the view screen. The monitor tilted, giving the crew of the *Avenger* a view of the entire room. It was decimated; lifeless bodies lay scattered around the deck. Their attention was immediately drawn to a body falling into the center of the room.

Barker got closer and squinted. The floor of the deck above had been ripped away entirely. Her eyes widened as the person turned and landed clumsily on its feet. It was a woman, who stumbled and straightened, then turned and assumed a defensive stance as a grey creature pounced down from above. She stumbled back under the onslaught, then pushed it off and across the room. It came back swiftly and launched itself at the woman, baring long, hook-like claws.

Barker saw contact made as prey and predator once again tumbled to the floor. She heard an inhuman screech, followed by the crack of bone.

"Janus!"

As the *Avenger* crew watched, the woman turned and smiled and Patrik scampered out of his hiding place to slap Janus on the back.

"We 'ave ta get out of 'ere, Patrik. They are coming."

He nodded. "They're always coming. Someone offered to help us."

Janus snorted. "They stupid, or just suicidal?"

"I dunno. Why don't you ask them?" He pointed to the screen.

Janus turned and walked over to the screen, tilting it to better focus on her face. "If ya people want ta kill yourselves doin' this, I will not object. I would like ta keep on livin'. Patrik given you the details?"

Masking her shock, Captain Harrison stepped forward and nodded. Because the man had been human, she had assumed that the entire crew was. However, Earth origins would not have explained the ship not being in their database. "Yes, he has."

Janus grunted and turned as more screeching came from the hole in the ceiling of the deck. "Let us go!"

Janus and Patrik ran out of the control room, leaving the view screen active for the *Avenger* crew to see a horde of grey go thundering through the gap, chasing after their prey.

Harrison turned and started barking out orders. "I want the plasma guns modified, a team assembled, and a shuttle launched within the hour."

As crew members dispersed to carry out the commands, Barker determinedly stepped forward and locked eyes with her captain. "I want to go."

Harrison debated briefly. "Very well. But be careful, Barker."

"I will."

~~*~*~*

Barker careened around the corner and slid to a stop in front of the doors to the docking bay. Despite the potential danger, she was excited – this being almost like uncharted waters. They were facing a new enemy, something that the Coalition had never seen before, which in that day and age was highly unusual. She had gotten a good look at the aliens as they had swooped down, and she agreed with Patrik: they looked like the spawn of Satan.

They were grey, with a slightly triangular head, two main eyes with an additional two stalk eyes, and a mouth that wasn't really a mouth. It appeared as if the aliens' teeth extended beyond almost nonexistent lips to form a hard beak with pointed edges. These strange teeth looked strong enough to split a human hand in two. Its main body was almost a formless lump, with four ant-like legs. It also had an upper body, with two forearms branching off just below the head and neck, and ending in very long, sharp looking claws that curled inward at the end. They were perfectly suited for tearing into flesh and bone. Small bumps covered the head and body, and the entire entity was covered in a slimy ooze, so much so that if the creature stood still for even a moment, a large puddle would form. There appeared to be small spikes along the sides of the body. As a whole, it looked incredibly dangerous.

Barker took a deep breath before she stepped into the transport area and looked around. Including her, a group of eight crew members was going to board the besieged ship. They were mostly security personnel, trained to fight. There was also one medic, who looked extremely nervous. "You all right?" she asked softly.

The woman flinched, then turned and saw Barker. "Oh! You startled me, Ensign."

Barker cringed. She hated being called "ensign", it just served to remind her how low in the chain of command she was. The only reason she had even been assigned a rank was because the ship was a USC vessel, Sol Division, owned and operated by the United Space Coalition's headquarters on Earth. The USC was a military based organization and required all ships, whether they were military or not, to follow their regulations.

"Sorry. You looked a little nervous."

"Yeah." The medic nodded. "I can't believe we're doing this. We aren't supposed to have to risk our lives. This is a tour ship, for God's sake! I didn't sign on for this!"

Barker was just about to open her mouth when a deep voice answered for her. "Tour ship or not, Captain Harrison is a captain of the USC, and they are under standing orders to help anyone in trouble. The *Avenger* may be a tour ship now, but it wasn't always."

Barker smiled up at Melvin Kodiac, one of her best friends.

The medic looked suspicious and squinted her eyes. "What do you mean?"

The blonde ensign turned away from her friend and back to the medic. "Didn't you know? The *Avenger* used to be one of the most powerful warships in the Coalition. They decommissioned it because it was too much of a security risk."

Any reply the medic might have made was cut short as the leader of their rescue team bellowed out his orders. "All right, people, let's move out. It's time to go and rescue the weak."

Barker saw Kodiac wince at the officer's choice of words. Major Commander Samson was a total ass who took every advantage of his rank. His view of the world was dismal, and he looked down on anyone who had ever gotten into a scrape of any kind. He was also something of a Human Supremacist, a group that was violently opposed to the inclusion of alien species in the Coalition.

The eight would-be rescuers loaded into the shuttle, took seats, and waited for launch. Barker gripped her plasma gun tightly and looked at the grim faces around her. She knew that most of them were scared; it wasn't often that they had to face an unknown threat. The condition of the ship in trouble hadn't been very encouraging, either.

The shuttle launched and flew steadily toward the ship under siege. As they approached the docking bay, their shuttle started to rock violently, throwing everything not secured onto the floor.

"What the hell is going on?" Samson yelled at the pilot.

"I don't know, sir. There seems to be some heavy turbulence around the ship."

"Well, make sure you get us through in one piece!"

"Aye, sir."

Hating the rocking and lurching with a passion, Barker squeezed her eyes shut. She felt a sympathetic hand on hers and blinked one eye open to see Kodiac smiling at her. She managed a weak grin in return, then breathed a sigh of relief when they finally docked.

Samson stood and looked at his crew. "All right, we're all going except you." He pointed at one buff young man. "You stay here and keep the shuttle secure. The rest of you, come with me. And remember, we are dealing with an unknown threat here. Keep your eyes peeled and don't hesitate to shoot at anything that is grey and screeches at you. Move out!" Samson took the lead and the rest followed.

Barker did as he had ordered and kept her eyes peeled, not out of fear, more out of fascination. The ship was marvelous, unlike any she had ever seen. She recognized that the bulkheads were falling apart and there were numerous holes in all the walls and numerous bodies in various stages of decomposition, but she knew that cleaned up, it would be a wonderful ship.

She felt her stomach churn at the sight of a body that was burned beyond recognition. Barker looked away swiftly, stepping carefully around some wires.

"So," Kodiac spoke up, "how do we find these people we're supposed to rescue?"

"Patrik said to use the computer," Barker offered.

Samson stopped walking and gestured at the blank walls. "Do you see any computers around here?"

"Well, no, but...Sandra?"

A sleek, feminine voice answered. "Yes?"

Samson looked around, trying to figure out where the interface was.

"Can you tell us where Everson Patrik is?"

"Wait, please." A slight humming came from the walls as the computer searched. "Patrik is on Deck Twelve, hallway 32, junction 67."

"What about Janus?"

"Janus is currently off sensors."

"Oh. What deck are we on?"

"You are currently on Deck Eleven, hallway 12, junction 45."

"Um..." Barker paused, thinking. "Could you tell us how to get to Patrik?"

"Surely. Take ladder 19. It is 30 feet forward on the right."

"Thank you, Sandra."

"You are welcome." The computer fell silent.

Barker looked up at a scowling Samson. He really didn't like it when someone showed him up. *Ah well, he'll just have to live with it.*

Samson growled and started forward. They had only walked 10 feet when a high screeching sounded down the hall. "Take cover and get ready to shoot!" The team obediently dove behind any cover they could find and raised their guns.

A squad of four creatures came bounding down the hallway, jumping off the walls and ceiling, almost flying through the air. The claws could apparently also be used as rappelling devices, the aliens burying them in the ceiling and walls to allow themselves to swing and jump. As if they could read each other's minds, all four stopped and looked around.

Samson didn't want to risk them calling for reinforcements, so he yelled, "Fire!" and stood and began firing his plasma gun at the quartet. The rest of the team followed suit, and soon the body count of the grey things rose by four. Samson stepped back into the hallway and shook his head at the creatures. "Come on. I don't want to have to deal with many more of these." He led them in a slow jog until they reached the ladder without further incident. They climbed up one level and checked to be certain that the area was clear. Samson looked around. "Now where?"

Barker spoke up again. "Sandra?"

The computer replied, "Take a right. Then your second left and third right. Patrik will be there."

"Thanks."

Samson grunted his acknowledgement and started off again, keeping his plasma rifle raised. He hated aliens, hated their smell and look, hated how sometimes they looked human but weren't. If someone walked on two legs, had two arms and a head, ten fingers and toes – that was human. Some species possessed those same attributes but rearranged them. To Samson, that was a travesty of everything that was human.

The commander rounded the last corner, then stopped as he heard the unmistakable charge of a plasma gun. Barker peeked around Samson and blinked. There he was, the man from the view screen – Everson Patrik.

He looked even more seriously injured than he had when they had seen him on the viewer. He was slumped on the floor in the corner, his gun tiredly held at the ready.

"Hello? Patrik."

Patrik tilted his head, recognizing the soft voice from his view screen conversation. He thought hard, trying to remember if that conversation had been real, if Janus had been real. He didn't think she could have been. Before she had fallen down through the ceiling, he hadn't seen her in days. He had lost all hope, his last consolation was to be blowing up the ship and taking all the buggers with him.

"Are you...really here?"

Barker moved forward and gently lowered the arm that stiffly held the plasma gun. "Yes, Patrik. We're here to take you to our ship. Try to remember."

He stared forward, trying very hard to do as she had asked.

Barker watched as he tried to jog his memory and she saw his eyes slowly lose their glazed look, just as they had on the screen.

"Yes...yes I remember." He nodded and slowly stood. He cocked his head, seemingly listening to something no one else was hearing. "You should move." Patrik said to the female medic who was standing at the corner of their alcove.

"Why?"

"Can't you hear it?"

Samson was about to order the woman to move when one of the grey creatures barreled around the corner, Janus right on its heels. "Get back 'ere, ya slimy bastard." Janus leapt and tackled the creature out of midair, taking both of them to the floor.

Barker watched as the woman got her hands around its neck, or what she assumed was its neck, and squeezed. She heard a pop and the thing went limp.

Janus unwrapped her arms and stood, angrily pulling something out of the thing's grasp. She scowled and put the string around her own neck, then turned and noticed the others for the first time. "Oh. So yer them would-be saviours?"

The blonde ensign blinked, getting her first good look at this alien. Janus didn't actually look that much like an alien. In fact, the only visible thing that labeled her as non-human were the platinum colored designs traced across her otherwise deep brown skin. They were mostly large blotches of color in odd shapes, with a few swirls making the rare appearance. They traveled up the sides of her neck and face, and above and below her eyes. The left arm of Janus's coat had been ripped off, and the bared surface displayed a large wound and the fact that the platinum markings covered her arms as well.

Janus stepped through the small crowd toward Patrik. She bent down so her blue eyes were on a level with his. "Ya all right, Patrik?"

"Yeah...yeah, I'm good. Let's get out of here."

Janus grunted and straightened. "Ya 'eard 'im. Let us go before we 'ave ta fight our way out." She had already started walking toward the docking bay when someone called, "Wait!" Janus sighed and turned back, aggravated. "Aye?"

"You're both hurt." Barker motioned to Patrik who had slunk up next to his friend.

Janus glanced at Patrik and raised an eyebrow. He shrugged. "We feel fine. Do not 'ave time ta play doctor. Come."

Barker sighed and followed the two crewmates; Kodiac and everyone else trailed behind. Samson ground his teeth together and followed. Control of the mission had just been snatched away from him, and by an alien woman to boot! He blew out a heavy sigh of frustration, but knew that it wouldn't do to lose his temper. He was on official business, and making a scene would simply get his ass chewed out by his captain. No, he'd tolerate the disrespect, for the moment.

Janus stopped in front of a small hatch and grabbed the handle. She pulled, growling when it didn't budge.

"Um...don't we need to go down a level?" Barker asked hesitantly.

"Aye, but this is faster." Janus grabbed the handle and placed one booted foot on the wall. Her second foot followed and she pushed off with her legs, her hands still wrapped firmly around the handle. She pulled, feeling the strain all along her body. "Agh...stubborn ship...open...right...now!"

With a final heave, the hatch popped off, causing Janus's body to fly through the air and land heavily on the floor. She winced and rubbed the back of her head before hastily getting up.

Patrik edged up next to his friend and peered down the chute. "Janus?"

"Hmm?"

"Didn't those things get into these shafts first thing?"

"Aye."

Patrik squinted into the darkness. "Soooo?"

"So, I am agoin' first." She stepped up to the chute and slid her long body in before anyone could say otherwise.

Patrik stepped back and blinked, then sighed.

Barker gulped and looked around nervously. She really didn't feel as safe now that Janus was gone. She stepped closer to Patrik, knowing it wasn't the time to make idle conversation, but it was preferable to hear people speaking rather than just listening to the eerie sound of electrical fires and the nervous breathing of those around her. Everyone was waiting in tension-filled silence, hoping to God they wouldn't hear a screech traveling toward them. Yes, any conversation was preferable to all that.

Patrik glanced to his right as someone edged up next to him. It was that blonde from the other ship — Barker was her name. "What?" he snapped in annoyance.

"Are you two the only crew left?"

"I wouldn't know. You'd have to ask Janus, she's been all over this ship. But I do know that she hasn't brought anyone back."

"I see." Barker nodded and paused a moment before speaking again. "What um...species is she?"

Patrik sighed and looked directly at the woman. He didn't blame her for asking; it was a logical question. There was Janus, looking all human and everything, the only noticeable difference being her interesting platinum whorls. But he knew from personal experience that, in Janus's case, looks were indeed deceiving. "I don't know."

"You don't know?"

"Isn't that what I just said?"

Barker pulled back, surprised by his outburst. "Okay, that's fine."

"It had better be." Patrik harumphed and turned back toward the chute.

~~*~*~*

Janus braced her legs in front of her and hoped that if she hit anything, her momentum would move it out of the way. She winced as she felt herself sliding over glass and all manner of debris.

The aliens had quickly overrun the waste disposal chutes after the crew had used them to carry out an ambush attack that resulted in the deaths of eight grey beings. After that, all such shortcuts between decks were blocked off, and the crew became as cattle being herded to slaughter. They were outnumbered and also didn't have a clue as to how to defeat their assailants. It had been horrible, some of the worst weeks of her life, and Janus had experienced some pretty terrible weeks.

Blue eyes popped open as she sensed the end of the tube coming up. Problematically, the hatch at the end was closed. Janus squeezed her eyes shut in anticipation of the jarring impact that was to come. She counted down in her head: *three, two, one, impact!* She let out a strangled yell as she felt the shock all through her sorely abused body. Thankfully, the hatch popped off and she was soon landing on a hard metallic floor. *Rokuer!* she swore silently.

She instantly bounded to her feet, in case there were any lurking beasties. Janus didn't expect there to be anyone in the room, it was after all only a storage room, but she scanned the area and sighed when it proved to be clear. She walked back to the chute and rapped loudly on it three times, signaling to Patrik that it was safe for them to come down. Then she turned to wait.

~~*~*~*

Patrik heard the signal and glanced over at the man who seemed to be the leader of the little rescue operation. He was fuming. In the spirit of diplomacy, a spirit he wasn't too interested in keeping alive, Patrik made a choice. "You can send your people down now."

Samson hardly looked at the man, just grunted and started booming out orders. "Single file. Line it up then, and let's get moving."

"Shh! Keep it down or they'll hear you!" Patrik hissed, not very pleased with the prospect of dealing with more aliens.

Samson glared but lowered his voice. A little. He wasn't frightened of the aliens; he didn't perceive them as being a significant threat.

Each one made their way down the chute, landing clumsily but safely, with some support from Janus at the bottom. Samson slid down last, still scowling when he landed.

Janus took a head count and noted that everyone was there. "All right we have ta..." She trailed off and took three steps forward, listening.

Samson started forward, almost yelling at Janus, "Hey! We don't have time to stand around..."

She rounded on him swiftly, throwing an arm against his throat and pushing him back against the wall. "Listen. I do not care who ya are on yer ship. Ya are nothin' 'ere. Ya 'ave no idea what is goin' on. If I 'ear someone, I will do all I can ta get 'em out a 'ere. 'Cause what ya see in front of ya is it! So, shut up before I throw ya out an airlock!"

Janus released him and went back to listening intently. She stepped up to a large pile of twisted metal that was blocking off a small closet. Very faintly, she could hear the sounds of weeping. It was human, and most definitely a child.

"Emmeline?"

Patrik gasped and surged forward until he was beside Janus. He strained to hear, just as Janus had taught him, but couldn't detect anything.

A tiny voice sounded into the silence. "J...Janus?"

"Honey, are you all right?" Patrik asked anxiously as he futilely pressed his hands against the barrier.

"D-daddy?"

"Yes, sweetheart. Are you okay?"

"I'm fine, Daddy, but I'm scared. I want out!" the young child wailed.

Janus quickly took over. "Emmeline, ya need ta stay quiet. We do not want them ta come back. I am goin' ta get ya out of there." She stepped back and looked speculatively at the large pile of debris and twisted metal. It looked as if it would be impossible to move, but she was determined not to let that child die.

Patrik was well aware of the gravity of the situation. When he looked at his friend, it was the father in him that spoke. "I need my baby, Janus."

"Aye. And I am goin' ta give 'er ta ya."

"But...but..." He gestured helplessly at the immovable object blocking his daughter's path to safety.

A loud screech interrupted the tense silence. Janus turned toward the hall from where the creature would launch its attack. She saw everyone else raise their weapons and cried out, "No! Do not shoot it!"

"Are you crazy?" Samson yelled.

"Just listen ta me!"

Samson reluctantly lowered his weapon and gestured for the others to do the same. Janus stepped toward the door, but stopped when a hand grasped her arm.

"Janus, you can't! It almost killed you the last time!"

She looked into her friend's hazel eyes and smiled quietly. "Aye, it did. But it is the only way ta get yer daughter out, so, let go." Janus shook her arm free and moved forward.

It was only moments before the creature came sliding around the corner, its four strange, beady eyes focusing solely on Janus.

Janus taunted the creature as it prowled around her. "That is right. Ya remember me, 'ow could ya not? Only spent the last week 'untin' us. Come on." She started backing slowly toward the barrier between Emmeline and Patrik. Janus didn't take her eyes off the alien as she waited for it to lunge. When it did, she was ready.

The grey being jumped and Janus threw her hands up, capturing it around what served as a neck. She dug her fingers in, and there was a reaction almost immediately.

Patrik and the rest watched as a bluish cloud slowly appeared around Janus's hands. The platinum markings on her skin darkened for an instant before glowing silver as Janus assimilated the energy from the alien's body.

* ~ * ~ * ~ * ~ *

Barker watched in amazement as Janus dropped the alien and turned to focus on the pile of metal debris. Janus's body rocked slowly from side to side as the newly absorbed energy was dispelled toward the barrier. Slowly, the pile rocked, and then moved away from the door, as if under its own power. Seconds later, the blockage was resting against another wall, the door was open, and Emmeline was free.

Patrik ran to his daughter and scooped her up, then held her close as she cried against his shoulder.

Janus was suddenly hit by the shock of having processed so much foreign energy through her body. She fell over onto her side and shut her eyes, gasping for breath and trying desperately to order the chaos in her mind.

She hated absorbing their energy. For whatever reason, the life force of the grey aliens was totally incompatible with the workings of her energy transfer, and, as Patrik had intimated, the results had nearly been deadly. The first time she had directed her powers toward them had been several days earlier, near the beginning of the attack, and she had used the innate weapon that had always worked flawlessly for her. Her energy burst had taken out two decks and at least twenty-four aliens, but she was unconscious for nearly three days afterwards. That in itself was highly unusual. When she awoke on the medical deck, one of the last places to fall to the attackers, Janus had been shocked to learn of her extraordinary negative reaction. She didn't remember any of it.

Now recovering from the smaller energy expenditure, Janus gasped and rolled over onto her back. She blinked up at the ceiling as her mind slowly started to clear. Looking at the debris around her, she fuzzily decided that it was despicable how dirty the ship was.

A gentle patting on her cheek brought Janus's mind screeching back from where it had been floating in recovery. Cloudy blue eyes looked up into hazel ones that were a replica of Patrik's.

"Janus, you okay?"

"Aye, little Emm. I am fine now. 'Ow about ya?"

"Mmkay. Thank you for getting me out, Janus."

Janus slowly sat up, wincing as her body protested. "But a course, Emm. I need ya ta 'elp keep yer pa in line, right?"

When the little girl giggled and wrapped her skinny arms around her hero's neck, Janus closed her eyes in relief, seeing that Emmeline was none the worse for her internment. Janus had been worried about Patrik since his daughter had disappeared, and she knew that he would be in a little better shape now that his entire family wasn't gone. Emmeline in her arms, she stood and looked around, seeing compassion on most of the faces in the room. The single exception was Samson. His look was one of contempt. That didn't matter to her.

"All right...let us get out of 'ere. This way."

Barker was in awe of Janus. The display of raw power and caring was something truly new. She had never before encountered such a species. There were numerous races that had mental abilities of some kind, but none that actually absorbed energy from other living things. And typically, people who had advanced mental capabilities – as Janus did – were weaker physically, but Janus was very strong. She did not carry any gun that Barker could see, but was nevertheless victorious in combat. And she spoke...Barker scrunched up her face, trying to place it. Janus spoke as if English was not her first language, which was understandable, but she seemed very familiar with the dialect. And she almost sounded like someone from Earth. It was a puzzle, and one thing Ensign Connie Barker liked was puzzles. She was very much looking forward to talking with the woman.

* ~ * ~ * ~ * ~ *

Janus stopped and peered around the corner. The docking bay was only twelve steps in front of them, but it didn't feel right. Reaching it had been too easy. She knew the aliens were undoubtedly aware that more people had arrived on the hapless ship. There was no way they were oblivious to that fact. And it wouldn't turn out to be much of a rescue if she led their rescuers directly into an ambush by the enemy.

She sighed and rubbed her head, trying to get rid of the headache that would have dropped a Zwkonian Ruper. And those things were huge. *Ah well.* Janus looked down at her left shoulder, which had previously exhibited a large wound. *One good thing about absorbing that energy, I'm healed.* She was glad. The injury had been worrying her for a while and she was happy to be rid of that annoyance, even if the price was a horrendous headache.

Tentatively, she extended her senses, well aware of the effect the aliens had on her in that respect as well. She probed the area, but did not detect anything out of the ordinary. Janus motioned to Samson that he could proceed with his rescue, which he did.

They edged quietly but quickly down the hall, covering the short distance without incident. One by one, they filed into the docking bay and stood before the shuttle. When the door suddenly popped open, guns were raised instinctively, only to lower when the young man who had been left behind to guard the ship cautiously poked out his head.

Samson stepped forward. "Everything been okay here?"

"Fine, sir."

"Good. All right, everyone on!" The team gratefully piled into the shuttle, settling down with relief and glad beyond measure that the nightmare was over.

Patrik and Emmeline right in front of her, Janus filed in last. As they stepped inside, she gave Patrik a slight nod and he nodded back. The airlock door closed and the shuttle immediately launched, the artificial atmosphere cycling and soon taking on the regular properties of the *USC Avenger* rather than that of the damaged ship.

Patrik set his daughter down and removed a small remote from his pocket. He counted down in his head, and when he knew they were far enough away, pressed the button. An explosion rocked the shuttle, causing a few people to stumble.

Samson surged up. "What the hell was that?"

Patrik's tone was calm. "I blew up the ship."

"What on earth for?"

"To kill those things and keep them from following."

As Samson was about to retort, Patrik turned away from him and stepped forward to where Janus was kneeling on the ground, gasping for breath. He knelt down beside her and grabbed her hand.

"Pa...Patrik...I can..." Janus gasped, looking at her friend with wild eyes.

"What? Janus, what's wrong? I don't..." He watched helplessly as Janus fell to the floor, unable to breathe.

Barker hurried toward them. "We have to do something; she can't breath!" She turned on the medic. "Can't you help?"

"No!" Patrik yelled, "No, no medical treatment."

The ensign rounded on him. "Are you crazy? She'll die!"

Patrik wasn't listening; he was staring down into his friend's blue eyes, thinking furiously. *Come on, Patrik,* he berated himself. *Think! You should know what to do. What's wrong?*

His mind had been living in a dead zone for the last several weeks, and his brain was inconveniently having difficulty retrieving important information – like what was deadly for his friend.

Janus stared up blindly. It had been ages since she had had such a reaction, and she had been lulled into a state of complacency. She had taken for granted the friendly atmosphere of her ship, and the people there who knew what they could and could not do. Now she felt the elevated oxygen levels making her limbs heavy, and her mind started floating away. She could see the bewilderment in Patrik's eyes, knowing he was her only chance for continued survival.

Patrik listened as Janus's breathing became raspy and almost stopped. And then it hit him. "Oxygen!" He sprang up and looked about wildly. "You need to lower the level of oxygen in the air! Now!"

Samson looked at him in disbelief. "What? No way, it'll kill us."

"It will not. It was like that on my ship; we didn't even notice. It shouldn't be a big difference," Patrik snarled.

Barker was already taking action, accessing environmental control. "How much?"

"It shouldn't be above 18.5 percent."

She quickly made the adjustment and watched as Patrik knelt down next to his friend. Emmeline edged over next to them as well and plopped herself down next to Janus. She grabbed the large hand and started tracing the dull platinum markings there.

Patrik sighed in relief as he heard his friend's respiration rate pick up almost immediately. The large body shifted on the floor and he knew Janus would be out for a bit. He remembered the last time this had happened, almost six years earlier.

They had been embarking on a shuttle mission to another planet. It had been a newer shuttle, and no one had changed the regulation of oxygen. Within a few minutes of entering the ship, Janus had lost consciousness, but that time he had known what to do right away. Even so, she had been out for almost twenty minutes.

Emmeline smiled as the pretty silver marks on Janus's hand started getting brighter, more normal. When Janus was nice and healthy, they almost reflected light. Emmeline frowned as she recalled that Janus hadn't been so healthy in a long time and she'd missed it. *Maybe now that all the bad things are gone, Janus will get better and start acting normal again. Maybe Daddy will too. That would be good.*

Barker knelt beside Patrik and spent a moment looking at the now peaceful face. *She is really nice to look at,* Barker decided. "Is she going to be all right?"

"Yeah." Patrik nodded. "She'll be fine. Especially now that she's in a..." He tilted his head, looking for the right word, "healthy environment. Janus is a survivor." He nodded in affirmation and then seemed to zone out.

Barker stood and walked over to where Melvin Kodiac was sitting. She didn't know what Patrik meant by that – a healthy environment – but she was going to find out.

Chapter 2

Captain Harrison looked incredulous as Barker made a quick and detailed report along with her request. The entire thing was a little surreal, especially the part about this Janus character absorbing an alien's energy. But she had seen and accepted some pretty wild things in the past. If Barker said it really happened, then she believed it. "Okay, so what do you need me to do?"

"Lower the oxygen levels in the atmosphere, make sure it's not more than 18.5 percent. We won't even notice."

"And this needs to be done because...?"

"So Janus can breathe. Right now, she's still lying in the shuttle and Patrik won't leave her."

"I see." Harrison paused for a moment and pursed her lips. "All right, that's fine. But after you get them to the infirmary, I want to know more about the people who are on my ship. Understood?"

"Yes, ma'am. Understood."

"Good. Dismissed."

Barker smiled as she left the room. By the time she got back to the shuttle, the oxygen levels had been changed. Janus still hadn't awakened, but Patrik was adamant that she would soon. Barker and Patrik carried Janus between them to the infirmary and placed her on a bed. Patrik and Emmeline were then immediately surrounded by a plethora of medical personnel.

Patrik sat quietly as the staff tended to his cuts and ran scans. An occasional "ooohh" and "aahhh" floated to his ears. *I can only imagine what is coming up on those screens.* Emmeline sat quietly while she was poked and scanned, just like she knew Janus would. When she was done, she stared up at her papa for a long moment. He smiled and nodded. Emmeline jumped down and crawled up next to Janus.

Barker smiled as she watched the child, and then turned toward Patrik. "Lovely daughter you have."

He smiled a little, his eyes staying locked on her small frame. "I know."

Barker wasn't sure, but she thought he was a lot more relaxed now that the danger had receded and he had his daughter back. "How long was she missing?"

"Five days, maybe. We were hiding out in a small room while Janus went exploring on the irradiated decks. One day, the door was just ripped right off the hinges. I fought as hard as I could, but I wasn't a match for three of them. I told Emmeline to run, run and hide. And she did." His voice got quieter and quieter, until he was almost whispering. "I thought she was dead because Sandra couldn't find her. The only reason she survived was that she hid in a supply closet. Had lots of food and water." He was quiet for a moment, just thinking. "Anyway, that's when I went to the bridge, and I stayed there until you called and Janus showed up." He shook his head slowly, his eyes dull. "I thought I was all alone."

Barker swallowed hard. She hoped she would never have to go through something like that. "Forgive me for asking, but my captain would like to know as much as she can..." Her voice trailed off, her silence asking for his permission to continue.

He inclined his head slightly.

"Well, it just didn't seem like those invaders were that dangerous. We didn't have much of a problem defeating them, and Janus seemed to handle herself pretty well."

Patrik squinted as he tried to recall events that seemed as if they had happened so long ago. "When they first came, it seemed like there were hundreds of thousands. They just...overwhelmed us, sweeping through in groups of ten and fifteen. We had no idea how to fight them; our conventional weapons were almost useless. It was a fluke – finding out about the pesticide. There was a fight in a supply room and one man shot open some containers that were in there. It spilled over the aliens and they immediately retreated. We were lucky he made it back to tell someone else. But by then, it was too late." He turned and looked at Barker. "And you're right, Janus does handle them pretty well. She always seems to know what to do. If she had been able-bodied at the start of it all, everything might have been different."

"Wait, wait, what do you mean, able-bodied?"

"Remember when she absorbed that alien's energy?"

"Yeah."

"And I said it almost killed her the last time?"

Barker nodded silently, a sense of dread filling her.

"Well, she tried that same thing right near the beginning. Was out for three days. By the time she woke up, more than half our crew was dead and the intruders had infested the entire ship. No chance...we had no chance." He shook his head again. "But you guys, you guys knew how to kill them and were prepared. You also had less of them to deal with."

"What do you mean?"

"When there were only five or six of the crew remaining, the main force of aliens departed the ship. Just small groups stayed behind, hunting us."

"Hunting?"

Patrik nodded. "I've seen those things rip through walls and bulkheads, tear a man in two with surprising ease. We were being hunted, toyed with, stalked. It was worse than just getting your head ripped off." He fell silent after that and just sat staring at his daughter.

Janus awoke slowly, and, out of long habit, she stayed perfectly still and quiet. She listened as far off sounds became louder and more distinguishable. She extended her senses through the room and sensed a body cuddled up to her side that she quickly identified as Emmeline. She could hear Patrik's low voice not far from her and was aware of the movement of other bodies in the room.

It was an art, really, learning how to control her acquisitions so that she picked up only what she wanted. Her hearing was incredibly sensitive. The fluttering of an insect's wings or the gentle breathing of an animal of any kind, all of it she could pick up by simply focusing in on certain things and blocking out others.

In one smooth motion, Janus sat up and opened her eyes. She felt Emmeline's little arms wrap more tightly around her waist. Janus looked around and readily determined that she was in a medical bay of some sort. Her attention was drawn by the approach of Patrik and Barker.

Patrik stopped in front of his friend and smiled. "Hey, you okay?"

"I am fine."

"You scared me, you know. Something like that hasn't happened in a long time."

"Aye."

Barker cleared her throat and looked down at her shoes for a moment. When she glanced back up, she was looking directly into Janus's blue eyes. "My captain wishes to speak to you both as soon as possible."

"Aye."

Barker nodded and then looked at the anxiously hovering medical personnel. "Would you consent to having a medical exam?"

Janus looked at Patrik for a moment and then back at Barker. "Why?"

"Well, for starters, it's our policy when we take on passengers. That way, if something happens due to a pre-existing medical condition, we are not liable."

Blue eyes squinted as Janus focused fully on Barker. "Liable? I do not understand."

Barker blinked and pursed her lips, her eyes shifting from Janus to Patrik. She was just beginning to realize that despite Janus's human appearance and Patrik being humanoid, there were probably going to be just as many cultural problems as if they were both foreign aliens. "Um...well, it's this thing we have here: when something bad happens to someone, and that person thinks another person or group of people are responsible, they can take legal action."

Janus raised her head for a moment and then nodded.

"You don't understand, do you?"

"No."

Barker glanced helplessly over at Patrik. He just shrugged. "It's not important. Anyway, aside from the legal implications, you seem to have a unique physiology that we would like to learn about. So, may we?"

Janus blinked, then replied, "Aye."

Barker smiled. "Good. If anything makes you feel uncomfortable, just say so and we'll stop."

"Aye."

Barker and Patrik stepped back as two medical personnel came forward with some equipment.

Patrik looked around and then leaned down next to Barker. "Um...Janus won't be able to tell you much about herself."

"What do you mean?"

"She doesn't really care how or why she or anyone else works, just that they do. You know?"

"Yeah. I think I do."

The doctor stepped up to the bed where her remarkable patient was perched and waiting. "Hello, I'm Doctor Cobb."

Janus only inclined her head.

Doctor Cobb smiled and pulled out a triangular scanning device. "So, what can you tell me about your physiology?" She glanced up to see a raised eyebrow. "Uh...your body and how it works."

"Nothin'."

"Nothing?"

"Nothin'."

"Then how do you know what you can and can't do? Barker tells me you actually absorbed alien energy and used it to move a large slab of metal."

"Aye."

"And that after you absorbed that energy, a wound that you had was healed." As the doctor spoke, she pushed aside the ripped material covering Janus's shoulder. The only sign of an injury was the dried blood on clothing and skin. "Amazing."

"I was taught by me people. Just as ya are taught. And it is instinct."

"I see. Well, you must have some understanding of what you can do."

"Aye."

"Care to share? How did you absorb the energy? What do these do?" Tina Cobb questioned as she ran her fingertips along the silver marks on Janus's skin.

"I just do it, and they are a part of me." When Doctor Cobb looked questioningly at her, Janus sighed and decided to throw the human a bone. "Everythin' 'as energy: plants, animals, even this ship.

My people thrive on that energy, we use it ta 'eal and power our more complex abilities, like *marcontin*."

"*Marcontin*?"

"It is what we call movin' objects with our mind."

"I see. Humans call that telekinesis. So, this energy – do you feel it like a living thing, or do you just know it's there?"

Janus squinted for a moment and lowered her head. She had never given her abilities much thought, and now tried to think of a way to explain them. "I feel it. It is like a current that runs through everythin'. Some things have a stronger current than others, and when I touch somethin', I feel it against my skin. Everythin' is connected ta it in some way." Janus looked up at Doctor Cobb and the other people in the room, surprised to see the fascination on their faces.

"How?" At Janus's confused look, Tina hastened to explain. "How is everything connected, how do you know?"

"It is tied in with my senses. When somethin' abnormal 'appens, even as simple as droppin' that scanner," Janus pointed to the triangular device in Tina's hand, "it disrupts everythin' else, makes waves in the current that I feel."

"So you channel this energy and it does...what? Besides letting you do *marcontin*."

"It strengthens us by 'ealin' us; it allows for superior defense because ya can sense an attacker, 'ear 'em breathe, feel their steps. We can survive in an environment without the current for a long time, but livin' without it would be difficult for us since we do not often 'ave ta do so. Most of my kind would not last long."

The door to the medical bay whooshed open and Captain Harrison entered. As she strode into the room, she noted the expression on Doctor Cobb's face. "Everything all right, Doctor?"

"What? Oh! Yes, yes, ma'am, everything is just great." She nodded enthusiastically and stepped to the side to make way for the captain.

Harrison smiled as she got her first good look at Janus. *Very interesting.* She walked over to the woman and extended her hand. "Hello. I am Captain Harrison of the *USC Avenger*."

Janus's eyes, cold and calculating, scrutinized the captain. "You are Coalition." As soon as the officer had walked in, Janus had gone on alert. The uniform had changed over time, but she still recognized the emblem on Harrison's clothing, still had a vivid recollection of the events that had happened to her so long before.

Harrison stopped short, surprised that Janus knew she was a captain in the United Space Coalition and leery of the expression on the alien woman's face. "I am. Is that a problem?"

Janus stared at the captain, well aware that she was judging the woman based on the group she belonged to rather than as an individual. She knew that the Coalition of her memories was far different from the one that existed in the present, and even back then it had only been a small group of people who were responsible, and she also knew that she was not, in all likelihood, in danger from these people. And she didn't care about any of it.

Janus had a long, long memory, and when she confronted her past, logic never won out. Her heart did, as well as her feelings of hatred, rage, and suspicion.

"Aye. It is a problem." Janus's tone was curt, and, she walked out of the medical bay and never once looked back.

Harrison shook off her initial shock and turned to Patrik. "What the hell was that? I hope your friend realizes that she is a guest on this ship, and if she wishes to remain as such, she should show some respect. I simply will not condone behavior like that!" Harrison pointed at the door through which Janus had disappeared.

Patrik pursed his lips and stepped forward. "Janus will do the right thing in the end. As far as I'm concerned, her response was completely justified. I will not stand here and let you speak badly of her, when you don't have the faintest idea what caused her reaction."

He almost snarled the last sentence and Barker winced slightly at the re-emergence of the man she had met on the com screen and the ship. It seemed Patrik was very protective of both his family and Janus.

"And I suppose you do?" Harrison retorted.

"Yes, but it's not my story to tell. You will get nowhere with Janus with the attitude you just displayed. In fact, that will only help make her opinion of your precious Coalition more valid. The only knowledge she has of you and your...organization...is negative. What you do here will either change that opinion or reinforce it and make her hate all of you with a passion that is unmatched. Of course her initial reaction is going to be to walk out, to hate you, even though she knows that logically she shouldn't."

"Does she know that? How well do you know Janus?"

"Yes, Captain Harrison, she knows that better than any of you ever will. Janus is the most objective person I know, except when it comes to her past and the part the Coalition played in it. And I know her well, thank you very much. I hope you know, *Captain*, that Janus is probably the greatest ally you could ever hope to have, especially if those...things...start attacking you. It is in your own best interests to be patient with her." Patrik stared back at Harrison defiantly.

The tension between Patrik and Harrison was thick. It was obvious that Patrik had his own temper and didn't have as tight a lid on it as Harrison. And they pushed each other's buttons.

Barker watched Harrison closely, knowing that her captain had a monumental temper, that once unleashed wasn't very pretty at all. She could see a slight twitch at the corner of Harrison's eye, testament to her ire. But to the captain's credit, she calmed and gathered herself. Barker blinked as Harrison turned and looked at her.

"Barker, please go find our guest and make sure she is all right. Then if you could, bring Janus back here."

"Yes, Captain." Barker hurried out of the room and wound through the passageways of the *Avenger*, just letting her feet direct her. She didn't have a clue as to where Janus might have gone, since the woman didn't know the ship but obviously wanted to be alone. The ensign found herself entering one of the observation decks. She saw a form in the shadows, leaning against the wall. "Janus, is that you?"

A head turned and eyes locked onto Barker, who couldn't repress an involuntary gasp at seeing the shining silver colour of them. It reminded her of seeing a cat in the dark with a bit of light reflecting in its eyes.

"Barker? Ya all right?" Janus stepped out of the shadows and toward the woman. She saw the slightly perplexed look on the ensign's face and wondered what was bothering her.

"Yeah, I'm fine. It's just...your eyes were silver."

"They do that in the dark."

"Why?"

"I do not know." Janus shook her head and stepped closer to the woman. "This is a big ship."

"Yeah, I guess."

"Ya been on it long?"

Barker sighed. "A while."

"Ya do not like it?"

"No...it's fine. I guess I'm just getting a little bored with it, is all." Barker cocked her head, interested in what Janus would have to say now that she appeared to be in a more talkative mood. "How about you? Were you on that ship long?"

"Aye. Comin' up nineteen years. I will miss 'em all."

"Guess you lost a lot of friends, huh?"

"Aye."

Janus turned and walked over to the large viewing window. Barker followed. Janus squinted out of the window and saw a structure – not very far off – that looked familiar. As she identified the outline, her eyebrows lifted and she felt an irrational wave of dread.

Watching with interest, Barker saw the reaction in Janus's face and eyes, something so strong she couldn't hide it.

"What is that?" Janus's voice was barely audible.

Green eyes flicked out the window momentarily before settling back on Janus's face. "I think you know what it is. Probably better than I do." She had a hunch, a suspicion that was nothing more than a gut feeling, so Barker decided that just blurting it out would be inappropriate.

"Why are ya 'ere?"

"The ship?" When Janus nodded, she answered, "This ship brings civilians of Earth, or anyone who wants, to see the prison. It's a tour."

"Why?"

"Because it's an important part of Earth history. Just think of it, all those people locked up for no good reason with wardens from Earth having control over life and death. It is the single greatest injustice in our history since some of the goings-on in the nineteen hundreds during the second great war. So of course people want to see it and learn about it, even if their interest is based in morbid curiosity." Barker watched Janus watch the prison. "Some of the things that happened..."

"Ya do not need ta tell me!"

Janus jerked away from the window and stalked out of the room as sad green eyes watched. Barker pursed her lips for a moment before following. "Guess that answers that question," she muttered, suspecting that Janus knew of someone who had been held in the prison. It certainly explained what Patrik had said about Janus's opinion of the Coalition. Barker broke into a light jog to catch up, and placed a hand on Janus's arm. She felt the muscles tighten and flinch, and Janus stopped. "Listen, Janus, I'm sorry..." Barker stopped as angry blue eyes stared into hers.

"I do not want ta 'ear it. I know what 'appened, and I do not like being back 'ere."

"Listen, I'm sorry, okay? If you don't want to talk about it, then that's fine, but please don't storm off in a fit of pique. I think you could have a lot to offer us, and I'd like for us to be friends."

"I do not know what ya think I can offer ya. I do not 'ave a 'ome, or a ship, or money. I just want ta go back."

"Back to where?"

Janus turned and looked at the persistent human at her side. Her jaw worked for a moment before she sighed. "Ta where we came from."

"Where is that?"

The dark head turned and looked back toward the observation deck. "If that truly is the prison, a long way from 'ere." Janus started back down the passage.

"Argh! I have never in my life met someone who could be so vague!" Barker trotted back up to Janus. "We could probably get you home."

"'Ow?"

"We have this generator thing. You punch in coordinates and a wormhole opens."

"A wormhole?"

"Yes."

"Yer people built this?"

"Yes, it's what ensured our entrance into the Allied Planets treaty."

"Aye."

Barker looked up at Janus, hearing a slightly different inflection in her voice. Up until now, "aye" had meant "Yes". "Was that a good aye or a bad aye?"

"Good."

The blonde head nodded. "Good. The captain wants to see you."

Janus just grunted and changed course back to the medical bay, having a good sense of where she had been.

They whooshed back into the medical bay, Janus throwing a slightly annoyed look at the door. It made sound, unnecessary sound. She didn't like it. She looked around to see Patrik on the bed with his daughter and Harrison in quiet conversation with Doctor Cobb.

Harrison looked up as the door opened, then turned back to Tina Cobb. "So, they're both in good health?"

"Aside from not having had a decent meal in the last while and some dehydration, they're fine. Patrik has some cuts and burns, nothing serious. Janus doesn't have a single mark on her, but there is dried blood, so what Barker and Samson reported to you is true. She absorbed energy and it healed her. If you want anything more than that about her physiology, you'll have to give me a few hours to process it all. The child is fine, perfect health."

"Great, thanks a lot."

"Just doing my job, Captain. Now, go make nice."

Harrison smiled at the doctor and turned. Cobb was right. She had made amends with Patrik, the two of them coming to an uneasy truce; now it was time to do the same with Janus. She didn't think it would be as easy. She could see the mistrust in those blue eyes, the veiled anger, and the rigid way Janus held her body – as if she associated pain with people like Harrison.

The captain stepped up to Janus and smiled. "I'm sure you have your reasons for your actions during our previous meeting, and I respect that. It is up to you whether or not you wish to share those reasons. Despite that, I'd like to hear some more about you and your people. No one has ever encountered a species quite like you before, and I'm curious."

"Ya 'ave."

Harrison tilted her head a bit. "Have what?"

"Seen us before. Ya 'ave, ya just do not remember. 'Umans 'ave short memories and shorter life spans." Janus made her statement quite factually, ensuring that no one could possibly take offense.

"Well, if you say so. I'll have to look into it. Doctor Cobb has told me about this energy absorption you do. It's very interesting."

"Why?"

Harrison blinked at the question, having not anticipated it. "Well, we like to know how and why things work, and no one has ever been able to do what you did. It's something new and exciting. I have to admit, though, that I'm a little skeptical. I mean, absorbing alien energy and healing..."

"Why can ya not accept somethin' on the word of others? Surely

Barker and the others reported. Why must ya see it, before ya can believe it?"

Harrison didn't have an answer, and the expression on her face showed that she was suddenly off balance.

Janus sighed and glanced at Patrik. She raised an eyebrow; he shrugged in response. Aware that everyone was watching, she lifted her hand up to waist level. She rubbed her fingers together for a moment, and then moved her thumb over the tips of her other fingers.

Barker's eyebrows raised as she saw a faint blue tinge appear in Janus's fingers, just like the cloud that had formed when she took in the alien's energy. As she watched, the tint became its own mini-cloud, then burst upward in a cloudy flame shape. It looked like a tongue of fire was coming out of Janus's fingertips, except it was blue instead of red and orange. "Wow."

Janus smiled and raised her hand, turning it around and separating her fingers so an individual flame came out of each digit. She focused in and raised the intensity, making the flame larger and then smaller.

"How...how do you do that?" Harrison asked quietly.

"I do not know; I just do. It is the energy in my body, I focused it 'ere, made it stronger so ya could see."

"Is it electricity?"

Janus threw Harrison a look at the question she obviously deemed to be stupid. "No. It is energy, like I said. The energy in all things."

"Can I...?"

Janus turned toward Barker at the quiet question, and Barker hesitantly clasped Janus's wrist and brought the hand closer to get a better look. "It looks like fire."

"It is not. It does not burn. Touch it," Janus encouraged softly. For some reason, she wanted to make Barker happy. It was strange, really. She never much cared for people she had just met and hardly knew, but something in her surged when she looked at the blonde.

Barker looked up and smiled before carefully waving her finger through the blue cloud. It didn't hurt, so she moved her finger in and kept it there. The sudden surge of energy traveled up her finger and arm and hit her in the chest. She felt it, felt it send blood pumping through her body and make her want to jump off the walls, start doing jumping jacks, or run a marathon. She jerked back, startled, and then grinned. "Whoa! That was...incredible."

Janus smiled and then closed her hand into a fist, in effect, extinguishing the flame. "'Appy, 'arrison?" The captain just nodded mutely and left the medical bay.

Barker smiled and then motioned to both Patrik and Janus. "Come on. I'll show you to some quarters."

* ~ * ~ * ~ *

"Well, here they are. Feel free to make yourselves at home until we get back to Sol."

Janus cocked her head, curious. "I thought ya were from Earth?"

Barker smiled. She found Janus's persistent questions amusing. She knew that if she were in an unfamiliar environment, she'd be asking a lot of questions too. "People from Earth call it Earth because, well, that's what we named it. But the Grogarians, who initiated the treaty between the Allied Planets and the USC, and were also the first species to make formal contact with Earth, called it Sol. So, that's how we are listed in all the treaties, because everyone is familiar with that terminology."

Janus grunted and started wandering around the room, poking into things like a mischievous puppy. Barker thought it was pretty cute. "Oh. There are clothes in there," the ensign pointed to the door by which Janus was standing, "if you want to change. Yours look like they've seen better days."

"Aye."

Janus opened the door and rifled through the contents of the storage cabinet, then removed pants and a shirt. A closer look at the clothing and she noted that they were nearly a replica of the crew uniforms. Janus shook her head. *I will not don the markings of the Coalition, no matter how much they might have changed over time.* She threw the clothes on the bed with another shake of her head.

Barker cleared her throat, realizing it would take more than some friendly words from Captain Harrison to change Janus's mindset. "Well, I'll let you three get settled. The room is yours until we get back."

"How long will that take?" Patrik asked from his position sprawled out on the bed, Emmeline resting on his chest.

"We can't wormhole from here, it's a pretty dead area of space. It'll take about a day to get out of this area and then a few hours once we worm, 'cause we can't go directly to the planet."

"Okay. And Barker, thanks."

"No problem."

She whooshed out of the room, leaving the only survivors of a vicious attack to stare at one another.

Patrik groaned as he relaxed completely onto the bed. "God, Janus, do you know how long it's been since I've been able to sleep in a bed?" He thought for a moment, then smiled. "Of course you do, it's been the same amount of time for you." When he got no response, he looked around and realized Janus was not in the room. He listened for any sign of her whereabouts, and realized that his friend was using the small, attached bathroom to shower and remove several weeks' accumulation of grime and blood.

Janus showered quickly and Patrik's eyes tracked her around the room as she moved back and forth between the closet and bed, a towel wrapped around her. She was pulling out clothes and putting some back, all seemingly without listening to him, though Patrik knew she was aware of every word. Janus was like that – a very good multi-tasker. "What are you doing?"

"Gettin' clothes," she stated, still moving articles of fabric about.

"What's wrong with those?" He pointed at the pair of pants and shirt in her hand before she shoved them back in the closet. Janus didn't answer, just kept rearranging. Finally, she selected a set that passed her scrutiny.

Patrik got comfortable again, but his head popped up when he heard fabric tearing. "Now what are you doing?"

"Still gettin' clothes," she mumbled.

Intrigued, Patrik sat up and watched.

Janus finally finished fiddling and dropped her towel. She ignored Patrik's startled squawk and him covering his eyes while she donned the new clothing, then straightened the hem of her shirt with some satisfaction. "Ya can look now."

Patrik hesitantly removed his hand, then smiled. Janus had found a much older issue Coalition uniform amongst the current ones, and she'd ripped off the sleeves, and the insignia along with them. Unlike the solid black uniforms, Janus's pants had a wide red stripe down the outside seam of each leg and a thinner one across each thigh. He tilted his head sideways to get a better look. "You look..." he pursed his lips before they shaped into a gentle smile, "...intimidating as hell." He looked into her vivid blue eyes. "Trying to make a statement?"

"No, just...assertin' my free will." The wicked grin on her face belied her assertion. Janus was indeed out to make a statement: that she was a free person, not to be trifled with, and that these people had no hold on her whatsoever.

An answering grin spread across Patrik's face as he read the truth in her eyes. "Go give 'em hell, Janus."

She tilted her head slightly in acknowledgement before striding confidently out of the room. The whooshing door seemed oddly muted.

~~*~*~*

Captain Harrison settled into the desk chair in her office, then keyed the communications system.

"Yes?"

"Doctor Cobb, I want you to get me a complete work-up on this Janus. Everything medical you can tell me, I want, understand?"

The smile was evident in the answering voice. "Already in progress, Captain."

"Good." Harrison paused for a moment before asking, "Do you know which crewmember would be the best at going through the database and looking for particular references to people or events without a specific search parameter?"

"Probably Lieutenant Melvin Kodiac, Captain."

"All right. I want you to get him down to the medical bay and tell him to start going through all our records. He's looking for any and all reference to Janus and her silver-streaked people. Janus claims we've come in contact with her kind before, and I want to know when, why, how...the works. Understand?"

"Yes, ma'am. May I ask why the sudden interest? I'm sure Janus would tell you if you asked."

"Maybe. But since we don't have any recollection of ever encountering such a people before, it was likely before her time, as well. I want the actual reports from the people who were there."

"I would suggest, Captain, that you also speak with Janus. We both know that the Coalition of the past had many faults. Our records will only tell one side of the story."

"I'll consider it. Thank you, Doctor."

After the captain severed the com link, Tina Cobb's ensuing silence spoke volumes. She did not approve of her captain only looking at one side of the situation, especially when Harrison was well aware of the many past transgressions of the Coalition. She only hoped that Harrison would not make any rash decisions that would alienate a potential ally as powerful and gifted as Janus.

The ship's doctor suspected that any insult to Janus would affect Ensign Barker as well. There was something there, running between the two of them, she could almost see it, but then again, it might have been some reaction caused by Janus's strange chemical makeup. Tina sighed at her indecision as she put out a ship-wide call for Lieutenant Kodiac to come to the medical deck. They both had work to do.

After she terminated the call with Doctor Cobb, Harrison sat back in her chair and considered her medical officer's parting advice. Cobb had a point, about any archived information only relating one side of a story. But her relationship, if she could even call it that, with Janus was very tenuous. Harrison didn't see any point in angering the woman with questions when she was not yet certain that they had made contact with such beings before. And if they had, what the substance of the contact was.

To herself, Harrison admitted that she was wary of Janus and her people. They were obviously a very powerful species, one that could either be the greatest threat or greatest ally the United Space Coalition, or Earth, had ever had. If it proved to be the former, Harrison would risk her life to protect the Coalition. The USC was what she lived for. If she did nothing, she would lose that life, and if she died defending it, she'd have lost her life, as well. Captain Harrison of the *USC Avenger* hoped to God that Janus and her people were friends. It never even crossed her mind that they could be neutral.

* ~ * ~ * ~ * ~ *

"Doctor Cobb! Doctor Cobb, come here please!"

Tina's head popped up at the sound of Kodiac's voice. "What is it?"

"This is something you should see."

Tina walked over and looked at the console Kodiac had been working at for the last hour or so. Her brow furrowed as she realized precisely what was so important. "Oh, my God! Call Captain Harrison; she needs to see this."

Kodiac nodded vigorously and keyed the com system.

Minutes later, Harrison strode into the medical bay. "What is it? What have you found?"

Tina stepped back and gestured to the computer. "See for yourself."

Harrison approached and focused on the screen. Her eyebrow raised as her brain immediately registered what her eyes were looking at: a file from the Marson Alpha IV prison. She scanned down to the high priority stamp on the file, and the second eyebrow lifted. Finally, her eyes focused in on the picture of the prisoner to whom the file belonged, and her heart skipped a beat.

Janus.

Chapter 3

Janus wandered down the hall, taking in the attributes of the ship as some of the more curious passengers took her in. Their blatant observation and speculation got under Janus's skin in the worst kind of way. She supposed she was an unusual sight, especially since she hadn't been there from the beginning of their tour. Though in her opinion, humans as a species were far too curious for their own good. It was something she had noted about Patrik, Emmeline, and the other humans she had been living with on the ship. She had learned to tolerate their interest because she knew them and they knew her.

As she rounded a corner, she experienced an extreme sense of danger; something was not right. Before she could react, Janus found herself pinned up against the wall by a big brute of a man. *Samson.*

"So, not as tough here, are you?"

Janus looked steadily back at him, acknowledging to herself that the strange environment with all of its strange inhabitants was playing havoc with her senses. All of them. There were certain things that people did that made waves in the energy. Janus had learned all of the patterns her former crew had made. Now all the new people were creating patterns that weren't harmful and she hadn't automatically recognized them as such. It annoyed her.

"What's the matter, suddenly can't speak?" Samson paused expectantly and growled when he got no answer. "You just watch yourself, alien. There are people who don't like you and your kind. People who would rather see you dead than a walking degradation to all that is human."

Janus looked into his eyes, remaining calm as she spoke. "Did ya ever think that it is my people who are degraded by ya? We 'ave existed a lot longer than ya. Maybe we are ashamed ta 'ave an inferior being evolve lookin' like us. Did ya ever think of that? 'Umans are not the best species in the universe. Ya are the most arrogant, confrontational, cynical, malicious, treacherous, idiotic, and inferior...beings...alive. Why do ya think it took so long before anyone made contact with ya? 'Cause ya live in one of the most isolated, trashy parts of the universe." Janus looked hard into Samson's eyes and moved her face closer to his. "Ya are nothin' to us. My people could care less about Earth." That said, Janus raised her legs and kicked Samson just above his kneecaps, breaking his hold on her.

He stumbled back, regained his balance, and spent a long moment glaring at the composed alien before turning and angrily stomping away. He almost bumped into a small body standing in the main hallway. "Watch it," he growled, never once raising his eyes.

Barker turned and watched Samson's retreat before peeking around the corner, where she saw Janus leaning casually against the wall. She let her eyes run over the tall form, appreciating how Janus was dressed before moving forward. "You should be careful, you know. Samson may seem all talk, but he isn't. He has a depressing amount of power planet-side. You could be in some real trouble."

"Ah do not plan on goin' ta yer Earth."

"Why?"

"Wall..." Janus rubbed her nose for a moment and smirked. "Fer one, ah kinnot breathe the air."

"Oh, right. Yeah, I guess that's a good enough reason." Barker looked up at Janus and noted the bright sparkle in her eyes and twitchy behaviour. "Do you thrive on conflict?"

Janus raised a questioning eyebrow.

"I just realized that your speech is more...um, well you're butchering the English language more than you have before and you can't stand still." Barker looked pointedly at Janus's clenching fists and shuffling feet.

"Ah like a good fight. But ah dinnat git ta fight 'im, and when mah blood starts pumpin', ah tend ta speak...um..."

"Differently?"

"Aye. Ah kin take care of meself, Barker. Do not worry 'bout me."

The blonde head nodded and Barker turned to leave. She paused and looked back over her shoulder. "Was it true, what you said about humans and your people? Does your race really think that about us?"

"Aye. It tends ta be the initial impression 'umans make. But if we git ta know them well, we git over it. It is people like Samson who give the rest a ya a bad name."

"Yeah." Barker nodded again and started down the hallway, thinking over everything Janus had said — both to Samson and to her. She took three more steps and then turned on her heel to face the woman still watching her. "Come on, I'll give you the nickel tour."

Janus joined her, head cocked. "Nickel? What is a nickel?"

Barker started walking as she considered her answer. "It's both a mineral and coin we have on Earth."

"So, why is this tour a nickel tour?"

"It's just an expression we have."

Janus squinted as she considered the information, then turned to Barker.

As Janus opened her mouth, the petite blonde covered it with her hand. "Shhh. I'm not going to get into this with you. It's not important."

They continued down the hallway in silence.

* ~ * ~ * ~ * ~ *

Harrison leaned forward to scrutinize the photo image more closely. It was definitely Janus – the same straight nose and strong jaw, the same blue eyes. Harrison squinted. No, not the same eyes. The eyes in the picture showed many things: fear, hatred, disgust, anger. Now Janus's eyes were shuttered to the world, showing only a wariness and suspicion of everything and everyone she did not know. It was obvious the prison had changed her, but prison very often changed people, and never for the better. There was a large bruise along Janus's left eye and several nasty cuts, the worst along her nose. Her face appeared haggard, her cheeks sunken. When Janus had been arrested, she had put up one hell of a fight and had not been in a "healthy" environment, as Patrik had termed it. If she had, her injuries would have been healed.

The captain straightened and shook her head. "It doesn't make any sense. The prison was abandoned fifty years ago, at least. And this record says that Janus was incarcerated there for twenty. That would make her more than seventy years old. The woman I met doesn't look any older than twenty-five."

Doctor Tina Cobb sighed and looked up at Harrison. "The medical evidence supports the file. Janus and her people live considerably longer than humans. I couldn't tell you how long, but it's a long time. That would explain her comment about our short life spans. In comparison to them, our lives are over in the blink of an eye."

Harrison grunted, then spoke. "I want to talk to Barker, then Janus. I want some details about this."

"Details?" Cobb asked. "Captain, I really don't think it would be wise to make an issue out of this. It happened a long time ago and Janus probably would not take kindly to being asked about it, especially by an officer of the Coalition. What purpose would it serve?"

"What purpose? For one thing, we might actually get some closure on the issue! And according to this file, Janus was one of the leaders of the uprising. Do you have any idea how many people died that day?"

Melvin Kodiac edged forward and raised a finger. "If I might venture an opinion, Captain, Doctor Cobb is correct. We all know that the Coalition back then was nothing to be proud of, and you have no authority over Janus. She was one of the many who were locked up just because she was in the wrong place at the wrong time. All you will accomplish by raking up ancient history is to alienate her."

"Thank you, *Lieutenant*, for your opinion. The next time I want it, I'll ask for it. Now, someone get Janus and Barker up here."

* ~ * ~ * ~ * ~ *

"All right, this is Earth right here." Barker pointed to one of the many circles on the huge view screen. "And this is where we are right now." She pointed to a second spot that was virtually in the middle of nowhere. "Now, can you tell me where you're from?"

Janus stepped up to the console and spent a moment looking at the controls before she started scrolling through the star charts. When she reached the outer reaches of what the Earthlings had charted, she raised her head. "This is all ya 'ave explored?"

"Yes."

"Aye, ya 'ave 'ardly even..."

"Scratched the surface?"

Janus looked up into Barker's eyes for a long moment, then smiled. "Ya 'ave not even nicked the surface." She shook her head. "My 'ome planet is too far from what you 'ave 'ere ta give ya an idea. But ya see this outpost 'ere?" Janus pointed to one right on the edge of the chart. "If ya go 'bout sixty light years this way, ya will hit a planet I spent a lot of time on. And Patrik, 'e is from this planet's sister." Janus indicated another floating circle along the outer reaches of the known galaxy.

"Jeez." Barker looked at the places Janus had indicted, noting the astronomical distance between them and the little circle that was labeled Sol. "We really have a lot to learn, don't we?"

"Aye. Yer planet is in the *yarkens*, as my people call it."

"*Yarkens*, what's that?"

"There is no direct translation. It means distant, empty region, inferior."

"Inferior?"

Janus glanced over at the ensign. "I do not make the words up, I just use 'em. Inferior meanin' that we do not deem the beings there worth our time."

"Kind of arrogant, aren't you?"

"No." Janus shook her head. "Just confident about our place in the universe."

Barker nodded and then stood, moving around to stand next to Janus. "So, if your ship was from so far away, how did you get all the way here? It would seem that you didn't have a clue where you were, and you definitely weren't expecting to see the prison."

"Aye, we did not know. The aliens, they moved us."

"Moved you?"

"Aye. Near the beginnin' of the battles, our ship shifted and it was like a big wave 'ad run us over. We stopped, but our sensors were down so we did not know where we were. It was not that important; we were sure we were to die."

"Wow! So they took you from way over there, to here, in seconds?"

"Aye."

There was a short, respectful silence. "That's some power these things have."

"Aye."

The door whooshed open and they turned to see a nervous looking young ensign standing there. "Barker, the captain wishes to see you and your guest in the medical bay...right away."

"Thanks. Do you know what's up?"

"No, but she seemed very, um...angry."

The duo paused as they headed to the corridor. "Really?"

He nodded. "Be careful, Barker." Then his eyes shifted up to Janus's face. "You too," he whispered, and then he was gone, scurrying down the hall like a terrified mouse.

Barker watched him, perplexed. "What was up with that? Be careful, what does that mean?"

"I do not know, but ya should take yer allies where ya can."

"Yeah." She breathed the word out and then started toward the medical bay, Janus close on her heels.

The duo stepped into the medical bay together, stopping and waiting until Captain Harrison motioned them both forward. They exchanged uneasy glances before moving up to where Doctor Cobb, Melvin Kodiac, and the captain stood. For one long moment, they stared at each other in silence, and Barker noted that Janus was the object of much scrutiny.

Harrison stepped forward, looked at Janus, and cleared her throat. "Something has come to my attention that I wish you to verify."

"Aye."

Harrison rotated the screen to face the alien and Barker, Janus's file still on display. "We came across this, and I'm wondering if it's accurate."

Barker raised an eyebrow as she identified the source of the file, and she turned her eyes to Janus.

Janus took a step forward and looked at the file, the picture and the words printed there, and felt that time of her life come rushing back in a painful wave. "Aye, it is. Is that a problem?"

"Yes. You escaped a United Space Coalition prison. Not only that, you were one of the ringleaders in the uprising. You are responsible for the deaths of dozens of USC wardens and officers, all of which is considered a felony against the USC and people of Earth. I have every right to arrest you and throw you back in prison."

Barker's eyes widened at the implications of Harrison's words and she mentally slapped herself for having pushed Janus into a conversation about the prison. Her reaction now made perfect sense.

Janus stood very still and very quiet for long seconds. Her head remained down, eyes locked on the screen displaying her file. Then very slowly, very precisely, her head lifted and cold eyes drilled into the captain.

Barker would have sworn she saw them flash silver.

"Ya 'ave no such right, *Captain 'Arrison.* Ya know as well as I do that Marson needed destroyin', but yer people would not dare touch it, not dare acknowledge what it 'ad become. Ya 'ave no idea the things that went on there, and ya 'ave no authority over me!"

"I do. You and your fellow prisoners took justice into your own hands. You were judge, jury, and executioners! No matter what happened in the prison, you are guilty of murdering the staff there, as is everyone else who escaped!" The captain and Janus squared off.

On the sidelines, Doctor Cobb and Melvin Kodiac were considering the heated exchange. They shifted subtly, moving further away from the captain and closer to Janus and Barker.

"It was our justice ta take, our lives that were on the line. It was us who watched friends and family," she choked on the word, "be tortured and killed. Do not dare stand there and claim we would 'ave been saved or 'elped or compensated by yer precious Coalition! Ya should know better; I do. So does Barker and anyone else who took the time ta learn what really 'appened. I 'ave seen the darkest side of your precious USC, and from what I kin tell, it 'as not changed. Ya are blinded by loyalty, 'Arrison. I am not stayin' 'ere." Janus turned on her heel and whooshed out of the medical bay before anyone could even take a breath.

Barker glanced at the fuming captain who was rubbing her neck. Next, she looked at Kodiac and Doctor Cobb, who seemed to be supporting Janus. The issue was apparently strong enough to divide the crew, and that was not a good thing.

"Janus is right." Barker looked up and locked eyes with Harrison. "Righter than you could ever imagine." Then she turned and walked calmly out of the medical bay, with Kodiac and Cobb following.

~~*~*~*

Everson Patrik jerked awake and rolled over. Having forgotten where he was, he almost fell off the bed. He grabbed the bed frame and glanced to his right to see his daughter curled up there in a contented sleep. After Janus had left, they had both showered and settled in for some much needed rest. But he was awake now, and for a reason.

It had taken him a long time to get used to the feeling, an awareness of Janus in the back of his mind. As far as either of them could tell, it had originated after Janus had saved his life by using some of her own energy to heal his wounds. The feeling was nothing concrete or easily described, just a sensation that eventually became normal and not worth noticing, except when Janus was upset, or extremely sad, or overjoyed. Then the feeling blasted to the front of his senses, either making him giddy and bouncy, or anxious and scared.

Right now he was anxious and scared, which meant that Janus was not happy or relaxed or content. She was pissed as hell and ready to blow. And that meant, she'd probably be walking through the door right about...

The door to the room whooshed open and an angry Janus stiffly stepped through it. Patrik rose and walked over to where she was standing, looking like she really wanted to hit something. "Hey, what's up? What happened?"

"We are not stayin' 'ere."

"Why?"

"'Arrison 'as found my Marson file. She is not pleased and neither am I."

"Okay. You know I don't have a problem with that, but how are we going to leave? We don't have a ship, and I don't think they'll give us a shuttle if the good captain has as big a problem as you say."

"Then we steal one." With that, Janus moved over to where Emmeline lay and gently picked her up, not bothering to wake the girl.

Patrik pursed his lips and nodded. "All right, works for me."

They turned and stepped into the hallway, and ran right into Barker, Cobb, and Kodiac. "We are not stayin'."

Barker nodded. "Yeah. I know. Come on, we'll help you leave."

The ensign started off down the hall, with everyone else trailing. They had almost made it to the shuttle bay when the entire ship rocked violently, throwing Patrik and Barker to the floor. Janus stumbled and braced herself against the wall, careful not to hurt Emmeline.

A voice came over the ship-wide com system. "Attention all hands, we are under attack. Repeat, we are under attack. All officers report to the bridge."

Janus cocked her head, carefully extending her sixth sense, probing the energy flow outside the ship. She shook her head, trying to dislodge the unsettling feeling the creatures created. "It is them." She did not need to elaborate.

Barker struggled to her feet and grasped Janus's arm. "Are you sure?"

"Aye."

"Ohh no, nonono, no...not again." Patrik shook his head violently and hugged his legs to his chest.

Janus handed Emmeline to Barker and knelt in front of Patrik. "Patrik! Ya 'ave ta keep it together. We will get through this. I promise ya."

He looked up into her eyes, got lost in their confident depths, and nodded.

Janus stood and helped him up. "Good." She then turned to the other people in the hall. "Doctor Cobb, ya should go ta medical. They will need ya there. Someone should tell 'Arrison what is 'appenin' and get those guns modified."

"I will," Kodiac said, and ran down the hall toward the bridge.

"Barker, is there somewhere ya can put the noncombatants that is easy ta defend?"

The ensign thought for a moment and then nodded.

"Good. Get 'em there and set up a defense. Patrik, ya should put Emmeline there and then start fightin'. We do not 'ave long 'til they will be on the ship."

Patrik nodded and swooped up his daughter, who was awake and looked frightened. "Right. What about you?"

"I am goin' ta try and keep 'em from advancin' too far."

"All right." Patrik turned down the hall and then threw a parting comment over his shoulder. "Be careful, Janus. We need you."

Barker looked up, her green eyes nervous. "He's right, Janus. If we're going to get through this, we need you. Watch your back."

Janus nodded and Barker turned and caught up with Patrik. She watched them go for a moment, sending a quick prayer to *wiparia*, then she closed her eyes and focused in on the energy again, pinpointing where the aliens were most likely to board. Janus turned and started running, following the unwavering line of disturbance in the natural order of things. The creatures were like that – just their mere presence screamed that something was wrong, and that made Janus think that they were not from any nearby star system.

She went up two decks and made countless turns, passing people who were scurrying about with no real purpose. She finally rounded the last corner just as a loud screech filled the air and the bulkhead was torn off. Janus straightened and let the rest of the world drop away, focusing only on the imminent threat.

As dozens of grey bodies dropped through the opening and surrounded the lone being who stood so bravely in their midst, unarmed and unprotected, Janus prepared herself for the fight of her life.

* ~ * ~ * ~ * ~ *

Melvin Kodiac slid around the corner and stumbled onto the bridge. Quickly noting the absence of the captain, he ran up to Commander Proparian and began to brief him. "Commander, listen to me. We're being attacked by the same creatures we rescued those people from. You need to make a ship-wide announcement to modify all the plasma guns." He got it out in a rush and then sucked in a huge gulp of air.

Steady blue eyes looked at the lieutenant, then the commander gave the order. His deep voice echoed through the bridge, and soon the rest of the *Avenger* crew knew what to do. "Where's the captain?"

"Last I saw, sir, she was in the medical bay."

"Okay. I'm sure she's on her way here."

"Permission to join the fight, sir."

"Of course. Go show these bastards what the Coalition is made of."

Kodiac sketched a salute and ran off the bridge to the nearest weapons locker. There he found crew members already modifying guns and others picking up weapons and the radios that the tactical officer was using to organize the crew. Kodiac picked up a radio just in time to hear Barker's voice.

"All ship's personnel, please escort all civilians to the observation room on Deck Three. Security Detail Delta, please report to the same location with full defensive weapons array."

"Barker, it's me, Kodiac. I'm on my way. Do we have most of the passengers accounted for?"

"Yeah, about eighty-five percent of them are here. They're scared, but I have to give them credit for not panicking."

"Okay, I should be there in ten minutes. Kodiac out."

The radio fell silent as Melvin Kodiac stepped into the hall on his way to Deck Three.

~~*~*~*

Doctor Cobb ran down the hall to the medical bay, her primary responsibility. The room was designed to stand up to any attack, a place where the wounded could recover in safety. The walls, floor, and ceiling of the bay were reinforced with extra layers of steel and titanium. If what Janus and Patrik had reported about the creatures that had destroyed their ship was true, that might not be enough.

She hoped that Janus was wrong and that they wouldn't be overwhelmed with casualties, but she knew that was just wishful thinking. Cobb raced around the room, pulling out equipment and weapons and alerting her staff to be ready for anything. She scooped up a tactical radio, knowing if someone were seriously hurt they would call for help on the special med channel. While making a final check of their preparations, the doctor noted that the captain was no longer in the med bay. "Hey, Bobby, when did the captain leave?"

The young man thought for a moment. "About five minutes after you did."

The chief medical officer nodded and started moving things about nervously. "I hope she got back to the bridge safely," she muttered to herself.

Cobb hated waiting. It had to be the most nerve-racking thing in the world. She would much rather be trying to save someone's life than anticipating a call for help.

Just then the door whooshed open and two men came in, one supporting the other. "A power conduit blew right in his face."

"Bring him over here and help me get him on the table. Bobby, I need your help!"

Doctor Cobb let everything fade out as she focused on the injured man, who was in a fight for his life.

* ~ * ~ * ~ * ~ *

Barker and Patrik were attempting to round up the remaining passengers and take them to safety. Along the way, they attracted enough attention for the word to spread, and they had quite a large following as they approached the observation room on Deck Three. "In here, everyone hurry!" Barker directed. The civilians poured in and situated themselves around the room.

Barker scanned the gathering and took a quick count. She nodded, pleased with the number of people who were now relatively safe. The observation deck had come to mind because it was right above the bridge, and hence had reinforced walls. The floor was also thicker than most, and since it was one of the many viewing rooms, there were fewer bulkheads the creatures could rip through to gain entrance. All they had to worry about was one wall and the ceiling.

In preparation for any eventuality, as ranking officer, Ensign Barker walked over and opened a compartment in the floor. She pulled out a few tactical radios and a cache of plasma guns. "Patrik, give me a hand." He joined her in modifying the weapons. When they had finished, she scanned the room for potential allies. Most of the faces that greeted her were nervous and frightened, but they were eager to help. There were ten extra plasma guns, and Barker needed to enlist ten civilians to wield them.

She stood and raised her arms, asking for quiet. "Listen up! I know you're all afraid, and you should be. But if we're going to get through this, I need your help. Now, can anyone here shoot?"

Several dozen hands were raised high into the air.

"Well and accurately?"

Hands dropped, until only seven were still raised.

"Okay, you seven, come up here and get a weapon, then spread out. Some of you cover the door, others just be prepared to fire. These things could come through the wall or out of the ceiling. Help *is* on the way."

People started to move, glad to have something specific to focus on, as Barker turned back to where Patrik was kneeling and talking quietly with Emmeline. She watched as he nodded and then leaned forward, wrapping his arms around the small girl in a strong, heartfelt hug. Barker felt a pang in her heart at seeing tears in his eyes. When he stood and turned to her, she stepped forward and clasped his arm. "I'll take care of her, I promise." She handed him a gun and radio. "Here, go look after Janus. Tactical is on channel three, medical is four. Be careful."

A small smile curled his lips as he moved forward and impulsively hugged the little blonde. Barker was stiff with surprise for a moment before she gratefully returned his embrace.

Patrik pulled back and looked into her eyes, seeing, for a brief moment, a strong will to live and something more that he couldn't identify. "You be careful too, Barker. And don't worry about Janus, she's been in tougher spots than this."

Barker nodded and watched him as he turned, ruffled his daughter's hair one last time, then stepped out into hell.

Patrik heard the door whoosh closed behind him and found he was starting to hate unnecessary sounds as much as Janus did. He abruptly turned his head. He hadn't seen anything out of the ordinary, and yet, on the edges of his hearing, he was detecting something – a clattering and faint yelling, testament to the presence of the intruders. It was coming from above him, and Patrik spent a moment using that feeling in the back of his mind to look for Janus. A sudden surge of feral joy blasted his mind, intensifying the awareness and making it easier to track his friend. *Yes,* he decided, *she's up there.* Janus relished fighting; it satisfied something inside her that he didn't understand, that he didn't think he wanted to understand. Patrik moved toward the upper decks at a slow jog.

~~*~*~*

Melvin Kodiac ran down the hall toward the observation room on Deck Three. He smiled as he considered the location. *Great thinking, Barker.* He really didn't want to have to fight these things. He had seen what they had done to the other ship and had gotten his fill of grey creatures then. But if they were here, then he didn't have a problem fighting. Not at all.

Kodiac rounded a corner and saw Patrik running towards him. They exchanged a nod as each remained focus on his objective. *Strange man,* Kodiac thought. His behaviour went from one extreme to another in a matter of seconds. But Kodiac figured that maybe Patrik was entitled, after having gone through a really rough time and, according to Barker, losing most of his family and all his friends, save Janus.

However, it apparently hadn't affected Janus the same way. Kodiac considered the woman for a long moment as he finally reached the observation room door. She was fascinating, something of an enigma. *And she is probably much stronger than Patrik, with many more defenses. She'd have to be, to survive Marson and come out intact, still able to function.* A close friend of Barker's, he loved to hear about her research, and he knew all about the prison and its horrors.

Kodiac stepped through the door and looked around, smiling at the sight of armed civilians stationed around the room, serious looks on their faces. *Great going, Barker. Maybe you should have joined the USC instead of studying history.* He scanned the room and finally located the blonde ensign talking to a young girl, who looked frightened and concerned and a little resigned, all at the same time. *Curious mix in one so young.*

He approached and Barker looked up, flashing him a happy little grin before turning back to the child. They exchanged a few more words before Barker motioned him closer. He knelt and smiled at the child. "Hello," he said. "We haven't been properly introduced. I'm Melvin Kodiac."

"Hi," she whispered. "I'm Emmeline Patrik." She stuck out a little hand and he accepted it with a smile.

Kodiac looked more closely at her eyes and decided he would have guessed her to be Patrik's daughter, even if he hadn't been told. "It's very good to meet you, Emmeline. How old are you?"

"Eleven."

He smiled broadly. "Wow, that's great. Eleven is a very good age to be."

Barker placed her hand on Kodiac's shoulder and turned to Emmeline. "I have to talk to my friend for a minute. Will you be okay?" When the child nodded immediately, Barker smiled and stood, pulling Kodiac up with her. They took a few steps away to a relatively private corner. "Where is that tactical team?"

"They were right behind me. They should be here soon. She seems like a real little trooper," he said, motioning to the child.

"Yeah, she'd have to be. I think she understands this situation better than most of us, having been through it before."

"Hmm."

A strangled yell broke the tense quiet and the duo turned to see a grey body ripping though the wall. As Kodiac fired his plasma gun, Barker ran back to Emmeline to protect the child. "Everyone get ready to fight!" she yelled as she raised her gun and keyed her radio, "This is Barker. We're under attack in the observation room on Deck Three. Where the hell is that tactical team?"

As three grey attackers forced their way into the room, nine people armed with plasma guns started firing at the same spot, dropping the creatures before they could get very far into the room.

Kodiac turned his head toward the people behind him and sucked in a breath. "If we can keep this up, we'll be all right. Drop 'em as soon as you see 'em." He turned back to the hole as more intruders tried to enter. The shooters all kept their heads, and soon the small band of creatures had been terminated, with no human casualties.

Just then the door whooshed open and the tactical team surged in. "Where?"

Barker shook her head as Kodiac spoke up. "We've neutralized the threat for now. Spread out and try to cover the whole room. Stationing some people in the hall might be a good idea, too, in case anyone comes running for cover."

The sheepish looking group did as Kodiac suggested, three of them returning to the hall while the other eight positioned themselves among the civilians.

Barker sighed and looked down at the child tucked under her arm. "You okay?"

Emmeline looked up with big hazel eyes and just smiled a little before looking back at the door.

~~*~*~*

Patrik hoped that the creatures had only broken through in the one spot on the deck above, prayed that this encounter wouldn't prove to be history repeating itself. He started running, making his way toward the sounds of battle. Soon he could hear their awful screech, smell their stench, and taste the foulness of the air. He rounded the last corner and pulled the trigger in pure instinct. Patrik blinked as the creature fell to the ground, dead. He looked up, seeing two more headed his way with deadly intent. A gleam appeared in his eye and a snarl twisted his lips as he remembered his wife and son, and soon Everson Patrik was charging into battle, an inhuman roar sounding from his throat as he exacted his revenge.

~~*~*~*

Janus ducked and surged backwards as the first of the group of attackers came at her, claws extended. The talons missed her stomach by mere inches and she swung back, grinning as she nailed it right in the head. She turned and kicked out, breaking another's legs and watching it fall to the ground.

Her blood was pumping now, and with a healthy ship full of people and energy to draw from to keep her in one piece, Janus was an unstoppable force. She continued the deadly dance, swinging and kicking, impacting with force enough to break bones and rupture organs. Her eyes flashed silver as the creatures started to fall around her, the slime that was their life's blood oozing onto the floor.

A few had gotten past her, but in the grand scheme of things, it wasn't that important. There were plenty of people throughout the ship with the means to dispatch a few creatures. She kept her sixth sense on alert for any major disturbances in the energy that would indicate the creatures were boarding en masse. Janus hoped to stop that from happening. The creatures would win if enough of them were able to spread through the ship and overpower the *Avenger* crew through sheer numbers.

Janus grunted as one of the aliens lunged and brought her to the floor with a thud. She looked up into its eyes and saw a coldness and hatred there that chilled her to the core. It screeched as its claws were raised, glinting in the light. They flashed down at her head with lightning speed, but she managed to twist her body to the right and she heard the claws dig into the floor. It tried to pull back, then screeched again as it realized it was stuck.

Janus grinned and gripped its chest, then pushed upward with a yell of her own. The arm was ripped from its body, the claw still firmly anchored in the floor. Janus bounced to her feet and quickly prepared for the handful of attackers that remained. They rushed her as a group, and she yelled again before wading gleefully back into the fight.

Chest heaving, she looked around at the remains of the struggle. Grey bodies were scattered everywhere, their slimy gore liberally coating almost every exposed surface. Janus took stock of herself, glad to see she remained unscathed, and that her energy level was still up. She probed the ship and was pleased to detect only a mild disturbance in the energy field. That meant the creatures were losing. She nodded, satisfied, and then turned her eyes to the large hole in the bulkhead.

Assessing the torn metal, Janus thought about the strength it would have taken to do such damage. *Maybe,* she considered, *maybe that takes a lot more out of them than we thought. If ripping these holes drains them, these things must have more than one weakness.* She pursed her lips while her mind worked, then she surveyed the gaping hole. She finally nodded and positioned herself below the hole, roughly in the middle. Janus lowered her head, closed her eyes, and concentrated, all the while rubbing her hands together. She sucked in a deep breath and raised her arms, fingers splayed, concentrating on channeling the energy. Janus kept her eyes closed, envisioning her actions in her mind's eye. When she opened her eyes and lowered her arms, she was pleased to see that the large hole had been mended. She smirked and then took off down the hall — toward the sounds of fighting and her friend Patrik.

Janus ran down the hall, slowing as she came upon some dead carcasses she hadn't been responsible for, some still smoking from the blast of a plasma gun. She continued around a corner and stopped when she saw Patrik standing in the middle of the hall, looking around. "Patrik! Ya all right?"

He looked up, a little stunned. "Yeah, I'm good. They didn't touch me. I did all this?"

"Aye." Janus came up to him and clapped his shoulder. "Thanks. Ya stopped the ones that got away from me."

"Yeah."

The ship lurched suddenly, sending them both to the ground. Janus landed directly on top of a dead creature, which she glared at for a long moment before standing. She reached down and hauled Patrik up next to her. The ship lurched again as it came out of its high speed mode.

Janus looked around as their surroundings settled into a deceptive quiet. "Ah do not like this."

"Me either. That felt very familiar."

"Aye. Let us go. There are still some creatures 'ere."

Patrik nodded and they started down the hall, following Janus's awareness of the intruders. They rounded one corner and stopped suddenly. "What are they doing?"

"Ah do not know." Janus studied the two aliens who were crouched over a console in the wall. "Shoot 'em."

Patrik obliged, raising his plasma gun and downing the saboteurs in an instant. "We should tell someone about what they're doing."

"Aye. Kin ya radio someone on that thing?"

Patrik keyed his radio, "Anyone there? Barker?"

"This is Barker. What is it, Patrik?"

"Well, for starters, those things moved us."

"Yeah, we're outside a planet and *a lot* of outposts."

"Well, maybe we can get some help. The aliens that are left are destroying the ship's systems. Janus and I just took two of them out."

"Mm... Okay, thanks for the update, Patrik. Barker out."

Patrik looked up at his friend and nodded. "We better keep going."

"Aye."

* ~ * ~ * ~ * ~ *

Captain Harrison had been taking a walk, thinking about what Janus and Barker had said, when she'd first heard the ship-wide announcement about the invaders. She ran along the corridor until she came to a supply room. Ducking inside, she was grateful to find a modified plasma gun along with a tactical radio sitting on a shelf.

As she stepped back into the hall, she shook her head. If she was jumping to conclusions about Janus, if her desire to uphold the laws of the USC was blinding her to the truth, none of that mattered at the moment. Her ship was under attack and she was determined to save it. She was four decks away from the bridge, and she hadn't seen another living soul since the attack had started. The captain hoped that trend would continue and she wouldn't have to deal with any intruders.

Harrison made her way swiftly but cautiously, and sighed in relief when the door to the bridge came into view. She was five steps short of her objective when the entire ship jolted abruptly to one side, and vibrations made their way through the bulkheads and rattled her teeth. A few seconds passed before the ship jolted again, and sent the captain sprawling. There seemed to be an eerie calm, like right before a storm as she struggled to her feet and ran the last few steps to the bridge. She entered just as Commander Proparian was demanding to know what had happened.

The Ops lieutenant answered, bewilderment clear in his tone. "Sir, it appears that we've changed positions. I don't recognize this region of space, and the sensors say this area isn't in the database."

Harrison stepped up next to the commander and shared a look with him. "Lets get a visual, Lieutenant."

"Yes, ma'am."

The view screen blinked to life, showing a large planet in the distance with several outposts and ships floating about.

"Captain." Lieutenant Thorp's voice broke the silence. "According to these readings, we're several million light years from where we were."

"What? Those aliens moved us?"

The commander stepped closer to the screen and said quietly, "Moved us clear across the universe."

Chapter 4

"No." Harrison shook her head and moved back to her seat. "This doesn't make any sense. Why would they relocate us? For that matter, we don't know for sure it was them. Maybe there was some kind of anomaly or wormhole or something."

"Captain, we're getting a communication from somewhere in the ship."

"Put it through." Barker's face popped up in a corner of the large central view screen. "Barker, everything okay down there?"

The ensign blinked for a moment, then replied, "Yes, Captain, we're good here. I see those aliens moved us. Any idea where?"

"Somewhere quite distant. How do you know it was them?"

"The same thing happened to Janus and her ship."

Harrison sighed and rubbed her forehead. "Yeah, right. Well..."

"Captain!" Lieutenant Thorp yelled. "I'm losing power to internal sensors. All the systems are malfunctioning."

"What? Why?"

"Captain!" Barker's voice broke through the noise. "It's the creatures. We just got a report from Patrik and Janus: those things are pretty much ripping the wiring out of the ship."

The captain turned back to the screen. "All right, Barker. Thanks. Try and keep those civilians safe." She turned, grabbed her tactical radio and set it to go broadband. "All tactical teams, this is the captain. Commence an immediate sweep of all the decks. We have reports that the intruders are destroying wiring throughout the ship."

Commander Proparian spoke up. "What are we going to do?"

Harrison turned back to the screen where the large planet was still displayed. "Get some help. Set a course; send a distress message as soon as we're close enough. Hopefully, we aren't in a hostile area."

"Yes, ma'am," the helmsman replied.

"So," the commander said, "why do you think they're ripping out our wiring?"

The captain sighed. "Overrunning us isn't working, so I guess they want us dead in the water, blind and defenseless. Can't see 'em coming, can't stop 'em."

The commander grunted.

"Three ships approaching from the port bow!"

Harrison's head popped up. "Let's see." A visual appeared on the screen. "Do we have weapons?"

"Yes, ma'am."

"Target the lead ship and fire."

"Direct hit. No effect."

"Evasive maneuvers; get us to that planet!"

* ~ * ~ * ~ * ~ *

Patrik and Janus continued moving throughout the ship, encountering and destroying multiple teams of two and three creatures. Eventually they rendezvoused with more tactical teams, and Janus was pleased to hear that there were very few human casualties. Her joy at that news was quashed when the ship rocked violently, electrical systems exploded, and an enraged screech filled the air.

Patrik leaned against the wall and looked around through the smoke. "They're firing on us!"

"Aye." Janus straightened as something caught her hearing.

"What? What is it?"

"Someone..." Janus looked around and cocked her head, "someone is in trouble." She sped down the corridor.

"Janus! Janus!"

"Git back ta the bridge. We might be closer ta 'ome."

Patrik blinked as he thought about that. It made sense. The creatures moved their victims so they would be far away from home and any allies. It was the best way to demoralize their victims in a fight – the sure knowledge that there would be no last minute rescues, no cavalry, no resources that were readily accessible. Once the aliens destroyed their target, that was it. There was no one else to deal with because, quite simply, there was no one left. The people of Earth would not know what had happened to the *USC Avenger*, wouldn't know where to send any search party. They would be forced to conclude that it had just disappeared.

In light of all that, it would make sense that the *Avenger* had been sent closer to that quadrant of space from which he and Janus came, as Earthlings had no knowledge of the area. His mood lightened, Patrik nodded and started toward the bridge.

* ~ * ~ * ~ * ~ *

Janus ran down the hall, following a sound on the distant reach of her hearing that was getting steadily louder. They remained under attack, which periodically caused Janus to lunge and stumble in an effort to stay on her feet. As she passed com screens on the wall, their flickering or blacked out state was mute testimony to the considerable damage the aliens were wreaking. She shook her head, hoping that they were in an area inhabited by friends and not foes. If they weren't, then her fate, along with Patrik's and everyone else's on the *Avenger*, was pretty much sealed. They would lose this battle and die. And she really wasn't ready to die yet.

As she stepped through a final door, the ship shuddered, sending her to her knees. Janus stayed there, listening. Someone...a woman, yes, a woman was yelling for help. She was very near. Janus turned her head and spotted an access panel almost concealed behind a large mass of wiring and twisted metal. She crawled over and pawed through the wreckage, finally uncovering the panel. Janus wrapped her hands around it and gave it a healthy yank, which popped it off its hinges.

Light and smoke streamed up from the hole and made her squint as she peered in. There was a fire burning in what appeared to be an engine room of some kind. Janus saw a woman crouched behind a protruding piece of metal, the fire creeping steadily closer. "Are ya all right?"

"Yes. Just please, get me out of here! This power relay is about to blow."

"Aye, just 'ang on." She studied the small room below. Torn metal was hanging from the ceiling and wiring was draped around like cobwebs, crackling and hissing with electricity. The trapped woman was running out of time, so Janus decided just to jump and see what happened. She stepped back as far as possible and took three long, running steps.

The woman shrieked as Janus sailed over the fire and landed, knees bent, right beside her. Janus hopped a little and turned. "Come on, we 'ave ta go." She glanced up at the power relay, sensing a build up in energy around her that would soon result in an explosion.

The woman shook her head violently. "I...I can't go through that."

Janus got down on a level that put her eye-to-eye with the woman. "We 'ave ta." She could hear an eerie humming from the relay, and her sixth sense was thrumming with warning. "If we do not, we will die. Ah will carry ya; ya will be safe. Ah promise."

She extended her hand and the woman stared at it, her eyes tracing the platinum markings there and on her saviour's face. She took a strange comfort in seeing them. She grasped the large hand and was pulled swiftly to her feet.

Janus wrapped her arms around the woman and picked her up, feeling the energy around them about to explode with the relay. She could feel the fire heating her skin and singeing her hair, causing sweat to bead on her forehead and arms. Preparing herself, Janus gathered as much momentum as possible and leapt over the fire, barely clearing the flames. She stumbled when she landed, but refused to fall and possibly cause injury to the woman in her arms.

The power relay was screeching almost like the aliens, signaling to the engineer in Janus's arms that it was seconds from exploding. Janus sensed it as well and stumbled over to the opening to the upper deck.

She crouched and leapt upwards just as the relay exploded and sent violent shockwaves through the blanket of energy surrounding her.

At a distinct disadvantage because she was not able to use her arms to grab onto something, Janus maneuvered her body hard to the right so she wouldn't land back down in the hole. They landed with a thud and Janus rolled, immediately covering the woman's body with her own. A large fireball blasted up through the hole and spread outwards. Janus stayed crouched over the woman, hearing her whimper and feeling the heat surround them.

After long moments of fiery silence, Janus rolled over onto her back and exhaled loudly. She stared up at the ceiling, now charred a deep black. Crackling and hissing came from the engine room, and Janus could smell melted plastic along with a myriad of other scents.

The woman beside Janus coughed and rolled over to lean against the wall. "Oh, my God!" she whispered as she stared incredulously. "How did you...? That fireball blew through here; it surrounded us. I could feel it. How are you alive?"

Janus cleared her throat and ignored the woman's apparent awe. "Are ya all right?"

"Wh...? Yes, I'm fine."

"Good." Janus stood and brushed herself off, which only managed to further smear the dust and soot. "Ya should do somethin' about that fire." She turned and started back toward the bridge, leaving a worshipful engineer staring at her back.

~~*~*~*

"Captain, those ships are coming around again. We can't withstand another pounding."

Captain Harrison growled under her breath and sent her first officer a look that clearly communicated her thoughts. "I'm out of ideas, how about you?"

Commander Proparian shrugged his broad shoulders and shook his head.

"Captain, another ship is approaching. I can't get many readings, but it's huge and it's coming from the planet."

"On screen."

The view screen came grudgingly to life and showed a massive ship on an intercept course with the *Avenger*.

"It's charging weapons! It's firing!"

"Brace for impact!" Harrison yelled.

The ship fired, but not at the *Avenger*. Three precise shots destroyed two of the attacking ships and there was an endless moment of tense silence before the remaining attackers fled.

The door to the bridge opened and admitted a harried looking Everson Patrik, who turned his attention to the large ship on the screen and whooped, pumping his fist in the air.

Harrison turned and looked at him, her eyebrows raised. "You know these people, Patrik?"

He grinned and stepped closer. "Oh, yeah. That ship is unmistakable. It belongs to Quip'lee, Totarian Commander of the Ninth Fleet of Jopus."

Harrison opened her mouth and closed it a few times before blurting out, "What?"

Patrik just continued to smile. "Don't worry. Just know that he's a friend."

"We're being hailed, Captain," the Ops lieutenant said.

"All right. Let's meet this Quip'lee."

The screen popped to life, displaying a being with a flat nose, ridges along his jaw and small spikes along either side of his neck, and long hair pulled back off his face. His eyes, an interesting purple, were registering surprise at seeing a human.

"Greetings. I am Quip'lee, Totarian Commander of the Ninth Fleet of Jopus. Are you in need of assistance?"

"Yes, we are."

The man nodded, a ghost of a smile playing over his lips. "I thought as much. Have you been fighting the Ebokras long?"

"If that's what these things are, no. We were first attacked today and they moved us here."

"I see. Then, you would not have lasted long. May I ask with whom I am speaking?"

"Oh, sorry. I am Captain Harrison of the *USC Avenger*, Sol Division."

A low growl came from Quip'lee's throat, and his mouth eventually formed the word, "Coalition." Then he recovered himself and looked directly at the view screen. "My apologies, Captain Harrison. The Coalition is not looked upon favourably by the people in this system, and I myself loathe it. But that is not fair to you." He bowed his head slightly in apology.

The tone in his voice when he had said "Coalition" was similar to the one Harrison had heard from Janus and Patrik. It rankled, but she was beginning to think there might be some legitimate reason for their disparaging attitude. Diplomatically, she replied, "That's all right, Commander. I seem to be getting that reaction a lot lately."

Just then the bridge door whooshed open to admit a sooty Janus. "What in the name of *wiparia* happened to you?" Patrik blurted without thinking.

Janus shot him a look before turning her eyes to the man on the view screen. "Quip'lee." She smiled. "It is very good ta see ya again."

"Janus, is that really you, or have I taken leave of my senses?"

"Aye, Quip. 'Tis me. And Patrik." Janus pulled her friend into Quip's view.

"Oh, my. We thought you were all dead. This is marvelous news, marvelous." He smiled brightly. "Where are the others?"

Patrik shifted uncomfortably and Janus sighed. "This is it. Only me, Patrik, and Emmeline survived. These people 'elped us."

Quip shook his head and scowled. "This is not good, Janus. We are losing to the Ebokras; the outer planets and species are falling. Jopus and the surrounding planets have remained strong only because all the major military is here."

Janus cocked her head and stepped closer. "Ya cannot be losing. Surely everyone 'as agreed ta 'elp. Everyone is in danger from 'em. What about my people?"

Quip's purple eyes looked upon his friend sadly. "Despite my desperate pleadings, they have remained uninvolved."

"*What!*" Janus yelped. "They kin not be that stupid. Do they think they will be left alone? 'Ow could they allow this ta 'appen? My father–"

"Is dead." Janus raised her head to stare at Quip'lee. "He's dead, Janus, I'm sorry. We tried to contact you, but we didn't even know if you were alive, let alone where you might be. Things have changed significantly for your people since you were last home."

"'Ow...'ow did 'e die?"

"He was on Lupadia, helping with a relief mission after an attack. The Rokarians launched a new explosive device the day after he got there; destruction was instantaneous. They never had a chance. Rokarian government called it a field test; everyone else called it genocide."

"'Ow long ago?" she whispered, just loud enough for Quip to hear.

"Almost two years now."

"Was anythin' done?" When the Totarian Commander of the Ninth fleet of Jopus did not answer, Janus raised her eyes and yelled, "Was there?"

"No, nothing was done."

Quip watched as rage filled every line of his friend's face. Her eyes flashed and the marks along her arms glowed. He understood. It was inherent in Janus's species – a great anger that accompanied the death of any one of their own. Vengeance was practically inscribed in their DNA.

"Janus!"

She looked up at him and waited.

"You will have your vengeance, but it's been two years since his death; it can wait. We need your help here, to beat the Ebokras."

Janus sucked in a breath, then nodded. "Ya are right, Quip. 'Elp these people; their ship needs a lot of repairs." Then she left, her platinum designs still glowing with anger and hatred. Patrik followed.

Harrison watched them go and then turned back to Quip'lee. "What about any of those creatures still on the ship?"

Quip smiled. "I have scanned your ship many times, Captain.

Your crew did an admirable job of keeping them at bay and destroying them. And they are called the Ebokras. I have called a tow ship that will take you to the main repair complex on Jopus Prime. There, you will have access to all the parts and any help you will require to fix your vessel."

"Thank you, Quip'lee. We are deeply appreciative."

"Any friend of Janus is deserving. And please, call me Quip. No one adds the 'lee' except my parents."

Harrison nodded. "As you wish. Oh, there is one more thing I would like to ask."

Quip raised an eyebrow in question.

"I want to stay, help you fight the Ebokras. It sounds as if you could use all the help you can get."

"You are correct, Captain, but why would you want to get involved?"

"I became involved when I rescued Patrik and Janus, and it became personal when they attacked us. But more than that, if you lose here, they will eventually come to Sol and we won't be able to defeat them."

Quip nodded. "If that is what you wish, Captain." He smiled. "I look forward to working with you. The tow ship is here; I must go. Quip out."

The transmission ended and Harrison turned to her first officer with a hesitant smile.

~~*~*~*

Janus strode through the door to the observation room on Deck Three and scanned the area. All things considered, it did not look bad. There was some damage from weapons fire and a large hole in the wall, but it appeared as if the Ebokras had caused few deaths.

She saw Barker at one end of the room, sitting on the floor with Emmeline cradled against her chest. *They look...adorable.* Janus blinked. *Adorable? Since when do I use that word?* She shook her head in bemusement as she walked over and knelt in front of them.

"Hello, Janus. You all right?"

"Ah am fine. Ya?"

"We're both good. What's going on?"

"They sent us closer ta 'ome."

Barker spent a moment looking at Janus as she considered that. "Your home?"

"Aye."

"So, the attacking ships?"

"Quip chased 'em off."

"And he's a friends of yours and Patrik's? With a lot of firepower."

Janus smiled as she replied, "Ya could say that. The *Avenger* is being docked on Jopus for repairs. I think 'Arrison is goin' ta stay, ta fight the Ebokras."

Barker waved her hand for Janus to stop, "Whoa, you're leaving too much out. What's Jopus?"

"Planet."

"We're docking on a planet?"

"No. Jopus Prime is the main space station. We are dockin' with it."

Barker nodded her understanding before continuing, "And you said the aliens are called the...the Ebokras?"

"Aye."

"Janus, no offense, but you don't look all right. What happened?"

"Power relay exploded. An engineer was stuck in it; I got between 'er and the blast."

Green eyes studied Janus's burnt clothes and sooty skin; her silver markings stood out with shocking clarity. "Oh." Barker breathed the word out softly. "Living fire shield. Interesting."

Janus grunted, then turned as Patrik came through the door.

He smiled when he saw his daughter safe and sound, cradled in Barker's arms. "Hey, guys." He stroked his daughter's hair, a tender smile softening his face. His eyes flicked up to Janus for a moment as he spoke. "Good to see Quip again, huh?"

"Aye."

"Quip? Who's Quip?"

Patrik looked at Barker. "Sorry, he's the captain of the ship that came to our rescue. An old friend."

"I see." Barker looked up as Janus abruptly stood and turned. "Where're you off to?"

"I 'ave ta go." With that terse statement, Janus strode purposefully out of the room.

Barker cocked her head at Patrik as she shifted Emmeline's weight off her diaphragm so she could breathe more easily. "What's up with that?"

"Janus is...she's dealing with something."

"What?"

He sighed and looked down at his slumbering daughter. "She just found out that her father died. So she's kind of edgy and...stuff."

"Stuff? Patrik, you're being evasive and you aren't doing a very good job of it. What's up?"

He blew out a breath and shuffled around so they were sitting shoulder to shoulder. "Look, there is a lot about Janus that I don't know. She's private, and she really doesn't like to talk about herself or her people. But, I know that they're big on vengeance. Janus's father was murdered, along with a planetful of other people, and her instinct is to go hunt the murderers down and kill them. But she needs to stay here and help Quip fight this war, so she's battling her compulsion to exact revenge."

Patrik stopped and waited, not sure what Barker would say to that. As far as he could tell, she was a very moral woman with high standards. The last thing he wanted was to diminish Janus in Barker's eyes, especially when he didn't know all the particulars himself.

"I see. It must be a pretty strong feeling to affect her so deeply."

He nodded and stated quietly, "Bone deep, Barker. Bone deep." Then he stood, picked up his daughter, and left.

Barker watched him go, her eyes tracking him through the milling bodies and out into the hall. She sighed and let her head thump back against the wall. *What a mess.* She buried her face in her hands. They were halfway across the universe, in the middle of a war, and there she was trying to figure out their two mysterious passengers.

What a mess, indeed.

~~*~*~*

Doctor Cobb wrapped her arm around her patient's chest as he convulsed. "Bobby, I need some help over here!"

The corpsman ran over and grabbed the man's legs, quickly pinning them down and then moving up the jerking body to stabilize it. That freed Doctor Cobb to start treating his injuries.

"How is everything else?" she asked, staying focused on her work.

"Good and not good. All the people on beds one through four are stable and resting comfortably. Bed five is critical, six looks like she'll end up a vegetable, and seven is..." He trailed off, his eyes shifting to bed seven where a large man was yelling and thrashing about. "Seven is completely out of his mind."

Cobb sighed and shook her head as the convulsions stopped and her patient laid still. "It could be a lot worse." She addressed the nurse who was hovering at the head of the bed. "He should be all right now, but keep him restrained and keep a close eye on him. Let's go look at our critical on bed five."

They proceeded to the man whose chest had been ripped open. Blood was dripping sluggishly onto the bed, and damaged organs were visible beneath torn skin and broken bone. Cobb shook her head and sighed heavily. "I can't do anything here except keep him knocked out until he dies."

Bobby's eyes filled with sorrow as he looked at the man, a good friend. "Are you sure, Doc? I mean, he...he's a father. Three kids back home, a wife. Oh, God, what will Susan do?"

"The damage is far too extensive. I'm sorry, Bobby. It is not within my capabilities to heal him." Cobb heard the door whoosh open, and hoped that it wasn't another victim of the cruel creatures. She looked up and her brow furrowed as she saw Janus enter and stop, her blue eyes scanning the room and seeing... Cobb wasn't sure what Janus was seeing. And then the tall alien's eyes landed on her and her dying patient.

Janus walked over to them. She didn't say a word, just stopped by the side of the bed and looked down at the man whose breathing was getting shallow and raspy, a death rattle in his lungs.

And from that moment forward, Doctor Tina Cobb – who had always considered herself a scientist and a woman of logic and reason – would look upon Janus with awe and wonder, as a miracle worker.

Janus reached out and placed her right hand on the man's forehead, her left directly above the destruction that had been his chest. She closed her eyes and concentrated, focusing down deep and ignoring everything and everyone else. Janus's body tensed as she drew from the energy around her – all the living beings, and an entire colonized galaxy outside the ship – and channeled it all through her body and down her arms, out her hands and into the body of the mortally wounded crewman.

Bobby watched as a blue mist appeared and his friend's chest slowly started to change. Organs were placed back into their proper positions, bones knit, torn muscle was mended, and finally, skin was stretched over the healed wound and sealed, leaving behind a red but undamaged surface. Then Bobby raised his eyes up to Janus, seeing the fierce concentration and light sheen of sweat that had broken out on her face and arms. Those odd silver designs were glowing brightly, and he fancied he could feel heat being generated by them.

Janus closed her hands into fists and opened her eyes. She looked closely at the patient and cocked her head as if examining something. Then she nodded. "'E will be all right," she said quietly before moving on to the next bed.

Cobb and Bobby followed as Janus stopped and stared down at the woman who might never wake up, and if she did, would be suffering from severe brain damage. "What 'appened ta 'er?"

Cobb stepped closer and rubbed the back of her neck. "We don't know. A crew member brought her in, said he found her already out cold. There is severe neurological damage. I was going to take her off life support and just let her die. She wouldn't want to live like this." Cobb gestured to the bed and then fell silent.

Janus leaned over, her face inches from the woman's, and stayed there for several minutes. When she straightened, she faced Doctor Cobb and stood quietly for a long moment, thinking. "Do not."

"What?"

"Do not let 'er die. She will wake up and be all right."

"Are you sure?" Cobb was skeptical and it showed in her voice.

"Aye. Give it two days. If nothin' is different, then ya can let 'er die."

Cobb blinked. Her eyes flicked between her patient and Janus, then she nodded slowly. "Okay. Two days."

Janus nodded and then moved on to the bed occupied by the large man who was setting everyone on edge with his screaming. He had started by yelling obscenities and had then moved on to condemning the ship, Captain Harrison, and anything else that occurred to him. Now he was unintelligible, his voice hoarse and high-pitched.

Doctor Cobb stood back and watched as Janus stared at the man, again seeing something that no one else could. It was very strange, and Cobb would have admitted that Janus made her more than a little nervous. But if Janus's heritage allowed her to save the lives of otherwise terminal patients, then Cobb wasn't about to denounce it.

Janus moved forward, intent on doing something to help the man.

Cobb stepped forward to stop her. "Janus, there's an..."

Janus stepped through the restraint barrier and up to the bed.

"...energy barrier there." Cobb decided to just watch and see what happened. Janus appeared to know what she was doing.

When he saw an intruder in his domain, the large man abruptly stopped his raving. His large brown eyes locked onto Janus's, and he lay there, almost fascinated.

Janus moved forward slowly, her motions smooth and unthreatening. She inched closer and closer to the bed until she was within arm's reach. The man lunged at her, but Janus was faster and she latched onto his arm, moving around and pulling it up behind him. He started thrashing about, kicking his legs and swinging his other arm, but he couldn't make contact with his captor.

Ducking her head down behind his thick neck to keep from getting hit, Janus held on tightly. She reached out and grasped his square jaw with her other hand and closed her eyes. This, this was something that she hadn't done before. She had healed countless physical injuries, but never had she ventured into the mental realm. It was a very delicate thing to manipulate, and Janus knew many of her people who had tried and ended up with their own minds disrupted beyond recovery. She didn't want to end up like that, but she also didn't like to see the man suffer. He was losing his mind because of what had happened, and somewhere deep inside he was aware of that. Janus couldn't think of anything worse – knowing you were losing your sanity and being helpless to stop it.

The large body stilled as Janus stood there, once again drawing on the energy around her. Her own personal energy was far too limited in magnitude to help these people; their injuries were too severe. Besides, that one time she had used it to heal Patrik, the result had been a strange mental link that had caused her friend some problems. She preferred not to force that on anyone else, wouldn't even risk it on the off chance that it had been a singular occurrence.

Cobb watched with concern as Janus stood there for far longer than she had with the other two. Healer and patient both appeared to be statues, not moving except for the gentle rise and fall of their chests. She didn't know what to do, whether it was normal behaviour or if

Janus was in trouble. Even if she was, Cobb wouldn't know how to help her. So she watched, wanting very much to bite her nails, or climb the walls, or start demanding some kind of reassurance that everything would be just fine.

The minutes ticked by, each one seeming like an hour to the nervous doctor. Just as she was about to step into the alcove that contained her patient, Janus released him. His body slumped back onto the bed as she moved back through the energy barrier. She leaned against the wall, breathing heavily. Cobb approached, seeing the strain on Janus's face and that she was sweating profusely. "Are you okay?"

Janus nodded, her eyes closed. "Aye." She straightened and took a step, and her knees almost buckled.

"Whoa!" Cobb moved forward and got her arm around Janus's body. "Easy. Come on, sit down over here." They moved to an empty bed where Janus sat, her arms at her sides and elbows locked, as if that was the only thing keeping her upright. "Now, are you going to be okay?"

"Aye."

"Janus." Cobb waited until her newest patient looked up. "Don't lie to me. When you walked in, you looked terrible, and now you look even worse. You almost collapsed."

"I 'ave never done that before."

"Healed people?"

"'Ealed a mind. I do not know if it worked."

Cobb looked over at the patient who was now resting comfortably and was blissfully quiet. "Well, you must have done something right. Just rest here and let me check you out."

"Doctor Cobb, ya do not need ta..."

"Please, Janus. I'm a doctor. If nothing else, it will make me feel better."

Janus ducked her head in an accepting nod and sat quietly while Cobb pulled out her diagnostic scanner and started working. Janus wasn't sure how it happened, but she eventually ended up lying down with Cobb still puttering about. She closed her eyes and blocked out the rest of the world as her mind started to float about. All the healing had taken a greater toll on her than she'd estimated, and she welcomed the respite.

Cobb crossed to the computer and started comparing the newest scans with the ones that she had taken of Janus when she and Patrik had first arrived. She didn't know much about Janus or her body, so it was the only way to get some idea of her current condition. Cobb saw Janus stretched out and looking barely conscious, and her concern showed in her eyes. If something was seriously wrong with their new ally, Cobb doubted that any future confrontations with the aliens would have a favourable outcome.

～～*～*～*

Barker dodged one of the clean-up crews and continued down the hall at a fast clip. All things considered, she thought they had survived the attack in pretty good shape. She turned a corner and almost bumped into a tall form that was not moving. Barker looked up and made eye contact with a suspicious Major Commander Samson.

She blinked, taking a moment to register his presence. She hadn't seen him since his confrontation with Janus in the hallway before the attack had begun, and she suspected he had been up to no good. He looked like everyone else – dirty and strained from the fight, but relatively intact. "Sir, you should get that arm looked at." She nodded at the obviously broken limb he was cradling.

"I was just on my way to medical, Ensign." He moved past her and then stopped. "Where were you during the fighting?"

"Deck Three, protecting the passengers. You?"

"Fighting, just like everyone else. I assume you did all right, since no one has been ranting about dead civilians."

Resenting his insinuation, Barker's eyes flashed. "Of course, sir. I've had basic training, just like everyone else."

"Doesn't make you a soldier." He walked off down the hall, the heavy tread of his boots echoing off the metallic floors.

"I don't want to be a soldier," she whispered, not knowing why that was suddenly so clear. "But I'll do what I have to."

"Hey."

The voice startled Barker, causing her to swing around, fists in the air.

"Whoa! I'm unarmed!"

Barker lowered her hands when she saw it was Patrik standing in front of her. "Jeez, don't sneak up on a person that's just been through an attack. Where are you headed?"

"Medical bay. Something's up with Janus."

"What kind of something?"

"Dunno. That's what I'm going to see."

"Come on. I'm going with you."

They were walking down the hall toward the infirmary when Patrik decided to ask. "You always talk to the air?"

"What? Oh, no. That was meant for Samson. A major pain in the ass, but he's technically my superior, so air-talking is a means of self-preservation."

Patrik grunted his understanding.

They entered the medical bay and paused as they scanned the room. Patrik saw Samson lurking in the back, his arm in being tended to by a nurse. Barker spotted Janus first and Patrik immediately broke toward the still form lying on one of the beds. At seeing the strain on his friend's face, he instantly became very worried. "Janus? Hey,

Janus!"

"Patrik."

He turned to see Doctor Cobb standing behind him.

"As far as I can tell, she's out cold."

Barker joined them and glanced down at Janus's pale face. "What happened?"

"She was using her...unique abilities to heal some patients and after the last one, she almost passed out. I convinced her to sit down, and then she just faded. I scanned her and there is a definite difference between this scan and the previous, but I couldn't tell you if that's good or bad."

The ship rocked gently, the motion far different from the previous jolts caused by the Ebokras' attack. Several noises followed and Barker looked around curiously. "What's going on?"

Patrik looked up from his position over his friend. "We're docking at Jopus Prime."

Barker nodded in acknowledgement, still overwhelmed by the idea that she was millions of light years from her home, her family, and everything and everyone she had ever known, other than the people on the *Avenger*. She now had a better understanding of what Janus, Patrik and little Emmeline must have felt, so far from home with no immediate way of getting back.

It was scary yet exciting, a massive concept to absorb all at once. Barker knew it hadn't all quite sunk in yet, and couldn't imagine what would happen when it did. For a very long time, the universe known to Earth had been very small – consisting of the Milky Way Galaxy and nine known planets, plus a sun. As time passed, humanity slowly gained an awareness of something much bigger and greater than themselves, and endeavoured to explore that something to gain an understanding of it all. Learning about new things and exploring that newest and last frontier was one of the most basic human urges, an urge that pushed the people of Earth far past their self-imposed limitations and into a new future.

All of the work and perseverance finally paid off with the arrival of the Grogarians, a species that came to them and offered a great wealth of knowledge and a place in a universal community amongst planets and species previously unknown to humanity. Barker realized that the Grogarians had not told the people of Earth many things, and it was her hope that they had done so, not because it was their wish to deceive or manipulate, but rather because humans had not been fully prepared to deal with the enormity of the universe and everything it held. They had truly been like a newborn, taking its first tentative steps into a new world with hardly even the guiding hand of a benevolent parent. The inherent dangers that co-existed with the potential benefits were unfathomable for the human mind. To have been exposed to it all when they were not ready to deal with it would have made humanity bitter and untrusting of the positives the universe had to offer.

In addition, learning that their status in the universe was as a tiny planet hardly worth noticing, part of the *yarkens* as Janus had said, that would have taken all the joy from the newborn, all the wind from humanity's sails, and left them dejected. They would not have explored, not grown or developed, never had the opportunity that they now had to become – at some time in the future – a force to be reckoned with.

Barker's thoughts whirled with those new realizations, triggered by a casual explanation from a man who knew the universe in its entirety and still managed to find joy in life and smile, even after tragedy had struck in his own family. She decided that while this was a new world, filled with its own share of heartache and danger, maybe it was worth exploring.

Floating in peaceful nothingness, Janus became aware of the proximity of Patrik and Barker. Patrik was easy to identify because of their mental link, but Barker... In a tiny corner of her semi-conscious mind, Janus was a little concerned at what was developing there. Whenever the ensign entered a room or came close to her, she felt an odd tingle and the energy around her suddenly surged with new life. It was very strange, simply because she had no idea why it was happening or what it meant. And that bothered the didactic Janus.

But, that didn't matter at the moment. There were important things she had to do. Janus slowly came back to herself, feeling much stronger and more alert. She sat up and glanced around, assessing the room before the occupants became aware that she was awake.

"Janus!" Patrik's happy voice was swiftly followed by his body popping into view. "Hey. How ya doing?"

"I am all right."

Barker came closer and looked at Janus, her green eyes shining with concern. "Are you sure?"

"Aye." And Janus, startlingly, found herself bestowing a slight smile on the blonde ensign.

Cobb stepped forward and cleared her throat. "I hate to be the bearer of bad news, but there are some big differences between my successive scans of you, Janus. I don't know what it means, but I really think you should get it checked out."

Janus inclined her head, knowing there was a doctor on Jopus Prime with whom she was on very good terms and who had an excellent knowledge of her and her people. He would be able to determine if something was wrong. "I thank you, Doctor Cobb."

"No, Janus. I thank you. You saved a lot of lives today, and I mean more than just these people's physical bodies."

Janus nodded again as she stood, though she did not understand what the doctor meant. She turned to Barker and Patrik, and focused in on the blonde. "Can I interest ya in a tour of Jopus Prime?" She wasn't sure where the question had come from, but upon reflection, decided it was as good an idea as any. Since Barker was going to be there for an undetermined length of time, she deserved to know the lay of the land.

The blonde woman grinned happily at the invitation and nodded. "I'd love that, Janus. Thank you."

Janus smiled a little, and the three of them walked out of the medical bay.

* ~ * ~ * ~ * ~ *

"Oh, my God! It's...indescribable," Barker breathed in wondering awe as she gazed down at the planet.

They were standing at one of the windows of Jopus Prime, the one with the best view of the planet. It was massive, painted in swirling greens, purples, blues, yellows, and almost every other colour imaginable. It was heavily green, purple, and blue but all the other shades were mixed in somewhere, creating a stunning effect that left the usually talkative woman speechless.

"Aye. Ya should see it from the surface when the sun sets. Incredible."

Barker detected an almost happy, contented note in Janus's voice that she had never heard before. She had not considered Janus the type to appreciate the more basic indulgences, but it seemed that Barker was in for many surprises. "So, is that it?"

"Aye."

"It's an amazing space station, especially compared to what humans have made."

Patrik stepped up behind them and clapped his hands down on their shoulders. "Since the tour is over, I'll take Barker from here and you," he looked up at Janus, "will go and see the good doctor. Right?"

Janus sighed. She didn't really want to go to a doctor, but she knew Patrik was worried about her and she owed him the peace of mind. Plus, it wouldn't be fair to Quip to get involved in anything if there was a chance she might be ill. "Aye." She turned to go.

"Janus?" Barker waited until blue eyes looked back at her. "I had a really good time. Thank you for showing me around."

Janus simply dipped her head in acknowledgment and continued on down the hallway.

Barker looked up at Patrik's face, seeing there a slight relaxation in the strain that had been present since they had met. "Bet it feels good to be back home."

"Mm. This isn't really home, but yeah, it's great to at least be in our own solar system."

The blonde nodded as they started walking. "So, where is home?"

"Well, for the last twenty years or so, it was that ship. That's where my family and friends were. I was born on a planet about thirty light years from here, but we left when I was really young. My parents are dead, so my wife and children were my home. Until Janus came along. Now, I'm not really sure." They proceeded in silence for a moment before Patrik turned an interested eye on his companion. "And you? Anyone back on Sol worrying about you?"

Barker pursed her lips for a moment and sighed. "My parents will get worried, I suppose. But other than that, I'm an only child."

"No significant other?"

"Nah. I was focused on my work for a long time and being posted on the *Avenger* wasn't exactly conductive to building a relationship."

"Will you miss it?"

Barker stopped walking abruptly and really thought about the question. Sure, she would miss her parents but not for a while. They were never in the habit of seeing each other on a regular basis, and accepted the fact that since they lived on different ends of the planet, any visits were short and sporadic. She had few close friends back on Earth, mostly just acquaintances. Melvin Kodiac was the only person she would categorize as a "best friend", and he was there with her. When she stopped to think about it, Barker realized that the time she had been spending planet-side had been decreasing over the last year or so, so as to become almost nonexistent. She could hardly remember the security code for her little apartment in Madrid, or the call number for the pizza parlor she practically lived off of for two years. It was an unsettling thought, and yet it came with a realization that brought her peace: she had outgrown Earth and all it had to offer.

Barker had known for a while that she was becoming increasingly unhappy with her life, and was aware that she needed a change. She hadn't the faintest idea what the change would be, but now that she was there at Jopus Prime, Barker had the suspicion that nothing on Earth or in the Milky Way Galaxy could satisfy her.

Quite aware of Patrik's penetrating hazel eyes on her, she finally answered, "No."

"Not at all?" He was somewhat amazed by her precise, blunt, one word answer. Then she looked up at him, and Patrik saw in her emerald eyes an understanding and an acceptance of a truth she just then discovered for herself.

"There's nothing left there for me." And then she smiled, a strangely contented grin, as if she knew some great secret that no one else did, a secret that was the key to life.

Patrik decided not to try and figure it out, he simply took a page from Janus's book and nodded. They continued down the hall in silence, Patrik accepting everything she had told him and Barker marveling at the new sense of freedom she felt.

~~*~*~*

Doctor Omelian'par looked up as a shadow fell across his desk.

His eyes widened as he identified the tall form standing in his doorway. "Janus, come in, come in." He bustled over to the woman, noting that she looked worlds better than the last time he'd had cause to treat her. *What an awful case that was.* He shook his head at the recollection.

Janus moved in hesitantly. She wasn't fond of doctors. She believed that if something was wrong with her – especially due to natural causes – then it should be able to repair itself naturally. The only time that philosophy was called into question was when her life was threatened by something uncommon. To Janus, that meant when she found herself in a situation that was not the norm. Her definition of the norm was not fixed, so it really came down to what she thought. She felt fine, better than she had in ages really, now that she had recovered from the strain of healing three people.

"Well, what seems to be the problem?"

"There is no problem."

"Then what–"

"A doctor 'ad two scans of me. They are different and she does not know why. I promised Patrik I would come see ya."

Omelian'par blinked for a moment, then sighed. Janus was as blunt and condensed in her explanations as always. "Why don't you just sit down and I'll take a look."

Janus sat and looked around the office as Omelian'par prepared the examination. He was a nice man, and she had always thought highly of him, even when she had cause to be cursing at him in three languages he had never heard before, the poor guy. She really didn't know why he put up with her, especially after that last time. He was the same species as Quip'lee, not a race one would ordinarily picture in the role of kindly physician, but Omelian'par had proven his exceptional bedside manner many times over.

As the doctor activated his equipment, he noticed that Janus had zoned out on him. He was not concerned; she always did that. After a few moments, he looked at the results and his purple eyes widened at what he saw. He rechecked the results, knowing that his degree of certainty would be one of the first things Janus would ask when he briefed her. When the screen insistently showed him the same reading, Omelian'par considered the implications and how Janus might react.

She had grown up around it, he knew. But still, it was not a condition that often occurred among her people and thus its presence could be truly terrifying. Janus's potential reaction was as much a mystery to him as anyone else. But if she embraced it, then...then it would prove to be the most wondrous and magical thing she could ever hope to experience. Omelian'par only hoped that Janus would see it that way.

He sighed and walked over to her. Knowing that anything more was likely to get him knocked through the bulkheads, he placed a very gentle hand on her arm. As he waited for her to come out of her self-imposed trance, he gazed at her silver markings, tracking the intricate design down her forearm, across her wrist, and onto each and every finger. Omelian'par's head jerked up as he felt Janus move and saw that she was staring at him with a question in her eyes.

"Come." He walked over to the console on which the results were displayed and waited for her to join him.

Curious about the odd look in the doctor's eyes, Janus stood, walked over to the monitor, and looked down. There she saw something she had learned about as a child from her parents, something she had believed she would never set eyes on again.

Omelian'par remained silent, knowing it needed no explanation, knowing Janus knew exactly what she was gazing at.

"Are ya sure? Did ya... I... recheck?"

"Yes, Janus, I ran it several times."

"It cannot be. It does not happen ta us."

"That's not true, Janus, and you know it. The only question you have to ask yourself, is: what are you going to do now?" When she looked up at him, he felt a flash of protectiveness at the bewilderment in her eyes. Then Janus turned and walked out in a daze.

Omelian'par watched her until she was out of sight. He knew there were a thousand different thoughts running through her mind. It was a shame, really, that Janus and her people knew little of one of the strongest emotions in the universe. Of being in love.

Chapter 5

Quip'lee looked up as he heard someone enter the room. He spent a moment looking at the faces of Patrik and the blonde woman, then nodded to himself. It had been a while since he had seen Janus and Patrik, and in truth, he had been concerned about them. He had not bought into the rumors of their deaths like everyone else had been so willing to do. Quip had too much faith in Janus's will to survive, her inner strength, to believe any such thing until someone showed him a body or related an eyewitness account. And Patrik...well, Patrik was as stubborn as hell. It had saddened him greatly to hear that Patrik's family was dead, that all he had been left with was little Emmeline. *Such a darling child.*

He turned his thoughts to the human woman who had walked in with Patrik. She seemed nice enough. She looked almost happy to be here and that baffled him. All the other humans were on edge and frightened beyond belief. Quip had heard several of them lamenting that this was not their war, but their Captain Harrison had made a decision and Quip was confident that they would all abide by it. However, this Barker person...something about her made him very curious and he wasn't sure why, or what was so fascinating.

Patrik slouched down into one of the many chairs around the table, listening as Barker bent to say a few words to him before she left. He nodded silently and glanced around the room full of people. In addition to Quip, Harrison was seated at one end along with several other military commanders and advisors who he vaguely remembered. They were all waiting for Janus. Patrik was a little worried about Janus. There was a strange feeling of confusion, disbelief, and happiness coming through to him from their mental link. It wasn't very strong, suggesting that Janus was dealing fairly well or at least managing to push her feelings down and ignore them. But still, it was a puzzling set of emotions that made him even more worried about his friend.

Just as Quip raised a questioning eyebrow at Patrik, Janus wandered into the room and took a seat, hardly looking at anyone and seeming very distracted. There was an extended moment of silence before Janus gathered herself and looked pointedly up at Quip.

"Very well. We have a major problem, as I know you are all aware. And the fact of the matter is that we are losing. We simply don't have enough ships or intel to mount a defense against the Ebokras. Thanks to the sacrifice made by our old friends," he indicated Janus and Patrik, "and the help offered by our new allies," here he nodded at Harrison, "we have a little more knowledge and strength. But unless something changes drastically in the next few days, it will prove to be far too little, much too late. Ideas?"

A light hum started up around the room as the people shifted in their seats and spoke all together, before one voice rose above the din. "Besides this odd vulnerability to pesticide, what else do we know of that can kill them?" The question was raised by Quip's immediate subordinate, commander of the fleet from Trugas, the largest continent on Jopus.

Janus spoke up. "Breakin' their neck, shovin' their nose bone inta their brain. Explosions, beheadin'...anythin' serious like that."

The woman who posed the question cleared her throat and looked at Janus. "Yes, all those things are fine for someone like you, but the rest of us would hardly last a second if we got close enough to fight hand-to-hand. And we don't have the means to just blow up all their ships on sight."

"What if we could find out where they were coming from and then blew that up?" This came from Patrik, who found himself the focus of the entire room. "What? They must have a base somewhere, right? A planet, a big starship, a space station – something you could infiltrate with explosives."

Quip inclined his head to one side as he regarded the young man who had lost so much. "Is true, but the problem would be *finding* that base. We haven't been very successful in tracking their point of origin."

"So the next time they attack, why don't we be waiting to lock on to a retreating ship and find out where it goes?" the commander from Trugas asked. "It should give us somewhere to start, even if all we find is a minor base. Right?" She looked around the room, seeing skepticism in almost every face. "We have to try something; our current plan obviously isn't working."

"She is right. It is the best idea I 'ave 'eard and 'as a good chance of workin'."

Quip looked at Janus and had to agree. Their options were limited. "Very well. Then someone has to modify our sensors for longer distances." He paused for a long moment and stared at the table. "And...that may not work, so we need something else. Come on, people, think! There is an entire universe out there filled with allies who haven't been touched by this war yet. Who haven't we contacted?"

Janus sighed as her mind once again lit upon the most logical conclusion that she could reach. She really didn't want to have to go back there, but...but this was worth it. She nodded her head slightly and then looked up, directly into Quip's eyes. "Do ya 'ave a shuttle?"

"Why?"

"I am goin' ta get us some 'elp."

"From your people?"

"Aye."

"Janus, we already asked them. Taykio is not very accommodating."

"Is that who is in charge now?"

"Yes."

"I never liked 'im."

"Me either."

"I will go. They 'ave as much stake in this as anyone."

"And if he insists on staying out of it all?"

Janus looked up then, her eyes intense and her platinum markings glowing. "Then it will be the death of 'im." Without another word, she stood and walked out of the room.

Quip sighed as he acknowledged the truth of Janus's words. He hoped she would be able to sway them, because without their involvement he did not anticipate a pleasant outcome.

Patrik slipped out of the room after his friend, knowing he really didn't have much else to contribute to the strategizing.

Seeing that the meeting was breaking up, Harrison stood and approached Quip. He looked up at the captain and waited for her to speak.

"The *Avenger* is a decommissioned warship; it was quite formidable in its day. I was speaking with one of your engineers earlier. You have some equipment and weapons that can easily be integrated to make us even more prepared to face the Ebokras. My engineers could have modifications completed in forty-eight hours. It would give you one more ship with a full crew ready to fight."

Quip considered Harrison's offer. It was just possible these humans and their technology and tactics might be what was needed to level the playing field. It would be something new that the Ebokras wouldn't be expecting, which alone would give them the upper hand. Besides, he had seen the ship. It seemed a waste to keep such an impressive specimen dry-docked when the captain was willing to commit herself and her crew to the fight. Even if the humans wanted to go home there was, at present, no way to send them. Quip nodded his consent.

* ~ * ~ * ~ * ~ *

The form leaning against the wall and gazing out the window was at once recognizable to Janus, and sent an odd tingle down her spine. Now that she was aware of what Omelian'par had diagnosed, Janus would admit to herself that she could feel it – a weak but persistent pull in the energy around her, unquestionably running between herself and Barker. It was a curious sensation, one she had heard described by her parents many times, and Janus clearly remembered the awe and joy in their voices.

She wasn't sure how she felt about it, about this anomaly affecting her. It was very rare and looked upon in many different ways by her people. Some saw it as a weakness and a curse; others, like her parents, saw it as the most precious and beautiful thing in the universe. Janus sighed, her eyes still glued to the relaxed silhouette. This wasn't supposed to happen. Her kind did not fall in love, did not make these kinds of connections.

Janus gathered herself and started walking toward Barker, deciding that the outcome would depend largely on the blonde ensign. If these...feelings...were returned, if this odd connection went both ways, then Janus would embrace it wholeheartedly because she knew she would not have a choice in the matter. It would happen anyway. That pull would get stronger and more palpable until they both just gave in and accepted the inevitability of it.

Barker felt someone come up behind her and she turned, surprised to see Janus. "Hey, I didn't think you'd be done so soon."

"Aye, we 'ave made a decision."

"Good. So what is it?"

"I am goin' ta my people and Quip will try ta track an Ebokras ship."

Barker nodded, trying to fill in some of the gaps in Janus's reply. "You want to find a base or something to destroy?"

"Aye, 'tis the idea."

"When are you leaving?"

"Soon."

Barker looked up into Janus's eyes and for the first time, detected an odd hesitancy there. She couldn't help wondering at its source. They had always been fairly comfortable around each other – no awkward silences, no tension – and it had been nice. Even the way Janus spoke was refreshing. Barker was learning that humans tended to mask their words with flowery language and whatnot, in hopes of deceiving whomever they were speaking to and furthering their own plans. She was getting tired of it all. But Janus never went into long-winded speeches; she gave you the stark, unvarnished truth.

The blonde woman reached out and placed her hand on Janus's arm, feeling the muscles tighten in response. "You be careful, okay? I know they're your people and you're quite capable of handling yourself, but...sometimes things happen."

Janus ducked her head. "Aye."

Barker raised her eyes over Janus's shoulder to see Melvin Kodiac standing there, waving his hand and gesturing her over. She nodded and looked back at Janus. "I have to go." Impulsively, she threw her arms around Janus in a brief hug and, after a moment's delay, felt a pat on the back. Then the ensign ducked around Janus's rock still body and trotted over to her friend. *Oh, Barker,* she thought, *that was bad. You know she doesn't like being touched, so you hug her? You're lucky she didn't knock you into space!* And yet, Ensign Barker stepped up next to Kodiac with a large smile plastered on her face.

"What are you grinning about?"

"Nothing."

He snorted. "Yeah, right. Come on. Harrison is converting the *Avenger* back into a warship. She wants all crew members there to help and be briefed on the operation of some new systems we're integrating."

Barker nodded and started her feet moving, throwing one more look over her shoulder to see Janus still standing there in apparent shock. She smiled again and started attending to Kodiac's update.

Patrik had been watching unobtrusively from his spot in a convenient doorway. He smiled as he watched Barker go, wondering if the woman knew what a challenge she was in for with Janus. He considered saying something to the blonde, fearing that she was in a position to get her heart broken. But first he had to speak with Janus.

Janus finally collected her scattered wits and focused on Patrik as he stopped in front of her and cleared his throat.

"You all right? You seem a little shaken up after that hug."

"Aye. I am fine. She just...she...surprised me."

"I can see that. So, what did Omelian'par say?"

She looked at him, debating whether she should tell him or not. "Nothin'. I am in perfect 'ealth."

Patrik tipped his head back, feeling that Janus wasn't telling him the whole truth. But she wouldn't keep a serious problem from him, so he was content to let it go. At least for the moment. "Okay." Patrik saw Quip coming down the hall and he stuck his hand out. "Be careful, Janus. I don't want to lose any more family."

She grasped his forearm and nodded. "Aye."

Patrik turned and went down the hall, giving Quip a nod as they passed.

Janus turned to look out the window, the familiar outline of Jopus oddly comforting. She felt Quip come up behind her but didn't move, opting to continue her study of the planet.

"It might not be as easy as you think."

"What do ya mean?"

"Janus, when was the last time you were home?"

She didn't answer, just swallowed a few times.

"Right. That's what I thought. Things have been changing there for a long time now. When your father died, it all happened faster. I doubt it will even resemble the place you remember."

"All the more reason ta never go back."

She said it quietly, and for a moment Quip thought he had imagined it. "Is that why you stayed away, Janus? Because you couldn't handle the changes?"

Janus stayed silent but Quip noted a slight ducking of her proud head, giving him all the answer he needed. He watched her draw a deep breath before turning to look at him. Janus stared at her friend for a timeless moment, letting down the barriers in her eyes for just a second and allowing him a brief glimpse of what she held inside. It was all Quip needed to understand, and he nodded.

"Shuttle's ready for you in Hanger 23." Janus started walking, but paused as his voice called out after her, "Come back to us, Janus." She resumed walking, and the last thing Quip saw was her strong back, shoulders held high as she prepared to step into a world she had left long ago. Janus was unaware of his desperate thoughts. *For the love of the gods, please come back to us.*

* ~ * ~ * ~ * ~ *

Patrik meandered down the hall with no particular destination in mind. He jerked backward as a head poked out into the hallway in front of him. Omelian'par. The doctor gestured him into the room and Patrik obeyed, settling himself on the corner of one of the beds.

Omelian'par shifted uncomfortably, aware that he was about to do something that went against his most basic ethics as a physician. But he was worried about Janus, and if she spoke to anyone it would be Patrik. The doctor was also confident that Patrik would keep a close eye on Janus and that settled his mind quite effectively. "Has Janus told you about anything I said?"

"No, just that there was nothing wrong with her. Why? Was that a lie?"

"No, no, she is very healthy. But I am a little concerned. Tell me, Patrik, what do you know of Janus's people?"

"Well, some, but the more I think about it, I guess she hasn't told me that much."

"Yes, I thought as much. She is very private that way. Has she ever mentioned her parents?"

He smiled and that gave Omelian'par his answer before Patrik could open his mouth. "She has. Actually, she has often spoken about them and their love for each other."

"Yes, yes. Have you ever heard stories about people meeting and feeling like they complete one another?"

"Um..." He paused, a little thrown off by the apparent change in the conversation. "Sure. A lot of species have a great desire to find that kind of mythical love."

"I have observed that. The popular term among people who believe in such things is half. Or, to find one's half. That is what Janus's parents were, Patrik. It was quite an amazing, and humbling, thing to see."

"Oookay, Omelian, where is this conversation going?" The doctor was doing an admirable job of dancing around whatever point he was trying to make, and it was getting on Patrik's nerves. He couldn't seem to tolerate that kind of thing anymore.

"Well, you see...the problem is that Janus...and her people, they don't...they don't..." He trailed off, the skin around his eyes twitching in agitation.

"They don't *what*?"

"They don't fall in love."

Patrik was still and silent for a long moment before he opened his mouth and managed to speak. "But that doesn't make any sense, Omelian, you just said that Janus's parents were halves...or each other's half." He shook his head in frustration, unsure how to phrase it.

"Let me finish, please, Patrik. Typically, yes, they do not fall in love, they do not make connections, they do not feel any strong emotion – except for the more destructive ones: rage, hatred, revenge. They are truly a violent race, but over time they managed to tame those impulses quite well. There is, however, a very small percentage who *do* fall in love. And I am not talking about trysts in the night; I'm talking about Janus's parents. That is the only type of love they can find. Which, I suppose, is why love amongst their race is such an extraordinary occurrence. Halves are truly rare. But when they do meet their half, recognition of the connection is almost instantaneous; it changes something very basic in their biology, in their very atomic structure." He paused to make sure that Patrik was still following and was gratified to see an extremely interested look on his face. "That is what has happened to Janus."

Patrik almost swallowed his tongue, and in doing so he choked and coughed as he looked at Omelian'par with large eyes. He finally caught his breath and promptly spoke. "Are you serious?"

"Yes."

"Are you sure?"

"Yes. I ran the results through ten times."

"Oh my." No wonder Janus had been acting so strangely. "Who is it?"

"I do not know. Why would I?"

"Barker." The name passed his lips in a whisper, and then something occurred to him. "Wait, wait. How do they know? How do they recognize this connection?"

"Janus's parents explained it to me as a pull in the energy around them that connected them both."

"Sooo, Janus's half," he cringed, thinking it was a strange word to associate with his friend, "is obviously not of her species. So this person won't be able to feel it like she does, right?"

"Correct. But I would assume that this person would have some extra awareness of Janus. This is not the type of thing one can just ignore, even without Janus's hypersensitivity to the world around her."

Patrik nodded absently, his mind running over the interaction he had observed between his best friend and the little blonde. He would admit that there had always been...something...there. He had felt it, but he wasn't sure if that had been because he knew Janus so well, or if it was some side effect of their mental link, or if it had just been that strong. He would have to think about that. "So, why did you tell me all this?"

"Even with Janus's exposure to love through her parents, she is totally unprepared to deal with something like this. And I would bet my reputation that if she talks to anyone, it will be you. Just tread carefully."

"Riiight. So why not just wait? If she did come talk to me, she'd have to tell me everything."

"In case you haven't noticed, Janus has an annoying tendency to leave things out of her narratives. Besides, if she doesn't come to you, it will still do my heart good to know someone is looking out for her."

Patrik nodded again, feeling like his mind was on overload. He needed to relax. He stood up and directed his footsteps toward his quarters for some quality father-daughter time with Emmeline.

~~*~*~*

"So," Melvin Kodiac looked up from where he was attempting to reconfigure the *Avenger's* targeting system, "how's Janus?"

Barker scowled at the console in front of her and then glanced up at her friend, "What do you mean, how's Janus?"

"That's exactly what I mean. I don't think questions get any simpler than that."

"Why should I know how Janus is? You really wanna know, go ask Patrik."

"Well," Kodiac cursed softly at the diagnostic data running across his screen, "it seems to me that the two of you have been spending a lot of time together and you looked pretty chummy, so I just figured..."

"Spending a lot of time together? Mel, you're losing it. We only picked them up a day ago, and in that time we've been attacked by evil, rampaging aliens and then transported across the universe. We haven't had a lot of time to sit and chat."

"Well, yeah, but despite all that, you talked a lot. And, I dunno...there just seemed to be something there."

Barker looked up sharply and then plopped down next to her buddy. "What do you mean?"

He blinked up at her and set down his tools, disregarding his work for the moment. "It just seemed to me that there was some kind of current running between you two right from the beginning. And Janus seems to like you. You're the only one from our crew she's said two words to...except Harrison and Cobb, but that was out of necessity."

"I'm also the only one who's really taken the time to talk to her."

"Right. So I figured you'd be able to tell me how Janus is doing."

Barker looked up, suspicious. There was something that he wasn't saying, that he was doing a good job of dancing around and alluding to. "Why do you care?" she shot back, trying to lure him out.

"Do you have a crush on her?"

It really was the last thing she had been expecting, so she sat and stared at him owlishly for a long series of seconds, then exploded. "*What!*"

Kodiac drew his head back and glanced around. They were essentially alone, so he felt confident in continuing their discussion. "You heard me. Do you?"

"What on Earth gave you that idea?"

"Hey, I'm not blind. I've seen you two talking. When you're with her, your face almost always has this incredible little smile and you seem really happy. And you seem to touch her a lot."

"I *always* touch people when I talk; it's my thing. It helps me explain things better."

"Yeah, I know, Barker, but the thing is – she *lets* you touch her. Even I can tell she's not a touchy-feely person, but she lets you, Barker. And that hug today in the hall? Whoo-boy!"

Barker thought about that for a minute. Janus always seemed to like her space, and communicated that fact very clearly in the way she stood and interacted with people – close, but not too close. Even Patrik. The most contact Barker had seen the man bestow on his friend was a shoulder clasp or a friendly swat on the back. "Okay, maybe you're right about the touching thing, but it's not something I can explain," she finished with a huff.

"You haven't answered my question."

"No, I don't have a crush on Janus."

"Are you sure?"

"Yes."

"Positive?"

"Yes, I'm positive! I do not have a crush on Janus, and you'd do well not to ask me again, bud!" Barker growled a little and then stood, brushed her pants off, and marched from the room.

Kodiac watched her go and then bent his head back to his task. "Sure, Barker. You just keep telling yourself that." A deep belly chuckle floated up into the air.

~~*~*~*

The blonde ensign walked blindly through the halls of the *Avenger*, a little miffed at Kodiac. *He just had to go and bring that up, didn't he? Had to say something that would get me thinking. Had to poke and prod until he got a reaction that gave him his answer.*

Barker halted and sighed. That's exactly what had happened – he had forced a totally emotional confession from her. No words required. *Damn it!*

She didn't want to have a crush.

Or be in love.

Especially not with someone like Janus.

Someone who would probably go away to some important war or other such thing and never come back.

Someone who'd leave and never say good-bye, or explain why they were going.

Someone who would find some greater cause that would always come first.

No.

Barker shook her head. She didn't want that. Didn't want the worry, or the heartache, or the pain.

Never again.

Damn him, damn Melvin Kodiac for making me realize what this is. For making it harder to ignore, to push down and lock away where it wouldn't ever be able to get out.

Barker sighed again and continued walking. Before she had acknowledged what she was feeling, she had been happy to be with Janus and talk with her and hug her. Happy to be happy. Because Kodaic had been right – being with Janus did make her happy and content in a way that had been sorely missing for several long years. But she had naively thought that it had simply been a friendship in the making – nothing more, nothing stronger. She had been wrong, and now Barker didn't know what to do.

She wound her way through the hallways, not paying much attention to where she was going. Her meandering finally came to a halt when she walked into a wall. Her blonde head shot up as she realized that she was in the middle of the hallway and that there shouldn't be a wall there. She was met with vivid, slightly amused blue eyes. "Janus."

"Barker."

"I thought you were leaving?"

"Aye. But I 'ad ta come 'ere first." She nodded at the door on her left and Barker saw that they were at the entrance to the medical bay.

"Oh. Well, I have to go. So I'll...um, I'll see you later."

"Aye." Janus turned her head and watched as Barker fairly flew down the hall as if she had to get somewhere really quickly. But Janus knew that wasn't true, since the woman had previously been off in her own little world. Janus could feel the cord that bound them together getting stronger as they spent more time in the same vicinity. And at the moment, there was a vague sense of upset coming down that link from the blonde. Janus couldn't help wondering at the source, thinking that maybe she was the cause. Deciding that she couldn't do anything about it at the moment, she turned and walked through the door.

As Janus entered, Doctor Cobb looked up and squealed with delight. "I was hoping to see you soon. I'd like you to meet some people."

The doctor pulled Janus over to the first bed where the man with the previously destroyed chest now rested, smiling and happy. He spent long moments expressing his gratitude to her for saving his life. The woman in the second bed was still unconscious, but Janus had predicted two days and tomorrow had yet to come. The man on the third bed surprised Janus by being incredibly soft spoken and friendly. Janus found herself enjoying the time spent speaking to him. She was pleased to see that her efforts to save his mind had been successful.

"You have no idea," he said, "what it's like to see yourself slowly losing your mind and not be able to stop it." And then he looked up at her and saw in her eyes something hauntingly familiar reflected back at him. He bowed his head and amended with a barely audible whisper, "Perhaps you do."

Janus spent longer than she had planned in the medical bay before she finally managed to pull herself away. She was just about to step through the door when it opened and Samson came through. At seeing her, he stopped and glared. Janus's body reacted instinctively to the perceived threat and she growled low in her throat, her lips pulling back in a snarl.

A cough broke through their shield of mutual hatred and disgust, and Janus stepped around him and out the door.

Samson stayed still until he was sure that...woman...was gone. He moved forward and stopped in front of Cobb.

She looked up at him and sighed. "Honestly, Dion, I really wish you wouldn't do that."

He scowled at hearing his first name from her lips. "Do what?"

"Be so hateful towards Janus. She has never done anything to anyone here to deserve such treatment, and seeing you act that way makes my skin crawl."

"We've had this discussion before, Tina, and I thought we had agreed to disagree. I'll do what I do, and you do what you do."

She looked up at him with sad eyes. "I don't know when you became so misguided, Dion."

He snorted and held out his arm. "Is this fixed yet?"

Cobb just shook her head and pulled up his sleeve, being none too gentle about it. She checked the device that had been strapped on to knit his broken bones and shook her head. "It's a pretty bad break. Leave it on until tomorrow, at least, then come see me." He nodded and turned to leave. Doctor Cobb reached out and clasped his good arm. "I wish you'd give Janus a chance. Talk to her, see that she isn't what you think."

He faced her fully, his visage going from passive to infuriated in the blink of an eye. "I don't want to give her a chance, or get to know her. I *know* what she is – an abomination to all of humanity!"

Now the doctor was getting angry. "Really? Is that how you sleep at night; how you justify all the things that your so-called friends have done, that you've been involved in? Is it? Because let me tell you something, Dion, from where I'm standing Janus is ten times the human you'll ever be!"

She took a deep breath and stepped closer. "You speak of human supremacy, of justice, and yet you're the same as every hate group that has ever existed in our history. You just don't want to accept anything that is different from you, anyone that might prove to be better or greater than you are. You're small, Samson, small and petty and hateful. Sub-human. One day those people you call friends, and your hate, will be the death of you. And when that happens, I won't be there to cry over whatever is left. You'll have gotten what you deserve." She released his arm and took a step back.

Samson stared hard at her for a long time and then his eyes narrowed. "So be it." He turned on his heel and walked out.

Tina Cobb sighed and sat down on one of the beds, suddenly feeling weak in the knees. *Oh, Dion,* she thought, *my dear, sweet, little brother. When did you lose your way? And why didn't I see it until it was too late?*

She looked down at the ring on her left hand, gently twirling it around on her finger. An image of her husband rose in her mind's eye, all shaggy blond hair and twinkling blue eyes. She smiled and felt a sense of calm fill her soul. *I'll get home to you soon, my love. I promise.*

* ~ * ~ * ~ * ~ *

The next morning, Janus left without a word to anyone. Her ship disappeared into subspace before the sun had risen on Jopus. She estimated a little over two days to get where she needed to be, mainly because there was a large grid of space around her home world where subspace travel was forbidden.

The ship was a basic shuttle with a light arsenal, two engines, incredible shielding technology, and very effective sensors. Janus was confident that if she ran into any trouble, she'd either be able to fight, or run and hide. She hoped that this trip would prove fruitful and she would arrive back at Jopus Prime with help. If not, well, she'd have a few choice words with her people before she left. And she wouldn't ever go back.

* ~ * ~ * ~ * ~ *

Late the next day, Quip'lee looked up as Captain Harrison entered the room in response to his summons. "The modifications to the *Avenger* are complete."

"Good. I want you to go out and test all the systems. I'll be sending the *Pro Re Nata* with you. Its captain... Well, I think you'll like him. Go to it, Harrison."

Harrison nodded and spun on her heel. She boarded the *Avenger* and they launched along with the *Pro Re Nata*. As soon as they were a few thousand kilometers from Jopus Prime, the com link was activated.

"Captain Harrison, quite an impressive looking ship you have there. Follow me to these coordinates and we'll get on with the testing to see if you have anything more than something nice to look at." The commander of the *Pro Re Nata* grinned as he waited for a reply.

Harrison blinked at seeing a human on her vid screen. From what she had seen, she didn't think there were that many humans in this region of space. "I assure you, Captain, the *Avenger* is much, much more than a pretty showpiece."

He nodded and the screen returned to a view of space. Harrison watched as the ship disappeared into subspace, and then followed. The USC *Avenger* arrived safely and in one piece. The screen came to life again.

"I guess we can assume that your engines are working just fine. I'm Captain Lang, by the way. It's good to meet you, Harrison."

"You too."

He smiled again and nodded. "All right, let's try out those new sensors, then targeting and weapons."

The rest of the day passed in much the same way, the *Avenger* completing every test imaginable with flying colours. Lang opened a channel one last time, "Awesome, Captain, truly awesome. The only possible test left for your ship is a battle situation, and I can assure you that will happen soon enough. Let's head back to base and maybe you'll let me buy you a drink?"

Harrison thought for a moment, then nodded. "Sure, why not."

Lang grinned before his ship zoomed off into subspace.

* ~ * ~ * ~ *

"Hey, Barker!"

The ensign looked up to see Kodiac headed her way. "Hey, bud, what's up?"

He sat down next to her and spent a moment looking around. They were in the cafeteria on Jopus Prime, and he had to admit that, as cafeterias went, this one was pretty damn nice. "Not much. I heard that you've discovered an affinity for the new targeting systems." He wiggled his eyebrows.

"Yeah. So?"

"So nothing. I just thought it was pretty cool. You sat down and started getting locks on those drones Lang released before some of the tactical officers who have been doing it for years."

"I see. And what were you doing during our ship-wide test?"

"Who, me?"

Barker smiled and shook her head. "Yes you."

"Nothing much. A little bit of this and a little bit of that."

"Spit it out, Kodiac," Barker growled out.

He immediately clammed up and pursed his lips, looking at Barker with a twinkle in his eyes. It was a twinkle she had long ago identified as Kodiac's "I know something you don't" give away. It made it very easy for Barker to know when he was holding back on her. "Well, if you must know, I had the opportunity to check out some more of this place's defenses. One thing led to another and before I knew it, I was in one of their fighters. Lang was impressed, I think." He grinned cockily and puffed out his chest.

"Kodiac, get to the point."

"All right, all right, geez. You, my friend, are looking at the new squadron commander for Beta team."

Barker blinked a moment as she stared at him. "You're a fighter pilot now?"

"Yes."

"With your own squad?"

"Yes."

"And you couldn't come up with anything better than Beta team?" Barker asked with rising disbelief. And volume.

"Um..."

She launched herself at her friend, wrapped her arms around his neck, and squeezed for all she was worth. "That's great, Kodiac."

"Um...Ba...Bark...breathe."

"Oh!" She loosened her hold and pulled back to look at him. "It is great, right?"

A large smile split his face. "Oh yeah! You have got to see their fighters. They are sooo cool. Small and maneuverable, but they pack one hell of a punch! It's like...like... I dunno what it's like but...it's awesome." He sighed dreamily.

"So what ship do you belong to?"

"At the moment, I'm still on the *Avenger*. I think Quip is trying to keep us all together, you know."

"Yeah...but?"

Kodiac looked at her, silent for several seconds. Then he sucked in a breath to blow out as a massive sigh. "I don't know, Barker. This place is wonderful; I love it. I don't know why, but something here makes me happy. Have you been down to the planet yet?"

"No."

"Oh, Barker, it's so beautiful. You should go. And when the sun sets..." He sighed again and slumped back in his chair.

"Yeah. Janus said something about that."

"I think I could stay here."

Barker looked up sharply at that and studied his face. She had to admit that he did look a lot more relaxed and content than before. "Do you mean that?"

He glanced over and then down at his hands in his lap. "Yeah," he whispered. "I do."

"Me, too."

Kodiac looked up in surprise. "Do you think we could? I mean..."

She shrugged. "I'm not sure. I don't think Quip would have a problem with it. The thing is, what's your situation at home?"

He shifted around as he considered that. "Well, I'm not indentured or anything. And there isn't anyone back there for me. But seriously, Barker, do you think the people of Earth would do anything? I mean, first they'd have to get here – which would take a hell of a long time – and then what? They can't demand that we go back. They're our lives; we have free will."

"Mm...that makes sense. Still, you'd do well to speak with Harrison when this is all over. And Quip." Barker stood and picked up the remains of her meal. "It's something to think about."

"It sure is," he murmured softly.

* ~ * ~ * ~ * ~ *

Captain Lang walked up to the table where Harrison was already seated. She stood as he approached, which caused him to grin and stick out his hand. "We haven't been formally introduced. Eric Lang, captain of the *Pro Re Nata*."

Harrison grasped his hand and replied, "Eileen Harrison, captain of the *USC Avenger*."

They shook and Lang grinned again as they took their seats.

Harrison opened her mouth before Lang could speak. "What does that mean, anyway?"

"*Pro Re Nata?*"

Harrison nodded.

"Well, I took some liberties with the translation and whatnot. It's Latin and it means 'for an occasion that has arisen'. I thought it was an appropriate name for my ship, considering my circumstances at the time."

Harrison nodded, thoughtful. "I see."

Lang grinned and continued with his original line of thought. "Well, I'm very pleased to meet you. We get a lot of new faces around here, but they're hardly ever human."

Harrison looked up and set aside her musings for later. "Yeah. I noticed that. But still, there are far more than I would have expected. And you used Latin for your ship's name, a dead language from Earth?"

Lang shrugged his shoulders, "There have always been humans scattered around. There are several colonies and planets that are strictly human with other species in the minority. But those planets tend to be pretty far from what most people would consider central areas, like Jopus." Lang shrugged and smiled, "You get used to being a member of a scarce species."

"Why?"

"Why do you get used to it?" he asked with another infectious grin.

"No, no. Why are there so few humans? And so scattered? I mean, we never even had cause to think there would be humans beyond Earth!"

Lang glanced around as his smile slowly faded. "I can't help you with the Earth or Latin connection. Latin has always just been around in old books and databases."

"But what keeps these colonies you mentioned from expanding outwards into areas like this? There must be a benefit to having a presence in what you call central areas."

"Several things. For one, this area is the native habitat of Quip'lee's species. You've seen him. They aren't the most friendly people and they have a bad reputation. So in that regard, I think it may be fear. A lot of the human settlements have chosen to limit their contact to trading goods and that's it."

"Annnnddd?"

Lang looked around again and then back at Harrison. "Does it bother you?"

"Excuse me?"

"The looks you're getting from the people here. I noticed you noticing them."

"Well," Harrison glanced around the room a little self-consciously, "I guess it did, at first. But I've gotten used to it. As soon as we picked up Janus and Patrik, I started getting those same looks and reactions."

"Do you know why?"

Harrison shrugged.

"Because of what you are: United Space Coalition."

"So why does everyone hate us? The Coalition has never been out this far."

"No, but that doesn't mean we haven't been as far as the Coalition...and Marson."

Harrison looked up at her tablemate, incredulous. "These people are giving me dirty looks because of Marson?"

"A lot of people from around here got caught up there: people's daughters and sons, sisters and brothers, wives and husbands. The remaining family members and friends grew up hating you, and they taught their children the same thing."

"But that was half a lifetime ago! Most likely, none of the people here even knew the ones who were in Marson. How can a society hold a grudge for that long?"

Lang's voice became impassioned as he expressed his anger at Harrison's obvious ignorance. "And what about people like Janus? How long do you think it has been for her? Hardly half a lifetime. Janus has to live with what happened there for longer than you or I could ever imagine." Lang leaned forward and looked right into Harrison's eyes. "That's what these people remember – the victims who can't find sweet relief in death. And that's why most humans stay away from this area."

"You blame an entire species for one planet's transgression?"

"No, but humans are much more unpredictable, selfish, conniving, and hateful than most. We tend toward those things without any provocation, without any wrong having been committed against us. We are vicious and evil and far, far more dangerous than people like the Ebokras, because we plan, and think it all through, and kill our family members without remorse or thought, or do unspeakable harm to our fellow man. That is the side of humanity that these people have been exposed to, that people like Janus – who were not even aware of the existence of the USC and were simply passing through, and yet they were snatched up like criminals – have been exposed to. And then you wonder how they could possibly look at us and feel nothing but contempt?"

Lang stood and adjusted his belt, "Maybe you should take a deeper look into your planet's history, maybe you should try and see things from Janus's point of view." Lang stepped forward and rested his palms on the table, arms outstretched. "Have you any idea of the things that went on there? Obviously not. Everyone here is aware of what happened on the *Avenger* between you and Janus. Only someone who is clueless or does not want to believe that the atrocities were committed would presume to have the right to take Janus anywhere because of what happened, as you just said, half a lifetime ago. Know one thing, Harrison, if you try anything, an entire planet – a planet that will stop at nothing to protect their own – will rally behind Janus, and you will most assuredly lose."

Harrison looked up into the man's eyes, only inches from her own. "You're bluffing."

"You think so? I suggest you err on the side of caution, because if you don't, it will all be a moot point." Lang left the threat hanging in the air as he straightened and walked out of the cafeteria, his strides long and purposeful.

Harrison heard the din around her rise as conversations resumed, and realized that they had been the object of much scrutiny. She found herself wondering how their meeting had become so hostile so quickly, and how Janus could be so beloved by an entire planet of beings.

Chapter 6

Navigation blew up, then the sensors and one engine. Life support failed. Janus cursed. She was not having a good day. First, she had detected a serious ion storm directly in her path. She had changed course, and that had led to her current predicament, which wasn't good at all.

Two Rokarian ships had dropped out of nowhere and blown out her subspace engines so she couldn't run. Then they had started in on weapons and sensors so she couldn't fight or try to limp away and hide.

"Damn stupid machine!" Janus yelled as she slapped the console. She looked again and sighed in relief. She had gotten the coordinates for a nebula locked in before the bastards had blown out navigation. "Now ah just 'ave ta keep the ship tagether," she muttered, and grabbed hold as her shuttle lurched again. Janus glared at nothing as she started analyzing the damage and guessing how much more they would cause before they left her alone. Hopefully, they'd leave and she'd be able to do repairs.

Something started to beep.

Janus looked around to see what else had gone wrong. "Shit." There was a hull breach, not a big one, but enough to start venting the minimal atmosphere she had left. Janus wasn't that concerned about life support, she could survive just fine without it for a while, but a hull breach was a much bigger problem.

She scooped up a repair kit and scrambled her way back to the damaged area. The vessel rocked again, almost sending her sprawling onto the hard metal floor. It only took a minute and the breach was sealed, allowing her to marginally relax. As she felt the ship slowing, Janus glanced over and saw that she was now inside the nebula. She had chosen this one specifically because the Rokarians were absurdly superstitious when it came to stellar phenomena. Janus was confident they would not follow her inside.

She sat on the floor and allowed her head to thump back against the wall. Two days she had been traveling without a single problem and on the third, everything just had to go bad. Janus shook her head as she rested and looked around. It didn't look too promising. Smoke was floating halfheartedly into the air, pieces of the ship were lying around, and Janus really didn't feel like fixing it all.

But she had a job to do, so she stood determinedly and decided what to fix first. "Sensors, navigation, first, then my second engine. Subspace kin wait. Then weapons...maybe." She sighed and started moving around, quite aware that she was in for a long day.

Janus wasn't sure how long the repairs took, but she knew it had been a while since she had begun to cobble together the necessary systems. She was now sweaty, dirty and tired, and the lack of an atmosphere was starting to make her feel lightheaded. Apparently, she had lost more than she'd thought with the hull breach, and she couldn't do more extensive repairs with the supplies she had on board.

She sat at the helm and considered her options. She had gotten the subspace engines fixed so she could, in all likelihood, engage them and head straight to her destination. *But that would be against the rules. You know that, Janus.* She shook her head. "Forget the damn rules."

Before she could reconsider, Janus started up the engines and was on her way. It only took a few minutes before she re-entered normal space to see something she had long ago thought she would never lay eyes on again. She leaned forward and studied her home for long moments. "It looks the same."

Janus stood and moved to the back of the ship, picked up a device and strapped it to her left wrist. One rule that no one ever broke was that regarding ship landing. No one ever landed on the surface without express permission from the head of the government. Janus tapped a few controls and was transported to the surface.

The city had not changed much over the years. It still had its tall buildings, adorned with the same platinum markings that covered the skin of the people indigenous to the planet. The roads were still dirt and very well kept. The plants and trees remained standing after thousands of years of existence, and there was a moderately high volume of people milling about.

Janus looked around at where she was and immediately recognized the waist high, stone retaining wall along the road and green hills beyond. "Of all the places ta end up, ah 'ave ta land 'ere." She noted the curious looks that she was getting from everyone and smiled a little. It had probably been decades since anyone had just appeared in the middle of one of their largest cities, and Janus was positive that the only thing keeping her from being arrested was that she obviously belonged.

She hoped that no one would recognize her and she could just go quietly on her way, speak to Taykio, and be gone. No muss, no fuss.

"What are you doin' here?"

Then again... Janus sighed as she turned to face the challenge. It wasn't anyone she recognized, so maybe he was just a vocal onlooker, unlike all the others. Janus stepped closer and raised an eyebrow when he took a cautious step back. That was new. Her people were not known for timidity.

A commotion at the other end of the square in which they were standing caused both Janus and the man to turn their heads. A small group dressed in the colours of the ruling family approached and stopped in front of Janus.

The man in the lead spent a moment looking at her and Janus got a distinct...Patrik would have called it "creepy feeling". Janus did not like this man.

"You will come with us." He turned, fully expecting Janus to follow.

She stayed where she was, her only movement the crossing of her arms in front of her. The man got three steps before he became aware that she was not following, turned and looked back at her. He scowled, and it was an expression Janus had gotten very used to seeing on Samson's face. This guy did not like her either. *Good.*

"Are ya deaf?"

"No." It was the first word Janus had spoken the entire time.

"Then come."

"No."

He moved forward until they were face-to-face, their eyes on the same level. "Listen, I have my orders—"

"No," Janus grabbed his shirt and pulled him forward, "ya listen. Ah just got 'ere, after a very bad day. I will go see Taykio when ah feel like it." He looked surprised. "Aye, I 'ave not been gone so long that I forgit whose colours are whose. I do not like 'im, either. Do not think ya kin tell me what ta do." Her last words came out in a low growl before she threw him to the ground and stalked out of the square, knowing exactly where she was headed.

"I do not know what you're expecting, Janus," he yelled after her.

Janus paused but didn't look over her shoulder. She could feel the shock wave that traveled through the assembled people upon hearing her name.

"But whatever it is, I do not think you will find it."

Janus kept on walking, the crowd parting in front of her, and she did not stop until she was far from the city.

The headstones, like all the others in the cemetery, were at once different yet similar to one another. Made of stone and shaped into the symbol of the family of the deceased, with more etchings around the edges and the center filled with large text that named the bodies lying in the ground, it was a pattern that all headstones followed. The only glaring, obvious difference was the shape – some geometric, others complex swirls, and a few that were letters from their language.

Janus focused on the two diamond shaped stones that were side by side – one of them, her mother's, was darker and more aged than the other. But her father's had its share of scrapes and dings, marks from the elements after two years of exposure. Janus ran her fingertips gently across the names etched in stone as she knelt in the grass.

She leaned forward and placed her ear against the flat surface of the lightly coloured stone. "I will avenge ya, father, I promise," she whispered, the words carried away by the gently blowing wind. Janus heard someone coming up behind her, but stayed in front of the stones, knowing she would probably never be back to pay her respects.

The person knelt down behind Janus's right shoulder and sat in silence, paying respect to the souls of the people before him. And then his voice, quiet and musical, rose to an almost silent whisper. "The ceremonies for them were beautiful. For your father, I think the entire city showed up. They were both very loved, Janus. Take comfort in that."

Janus's fingers lingered over her mother's name for another long moment before she sat back and turned her head to take in the form beside her. It was Gregor, an old friend. They had grown up together.

Gregor looked at his friend and a small sigh escaped his lips, "I could not believe it, when I heard who had appeared in the square. Everyone here thought you were dead. And then I heard how you manhandled Taykio's right hand, and I knew it was you. No one here has the balls."

Janus faced him fully and planted her elbows on her crossed knees. "'ow did it 'appen?"

"Taykio?"

"Aye."

"You know, Janus, just as well as I. Taykio has been making noise about how things should be ever since we were kids. When your father died and you were nowhere to be found, it just allowed him to take control and do what he had been raving about. We did not know he had accumulated such a following."

"And Nulas?"

Gregor winced at the mention of Janus's brother. "He has been less than accessible. After your father died, he shut himself away from the rest of us. He hardly ever comes out of his house and no one has been in since the funeral."

"'E let Taykio take over?"

"Let is such a bad word—"

Janus surged upward off the ground. "Let is a *perfect* word! The only way the rulin' 'ouse can change is if the line is destroyed or someone challenges fer it! Our line still exists, and Taykio is spineless; 'e would never challenge!"

Gregor stood as well and let his friend rant for a moment. "I know, Janus, believe me I know. But as far as anyone here is concerned, Nulas is dead. He is never seen, so he very well might be, and no one knew a single thing about you so what were we supposed to do? Taykio assumed control and anyone who protested was arrested. Only you or Nulas can challenge him with impunity, and he'll have to comply because you are the rightful leaders."

Janus looked over at him, her face composed and her eyes almost sad. "Ah am not stayin' 'ere."

"Then nothing will change."

Her eyes narrowed as she looked off toward the city for a long minute. "Maybe not." Then she strode out of the cemetery with Gregor hot on her heels. "Nulas still live in the same place?"

Gregor nodded.

"Good."

They arrived back in the city in short order, and it looked to Gregor as if Janus's memory had not suffered at all from her absence. She walked directly up to her brother's front door and started pounding on it with a clenched fist. The ruckus quickly attracted a curious crowd, everyone wondering who was pounding on the door of the evasive Nulas. And what response the intruder would receive.

"Nulas! Git out 'ere, ya coward! Ah swear if ya do not open it, ah will break the door down."

Nulas winced as he heard the pounding and the voice that sounded exactly like his father's only not quite so deep, and much, much more aggravated than he ever remembered hearing his father sound. It sounded familiar in another way. Almost like... "Janus?"

"Aye, now git out 'ere."

Oh, great wiparia, he thought. *She sounds just like him.* Even to the pronunciation, a replica of the accent their father had picked up while on a diplomatic mission to an underdeveloped farming planet.

Janus stopped pounding on the door and turned an annoyed eye to Gregor. He shrugged, not having any suggestions. They had tried countless times to get into Nulas's house, without success. Janus turned from the door and took two steps back into the street. She lowered her head for a moment and then, in one blinding motion, turned with her arm outstretched. A wave of energy rippled through the air and slammed into the door, breaking it from its hinges.

Janus gave a little nod of satisfaction. Ignoring Gregor's slack-jawed look, she stepped into the house. It was dark and smelled of dusty mold. The air was thick and Janus felt like it was pressing down on her; it was stifling. She moved forward quickly and identified her brother's form, picked him up by the back of his shirt, and hauled him out the door, then dumped him neatly in the middle of the street.

Nulas rolled upright and looked up at his sister, his eyes squinting against the bright sun. He blinked a few times before her face came into clearer focus and he was able to make out her features. He spent a moment reacquainting himself before he found his feet suddenly dangling off the ground again.

Janus held him up by the collar of his shirt and glared for a long moment. "What are ya doin'?

"Huh?"

"That!" She swiveled and pointed into his dank house. "What are ya doin' in that? 'Ave ya totally lost yer sense of self? Ah kinnot believe that ya let someone like Taykio just take over the planet. Ya know just as well as I what 'e is like. Ya 'eard the same stories from our parents and so what do ya do? Ya 'ide away like a coward! Ah kinnot believe it!" She released him and watched as he fell to the ground with a thump, a small cloud of dust rising around him.

He shook himself off and stood, facing her with a long absent fire in his eyes. "And where have ya been? I did not see ya coming back here after either of them died! You know I can not take his place."

Janus raised an eyebrow.

"I do not know a thing about running a city, much less a planet!"

"Ya know just as much as me; we grew up with it. And yer much better than Taykio."

"Well maybe I do not want it! Did ya ever think of that, Janus? Maybe I just want to crawl away and wait to die."

Fed up with his attitude, Janus almost snarled at her brother, "And what a waste that would be."

The crowd started murmuring and shuffling about, causing the siblings to turn as Taykio appeared with two of his personal guards. He strolled leisurely through the street and stopped when he came even with them. "Well, what a day this is. The two prodigal siblings have returned and are brawling in my streets. Will wonders never cease? Nulas, how very nice to see you again." He turned and focused solely on Janus. "Janus, you are not someone I ever expected to see here again. How have you been?"

Janus stalked forward – quite prepared to simply leave, convinced that visiting her home planet hadn't been such a good idea in the first place – and stared down at Taykio. They hated each other; it was no secret, especially between the two of them.

"Still not one for small talk, Janus? Fine, why don't you get to the point?"

"Ya 'ave 'eard of the Ebokras?"

"Those things Quip'lee was carrying on about, asking for our help. Of course."

"And ya said no?"

"Yes."

"That is it? Did ya even consider it? Or did ya just take it as an opportunity ta exercise yer will over these people? Ya do not know what is 'appenin' out there, do ya?"

"Janus, we are quite aware of the state of the galaxy and universe. We are not stupid, and if these...Ebokras? If they prove to be a threat, we will act."

Hardly believing her ears, Janus turned away from Taykio and faced the crowd of people. "What is wrong with ya? Do ya not remember who we are, what we stand fer?"

"You know our customs, Janus, we do not get involved in fights unless we are directly attacked. We are never the aggressor."

"Ya 'ave been attacked. I 'ave been attacked. These things 'ave killed my entire family."

"Janus, you still have family here. I do not—"

"Not *that* family, my adopted family, the people who 'ave been there for me more than ya 'ave." Janus looked around at the crowd of people. "What is wrong with ya all? What 'as 'appened ta change things? Ya would stand 'ere and watch everyone fall around ya and do nothin', even though we 'ave the power?"

"These people have made no direct threat against us. We remain untouched, so it is not our place to get involved."

Janus rounded on Taykio and almost yelled in his face, "And why do ya think that is? Ya think these people 'ave left ya alone out of the goodness of their 'earts!? They know ya can beat 'em, they know we 'ave the power ta stop 'em. So they are conquerin' everyone else first, makin' sure no one will be left ta 'elp us, and then they will come and overwhelm us and ya will curse yer stupidity and stubbornness as ya are all slaughtered. They will not let such a threat as us survive, and if ya believe anythin' else, ya are the stupidest man alive."

Janus turned back to face the watching throng. "The people I remember, the ones I called family and friends, would 'ave jumped inta action at the first sign of violence against any one of us. They would not 'ave spared anythin' in the fight. Will none of ya stand and fight? Not one will see this as the threat it is? And what will ya do when it is yer family dyin'? Will ya fight then?" Janus yelled, scanning the crowd, seeing the uneasy shifting. "Will ya? It will be too late. If ya wish ta 'elp, now is the time ta do so!" Janus paused again to look at the faces of people that had hardly changed since she'd last seen them, but she felt as if she barely knew them. She shook her head and blew out a disgusted breath.

"Ya 'ave changed. Ya 'ave not a shred of 'onour or morality between ya. Now I remember why I never came 'ome. Ya disgust me and I am ashamed ta be associated with ya." Janus shook her head and started walking to the exit of the city. "Good riddance. I 'ope that when they come and kill ya, ya will all burn in *targus*." Janus felt a perceptible shock move through the crowd at her parting words, and she smiled grimly upon feeling it.

Janus stopped in the square at the exact spot she had first beamed down. She turned and took one last look at the gathering, one moment to burn into her memory the bewildered expression on Gregor and Nulas's faces, the uneasy acknowledgment of her words as they were absorbed by the crowd, and the almost savage look of satisfaction on Taykio's visage.

Then she turned her eyes to the land and took in the hills, trees, and buildings. One moment to send a last look toward the cemetery where her parents lay; one moment to realize this would be the last time she would stand on this soil – the soil of her people, of her homeland. Then she raised her arm and tapped the controls, waiting for the shuttle to respond and whisk her off of this world. Her eyes lifted and latched onto those of her brother for a brief, intense moment of sibling understanding. And then she was gone. Forever.

* ~ * ~ * ~ * ~ *

Beep.
Groan.
Beep, beep.
"G'way!"
Beep, beep, beeeeeeppppppp!
"Argh! Fine." Melvin Kodiac rolled out of his bed and half walked, half stumbled across the room to his computer. Bleary eyed, he slapped at the controls a few times and finally succeeded in silencing the alert. It figured that after several days of skirmishes and battles where the *Avenger* was sent out dozens of times at all hours of the day and night, that today – when Quip had promised they would not be sent out unless it was critical – his computer would decide to take up torture as a hobby.

He scrolled halfheartedly through the data on his screen, only interested because he had no idea what it was. Kodiac did not recall leaving any outstanding search parameters, so his curiosity was piqued. A photo caught his eye and caused Kodiac to straighten up and start reading with more enthusiasm. "Holy shit!" He noted the location of the files in the database and flew out of his room and down the hall.

Kodiac stumbled to a halt just inside Barker's room, debating whether he really wanted to wake her up. It was important, true, but she loved to sleep and had been more than mildly testy of late. He had asked what was wrong and had hardly gotten more than a growl out of the woman. Kodiac suspected she was concerned for Janus, although she wouldn't admit it, and he was certain she'd bite his head off if he mentioned it.

He finally walked into her room and sat on the very edge of Barker's bed, gently clasped her shoulder and gave a little shake. "Barker," he whispered, then realized that was absurd. Why whisper when your intent was to wake someone up? "Barker, wake up!" he said, not in a yell but loud enough to jostle the blonde from her slumber.

Barker surged up in bed and looked at Kodiac before sighing and rubbing her face. "Jeez, whaddaya do that for?" she mumbled, irritated.

"I have to show you something."

"Now? For the love of God, Mel, couldn't it wait until morning?"

"Well, maybe, but I thought it was important and I think you will too. Come on." He grabbed her arm and started pulling her up and across the room. He quickly typed in the location of the files he had been reading and stepped back to give Barker some space.

She slapped at the controls much as he had until something caught her eye. After a few brief moments, she turned and looked up at

Kodiac. "Holy shit!"

He grinned. "That's exactly what I said."

Barker turned back to the screen and pursed her lips. "Do you have any idea..." Her voice trailed off and she shook her head. "Now what do we do?"

Kodiac peered at the screen and thought out loud. "I dunno. That's why I came to you. I wouldn't suggest going to Harrison, at least not yet. She's still a little," he waggled his hand back and forth, "iffy on the whole Janus issue. I don't think she'd react well to this."

"So who, then? Quip'lee? No offense to him, 'cause I kinda like the guy, but he's military and would probably look at us like 'What's the big deal?' Sooo..."

"Janus would be the ideal person to talk to." Kodiac suggested.

Barker turned her head to look at him and said simply, "Janus isn't here."

They both turned to stare at the screen for a long time until the same whispered name passed their lips: "Patrik." The duo scrambled out of the room, tripping over each other in their haste to exit.

~~*~*~*

Everson Patrik had been assigned quarters on Jopus Prime for the duration of the war with the Ebokras. He didn't have a permanent home, nor any family to go back to. He was sleeping soundly as the two schemers came to a stop outside his door.

"Wait, wait...what about his daughter?"

"What about her?"

"I don't want to wake her up."

Kodiac rolled his eyes. "You ever seen a kid her age? They usually sleep like the dead. Beside, we're up, might as well bring someone else into the late night party." He grinned and barged into the man's room with Barker right behind him.

They stopped as the bundle of covers on the bed stirred and a human form raised itself into the darkness. "Barker?" a sleep roughened voice called quietly.

"Yeah, it's me and Kodiac. We need to talk to you."

"Um," there were some shuffling noises as he got out of bed and walked over, "now? It's four in the morning."

Kodiac nodded. "Yeah, we know, we know. But it's important. Come on." He latched onto Patrik and started pulling him out of the room. The still bewildered man had little choice except to follow or risk losing his arm, leaving Emm to continue sleeping.

They walked through the almost silent halls, an eerie sight compared with the regular hustle and bustle of a normal day. The few people on duty who passed them threw the sleep-rumpled group an odd look or two, but didn't comment. They all finally sat down in the cafeteria where Kodiac, as the instigator of their late night meeting, got coffee.

Barker wrapped her hands around the cup and breathed in the wonderful aroma with relief. She noticed Patrik doing almost the same thing and smiled a little. After taking a moment to collect themselves, Patrik raised his hazel eyes and pinned Kodiac with a stare. "What's so important that you dragged me out of bed?"

"You remember when Harrison first found out about Janus?"

Patrik didn't need any elaboration; he nodded.

"Well, the captain found out about Janus and Marson because she had me scouring the database for a reference to Janus's people because Janus had said something about previous contact. Anyway, after the whole deal with their little fight and then the ship being attacked, I totally forgot. The search was still running and just today came up with more results." He stopped there and Patrik waited as Kodiac took a sip of his coffee.

Reading the apprehension on Patrik's face, Barker took up the narrative. "The incident with Marson may not have been what Janus was talking about. We found another reference to her people in the database, about them being on Earth."

Patrik spat out his mouthful of coffee and raised his eyes. "They can't survive on your planet. Are you sure?"

Barker nodded. "We saw a picture. It was definitely one of Janus's people."

Patrik grabbed a napkin and started soaking up the coffee as he considered the situation. "Fine, but why is this so important? Why tell me? I don't get what the big deal is."

Barker cleared her throat and leaned forward a little. "I study history, Earth's history. I could tell you almost anything you could possibly want to know about the time frames I study. This visit happened in that time frame. So why don't I know about it? Furthermore, why is it in the *Avenger's* database, but not in any archives on Earth?"

Patrik sat back and rubbed his face. "Listen, Barker, I guess this is all very interesting for you: a new discovery, history that no one knew about, something that might very well change...something on your planet. But unless you have more to say that I might deem important, I really can't scrape up the energy to care. Earth means nothing to me. I have never been there and I have no desire to change that. If you're fishing for more information about what Janus's people were doing there, you have to talk to her because I know nothing." He stood and pushed in his chair. "Now I'd really like to get back to bed."

"It's where you're from." Kodiac blurted it out and watched as Patrik's back stiffened and he turned, an odd look in his eyes.

"Excuse me?"

"Sit down," Kodiac's eyes flicked to the chair, "and we'll tell you."

He sat stiffly in his chair, holding his back ramrod straight, his hands folded in his lap and his total attention glued to the people in front of him. "Explain." One word, precise and fierce sounding.

Not liking the look on Patrik's face, Barker shifted. "Well, not you personally, but your ancestors. According to the information, the Platinum People came to Earth and were there for a year or two. In that time they did, I dunno...research about us, humanity, and what made us tick. When they were ready to leave, they had a list of people. Anyone on the list had the opportunity to take their families and go with the aliens." She paused and looked into his eyes. "Most of them did. There was a list in the database and the family name Patrik was there."

"That doesn't mean anything."

"I know. But there was also a list of the places the humans were dropped off to colonize. Janus mentioned your home planet to me once, and it is on the list."

Patrik looked at them and shifted a little. "Still, these people aren't scientists or colonists. From what I know, from what Janus has told me, this story doesn't make any sense."

Kodiac leaned on the table and looked at him. "That's one of the reasons we wanted to talk to you, to see if you could verify it."

"It's quite possible that you're a descendant of people on Earth. You could have relatives there; you have the right to know."

Patrik's eyes flicked around the almost empty room, bouncing from their earnest faces to the table and ceiling. Anywhere. He finally made a decision. "I want to see whatever you read. And I am going to talk to Janus when she gets back. And I am not going to regard this as anything more than a fantastic story until I get some corroboration." He stood as Barker nodded.

"That's fine, Patrik. I'm not expecting anything from you, I just thought you had a right to know."

He nodded as they trailed out of the cafeteria and into the halls of Jopus Prime.

~~*~*~*

Word of Janus's returning shuttle spread through the space station like wildfire. Patrik took off for the shuttle bay as soon as he heard, anxious to speak to his friend and see how her mission had gone.

In the early morning hours, he had read the files and had to admit that they appeared pretty official. But he had to wonder why an entire planet of people would forget something that should have been a historic moment for them, that should have been lauded in the history books as an example of how far humanity could go. He had to wonder why Barker, who was an expert on her planet and its history, had no knowledge of the event. And he had to wonder why Janus's people had bothered. From what he had heard from his friend, they did not hold humanity in high regard. But perhaps this experiment was the reason for that, perhaps the chosen few who had gone with the "Platinum People" – as Earth had called them – had fallen short of the expectations placed on them. And that was the catalyst for the now very well known opinion Janus and her kind had of Earth and its denizens.

Patrik watched as the shuttle landed and his brow scrunched as he noted that it was a little worse for wear. He became even more concerned when Janus did not step outside and greet him with her usual little smile and handshake or slap on the back. He entered the ship and his eyebrow rose as he saw, directly in front of him, a very large dent in the sturdy metallic wall. Patrik went deeper into the ship and soon found his tall friend sitting in the pilot's seat, her head leaning back against the wall and her eyes closed.

He didn't say a word, didn't touch her, hardly made a sound. He just sat on a console next to her, knowing that Janus knew exactly who was beside her and hoping she was drawing comfort from their friendship.

Janus finally sighed and turned her head to look at him, causing Patrik to note several things at once. There was a weariness in her eyes that he could not remember ever having seen before, an acknowledgment of things past and never to be reclaimed again. Another note of concern was the leather cord that Janus had always worn around her neck, tucked into her shirt. He had seen it once or twice – a medium sized, bronze coin with strange markings on it. There was a hole in the center through which Janus had threaded the cord. It now sat in plain view, on top of her shirt.

"Guess it didn't go too well," he stated, not really needing an answer but wanting to break the silence.

"No."

"So Quip won't be getting any help?"

"No."

Patrik looked down at his boots, very concerned. He could feel a strong melancholy around her that was not typical of his friend at all. One thing he knew was that when Janus was feeling something strongly enough for him to pick up on it, the emotions were usually off the scale.

Janus was very reserved and stoic by nature, keeping what she felt under wraps. Coupled with her species' tendency to not feel anything strongly except the more negative emotions, and Patrik could count on the fingers of one hand, the times anything other than hate or anger had come through their link to him. Now was one of those times.

"Did the shuttle piss you off, or what?" he asked, hoping to get more than a lackluster "no" in response.

A small smile flitted across Janus's face as she remembered getting back to the shuttle and feeling an overwhelming surge of hatred at the cowardice at her people. She had lashed out and planted her fist in the wall of the ship. It had made her feel a little better. "No. I was just takin' out my frustrations."

"I see. Well, I think Quip will probably want to see you, even though you don't have anything positive to report."

"Aye." Janus stood and turned to him. "'Ow 'ave things been 'ere?"

He shrugged. "As good as can be expected. We haven't suffered any significant casualties; the *Avenger* crew has proven to be very adept at this war thing. You can get a better report from Quip."

Janus nodded as she started moving to the exit.

"Oh, Janus!"

She raised an eyebrow at him.

"When you're done with Quip, I'd like to speak to you about something."

"Aye." Then she turned and with a purposeful stride headed toward Quip'lee's office.

Quip looked up with a smile as Janus stepped into his office and stood in front of his desk. "Janus, glad you're back. Any problems on the trip?"

"Nothin' I could not handle. Ya need ta fix the life support on my shuttle."

He smiled. "After all this time, don't you think I know that your shuttles always need some work? You seem to attract trouble." He gestured to the chair in front of his desk, a little concerned when she declined. That meant she didn't have a lot to say and wouldn't be in his office long. "How'd it go?"

Janus shook her head.

"That's a damn shame, Janus, a damn shame."

"Aye. What about 'ere?"

"Well, the *Avenger* has been working out very well. We've been winning most of our space battles, and even managing to beat them back when they get inside the ships. But we're still greatly outnumbered and we can't keep this up. Our efforts to track a ship have been...successful and not so successful." He glanced up for a moment to make sure he still had Janus's attention. "The first time, we lost the ship. We spent a day updating our sensors and tried again. We're following two vessels, but they are pretty far out and they haven't stopped yet."

Hearing something in his voice, Janus looked at him keenly. "What are ya thinkin'?"

"Well, either they know that we're following and they're leading us on a fruitless chase, or they have come from somewhere really, really far away."

Janus nodded. "I thought so. They make too much of a disturbance ta be from 'round 'ere." She fell silent and glanced down at her hand, idly tracing the diamond that was prominent in the center of other swirls and shapes. "What about diplomacy?"

Quip spluttered and looked up at her sharply. "You're asking that now?"

"Did ya try?"

"Of course we tried, Janus. We always try. They blew our emissaries all to hell."

"Just makin' sure."

"Why? What are you thinking?"

Janus looked up at him, her hand unconsciously going to the coin around her neck. "I 'ave one last option, but I am not sure if I want ta use it. I will get back ta ya."

She walked out before Quip could even think to ask what she was talking about. It left him wondering.

Chapter 7

Patrik didn't have to wait long before Janus strode through the door of his quarters and glanced around. He was sitting at the small computer table that was set to one side of the room. The files were pulled up, but minimized. He didn't get up or say anything, just watched as Janus took in the room. There was something else going on with Janus and he wasn't sure he even knew where to begin guessing what that something might be. She was almost hesitant, distracted, like she was making a life changing decision. Maybe she was; how was he supposed to know?

Janus finally walked over and sat down across from him. She threw Patrik a small smile and just waited for him to speak. It didn't take long.

"While you were gone, actually last night or very early this morning, Barker and Kodiac dragged me out of bed." He noticed the slight shift of her body at the mention of the blonde and quickly changed subjects. "What's going on with you two, anyway?"

She looked up and into his eyes. "What do ya mean?"

"I mean, the entire time you were gone she was acting funny, on edge and irritable. And she got even worse just a day or so ago. Snapping at everyone like they were her worst enemy." *And we won't mention the feeling of resigned sadness that I got from you right around that time, will we? No, Janus doesn't like to talk about things like that.*

Janus's gaze flicked about the room as her mind raced. *Do I want to tell him? Why not? He was the best person to talk to and might be able to help. Really, there was no reason not to,* she decided. "'As Omelian'par spoken ta ya?"

Patrik looked up, a little surprised. Then he remembered that Janus had known these people and their tendencies far longer than he himself had. "Yes. He told me. Are you mad?"

Janus shook her head.

Patrik felt a little sigh of relief pass his lips. He had been concerned that Janus would be angry about Omelian talking to him. If she were, she would have been able to cause the doctor a lot of problems. Patrik looked at his friend and saw the indecision and stark fright there and leaned forward. "Janus, I understand what you're feeling."

"Ya do not. Ya do not know what it is like ta look at someone and feel yer knees go weak, yer palms sweat, yer breathin' catch in yer throat, and yer 'eart start beatin' double time and not know what it means, or what ta do about it. I 'ave lived longer than ya can conceive and nothin' 'as scared me more than this, so do not claim ta understand."

Patrik pursed his lips and looked down at his lap for a moment. "You're right, I don't know about all that," he looked up and into her eyes, "but I do know what it is to be in love. Janus, this all isn't going to just fall in place. Barker is human and it can take us years to realize we are in love, very rarely does it happen in a day. And she could be totally oblivious to her feelings, although she doesn't strike me as the type. Or she could have a history where she was hurt and it's keeping her from acknowledging you and her feelings. So I suggest you do something."

"Like what?"

"Humans have something called dating, or courting, wooing. Whatever."

"Wooin'?" Janus looked skeptical and rather perplexed, causing Patrik to start laughing. "'Ow do ya woo?"

"It's simple. When I was dating my wife, I gave her flowers or chocolate, and spent time with her. It doesn't really matter what you do, Janus, as long as you spend time with Barker and get to know her, show her that you're interested in a relationship. Hopefully, the more time she spends with you, the more she'll realize and accept her own feelings."

"'Opefully?" Janus asked, her eyebrow raised.

"Yeah. But it should happen. I mean – this half thing isn't a mistake?" Patrik winced as he heard the question in his own voice and saw the reaction on his friend's face.

Janus leaned forward and stared into his hazel eyes, her face and voice very serious. "With us, it is always very real. There are no mistakes. Ever."

Patrik raised his hands. "All right, I was just making sure. Of course, you could always just talk to her and tell her what's up."

"No."

"Why not? It seems like a nice fast solution to me."

"Barker 'as ta realize and accept this on 'er own, or else it is not the same. Promise me ya will say nothin'."

Patrik sat quietly for a moment and nodded. "I promise. But you'd better start wooing, you hear me?"

Janus smiled. "Aye."

They fell into a brief silence, both of them feeling a little better now that the secret was out. Over the course of their friendship, they had gotten to the point where they told each other everything. Maybe not right away, but the truth always, always came out. And not by way of some slip of the tongue, but because they chose to share, because having a secret between them always caused a slight tension. They always knew when the other was holding back, but had long ago come to an understanding: not to push, or lay on the pressure, or be intrusive; just to wait patiently until whomever had the secret was ready to share.

The only exception was Janus's past and her people. She shared little information about that, and then only when it became necessary for Patrik to know. For his part, he had long ago resigned himself to not being privy to that part of her life. That was just fine with him, because he knew without a doubt that there was much more to Janus than what species she belonged to.

Janus leaned back and looked speculatively at her friend. "What did ya want ta talk about?"

"Oh, right! As I was saying, they pulled me out of bed claiming that Kodiac had found this all-important reference on the database that I had to see. They told me some interesting things, so I had a look at the information myself."

Janus raised an eyebrow.

"But I'm still skeptical. It just doesn't seem to fly."

"Why not?"

"Because it involves your people and contradicts things you've told me about them."

That got Janus's attention, causing her to sit upright in her chair and lean across the table. "What?"

Patrik had expected that reaction and had decided to let Janus read the information herself, rather than relating it to her. With that in mind, he simply turned the computer screen around and maximized the files. As Janus started to read, he sat back. And waited.

Janus read rapidly, her eyes flying over the words and her mind absorbing every minute detail. It had happened a long time ago, almost six hundred years, but Janus knew of it. The picture that accompanied the assortment of articles was someone she recognized. It took a moment or two of staring before the face triggered a memory and a name. She looked up at Patrik. "That is my grandfather."

Patrik's eyebrows rose as he scooted around to sit next to Janus. He looked at the picture of the distinguished looking man, now seeing the family resemblance. Sort of. The jaw was the same shape, the hair, the same dark black, but it was the eyes that were the giveaway. Only a shade or two lighter, but with the same fierce intensity that Janus's eyes held. He looked up at his friend, waiting for an explanation.

"We were not so stubborn back then, and 'e decided ta explore, see what was out there. Everyone was surprised to find a race of beings so like our own but so different. They decided ta expose themselves ta the Earthlin's, learn about 'em. Apparently, someone decided they 'ad a lot a potential, but bein' on Earth was 'oldin' 'em back. So they gave certain people a choice ta be taken ta other empty planets fer colonization. Many went, but somethin' went wrong. I am not sure what; my father never said. Our people turned cynical and very xenophobic for a very long time. Things started ta change when my father took power. 'E started takin' us inta the world again. Taykio thinks we should go back ta 'ow we were before my father's time, isolated." Janus shrugged a little.

Patrik sat back and just thought for a moment. "That's interesting."

"Aye."

"So you have no idea what happened? Or why Earth doesn't remember?"

Janus turned a confused eye on him.

"Barker, she studies history and has no knowledge of this."

"I am not sure. It might be possible that someone went there and made 'em forget us."

"Can you do that?" Patrik asked, stunned.

"Aye."

"But why? I don't get it."

Janus leaned back and stared at the ceiling as she thought. "Maybe whatever 'appened was so bad that it would not be good fer Earth ta remember. Maybe it would 'ave poisoned 'em toward other space civilizations. Maybe they were given the choice and chose not ta remember. I do not know."

"Is there any way to know for sure if someone is from the families that went? I need to know if I'm from Earth."

Janus looked at him and shook her head. "I kin not 'elp ya there."

Patrik nodded, and then something occurred to him. "You should tell Barker."

"Aye," Janus responded, not all that pleased with the thought, remembering how the ensign had been acting around her before she left. But Barker needed to know, and truthfully, Janus knew that the determined little blonde wouldn't stop until she had the whole story. The ensign's curious nature was doubtless fully engaged, and Janus had no desire to leave the woman hanging with no answers.

She departed, leaving behind a thoughtful Patrik.

It was easy enough to find Barker, not that Janus had thought it would be difficult. She was surprised to note that the pull between them was noticeably stronger than when she'd left. As far as Janus knew, the connection didn't normally grow stronger while the two people involved were separated.

Barker was sitting in the cafeteria, listening with half an ear to what Kodiac was saying. Something made her look up and across the room to see Janus hovering outside of the door. The blonde sighed, knowing she would have to speak with Janus and that she had to take care not to vent her frustrations on her friend. She had decided that Janus deserved more than a brush off or a flimsy excuse. Despite her budding feelings, Barker was going to keep a tight rein on her feelings while around Janus and tolerate the discomfort that would cause her. After all, Janus was worth it.

After a brief moment of hesitation, Janus proceeded into the room and sat down across from Barker.

The blonde looked up and smiled. "Hey."

Janus nodded. "'Ello."

Seeing something different in Janus's face, Barker leaned forward a little. "How'd it go?"

A negative shake of the head related the outcome of her mission. "That sucks."

"Aye." She shifted and placed her elbows on the table. "Patrik showed me what ya found." Her eyes flicked to Kodiac for a moment then back to Barker.

"Anndd?"

"It 'appened."

Barker's eyebrows rose as she waited. "That's it, that's all you have to say?"

Janus shrugged. "Aye. It was a long time ago. I do not know more than ya do."

Barker sighed. "Okay, that's fine. At least we know it happened. Maybe if we do some digging, we'll find out more."

Janus cocked her head as a potential avenue of information occurred to her. "Ya might want ta see Cobb."

"Why?"

"There might be some medical records that she could verify."

The ensign considered the suggestion. It made sense that anyone who had gone with the aliens would take some kind of physical before going, maybe even blood tests, and that would all be on record. *If Cobb could locate those, it might be possible...* Barker's thoughts trailed off as her mind lit upon the same conclusion Janus had arrived at. She stood and looked at her tablemates, smiled, and then almost ran out of the room.

Kodiac looked over at Janus, who gazed back with a slightly raised eyebrow. He pursed his lips and nodded. "Yep, Barker just figured something out." Then he too left the cafeteria.

Janus watched him go, then turned her attention to the table top for a long moment. Her hand reached up and grasped the bronze coin, turning it over in her fingers. She nodded and started off to Quip's office.

* ~ * ~ * ~ * ~ *

"So, let me get this straight. You want to—"

"Quip! Does it really matter? All ya need ta know is that I am gettin' ya some 'elp. Is that not what ya wanted?"

Quip looked up at his friend, surprised by her unusual lack of control. "All right, Janus, you're right. It doesn't matter, not really. So where are we going to do this?"

"In yer conference room."

"Who should be there?"

"Whoever ya think is important."

"All right, Janus. Give me five minutes to get everyone there and then you can do whatever it is you're going to do."

Janus nodded and headed for the conference room. True to his word, five minutes later all the chairs were filled with military commanders and advisors of Jopus. Quip glanced around to see that everyone was present, and then nodded at Janus.

She stood and moved around to the computer at the head of the table. She sat typing commands for long moments as the entire room watched, curious. After several moments, Janus straightened and moved back to her seat. There was a short, collective silence as everyone wondered what was going on.

"What did you do?"

Janus shot a glare at the person who had spoken and then turned her attention back to the table. A few moments later a large, floating, almost invisible circle appeared above the table. It was the long range communication bubble. The bubble continued trying to contact the coordinates it had been given, then stopped suddenly.

A mechanical voice broke the stillness. "Error. Restricted channel. Error. Please correct. Error."

Janus stood and went back to the controls. She removed the coin from around her neck and spent a moment studying it before she punched in a series of commands.

The mechanical voice paused in its message, followed by a low whirring sound. "Accepted. Channel open. Verification: P9R66HO77JA5X.0038. Request conference, sending inquiry." The bubble split off into four smaller sections, leaving the larger main bubble still spewing commands. "Waiting for reply."

Quip looked up at his friend, totally baffled by what was happening in his conference room. Janus simply raised her eyebrow at him, a silent admonition telling him to be patient and wait. Quip huffed and turned his attention back to the floating bubbles. He was never a very patient man at the best of times, and this was very difficult for him.

Finally, the main bubble spoke again. "Accepted. Reply answered. Awaiting verification." There was an expectant pause. "Accepted. Establishing link."

One of the smaller bubbles shimmered, slowly bringing into focus the expectant and curious face of a middle aged human. The man blinked as he looked around the room, trying to figure out who had called the conference meeting. A large grin split his face when Janus stepped into his line of sight. "Well, colour me surprised. Janus, how the hell have ya been?"

A small smile quirked the corners of her lips as she looked at her friend. "I 'ave been better, but I 'ave also been worse."

"So what's going on? I never expected any of us would have to use this." He lifted a chain around his own neck and waggled it, showing the occupants of the conference room that he too held a bronze coin.

"We should wait so I only 'ave ta say this once."

Just then the bubble chimed in again. "Accepted. Two replies answered. Awaiting verification." There was another expectant pause. "Accepted. Establishing links."

Two more smaller bubbles shimmered to life and cleared to reveal two new faces. A half whispered gasp in the conference room caught everyone's attention. "Cyborgs." The cyborg woman in question looked around and spotted the person who had spoken.

"Yep, cyborgs. You have a problem with that?"

The speaker's eyes widened to a comical degree as the attached head was shaken back and forth.

"Good," she growled.

Janus laughed a little. "Tryst, do not scare the advisors."

Tryst's head turned and a large smile spread across her features. "Janus! It's good to see you."

"Aye, likewise."

"Hey, what about me?"

Janus looked up at the third bubble, whose projection showed an orange striped face with high forehead ridges and sunken eyes. "Aye, Warber, it is good ta see ya too."

Warber grinned and looked at his own screen, which showed him the faces of all the speakers Janus had called on, as well as a good view of the people in the room with Janus. They all glanced at the fourth bubble that remained in its inactive state.

Janus looked up at the faces of her three friends. "'As anyone spoken ta Karton recently?"

Three negative headshakes were her answer and Janus's stomach sank. She threw another glance at the bubble and was just about to shut down the request when the main bubble spoke. "Accepted. Reply answered. Awaiting verification." After a final expectant pause, the mechanical voice said, "Accepted. Establishing link."

The fourth bubble came slowly to life, finally revealing the haggard face of an older gentleman whose grey eyes lit up from within upon seeing Janus. "I should have guessed it would be you to finally call us all together again." His bearded lips stretched into a smile. "You didn't think I was going to miss out on this, did you?" Karton asked, seeing in Janus's eyes the worry that had blossomed at his delayed response. "I knew it would happen, and nothing was going to keep me from being there when it did."

Janus grinned. Karton was exactly how she remembered him. Her eyes flickered over all their faces, seeing there a few more lines than the last time, a little more strain and a few more shadows in their eyes. But they were still the same people she had known so well, and that made her feel good.

Karton smiled. "Now, why don't you stop goggling at us all and tell us why you've called this little meeting. Although, I'm sure we can guess." He looked at his fellow bubble mates, seeing in their faces that they did indeed know.

Janus said one word. "Ebokras."

A slight murmur rose in the background of each of the bubbles, giving testament to the number of people who awaited their leaders' decision as well as confirming that most, if not all, have encountered or heard of this enemy.

Tryst gave the impression of leaning forward, closer to Janus. One eye narrowed, the other being covered by a cybernetic patch. "Just tell us where, Janus, and we'll be there ASAP."

"Jopus Prime."

Tryst nodded. "Tomorrow." Then her bubble went dark and dissolved into the larger one.

Warber's striped face nodded as he thought. "Two days. Looking forward to seeing you again Janus." His bubble disappeared as well.

Evril, the first man who had responded to the conference call, spoke next. "It'll take us a little longer, Janus. Three days minimum."

"Aye, Evril, take yer time." His bubble went dark.

Karton laughed out loud at the look on Janus's face. "You didn't think it'd be that easy, didja?"

"No."

"Come on, Janus." He smiled. "This is the very reason we made the agreement. This is why we made these." He lifted his own bronze coin. "And besides," Karton's voice got deeper, his face became deadly serious, "we'd follow you anywhere. All you had to do was ask." He stared at Janus for a long moment until her eyes lifted to meet his own. He nodded. "We'll arrive with Tryst." His bubble dissolved into the large one, which folded into itself now that it had performed its function.

Wondering what the hell was going on, Quip looked over at Janus. "Janus? What was all that?"

Janus stood and turned to him. "They are friends, good people. They will be what we need." She started out of the room, needing a little time to deal with everything that was running through her mind.

Quip stood quickly and took a step toward the door. "Yes, but where are they from?" he yelled after her retreating back. A single, lonely word floated back to him.

"Marson."

* ~ * ~ * ~ * ~ *

Patrik glanced up as a body plopped down beside him. "Barker? Something I can help you with?"

The blonde sighed and nodded. "Yeah."

He waited a beat, and when it became apparent that no more information was forthcoming, he prompted her with an impatient, "Sooo?"

"I just came back from seeing Doctor Cobb. She found some more information encrypted in the data files that Kodiac and I showed you last night. We believe it's DNA."

Patrik nodded, his eyes glued to Barker's face. She seemed different, almost subdued.

"Anyway, Cobb has it running in her computers and would like you to go to the medical bay."

"What? Me? Why?"

She looked at him then, a small smile on her lips, "So she can run your DNA against the other samples to see–"

"If any of it matches up. I get it." Patrik stood and pulled Barker up by the arm. "Let's go, then."

She followed behind him, her mind still light years away going over her earlier conversation with Janus. Well, not exactly the conversation, but what she had been feeling. No matter how hard she tried, she just couldn't manage to ignore the growing feelings that came blasting to the surface whenever she was around Janus. And that scared her. "Hey, Patrik?"

"Mm."

"You've known Janus a long time, right?"

He looked at her out of the corner of his eye for a moment before turning back to navigating the halls. "Almost twenty years. Why?"

Barker heard the suspicion in his voice and couldn't help but like him for it. It was nice to know that he was looking out for his friend. "Well, I was just wondering..."

Oh boy, Patrik thought. *I just know she's going to ask something that I don't want to answer. I can hear it in her voice.* "Look." He cut her off and stopped walking abruptly. "I know–" Someone jostled his shoulder and Patrik threw an annoyed glance at the man before pulling them into a doorway and out of foot traffic. "I know that you are very interested in Janus and frankly, so am I. But I will not betray her trust or confidence in me by talking about this behind her back. You should talk to Janus. I'm sure she'll give you the answers you're looking for."

Barker looked down at her shoes for a moment and sucked in a breath. "I'm sorry for putting you in an awkward position, Patrik, but Janus isn't the most forthcoming person, you know?"

An evil glint appeared in Patrik's eyes, complemented by a wicked smirk. "Well, maybe you'd have more luck if you were off this thing," he rapped his fist on the wall, "and in a little more private place."

She looked at him, seeing the mischief and glee in his face but not knowing the origin. "You think?"

"I do. One thing I can tell you is that the particulars of Janus's past and her people make her a little uncomfortable. Now, we have an appointment with the doc."

Their meeting with Cobb was...enlightening. Patrik sat very still while the good doctor took her samples. Barker saw the tension in his shoulders, the strain on his face. She couldn't imagine what the possibilities were doing to him. Finally, after an eternity of waiting, Cobb walked over and nodded. Just nodded. Barker saw the turning of Patrik's face and the almost physical impact as his hazel eyes locked onto her own. She saw his lips move for a moment but only managed to catch one word. *Wiparia.* She didn't know what that meant, but she supposed that it wasn't very important. Then Patrik told her to go and see Janus, to try and have some of her own questions answered.

And so the ensign found herself winding her way through the halls, following no pattern in particular in her search for Janus. Barker finally came to a halt outside one of the many quarters on Jopus Prime, wondering why she knew that Janus was inside. She knocked hesitantly, and was more than a little surprised when a familiar voice told her to come in.

Inside the darkened room, the blonde saw the customary bed and table but not Janus. She looked around a protruding wall and recoiled a little at what was there: Janus, hanging upside down by her legs from a sturdy bar stuck in two walls. She had her eyes closed, arms crossed over her chest with fists clenched, and she was swinging back and forth just a little.

"Janus?"

"Aye?"

Barker tried to hold back the laugh that was bubbling its way out of her throat. "What are you doing?"

"Meditatin'."

"Upside down? From your ceiling?" she asked, thinking that her friend looked very much like a gigantic bat.

One blue eye opened and focused on her as Janus's body slowly stopped swinging. "'Tis not the ceiling."

"Sorry, from two walls, then."

Janus just snorted and bent her upper body up so she could latch on to the bar with her arms, release her legs and then descend gracefully to the floor. She bounced a few times on the balls of her feet, and then turned her eyes to Barker with one eyebrow raised.

"I was wondering if you'd like to go down to Jopus with me. I haven't been yet, and I had so much fun when you showed me around here."

"Aye."

Barker blinked, a little surprised at the rapid agreement. A large grin split her face. "Great."

Janus just nodded and started out of the room. They arrived quickly at one of the transporter stations and were standing in a lush field before they knew it. Barker looked around, her mouth open.

"Wow! I never expected this."

"Most people do not."

The planet had no large buildings blocking out the sun, no smog in the air, and none of the noise that Barker was used to associating with civilization.

"Quip and 'is people 'ave a great respect for nature. Jopus reflects that." She gently turned Barker around and pointed. "There are a lot of people 'ere; they just preserve the land."

Barker looked to where her guide was pointing, seeing below them in the distance a bustling city center filled with wooden dwellings and people all laughing and doing business. She glanced over her shoulder to see the rolling hills and mountains in the distance, as well as a dense forest not far off. Then she looked up at the sky and felt a whole new reverence for the spectacular beauty of the view from Jopus Prime. The mixture of colours was vivid and Barker felt like reaching up and touching them, imagining how they would travel down her arm and paint her in a hodgepodge of lights and darks.

"The sun will set soon."

Anxious green eyes turned up at that. "Really? Oh, great!" Green eyes twinkling, she rubbed her hands together. "I have it on great authority from both you and Kodiac, that it's simply spectacular."

"Aye." Janus smiled and grabbed Barker's hand. "Come."

Barker let herself be led away, much more concerned with the warmth of Janus's hand in her own than with where they were going. When she felt a gentle tug on her hand, she looked up and saw that Janus was seated in front of a large rock. Barker sat, her hand still clasped gently by Janus, and spent an idle few moments staring at the sky.

They were shoulder to shoulder, and Janus could feel Barker beside her in so many ways – not just the living warmth of her body or the blonde's small hand in her own, but the pull between them was more intense than ever. She could smell Barker, everything from her clothes to her hair to the skin smell that was common to all people. Janus decided she liked it very much. She could also hear the ensign's heart beating faster than she thought a human's heart really should, and that worried her just a bit.

Barker swallowed. She was nervous, oh so very nervous. With them together and touching and so utterly alone, she didn't think she'd be able to ignore what she felt for Janus. *Maybe this wasn't such a good idea after all.* The thought flitted through her mind for a brief instant before she pushed it away and resolved to take advantage of the opportunity and squeeze as much enjoyment out of it as possible. Who knew when it would come again? She just needed something to distract her mind. Barker looked down at her hand and her eyes were immediately drawn to Janus's own darker skin with its unusual tracings. She lifted their entwined hands and started following the designs with her fingertips.

"Tell me about these?"

Janus looked over at Barker and then down at their hands. "What do ya want ta know?"

"What do these mean?"

Janus shifted so they were facing each other and spoke quietly. "Each large symbol, like the pentagon or triangle," she named two that Barker would recognize, "represents a family. The swirls show the lines within the family."

Barker's brow puckered as she tried to understand. "Which one is your family?"

Janus turned her hand over and pointed to the diamond there.

"Okay, so," the ensign placed a finger on the diamond, "your family line starts how?"

"Uh..."

Barker looked up to see an adorably confused look on Janus's face that almost made her burst out laughing. It then occurred to her that Janus probably had never explained this and didn't even know what she was asking.

"Let me put it this way – what act leads to creating a new family and adding a symbol to all the others?"

"My grandfather's grandfather decided ta break away from 'is father and start a new 'ouse, probably because they did not agree on somethin'. When 'e did, 'e took those loyal to 'im and all their belongings and started a new family. 'E chose the diamond ta represent it."

"All right, so the diamond represents him and his wife, and each swirl, their children." Barker looked down to see five main swirls branching off the diamond. "Right?"

Janus briefly considered correcting Barker's use of the term "wife", but decided that would start a conversation she wasn't sure she could risk having. "Aye."

"And each smaller swirl on the main ones show *their* children, correct?"

"Aye."

"So where are you?"

Janus bent her head and scrutinized the diamond for a long moment before pointing. Barker smiled as she realized how big Janus's family was. She looked closer and realized, "You have a sibling?"

"A brother, Nulas."

"What's he like?" The narrowing of Janus's eyes and slight twitch to her lips warned Barker before anything else that this topic was not open for discussion. "Never mind." She retracted the question and quickly returned to her original line of thought. "So, how does a new design get added. I mean, these are real, right?"

"Aye, they are a part of me. I do not know."

"Really?"

"Aye. I never much cared. There is..." She trailed off and thought.

That is not a good idea. I do not want 'er talkin' to Omelian'par.

"There is what?"

Right? That would be bad, very bad. Janus looked into Barker's eyes, seeing her curiosity and longing to know more. "A doctor on Jopus Prime who knows a lot about us. Omelian'par." Janus found herself saying the words before she could stop herself. Internally, she winced.

"I'll have to go see him, then."

Janus nodded.

Barker's appraising eyes flicked over her friend's face, taking in so many subtle things. Something was up with her and Barker didn't have a clue as to what it might be. Then she turned to see the beginning of the sunset. "Janus, it's starting." She nudged the other woman's shoulder and settled in to watch.

Janus shifted so she was once again leaning against the rock, her mind in a whirl. *It's starting? No, it started a long time ago.* She sighed, hoping Barker would realize what was going on soon because all these different emotions that she wasn't used to feeling were starting to wear on her. And the blonde ensign brought them out in her with hardly a thought. All Janus needed was a look or a touch, and she'd be filled with something she didn't understand. It scared her beyond belief.

Barker looked at her companion out of the corner of her eye and then tentatively reached over and grasped Janus's hand, pulling it over and holding it in her own.

Neither of them noticed the sunset.

Chapter 8

"What did you do to cause such a stir?" Patrik asked as he took a seat.

Janus briefly looked up from where she was bent over a data pad before ducking her head again. "What do ya mean?"

Patrik smiled. "Come on, Janus, everyone is abuzz. Granted, no one is quite sure what they're abuzz about, but there is a definite air of excitement."

"Aye, and why do ya think I 'ad somethin' ta do with it?"

"Well, if it were Quip or anyone else, everyone would know more. And I know I didn't do anything. So come on, Janus, spill it."

She dropped her pad and leaned back in her chair, taking an idle moment to study his face. He had been so young when they'd first met, so full of a fervor for exploring the universe. And he had accepted without question all that she was and all that she was not. And after everything, here he was by her side, a little older and a little more cynical but still with a bounce in his step, a twinkle in his eye, and a fairly congenial attitude. Maybe it was time to tell him a little more.

He watched as her face shifted minutely, revealing very little of her thoughts and feelings. He had to deliberately keep his jaw from dropping when she leaned forward and slid the bronze coin across the table to him. Patrik stared at her, and when he received a slight nod he reached out and very gently picked it up, cupping it in his hand like a precious stone.

"Do ya know what that is?"

Her voice was a quiet whisper and he felt compelled to answer in the same manner. "No, you never said, never let me see it."

"Fer good reason. I did not want ta remember."

Patrik didn't dare say a word for fear that she would stop short of any further revelations.

"After we got out of the prison, some people went 'ome ta try and reclaim their lives. Others just disappeared. But some did not 'ave a clue as ta what ta do. There were four distinct groups, each with a leader who 'elped rally us ta escape. Tryst led the cyborgs, Evril the psionics, Warber the warriors, and Karton all the odds and end people who did not fit anywhere. We made a decision ta 'elp each other, defend, ta unite if somethin' like Marson ever 'appened again. We made those coins that 'ave a com channel and verification codes ingrained in them so we would always be able ta reach each other. Those are the people I called for 'elp."

Patrik allowed the words to sink in slowly as he turned the coin over and over in his hands, feeling the texture and raised symbols that only Janus could understand. It took a long minute of silence before his brain started to work again. "But that was fifty years ago; how can they be alive?"

Janus turned the pad she had been reading and slid across the table, her face motionless and her eyes as icy as he had ever seen them. Patrik reached out and took the pad, surprised to note that his hand was shaking just a little. Hazel eyes looked down, taking in the pictures of four people, people he assumed matched up with the names Janus had given him. His eyes were drawn first to a woman, the alterations to her body painfully obvious. It had to be Tryst. Then he looked at a man whose face was covered in alternating orange and black stripes and although the structure of his bones had been altered, it was obvious he had started out human. The other two looked normal enough, so Patrik pressed the page button.

Scientific reports, journals, experimentation. The last word stuck in Patrik's head like a sick joke. He looked up, horrified to see the confirmation on his friend's face. "They were experimenting on you?" He looked again, seeing the protocols for countless procedures from genetic manipulation, to the integration of technological systems with biological, to the development of mental abilities. They had indeed been experimenting, and they had succeeded.

Patrik continued scrolling through the list, his stomach roiling with every new title he discovered. He was almost ready to throw the pad down when one last item caught his eye. It was labeled Fountain of Youth. A sick feeling of disgust surged through his body as he opened the file and started to read. Janus's picture was featured near the top, along with several other scans and test results. He finally got to the bottom, seeing there the list of test subjects and the first four names.

Tryst—successful
Karton—failed
Evril—successful
Warber—successful

And it all clicked. Patrik threw the pad on the table and glanced up, seeing on Janus's face a moment of unguarded pain and guilt. They had used her, used her physiology to extend these people's lives and suffering. Acting without thought, he moved around the table and just wrapped his arms around her shoulders as she collapsed against him.

There were no tears, or sobs, or nonsensical mumbling, just a tortured soul seeking comfort from a good friend for things beyond her control. It had been long in coming and Janus enjoyed the solid presence of the warm body that was wrapped around her own. Neither of them said a word, just held each other in nonjudgmental silence.

Patrik finally pulled back and knelt on the floor, looking up into Janus's blue eyes and seeing, for a brief moment, only a fraction of the suffering and pain she held within. Then he smiled shakily, pleased when she returned it. He cleared his throat and sniffled a little. "So, I take it they're coming?"

"Aye."

"And they'll fight?"

"Aye."

"And will we win, Janus? Will they be enough?" he asked, unable to hide the hopeful plea for a positive answer.

"They are some of the fiercest fighters I 'ave seen in a long time. If we do not win, if they are not enough, be sure that the Ebokras will not take us easily. I promise ya that."

* ~ * ~ * ~ * ~ *

Kodiac popped his head into Barker's room, his face all smiles. She was sprawled on her bed with her face in a book. "Hey."

She turned and smiled. "Hey, yourself. Come on in."

He did, pulling a chair over next to the bed and propping his feet up. Without warning, a mischievous grin crossed his features. "So, how was the sunset?"

"Umm...it was very..." How was she supposed to describe it? She remembered precious little of the actual setting of the sun; her attention had been fully engaged with the woman who had sat beside her. "Enlightening." *Ugh, horrible way to describe it.* She gave her head a mental shake.

"Right. Because we always learn so much when we watch one." Kodiac suspected he knew exactly what had distracted Barker, since he had seen her and Janus head down to Jopus together. But the last time he had brought up the subject of Janus, his blonde friend had almost taken his head off. And that was their deal – if one of them touched on a taboo subject, they were to drop it until the other person brought it up again. "Well, you can always see another one; it's not like Jopus is going anywhere."

Barker sighed and lowered her book, turned her head and gazed plaintively at her annoying friend. "Did you want something?"

His eyes widened in innocence. "Can't I just be interested in how your day was?"

"Not when you have a look like that on your face."

He heaved a sigh and sat back in his chair. "Fine, okay. But did you hear the other news?"

"Nope," she said, seemingly disinterested.

"Barrkkkeeerrrr!"

"Koooodddiiiaaaccc!" She threw him a smile over the top of her page and then nodded. "Fine, tell me. What's the big deal?"

"Well, the news is that Janus put in a call to some outlaw buddies of hers and they're all coming with God knows what kind of weapons."

Barker stopped reading and stared blankly at her page before she dropped the book to her chest and turned her gaze onto her smiling friend. "You're kidding, right?"

"Nope. That's one of the less extreme rumors. You should have heard the cafeteria before. Some people have pretty twisted imaginations."

The ensign sat up and leaned against her headboard. "So what's really going on?"

He leaned his elbows on his knees and lowered his voice like he expected there to be spies in the walls of the *Avenger*. "Well, no one has anything more than rumors and Quip isn't talking, neither are the advisors."

Barker snorted. "And I imagine that's doing tons to fuel the gossip."

"Yep, but Janus did call someone that has Quip smiling a little, so..." Kodiac wiggled his eyebrows.

"So, I guess we'll just have to wait and see." She scooped up her book and started reading again.

Kodiac didn't move.

She peered at him from the corner of her eye and sighed. "What?"

"Can't you just ask–"

"No."

"Why not?" he whined.

"Because at the moment, I'm not sure where I stand with Janus, and if she did tell me something it would probably be in confidence. And something tells me she's big on loyalty."

"But–"

"No!"

He sighed but still didn't stand up.

Frustrated, she threw down her book and turned to sit knee to knee with him. "Look, you want to know? Go ask Janus yourself." His eyes grew so wide, Barker thought his eyeballs would pop out of their sockets.

"Are you kidding? She freaks me out."

"Then I guess you'll just have to wait." She grabbed her book again and stretched out on the bed. "Now leave me alone, or if you're staying, be quiet." Her compact body wiggled around to get more comfortable, and a faint smile twitched her lips as Kodiac got to his feet and trudged out of the room.

Barker waited until she was done with her page before marking her spot and almost leaping out of bed. She slipped silently from her room and started toward the docking bay. She was navigating the halls of Jopus Prime, looking for one room in particular. The first thing she had done after getting back from Jopus was look at the directory for

Jopus Prime. Omelian'par had his office in one of the more remote ends of the space station, so it really wasn't that hard to find.

She stopped in front of an open door and stuck her head hesitantly around the door frame. The room was empty, so she entered, noting the up-to-date bio beds and equipment that she imagined Cobb would swoon over. Being a tour ship, the *Avenger* didn't get the money for new medical equipment like the military cruisers, but their medical bay was sufficient for their regular mission plan. Still, Cobb had complained many times about the distinct lack of all the new gadgets on the market.

Barker ran her fingers along the computer console, seeing that there was no dust and not a single speck of dirt to be found. She jumped as a voice came from behind her.

"Oh, you startled me."

She whirled to see an older man standing there, his face very similar to Quip'lee's. "I startled *you*? You startled *me*!"

Omelian'par smiled at the young woman as he stepped into the examination area. "I am sorry for that. Is there something you need?"

"Well, there is something you could do for me."

He came forward, anxious. "Yes, what is it?"

Barker was taken aback by his earnest voice for a minute before she remembered to whom, or rather what, she was talking. "Oh, no, there isn't anything wrong with me. I'm not in need of your services."

The doctor visibly relaxed at that and a smile creased his face. "Well, now that I know that no one is in any danger, please come..." Omelian'par trailed off as his eyes squinted and he unconsciously leaned forward. Then those same purple eyes widened and he pulled back. "Oh my, oh my, oh my! I should not talk to you." He shook his head, his long hair flying from shoulder to shoulder. "No, no." He whirled around and started back into his office.

Barker followed, confused. "Please, Omelian'par, I don't know what's wrong. If I've offended you in some way..."

"Oh, nothing like that. I just, I should not talk to you."

"Mind telling me why? Janus said you—"

"Janus? Janus sent you here?" That seemed to quell his anxiety as he sat behind his large desk and looked up with expectant eyes.

"Yes. I was asking her about the designs on her skin and she told me to talk to you. That you know a lot about her people."

Omelian'par blinked a little as that registered. Janus had sent Barker, her unknowing half, to him. To talk. Did she really trust him that much not to say things he shouldn't? Or was that what she wanted him to do? He shook his head and looked back up at the attractive blonde, who was looking at him with some concern. He smiled and gestured to the chair beside her. "Please, have a seat. I must apologize..."

"No, that's quite all right. I understand that there are some things about Janus that she doesn't like to talk about, and that you probably know about those things."

He ducked his head in acknowledgment. "You are an astute woman."

"I try."

She grinned and Omelian was charmed by the intensity of it, fueled in part by her connection to Janus. Internally, Omelian'par was amazed that the human was so unaware, but he had learned long ago that most humans were like that.

"I'm curious, how did you come to know so much about Janus's people?"

He relaxed back into his chair, a grin splitting his face. "Oh, now that is a story that I love to tell. Janus's father came here to Jopus. He had been spending a lot of time trying to reestablish contact with parts of the galaxy. We became friends and he returned several times, once with his wife." Omelian'par paused as his eyes took on a faraway look. "Wonderful woman. Full of life and spirit, full of love. When she died, I didn't know if Barlas — that's Janus's father — would survive. But he did. Anyway, Barlas had frequently spoken about his wife, and I felt as if I already knew her. When I saw them together, I was almost blinded by the strength of their love." He shook his head. "Amazing. They agreed to cooperate while I ran scans and tests; they helped me to understand some of the quirks of their species. It was mutually beneficial."

He nodded again and fixed his eyes on Barker's face. "One of the best couples I had seen together in a long, long time. I never thought I would see love like that again." *But when I sit here and look at you*, Omelian'par thought, *and know that you have no idea what is happening... I know that yours and Janus's connection will rival that of her parents.*

"Have you seen it again?" Barker couldn't keep the extreme interest out of her voice.

Oops, how to answer that? His smile was enigmatic. "Let's just say that I see something in the making."

The ensign accepted that and posed another of her many and varied questions. The time passed rapidly as they got involved in several lively conversations, but the focus of their meeting always seemed to turn back to Janus. And her parents.

It was late into the night when Barker stood, saying she really ought to go to bed. Omelian'par was both relieved and saddened. He had greatly enjoyed her intelligent company, but was finding it harder and harder to evade her more pointed questions. Those questions were leading more and more into the issue of love among Janus's people, and he really did not want to lie to the pleasant young woman. "Barker?"

Almost to the door of his office, she paused. "Yes?"

"If you found yourself in a situation like that of Janus's parents, what would you do?"

Barker studied the floor, giving the question her full consideration, taking into account her past hurts and her very real feelings for Janus. Which, she knew, she was avoiding. "I don't know if I'd be able to take the risk."

Omelian'par sucked in a breath at the answer. "Love is not something one can deny or ignore. In fact, it can drive a person to extreme distraction if left unrealized."

She nodded. "I know."

"'The cure for love is still in most cases that ancient radical medicine: love in return.' That is from Nietzsche's Daybreak, s. 415, R.J. Hollingdale translation."

Barker's head popped up at that and a smile crossed her face. "Nietzsche? Why, Omelain'par, I would never have taken you as a reader of ancient Earth texts."

A slight smile creased his features. "For all their brutality, humans have produced some of the greatest thinkers in the universe, with the most interesting ideas." His eyes ran over her face quickly as he thought. "Don't be afraid of your feelings, Barker. I have very rarely seen this type of love go one-way. Now, go get some sleep. And feel free to drop by anytime."

"I will." She nodded and continued out the door.

~~*~*~*

Quip'lee tugged on his sleeves and straightened his back, choosing to ignore the amused snort coming from beside him.

"Ya are not meetin' diplomats."

He threw a mock glare at Janus and huffed. "I like to make a good first impression."

"They are not easily impressed with ceremony, Quip."

"Well why don't you tell me what they are impressed with." He turned to face her, forgetting that their new allies were due to arrive any moment.

"Courage, bravery, morals."

"Morals?"

"Aye."

The air lock door slid open, catching Quip off guard and giving both Tryst and Karton a more natural first impression of him – hands on hips, with his usual half-serious, half-joking expression.

Tryst grinned as she saw who was standing before her and she stepped forward. She grabbed Janus in a long, hearty hug, which ended with a slap on the back. Then she turned to Quip and stuck out her right hand, which was covered with a myriad of technology. To his credit, Quip didn't bat an eye, clasping her hand just as he would any other. Tryst grinned again and gave a little nod.

Karton stepped forward next, his lips upturned in a slight smile and his greeting more subdued. He took Janus's hand and wrapped it in his own as they stared into each other's eyes. They stood like that for a long moment before he pulled her into a brief hug. Karton stepped back and shook Quip's hand, then turned to face the airlock.

Three large ships were docked in the bay, all of them unloading people and supplies. Everyone was busy and looked as happy as possible, considering the circumstances. A large man with darkly black skin loped forward and skidded to a halt before them. "We have everyone organized and ready to move out. Where do you want them?" He was looking directly at Quip.

"We have an entire section of the space station assigned for all of you. Janus will take you there."

"And our supplies?"

Quip's eyebrows rose. He didn't know what the man was talking about.

Karton cleared his throat. "We brought enough stuff with us to support ourselves for several weeks. And some extra for your contingent, just in case."

"Oh, well, that is very kind of you. I'm sure there's room in one of the cargo bays, I'll take whomever down and see about clearing some extra space."

The large man nodded and turned, sucked in a breath and yelled out a word that Quip didn't quite catch. The people perked up and started moving toward the door, falling into a single file with Janus in the lead.

Quip watched with some amazement as everyone walked past him in a manner that was very organized and controlled, very disciplined. He could see cyborgs, humans, and every manner of species in the crowd, all of them mingling and talking as if they were old friends. Quip turned as the large man came to a halt beside him again. "Shall we go see to those cargo bays?"

"Of course. I'm Tim." He stuck out his arm, which Quip grasped. "Quip'lee."

He smiled, his teeth a startling white against his skin. "I know."

~~*~*~*

"There's your answer, bud."

"Huh?"

"Huh?" Barker mimicked Kodiac, then slapped his shoulder. "Look" She pointed out into the hallway where a large group of very diverse people was walking by.

Kodiac turned and studied the seemingly unending stream of people as they moved past in ordered chaos. "Janus's friends?"

"I would think so."

Static broke into their conversation, "Attention, all personnel, man the following ships: *Pro Re Nata*, *Torken*, *Versai*, *USC Avenger*, and *Uto-*

pia. Prepare for launch to Sector Eight. That's the *Pro Re Nata, Torken, Versai, USC Avenger,* and *Utopia*. Man immediately and prepare for launch."

Barker grabbed Kodiac's arm and started pulling him down the hall. "Come on, come on, you big lug!"

Kodiac stumbled and cursed, trying to finish eating his sandwich as he followed behind the little blonde. He was grateful when they reached the ship and Barker had to let go of his arm as they went their separate ways – Barker to her tactical station and Kodiac to the fighter bay. He paused, mid step, and looked over his shoulder. "Hey, Barker!"

Her head whipped around. "Yeah?"

"Be careful." He saw a slight smile twitch her lips.

"You too." She raised her arm in a wave, reaching above the scurrying bodies that now filled the halls.

Kodiac returned the gesture and then started running down the hall to his post.

The *USC Avenger*, former tour ship and now restored battle cruiser, was ready and underway within three minutes of the initial call to arms. Captain Harrison took her chair on the bridge and watched as first the *Pro Re Nata* was launched, followed by the *Utopia*, then the *Avenger*, then the *Torken*, and finally the *Versai*. She gave the order to her helmsman and soon they were in subspace and zooming off to Sector Eight.

An inter-ship com link was established three minutes into transport, showing all the captains the grim face of Quip'lee, the Totarian Commander of the Ninth Fleet of Jopus. He looked at the faces awaiting his orders and sucked in a breath. "You should all know what is happening. We received a distress call from Sector Eight earlier today and dispatched two cruisers, one support ship, and a supply vessel. We lost contact with all the ships almost immediately after they arrived on the scene. Following protocol, I dispatched two reconnaissance shuttles who reported back with very grim news. As you all probably know, Sector Eight is on the outskirts of this system and we have so far been able to keep the Ebokras out. That is not the case anymore. Our reconnaissance shuttles reported a large horde of them infesting the sector. They had overrun the two planets there and most of the outposts.

"Your job is simple. The *Utopia* and *Avenger* will conduct rescue for our remaining people who have locked themselves in Outposts Twelve, Sixteen, and Twenty. As soon as you have recovered all survivors, you are to return to Jopus immediately, do you understand?" The two captains nodded. "Good. *Torken*, you are to cover the *Utopia* and *Avenger*. Captain Lang on the *Pro Re Nata* has something of an experimental weapon that we adapted from Rokarian technology that they used successfully at Lupadia to destroy several outposts and a planet. I think you all know why I was reluctant to use it before." There was a brief, respectful silence for all the souls that had been lost on that day. "Anyway, if our recon is still accurate, there is a large Ebokras mother ship in Sector Eight. I don't need to tell you all that this is the largest gathering of the enemy in one spot that we've ever seen. Captain Lang is to destroy it. Finally, *Versai*, you are to keep the enemy off the *Pro Re Nata* and just cause general havoc, which I know you're good at." Captain Heruks of the *Versai* grinned and nodded. Quip smiled a little. "All right, I chose you all for this because I have the utmost confidence in your ships, your crew, and you. Make us proud."

The inter ship link disengaged, leaving the five captains hardly enough time to mull over their orders before they dropped out of subspace and into the outer regions of Sector Eight.

"Everyone, this is Lang. You know what to do, and remember, whatever happens, follow the orders that Quip gave you. *Pro Re Nata* out."

Harrison watched for a moment as the *Pro Re Nata* moved off into the distance where visible debris was floating in space. It occurred to her that Quip had not said what had happened to the original ships that had been sent to Sector Eight. That knowledge sent a shiver down her spine. "*Utopia* and *Torken*, this is the *Avenger*."

"Go ahead, Captain."

"I'm reading you, *Avenger*."

"May I suggest a tactic? I'll take Outpost Twelve and *Utopia* will take Twenty. *Torken*, position yourself somewhere in the middle and act as our eyes so we can focus on the evacuation."

"Affirmative, *Avenger*. Moving to Outpost Twenty. *Utopia* out."

"*Torken* moving to defensive position. Out."

Harrison nodded. "Okay, Mr. Keith, set in a course to Outpost Twelve."

"Yes, Captain."

The silence was what was really bothering her, Harrison decided. She was used to nice, relaxed missions where there was always a hum of conversation and a feeling of camaraderie. But on a mission like this, where the stakes were high and the price of failure was unimaginable, even the beeping and hissing of the bridge controls were silent. It set her nerves on end.

"Is the outpost aware that evacuation is imminent?"

"Shall I send a message, Captain?"

"Yes."

There was a slight pause as the Ops lieutenant bent to his work. "Message sent."

As the *Avenger* crept cautiously forward to the outpost, Harrison cast an uneasy look at her first officer. Commander Proparian looked back, his own face showing his misgivings about the operation. "Have we received a reply yet?"

"No, ma'am."

Harrison pursed her lips. "I don't like this," she muttered. "What about the Ebokras? Any activity?"

Derek Chu, Tactical Officer, looked at his console before shaking his head. "No, Captain, there is minimal activity. The Ebokras seem to be ignoring us."

"What about the *Pro Re Nata*?"

"It's still moving toward its objective."

"Which is?"

"A large ship about nine minutes in front of us."

"How large?"

"Um..." The Ops. Lieutenant scurried to keep up with his captain's rapid-fire questions. "Almost one thousand kilometers wide?" His voice rose at the end as his mind tried to wrap itself around that concept of hugeness.

Harrison turned to look at him. "Are you sure?"

"That's what the sensors say."

The captain turned quickly and walked closer to the screen. "Then why can't we see it?" Her eyes widened as her mind worked furiously. "Mr. Keith, pull us back to our original entry point from subspace. Open a com to all the other ships."

"Link open."

"This is the *Avenger*, pull back immediately. This is an ambush. I repeat, pull back—"

Screaming was stilled by a large explosion that rippled over the com link as Outpost Twenty blew up, taking the *Utopia* with it. The end of the shock wave rocked the *Avenger*, causing its crew to scramble for something to hang onto.

Harrison recovered her legs and quickly sat as she listened to their link with the *Utopia* descend into static. "Retreat! We are compromised. Retreat!"

"Captain, I'm picking up several dozen Ebokras ships headed this way," Chu reported.

"Mr. Keith, take us into subspace."

"I can't. I don't know what's wrong, but something is jamming our engines."

"Then just take us away from here! The *Pro Re Nata*?"

"I've lost it, Captain. There is too much interference caused by the explosion and they might be jamming communications as well."

"Can we get a com to any of the ships?"

The commotion was interrupted by a broken transmission. "Callin...*Avenger*...this is...ken...damaged...head to...rendez...dinates...009.34.1.45...call...reinforcementsssssss." The transmission faded into a hiss of static.

"Did we get those coordinates?"

"Yes, ma'am."

"Set a course. Try and keep us ahead of that swarm. Monitor the subspace engines and tell me as soon as they're operable. Attention all hands, this is Harrison. We've walked into an ambush. The *Utopia* is gone. The status of the *Pro Re Nata* and *Versai* is unknown. The *Torken* is badly damaged. We're heading to a rendezvous site with lots of Ebokras on our tail. Fire at will. Do whatever you need to do to keep us in one piece. Harrison out."

She collapsed back into her chair and sighed, taking just one moment to rest. She had a feeling that she wouldn't have the opportunity to do so again for a long time. "What do you think?"

Commander Proparian turned his head at the question. "I think our odds of survival are slim to nil."

Harrison snorted. "That's why I love you, always the facts even when I don't want them."

"You didn't let me finish. Despite that, I *know* that this crew, ship, and captain pull off amazing things when times are at their worst. So ask me what I think when we get back to Jopus."

Harrison smiled. Her first officer never ceased to amaze her. Then the *Avenger* rocked under enemy fire and she turned her attention to the crisis at hand.

~~*~*~*

Patrik stuck his head into the just recently filled quarters and smiled as he felt a small hand grasp his thigh. Emmeline poked her head around her father's leg and peered into the room with the unashamed interest that only a child can muster. They moved further inside and settled against a wall as identical pairs of hazel eyes studied a certain individual.

Karton was well aware of the spectators but was intent on finishing his task before turning to Patrik and his adorable child. He had never met them before, but knew that anyone who had earned Janus's friendship and retained it for twenty years was certainly worth knowing. He finished stowing his belongings and turned to the father and daughter. Karton's bearded lips twitched as he took in the picture they made. *Almost identical.*

Patrik stepped forward and held out his hand. "Hi, I'm Patrik and this is my daughter Emmeline."

Karton shook the offered hand and knelt to meet the child's eyes. "Hello there."

"Hi."

"And how are you doing?"

"Good. You're Janus's friend?"

"That I am, young one, that I am."

Emmeline nodded. "Janus has nice friends."

Karton laughed, the deep sound reverberating off the walls. "Well, I hope I live up to that expectation."

"You will," she said with absolute certainty.

Karton looked into her eyes and saw a knowledge that far surpassed her age. "How do you know that?"

"I just do."

He spent another moment staring at her, gratified when Emmeline took no offense and stared right back. "Mm...I suspect you do, child; I suspect you do." Karton stood then and smiled when he saw the wary look on Patrik's face. "Come on then, sit down. I don't make a habit of keeping guests standing in my doorway."

Patrik took the offered seat and watched as Emmeline did the same.

"Now, what has brought you two to my new place of residence?"

"Janus, actually. We were looking for her, and since she was escorting you..."

"I see. Well, you will not find her here."

Patrik felt that Karton didn't mean the room in particular, but Jopus Prime as a whole. "Okay, and where might she be?"

"With her half."

Patrik opened his mouth a few times and then closed it, looking very much like a fish. "What?"

"Janus is exactly where she needs to be – with her half."

"Listen, Karton..."

Karton smiled, seeing Patrik's rising ire in his face. "Janus was here and then all of a sudden she took off running down the hall, right after the announcement to man those five ships. She is with her half."

"You mean Barker, on the *Avenger*?"

Karton smiled faintly and ducked his head. "If that is the person who has captured Janus's soul, then yes. And if the *Avenger* is where this Barker person is, then yes."

Patrik swore roundly and stood, knocking his chair over backwards. "Stay here, please," he said to Emmeline before running from the room.

Karton looked after the man with amused grey eyes, then turned his gaze to the child. "And why didn't you tell him that?"

Emmeline looked up at Karton, her young face a study in concentration. "Daddy doesn't like it when I use my gift."

"Because of your mother?" A gentle question which received an immediate affirmative nod from the child. "Well, let me tell you something, Emmeline. Your 'gift' as you call it, really is that. But even more, it's part of you and you should not deny it. I can help you, if you like."

Emmeline again nodded her head vigorously.

Chapter 9

The entire vessel shook again, sending the tall form stumbling. Janus growled low in her throat and continued down the hall. She had just heard Harrison's announcement and probably knew better than the captain how much trouble the *Avenger* was in.

She wasn't sure what had possessed her to board the ship. One minute she had been showing Tryst and Karton to their newly assigned quarters, and the next she had gotten a vague sense of unease, seemingly coming from everywhere at once. Following on the heels of that had been the call to arms, and Janus instinctively knew that she needed to be on the *Avenger*. Not just because that's where Barker was, but because something told her that she would be needed there. Janus had long ago learned not to question such feelings, just to follow them without thought.

And now she was very glad that she had, because the chances that the *Avenger* would get out of this situation successfully were, in her opinion, abysmally slim. If Harrison really was on her own without any of the other ships to offer assistance, Janus didn't think that the human had enough information on that region of space to survive for long.

The door to the bridge was only a few feet ahead of her and Janus could hear the raised voices, yelling out questions, answers, and all manner of data. She whooshed onto the bridge and just stood there, taking in the chaotic scene. Harrison was seated and watching the large view screen that displayed four Ebokras ships that were coming around for another attack. The rest of the bridge crew was diligently working at their controls.

"Mr. Chu, how are we doing?"

"Not good, Captain. Our weapons don't seem to be making much of an impact."

The ship rocked violently.

"Is there anything we haven't tried?" Harrison yelled.

"No, ma'am."

Another severe jolt sent a few people stumbling.

"Well, I'm open to suggestions!"

Janus studied the screen intently, taking in the formations of the ships and their attack patterns, the frequency with which they regrouped, and the *Avenger's* apparently useless weaponry. She didn't like what she saw.

An attacker fired, hitting the *Avenger* with enough force to rattle the walls. Electrical consoles began to explode, their hiss followed by the acrid stench of smoke and burnt plastic. Janus could hear the terrified and agonized screams of injured crewmembers throughout the ship, the sickening sound of twisting metal, the smell of blood. It all grated on her heightened senses, enough to make her want to scream, enough to make any person crazy. But Janus calmed her mind and blocked it all out, just as she had been taught. She turned her thoughts to the immediate problem and responded to Harrison's plea for an answer. "'Ide." Her voice, calm and unexpected, cut through the harried atmosphere of the bridge and made even the most frustrated crewmember take notice of her presence.

Harrison stood and turned, her face set and angry. "What are you doing here?"

"Ya kin worry about that later because if ya do not do somethin' now, it will not matter. There is a large asteroid belt around 'ere. It will block even the best sensors and give ya a place ta 'ide while ya make repairs and come up with a plan."

The captain turned toward Ops, where the lieutenant was already nodding. "Got it."

"Mr. Keith, set in a course, maximum speed."

"Aye, Captain."

Harrison turned back to Janus and pointed at her. "You, stick around."

Janus ducked her head in brief acknowledgement and leaned back against the wall to wait.

The asteroid belt was, fortunately, not very far away. It was dense, and the only thing that kept them from suffering more damage was their excellent pilot, but Harrison was pleased to note that the Ebokras were no longer on their tail. It gave them all some much needed breathing room and the opportunity to regroup after their mission had taken a very unexpected and unwelcome turn.

"Damage report."

"We have reports of eight dead and another twenty-seven wounded. Deck Nine has no atmosphere, structural integrity of Decks Five to Seven has been severely compromised. I can't even get a reading for Decks Two and Ten. Engines are at fourteen percent; shields are minimal, if working at all; sensors are down along with subspace engines. Our com signal still appears to be jammed."

Harrison sighed and rubbed her forehead. "All right, people, you all know what to do. Commander, you have the bridge." The captain turned toward her office and motioned Janus to follow.

They stepped into a medium sized room, Harrison immediately taking a position behind her desk while Janus lounged around the doorway. This really was, Harrison decided, the last thing she wanted to have to deal with. Her ship was pretty much defenseless, crippled and blind, and there was no help in the foreseeable future. Janus was an unknown element that the captain honestly saw only as a threat and liability.

Harrison rubbed her forehead again and collapsed, exhausted, into her chair. She stared at the alien woman standing so casually and confidently in front of her, and couldn't find the words to speak. Janus looked back, her face showing nothing, clearly communicating that this was Harrison's show and that she should take the lead. "Okay, Janus, it's obvious that we don't like each other. Right?"

"I 'ave formed no opinion about ya personally."

"Fine. But at this moment, I'm not that fond of you. I really don't want to have to worry about you or what you're doing on this ship when I have all these other problems. Frankly, I have to wonder why you're here." The captain paused, clearly expecting some kind of response.

Janus grumbled under her breath and decided it would be prudent to at least try and cooperate. "I am 'ere because I knew I needed ta be 'ere. Ya do not 'ave ta worry about me. Ya are allied with Quip against the Ebokras, and that makes ya a friend of mine."

"Friend?" the captain asked, skeptical.

A small smile quirked the corners of Janus's lips. "Not in every sense of the word. Ya may not want ta admit it, but ya need me 'ere. No one else knows the area of space, where ta 'ide or find 'elp."

Harrison sighed and accepted the truth of those words. "All right then. Nothing is going to happen until we get this ship fixed up. Are you any good at engineering?"

Janus nodded.

"Good, because I'm thinking our best option is to get those subspace engines up and retreat back to Jopus Prime as fast as possible. My people are still a little shaky on all the quirks of the technology. Dismissed."

Janus's eyebrow rose a fraction of an inch, but she left the room and started toward Engineering. It was going to be a long couple of days.

~~*~*~*

Janus sat back and rubbed her eyes. Things weren't going very well. Everything seemed to be in need of repair and there were only so many engineers and so much they could do. She thought she finally had the engines up and running, but she wasn't sure whether they would stay that way.

Rita Donahue, chief engineer and resident genius, gazed across the room at the tired figure that was sitting slumped against the wall. She hadn't known much about Janus when she had stepped through the door, but Donahue was glad that Janus was there. The engines were, on good days, very finicky and hard to keep in good working order. On a bad day, it was nearly impossible for even her to maintain them, and today definitely qualified as a bad day. "All right, folks, let's run this test!"

People started moving about and preparing to test their engines again. They had done so twice already, and twice they had been disappointed, so the atmosphere was understandably subdued. Donahue walked over and slid down the wall so she was beside Janus. "What do you think?"

Janus looked up at the engineer and her brightly coloured red hair, then shrugged. "I am not sure. I thought they would work before, but they did not."

"Only one way to know, then. Brad, start it up!" An eager young man looked up and stuck his thumb in the air, then bent to a control panel. The room quieted as the engines started up, the two main ones followed by five sub-engines filling the room with a low hum.

"Engines at twenty-nine percent, thirty-seven, fifty-six." The hum got louder. "Seventy-two percent."

Janus sat up straighter as something, a feeling, tickled the back of her neck. This wasn't going to work. She shook her head and stood, looking around the room with frantic eyes.

Donahue stood as well. "What's wrong?"

"I am not sure."

"Engines at eighty-nine percent." The hum suddenly turned into a high pitched whining sound that caused the engineers to wince and cover their ears.

Janus grimaced and started moving forward to a small knot of people who were standing in front of an open relay station. Something was very wrong.

"Shut it down!" Donahue yelled.

"I can't, engine power is still increasing! One-hundred percent, one-hundred and five!"

Janus broke into a run and launched her body into the air, spreading her arms and taking three of the engineers to the ground with her. She bounded up and grabbed the other two by the front of their shirts and pulled, just as the relay station exploded, followed by every other station around main engineering.

As she fell to the ground and saw the other stations explode, Janus was reminded of some silly human game Patrik had shown her once. Dominos. That's what it looked like: one station exploding and causing the one next to it to overload and shower the room with flames. She closed her eyes as they landed on the floor with enough force to rattle her teeth. The last thing she heard was the crunch of bone.

Donahue saw Janus take off and tackle her staff, she saw the explosions start, and dove behind a console. She threw her arms over her head and curled up into as small a ball as she could. The explosions rang through the air, one after another, followed by a few screams and the continued whining engine noise. At last the room quieted, and all she heard was the crackling of flame and the eerie creaking and groaning of metal. She lowered her arms and peeked up cautiously, satisfied that the ceiling was still intact and there was nothing blocking her way. Donahue stood slowly and looked around.

The lights were flickering and smoke was rising up into the air. The flames were valiantly trying to consume more air, but the fire control system had done its job and sprayed the engineering compartment with a liquefied foam. Everything was wet, there were puddles on the floor, and foam was dripping off the walls. Bodies were sprawled out all over the floor, some stirring and groaning, others very, very still. Donahue continued her visual diagnostic and groaned when her eyes landed on the almost gutted walls where the relay stations had been. She started toward the console where Brad had been standing and checked the engines to find that they were running at sixty-seven percent, despite the damage. *Well*, she thought, *it's better than we started out with.*

The com system crackled to life and Harrison's agitated voice flooded Engineering, "Donahue, what the hell is going on in there?"

She knelt and placed her fingers on Brad's pulse, sighing in relief at the strong, steady beat. "We had a bit of a...mishap, Captain." *Mishap! Try disaster.* "I need Doctor Cobb down here. We have injured and probably some causalities." A sudden image of Janus's flying leap flashed through her mind and Donahue stood abruptly. They had been right in front of a relay station. She started over to where she had last seen them and stopped short upon seeing a large piece of the wall lying in her path. A shoe was sticking out from underneath it. "I need some help over here!"

The people who had only been stunned by the explosions ran over in response to Donahue's yell. Four of them gathered around the large hunk of metal and put their backs into the lifting. The metal groaned and protested the entire way, but they eventually had it moved off to one side.

Donahue knelt and very gently checked the man's pulse. It was thready, but it was there. She rolled him over and found a large gash along the left side of his head and several burns along his neck and arms.

Someone groaned and she looked over to see a body lying only a foot away. It stirred and sat up slowly, rubbing its face with a shaking hand. Donahue moved over to the woman and knelt in front of her to be met with cloudy eyes. "Karen, are you okay?"

Karen groaned. "Oh yeah, Chief, just fine."

Donahue looked around; she didn't see anyone else. "Do you know where Janus and the others are?"

Karen shook her head and then winced at the movement. "No. It all happened so fast."

The door to Engineering whooshed open to admit Doctor Cobb and several nurses, all of them loaded down with medical supplies. They spread through the room, going first to the bodies that were still unmoving on the ground or with other concerned friends crouched over them. Donahue put up her arm and yelled for the doctor.

Cobb looked up and said a few words to the young woman she was with, then headed over to the red headed chief engineer. The doctor stopped first at the man and spent a moment injecting him and scanning before she moved over to Donahue and Karen. Karen checked out with only a concussion, so Cobb sent the woman back to her quarters and lifted her eyes to the chief engineer for a status report.

"Three of my engineers and Janus are missing."

"Missing?"

"We haven't found them yet, but they were around this area. I'm thinking they can't be in very good shape."

Cobb nodded. "As soon as you find them, call me over. Are you all right?"

"Me? Fine."

"Whatever you say."

Brad looked up from where he leaned on the wall and observed the room. *Oh, God, this is really, really bad.* He shifted his hand where he was holding a part of his shirt to his head and took a few cautious steps toward Donahue. He wasn't sure what had gone wrong, but he had a theory or two. He slipped and almost fell, but caught himself on the wall and looked down. A puddle of water. Brad was about to continue toward his chief when something about the water caught his attention. He squinted and carefully got down on his knees to take a closer look, bending to see in the dim, flickering light. It almost looked...red. His clouded mind thought about that for a long time until his body jerked upwards. "Doctor Cobb!" His voice came out in a high screech that caught everyone's attention.

Cobb looked up quickly to see a young man kneeling over a puddle of water with an odd look on his face. She stood and motioned to Bobby, who also started over. They arrived at Brad's spot with Donahue in tow and fell to their knees with a little splash. "What is it?"

"Look."

Brad pointed and Cobb did look. She saw the blood that was turning the water crimson and the large console that had fallen over. Cobb stuck her hand in a gap between the floor and console, swallowing when she felt warm flesh. "Let's move this thing, people; we have injured under it!"

* ~ * ~ * ~ * ~ *

Barker wheeled around the corner and bounced off something solid and warm before she felt her shoulder grasped tightly. She looked up into Samson's emotionless face and they continued down the hall together, not saying a word. She felt her stomach roil and her head start to pound: something was very wrong and she knew she needed to be in the medical bay.

They walked through the door and stopped in their tracks. The medical bay looked like... The only word that came to Barker's mind was "pandemonium". All of the beds were occupied and there were cots set out in all of the previously empty places. Nurses scurried about checking patients, helping Doctor Cobb, and quelling the concerns of friends. A few of the patients were wailing their agony into the din, but the majority of them were unconscious.

Barker felt her eyes drawn irresistibly to one bed that was off in the corner where a perplexed Cobb, nervous Bobby, and hovering Donahue were standing. She looked at the body that was lying on the bed and felt her heart rise into her throat. It was Janus. She hadn't even known that the woman was on the *Avenger*.

She immediately moved in that direction, getting more and more concerned as she went, her heart pounding and hands shaking. Harrison had announced the accident in Engineering almost two hours before, and here was Janus, lying on a medical bed unconscious and bleeding. It didn't fit with everything Patrik had told her, everything she had seen Janus do and come out of unharmed, everything Janus had told her. It just didn't fit.

Cobb looked up to see Barker, her eyes wide and face stricken. Then her eyes fell back to Janus's pale and unresponsive face and she cringed.

Barker stood next to the doctor and started her inventory at Janus's head. Her face was pale and sweaty, with a long scratch traveling from under her left eye to her jaw line. There was a myriad of other cuts, bruises, and burns along her arms, but Barker didn't see anything too serious. She continued her scrutiny, her entire body jerking as her eyes landed on Janus's midsection.

A large, roughly square piece of metal was sticking out of Janus's side, just under her ribs. Blood was spurting from around the foreign object and out onto the bed, soaking it through. Cobb's hands were liberally covered with blood, and there was a scattering of objects around, mute testimony to the doctor's efforts.

Barker reached out and gently placed her hand along Janus's cheek, feeling the cold and clammy flesh. She spent a moment just looking at Janus's face, staring and trying to forget the damage that was visible on the rest of the strong body. Just a few moments to pretend that everything was fine, just a few. She sniffled and slowly removed her hand, wiped her nose, and then looked at the gathered people. "What happened?"

Donahue spoke first. "There was an accident in Engineering. Janus knew it was going to happen and she started moving across the room to tackle five engineers who were standing right in front of a relay station. They would have been killed. Then afterwards, we couldn't find three of the engineers or Janus. When we did locate them, they were under this large console that had collapsed, all piled one on top of the other with Janus on the top, protecting them all."

Cobb cleared her throat. "I don't know what to do. As far as I know, Janus isn't supposed to get hurt like this, and any medical treatment I've tried hasn't worked. There is a lot of internal damage, even a severed artery, but I can't get in there to fix it or stop it. She just keeps bleeding and breathing, so... I don't know, maybe her body is doing exactly what it's supposed to be doing." Cobb shrugged helplessly. "If this were any human, they would have been dead before I got them back here, so I think it's safe to hope."

Barker made a small gurgling noise and turned back to Janus. "Can you leave, please?"

"Barker..."

"Leave! You can't help her, so just go!"

Cobb looked at Donahue and Bobby, then nodded her head. They dispersed quietly and left the doctor to face the emotional little blonde. Cobb gently placed her hand on Barker's shoulder, felt her stiffen in response but continued to stand there. "I'll come back and check on her regularly. If anything happens, you yell, all right? I don't care what it is."

Barker nodded and sniffled again. "You think she'll be all right?"

It was a small, sad voice that posed the question and Cobb felt her heart breaking. "I...I don't know. I don't know enough about Janus. I...I'm sorry." Cobb patted the ensign's shoulder and quietly brought over a chair, which she placed just behind Barker. She had a feeling that the medical bay was going to have a new fixture until Janus got better or... *No.* Cobb shook her head. *I will not think like that.*

* ~ * ~ * ~ * ~ *

"What do you want me to do?"

"I don't care what you do, as long as it's *something*!"

"Patrik, would you listen to yourself? We lost contact with five warships, five! Not to mention that we can't get a read on anything else in Sector Eight. I cannot, in good conscience, order more people out there!"

"Quip, we can't just leave them out there."

"I know you're worried about Janus but–"

"No. I'm not worried about Janus, I am very frightened for her. Something is *wrong,* but you obviously don't give a damn!"

"Now that's not fair. I've known her a long time and she means just as much to me as anyone else, but I will not order anyone else to risk their lives."

"You won't have to. Just ask them, Quip. Ask Tryst and Karton. From what I've heard, they'd follow her anywhere." Quip started to shake his head, which caused Patrik to stand so quickly he almost fell down again, dizzy. "Fine! You don't have to, but I will ask them and we will go."

He stormed out of the office and quickly moved down the halls of Jopus Prime. Before he knew it, he was standing in front of Tryst and relating his story. It wasn't much of a story since he really didn't know anything except what he felt, but that seemed to be enough for the cyborg.

She called out several names that he didn't recognize and everyone lurched into frenzied motion. Tryst told Patrik to go to Docking Bay Nine and wait while she went to see Karton. It wasn't long before three of their ships were manned, stocked, and launched on a rescue mission. Quip'lee did not try to stop them.

"So, what do we know?" Karton asked.

Patrik leaned forward on the table. "None of the sensors on Jopus Prime can get a read on anything in Sector Eight, nor can they get a message sent to any of the ships Quip dispatched. No contact has been made by any of the ships, and some people think it was a trap, an ambush."

Tryst grinned. "So we're going into hostile territory with no intel, no back up, and no idea where to look for any of them, right?"

"Um...basically, yeah."

"Great, my favorite kind of mission."

Karton laughed gently and shook his head. "Assuming we find the *Avenger* or any of the other ships, what then?"

"Help them?" Patrik suggested with a shrug.

The older man smiled. "Right. So – no plan, we're just flying by the seat of our pants?"

Tryst waggled her eyebrows. "Definitely."

"I can live with that."

Patrik perked up as he remembered something. "Oh, I suggest we don't actually go right into Sector Eight. Sounds like the Ebokras have something to jam communications and maybe other systems. We don't want to get caught in the trap when we're supposed to be the cavalry. And maybe we'll be able to gather some information from the fringes."

Karton nodded. "Prudent course of action. Tryst?"

She sighed and raised her hands. "Yeah, yeah, take all the fun out of it, why don't you?" Karton raised an eyebrow, which made Tryst squirm at the likeness between his version of Janus's trademark gesture and when Janus herself did it. "Agreed."

Karton stood and dusted off the front of his shirt. "Good. Now, how long until we arrive?"

"About ten minutes."

"Tell everyone to be on their toes and prepared to retreat at a moment's notice."

~~*~*~*

"Ba'ke?"

The raspy whisper leeched into her consciousness, but was not nearly enough of a stimulus to wake Barker from her exhausted sleep. It came again, a little stronger and accompanied with a slight tap on her arm. This time, the sound that hardly resembled her name brought Barker surging up so fast that her back seized up from being in one position for far too long. She grimaced and then swiftly forgot about the lancing pain as her eyes latched onto half-open, bleary, pain-filled blue orbs.

"Janus?" It took Barker a moment to realize she had spoken, her voice cracking and low. "Wha...what can I do?" Her eyes kept flicking from the familiar face down to the large piece of metal still sticking from her friend's midsection. The sight made her heart ache.

Janus raised her hand, very slowly and precisely, to rest gently on the piece of metal. "Take...out."

"What?"

"Take...it...out," she ground out between clenched teeth, pronouncing the words very deliberately so as not to be misunderstood.

Barker nodded. "Okay, if that's what you want." She tried to stand and stumbled, her legs rubbery and numb. It took only a moment to move a few feet and shake Cobb awake from her position sprawled on an empty bio bed. The ensign felt a moment of sympathy for the doctor who had only just gotten a moment of respite from the constant swarm of concerned friends, the cries of patients, and the unnerving presence of Captain Harrison.

Cobb jerked awake and stood immediately. "What is it?"

"She's awake and wants you to remove the metal."

"What?" Cobb walked over to the bed and bent to see Janus face. "I...Janus are you sure? That could cause some serious damage."

"I am not...'uman. Just...do it...now."

"Whatever you say, you're the expert." Cobb moved around, grumbling under her breath.

Barker knelt down and looked Janus in the eye. "What's going on? Why aren't you better?"

"Can ya not...see it?"

"See it? See what, Janus?"

"Streaks...the streaks."

"Streaks? Janus, I don't understand."

Janus moved so fast that Barker didn't even register the motion until the large hands were clasped on either side of her face. She started in surprise but remained still, her own hands around Janus's thick wrists. Totally ignoring Cobb's insistent voice, Janus very gently moved her thumbs over Barker's eyes and concentrated as she felt the blonde's eyelids close.

Barker stayed very still and waited, not having any idea of what was happening but trusting Janus to not do her any harm. It started slowly as a gradual increase of heat, seemingly coming from Janus's fingertips and engulfing her eyelids. The sensation got hotter and moved back to settle in her head, right behind her eyes, not painful but annoying, like an itch that you can't scratch. It lasted a second or two and ended in a sudden brief stab of pain that made her flinch backwards and give a slight cry.

She shook her head and rubbed her eyes before opening them to see Janus lying on the bed, very still and once again unconscious. "Is she..."

"No, same as before. What was all that about?"

"I...I don't know," Barker shook her head and blinked, rubbing her eyes and opening them again. She froze and blinked a few times, looking around the medical bay with something very close to disbelief. "Oh my God."

Cobb glanced up from her work, her brow creasing at the strange look on the ensign's face. "What?" She finished placing a bandage over the large hole in Janus's side, not sure if it would do any good but feeling better for it. "Barker?"

"Streaks," she said to herself and continued to gaze around, then looked over at Cobb and down at herself. Finally, she looked at Janus.

"Barker, what the hell are you doing? You look like you got a message from some divine being or something."

"Streaks, that's what Janus was talking about."

"And?"

"I can see...them. Yellow lines are covering everything – the walls, floor, beds, us, our clothes, everything except Janus." She looked down for a moment. "And her blood."

Cobb's eyebrows lifted as she nodded indulgently. "Right, okay. When was the last time you had a decent meal, or sleep?"

"I'm serious here! Look, do some doctor thing and find proof. Janus did something so I could see this, so there must be something different about me now that you can detect. Right?"

The doctor walked over and placed her hands on Barker's shoulders. "Listen..." She trailed off and leaned closer. "Close your eyes."

Barker did so and heard Cobb whistle softly under her breath. "What, what is it?"

"There are silver marks on your eyelids, just like Janus's."

"What do they look like?"

"Um...well, a diamond with these..."

Barker jerked out of Cobb's grasp and picked up one of Janus's hands. She pointed to the symbol in the middle of her hand and looked up at the doctor. "Like this?"

"Yeah, exactly like that. Do you know what it means?"

"It's the symbol for Janus's family. Now do you believe me?"

"Okay, okay, let's just think about this for a minute. I want to check your eyes out first and then...well, we'll have to decide what to do."

"Fine by me." Barker plopped herself down on the foot of Janus's bed and waited. "Get to it, Doc."

～～*～*

"What's the verdict?"

"As far as I can tell, your optic nerves and retinae have been altered in some way to pick up a larger spectrum of light than what is normally visible to the human eye."

"So you believe me?"

"Yeah, Barker, I do."

She smiled. "Good. Now what about Janus?"

Cobb turned to look at the still body. "That is a little more complex. The internal damage is healing, very slowly, but it is healing. I think she'll be up and around soon, because if she hasn't died yet, then I don't think she will."

Barker swallowed and felt her heart calm a little and the tight feeling in her stomach ease. "That's good."

"Yes, but what I can't figure is why this is taking so long. I mean, you said that on the ship her arm healed instantly."

The blonde head nodded.

"Right, so what's different?"

"Well, it might have something to do with these streaks. I mean, Janus said that it's the energy in all things that allows them to heal so quickly. Maybe this yellow stuff, whatever it is, has...altered the energy in some way so her body can't use it as fast."

Cobb opened her mouth and tilted her head to the side, shrugging. "I suppose it's possible, even plausible. You said the streaks were on everything except her, right?"

"Yeah."

The com system came to life, "All senior staff, please report to the briefing room immediately."

Barker sighed. "I was wondering when that was going to happen."

"Go. I'll keep on eye on Janus. And Barker? I'd suggest not mentioning these...streaks...to Harrison until we know a little more."

The ensign nodded. "Good idea."

Chapter 10

Harrison looked around the room and scowled. Her senior staff was assembling with their typical hurried casualness, but there was a distinct undercurrent of tension that was usually absent from their meetings. Everyone was finally present and seated, so Harrison leaned back and clasped her hands in front of her. Her brown eyes flicked from person to person, taking in each expression and hating that she could do little to alleviate the suffering of her crew. "I'm sure you all know about the accident in Engineering. Donahue, how are repairs and theories coming along?"

The redhead grimaced and squirmed in her seat. "Our walls and most of the relay stations are totally destroyed, beyond repair. Every time I take a look around, I'm surprised the ceiling hasn't fallen down on top of us. Amazingly enough, the engines are working and seem to be stable, but we still can't create a subspace field. We don't know why or what caused the accident."

"Keep working on it. Chu, what's our status with the Ebokras?"

"As far as I can tell, we're safe, but I can only get minimal sensor readings; there is some very serious interference. If we got the sensors to full capacity, I might be able to rig something up to work around the interference. Until that happens..." He shrugged.

Commander Proparian spoke up. "At last report, our weapons were at one-hundred percent, shields at ninety, so if the Ebokras wander in here looking for us, we should be able to fight them off."

Someone snorted. "Right. Like we did so well last time."

"With the asteroids, they can't launch a massive assault, and even without full engines we could hide pretty well."

"What about communications?" the captain asked.

"Nada, absolutely nothing."

Harrison rubbed her forehead and sighed. "Anyone heard from Cobb?"

Barker took the opportunity to lean forward and join in the discussion. "She's in the medical bay watching her patients."

The captain grunted and keyed the com system. "Doctor Cobb?"

"Go ahead, Captain."

"What's our status?"

"In total, eight have died and another twenty-six are injured. Of those twenty-six, I expect to release ten of them by tomorrow morning and another three are critical. The other thirteen are somewhere in between – ranging from a mild concussion or broken fingers to severe burns and internal injuries. Unless something unexpected happens, I'm confident they'll all make a full recovery."

Harrison grunted in approval. "And our guest?"

Cobb made a humming sound as she debated what to reveal to the captain. "Well, if things keep progressing as they have been, Janus will be up and as good as new in a few hours." There was a pause as Cobb's voice faded briefly, then came back, "I have to go, Captain. If you want any more information on Janus, you can ask Barker. She was here the entire time."

"Thank you, Doctor. Harrison out."

As the room fell into silence, Barker looked around and studied her crewmates with a practiced eye. The expressions on everyone's faces ranged from a mixture of shock, grief, and disbelief to rage and anger. Even Samson, who was the picture perfect soldier with an emotional detachment and the capacity to be cold and calculating when the need arose, a man who always had a caustic remark balanced on the tip of his tongue, looked shell shocked. It made Barker feel a little off balance, because in all the years she had been on the *Avenger*, the one thing that had never changed was Samson. He was like a relentless, unchanging force of nature – stubborn and narrow-minded in his beliefs, but a constant. To see him affected by a situation meant it was really bad and worth worrying about.

The ensign looked up as she heard her name and realized that the captain had dismissed everyone except her. Barker cringed as her mind swiftly supplied several scenarios, many of them outlandish and totally unrealistic, but they made her stomach turn nonetheless. As she focused on the captain, she found herself hard pressed not to laugh at the yellow streak that traveled right down Harrison's nose to end in a large, solid dot.

"Barker, let's cut to the chase, all right?"

"Sure."

"We both know that Janus is a touchy subject between us but I have to know a few things, so please view this simply as a captain taking care of her crew and not an attack on your friend."

The ensign gazed speculatively at Harrison, her green eyes wide and unblinking. "I'll try."

"First, how is she?"

"You heard Cobb–"

"Yes, but I'd like to know everything."

Barker's brow creased. "Well, it was kind of scary earlier because she just kept bleeding and bleeding and Cobb couldn't get it to stop. She said there was some very bad internal damage and a severed artery. But when Janus didn't die, we figured her body must have been doing what it was supposed to, right? Anyway, she was out for a...really long time before she finally woke up and told Cobb to remove the big hunk of metal."

"Metal?"

"Yeah. Janus jumped some engineers to get them out of the way of a relay station that was about to explode, and she must have gotten on top of three of them before a large console and part of the wall fell over. She took most of the damage and got this piece of metal stuck in her. After Cobb removed the metal, Janus just dropped away again. I guess she's healing fine. Slow, but fine."

"I see. And the accident, you don't think she—"

"No!" Barker stood quickly and glared. "Listen, Captain, Janus may be a very big question mark in this whole thing, but she's out to stop the Ebokras even more than you or me. Remember, it's her home and friends that are being threatened! She isn't the type of person to cause an accident just because she might not like you. She chose to be here, so you'd do well to accept that she's here to help!"

"Barker—"

"You said you're taking care of your crew. Well, Janus is just as much a part of this crew as anyone else. She is your ally and our best chance for getting out of here. Now, if you'll excuse me, Captain, I have to go see my friend!" Barker left the room in a huff and didn't stop until she was back by Janus's side.

Cobb looked up and smiled at the blonde woman who entered the medical bay and walked forward. "Okay, here's what I've done. I took into account the changes in your optic nerves and managed to rig up a system that should, hopefully, detect these streaks...or whatever they are. This scanner," the doctor held up the device, "should work. All we need to do is scan anything in this room and then Janus, and we'll know if I did it right."

Barker took the scanner and took a reading on herself. Cobb recorded it while the ensign moved over to Janus and scanned her, then relayed the readings. "So, this first reading is positive for these yellow things?"

Cobb squinted at the screen and typed in a few commands. "Uhmm," she mumbled absently.

"I don't get it, why do we need this? I can see them, so—"

"I got to thinking and started to wonder if maybe this isn't some kind of weapon that the Ebokras were testing. I have the parameters entered into the computer, and once I run a short range scan, we'll be able to see if these things are infecting all of space or just the ship."

"A weapon? But that would only be good for... Oh." Barker's eyes drifted over to Janus's body and paused before moving back to the grim-faced doctor.

"My thoughts exactly. We have every indication that the Ebokras aren't stupid, and from the things Janus has said and done, her people sound pretty powerful. The Ebokras wouldn't stand for having a species like that around unless it was under their control."

"How long will that scan take?"

"A few minutes."

The blonde ensign nodded and moved over to Janus's bed where she knelt and studied the woman's face, taking in the improved colour and lack of sweat. Barker peeked hesitantly under the soaked bandage across Janus's midsection and winced at the large wound that was still seeping blood. It did not look good at all. "Hey, Doc?"

"Yeah?"

"You've been checking for infection and stuff, just in case?"

"You bet."

"Good."

A beeping broke the silence followed by a grunt from Cobb. "We have a positive result for the streaks in space."

Barker sighed and leaned her forehead on the edge of the bed. "Wonderful," she murmured.

Cobb walked over to the ensign, placed her hand on the woman's back and gave it a gentle rub. "When was the last time you slept? In a bed?"

"Umm..."

"I thought so. Go on, get to your quarters and sleep, doctor's orders. I promise I'll call you as soon as Janus wakes up or if something happens."

Barker nodded and rubbed her eyes. "Yeah, okay. Sounds like a good idea." She struggled to her feet and walked slowly out of the medical bay and down the numerous hallways to her quarters. It was a simple matter of slipping into her normal sleeping attire and climbing under the covers. She closed her eyes and was asleep in an instant.

~~*~*~*

Karton walked onto the bridge and spotted Patrik hovering over the helmsman's shoulder, making him decidedly nervous. He went over to Tryst, who was watching everything with an increasingly bored expression. "What's going on?"

The cyborg turned and snorted. "Besides Patrik driving everyone nuts? Not much. We can get minimal readings into the sector, a lot of debris where the *Avenger* was supposed to be. We sent out a probe to try and collect some for analysis, and if all went well it should be arriving soon. I have them running scans, looking for likely hiding places, since that's what Janus would do."

Karton grunted. "Good. Any sign of those other ships?"

"Not really. We picked up some residual engine emissions leaving the sector that I have some people tracking for a destination. As far as we can tell so far, it's a Jopus fleet ship, but that analysis could change once we get more details."

The older man nodded and slowly sat down, groaning as his aging body creaked in protest. "And Patrik? Tried giving him some busy work?"

"Did I ever. That man has the attention span of a gnat. I have no idea how Janus managed to live on the same ship with him all these years."

Karton smiled a little. "It's that friendship thing, Tryst, just what Janus needed when she left us."

Tryst nodded and sat next to the bearded man, studying him with a knowing eye. "And you?"

"What about me?"

"Did you rest?"

Karton managed a growl that Warber would have been proud to call his own. "Tryst."

"What? Don't I have the right to be concerned for a friend?"

"Yes, but I do not want to be pestered or mother-henned to death. That's what my own parents are for."

Tryst sighed and leaned back in her chair. "I know, Karton, but I can't help it. Are you going to—"

Karton cut her off. "Yes, but in my own time, so don't you go and open your mouth about it."

She turned to him, her cybernetic eye whizzing and zipping, processing all manner of information. "You know I won't, Karton, but I also won't lie to Janus, and we both know how...perceptive...she is. Once she spends any amount of time with you, she'll become suspicious, and if she asks me I...I don't think I can lie to her. Even for you."

He inclined his head to the side. "I can accept that."

"Tryst! Karton! We have a positive final destination for the engine trail we've been following. And the ship is definitely a part of the fleet of Jopus."

The two commanders exchanged a meaningful glance and replied in unison, "Lock in a course. Be cautious."

* ~ * ~ * ~ * ~ *

Hearing one of her patients stir, Doctor Cobb looked up from her desk, which sat in one corner of the medical bay. When she saw that it was Janus, she stood and moved over to the bio bed, resting her hands on the edge as Janus very carefully looked up at her. "Hello there, how are you feeling?"

A grimace crossed her face and her lip curled. "Ugh."

Cobb nodded. "Yeah, that's pretty much what I expected. Anything I can do?"

Janus blinked several times as her eyes flicked around the room.

"I sent Barker off to bed." Cobb studied her patient and leaned her arms on the edge of the bed so her face was a little closer to Janus's. "Can you tell me what these streaks are?"

A pink tongue poked out between cracked lips as Janus opened her mouth slightly and shifted on the bed. "Infection."

"Okay, infection. Of what? It's not hurting us."

She shook her head slightly. "Wrong. It gets inta technology and spreads."

Cobb's brow wrinkled. "You're saying these things are responsible for our engine failure? And the problems with our communications and sensors?"

"With everythin'."

"And it will spread to Jopus Prime if we go back?"

"Aye."

Cobb stood and walked away a few steps, rubbing her chin and staring at the carpeted floor. She ran an idle toe across the floor, tracing and erasing design after design as she thought. "You're positive?"

A cough was her answer. The doctor swung around and a sheepish look ran across her features. "Sorry, Janus. Here." She retrieved a glass of water and brought it back to Janus who gulped it down greedily.

"I am sure."

"All right. So we need some way to kill it or something. Maybe I can rig something up." She mumbled for a moment and then remembered her promise to Barker. It only took a few seconds to send off a message to the blonde's quarters. "Barker's on her way to see you."

Janus slowly pulled herself up in bed to sit with her back leaning against the wall. "Ya did not 'ave ta do that. She can see 'em?"

Doctor Cobb looked up from her computer and pursed her lips. "She can. Why did you do that?"

"I was not sure if I would be all right. I wanted someone ta know what was 'appenin' so ya could survive."

"Surely you wouldn't have died? I may not know a lot about you, Janus, but I do know that you aren't one to die easily."

"The streaks affect us in a bad way. I did not know if I would be able ta fight it."

Cobb walked back over to the bed and took in her patient's greatly improved colour. She gently moved aside the bandage and saw, with great relief, that the previously gaping hole was now only the size of her pinkie finger. The skin around the wound was still red and slightly swollen, but the bleeding had stopped and the entire injury looked to be only days away from healing completely. That was, of course, on a human. With Janus, Cobb would be surprised if it took any longer than an additional thirty minutes.

The medical bay door whooshed open to admit a slightly frazzled looking blonde ensign, who had a scowl etched on her otherwise youthful face. She stopped in her tracks when her eyes came in contact with very clear, very alert blue ones, and her face broke into a huge grin.

"You're awake!" Barker moved over quickly and threw her arms around Janus's neck.

For once Janus was expecting it and managed to clasp her arms around the relatively small back of her friend. She stayed very still until she felt Barker start to pull away.

The blonde looked up at her friend's face, still smiling, and seemingly without noticing, ran her fingers along Janus's cheek. Barker cleared her throat after a moment and blinked a few times. "So you're all right?"

"I am fine, Barker."

"Good."

Cobb spoke up. "What was with the scowl, Barker?"

She looked up at the doctor, confused. "Huh? Oh! I just noticed that there are a lot more yellow thingies than when I went to sleep. And it gets a little annoying to walk around and see the entire ship covered in stripes and dots and swirls." She sighed and looked plaintively at Janus. "Do you think you can undo this?"

"I can, but not right now. I want ya ta be able ta see 'em, just in case."

"Great. Now that that's all cleared up, who wants to tell Harrison?" Cobb asked in an overly cheery voice.

* ~ * ~ * ~ * ~ *

"Anyone have any idea what we're looking at here?"

"Not really."

"Nope."

A fourth head popped up in between the other three and gazed at the view screen. "Wouldja lookit that," Patrik mumbled.

Tryst turned a sardonic eye on him and huffed. "Yes, it's very interesting, but we aren't getting any closer to finding Janus."

Patrik pulled back and moved to one of the bridge chairs where he sat and planted his elbows on his knees. "Whatever was wrong with her has eased a bit, but I still don't like the feeling I'm getting." His hazel eyes flew back to the screen and he squinted. "How far away is that ship?"

"A little less than a light year."

Patrik nodded to himself as he continued to study the vessel. It was very odd looking, like parts of it were missing. Scans indicated that the ship, which they had identified as the *Versai*, was completely intact. The longer he spent looking at the ship, the more he came to identify the pattern and what, exactly, was happening. Parts of the ship were shimmering out of sight, almost like the way in which a transmission becomes fuzzy with interference. "Hey, look at this, guys."

Tryst and Karton turned to him and then looked back at the screen.

"Okay, watch. You see the left port side."

"No."

"That's my point, we can't see it. But wait just another minute and we will, but the front will disappear." They waited in tense silence and sure enough, the left port side reappeared, followed swiftly by the disappearance of the entire front of the vessel. "All right, now after this, the middle will go away."

It occurred just as Patrik predicted, and they spent several long minutes following the pattern and ensuring that it did not change.

Tryst finally rubbed her head and groaned. "Yeah, okay, this is all very nice, but what is the point?"

Patrik stood and stepped closer to the screen, pointing up at the invisible sections of the ship. "There isn't any fire or debris or anything. These sections aren't destroyed, they're just leaving our field of vision. The *Versai* is fully intact."

Karton cleared his throat. "Intact maybe, but functioning? Definitely not."

"But they're our best bet for locating the *Avenger*. We've been running scans continuously and haven't even picked up a blip. At least these guys know what happened, and maybe their ship will give us some clue as to exactly what is wrong in Sector Eight."

"So you want to go in there and do what? Rescue them?" Tryst asked.

"We should try. They're right on the fringe of the sector. If we send in a shuttle, maybe it won't be affected by whatever is causing that." He waved to the screen and the distressed ship.

Karton tilted his head back and looked up at the ceiling, his lips pursed and foot tapping. "I suppose that it is worth a try. We don't have any other recourse at the moment."

Tryst nodded. "Yeah, okay, fine. Come on, Patrik, this was your bright idea."

* ~ * ~ * ~ *

"As soon as we're in range, run a more detailed scan of the ship, especially the missing parts."

Patrik nodded and shifted in his chair. He continued to tap away at his control panel and started analyzing the results of his scans. "I'm no expert here, but it looks like those sections of the ships are out of phase or something. In fact, the entire ship is, to a certain degree, but it's like whatever is causing it can't decide where to start and keeps moving through the ship."

Tryst looked up at the vessel, studying it with electronic detachment and efficiency. "Or whoever is still alive has found a way to fight it."

Patrik hummed in his throat, his eyes flicking over the different readouts assailing him. "That would be good," he mumbled absently. "We still good with engines and sensors?"

Tryst checked again and nodded. "You bet. Everything is at top power. We'll cross over the boundary into Sector Eight in about a minute. That'll be the real test."

"Remember to keep everything at low power."

Tryst nodded and continued to pilot the shuttle. One of their engineers had caught up with them just outside the docking bay and informed them that he had made a breakthrough. It looked like this thing, whatever it was, put out an energy reading of its own, which the engineer had recreated. He'd reported that upon exposing different types of technology to the conditions he had duplicated, the ones with the higher energy outputs had been attacked and disabled long before the ones with a more minimal reading. Tryst was grateful for the knowledge because although she loved a good fight, she hated not knowing who or what she was up against.

"Crossing into Sector Eight in five, four, three, two...and one." Both passengers grabbed onto whatever they could in anticipation of some form of turbulence. Two pairs of eyes looked up and around the shuttle when nothing happened, just the continued silence broken only by their breathing.

Like the eye of a storm.

Patrik breathed out a sigh of relief and dropped his arms. "Finally, something goes right."

"Let's keep going then, and hope our luck holds."

~~*~*~*

Rita Donahue stepped back and studied the large machine they had just finished tinkering with. Her eyes swept over to the three other people who were also gazing at the machine. "Are we sure this is going to work?"

Cobb shook her head. "No idea at all."

Janus rubbed the side of her jaw. "It is a start."

Barker stepped forward and leaned her head on Janus's shoulder. "And having a place to start is always a good thing."

Donahue looked back at the large, roughly rectangular object. It hadn't taken much effort to build, most of the supplies had been lying around. With the combination of Cobb's information and Janus's intuitive knowledge, Donahue felt it might actually work. But there was also a chance that it might not. "It's too bad we don't know more about these streaks."

"We encountered them a long time ago and never learned much. I am sorry," Janus said to the engineer.

Cobb tilted her head and sighed. At least Harrison hadn't blown a gasket like she'd thought the captain would. They had decided that all three of them would go and tell the captain about the invasion of the yellow things, and then focus on finding a way to stop it.

Harrison had really wanted to do some yelling, Cobb could see it in the twitching of her lip and clenching of her fist. But she had kept her cool, and Cobb was very glad for that. Maybe, just maybe, Harrison was coming to accept Janus and the fact that the entire situation was pretty much out of their control. All Harrison could do was react to problems as they arose and trust the only person who had a chance of saving the *Avenger* and its crew: Janus.

"All right." Donahue stepped back to stand with the others. "What do you say we test this thing?"

"Aye."

The four of them vacated the shielded room and took up a position in the hallway. They had decided it would be safest to test the machine somewhere where it could do the least damage in the event it blew up or...something.

Donahue looked up past Janus. "Ready?"

Janus inclined her head.

Donahue pressed a button on the small remote in her hand. The machine was designed to emit an energy pulse that Cobb figured should dispel the yellow streaks. They waited, listening for some sign of activity. When nothing happened, Donahue shook her head and sighed. "Great. It didn't even blow up!" She reached for the door handle but was stopped by a hand gripping her wrist.

"Wait," Janus said, her head cocked and listening to something no one else could hear. "We must go." She motioned to Barker and Cobb who started down the hallway, then started walking herself, Donahue's arm still firmly in her grasp.

The foursome reached the end of the small hallway and exited into the main corridor just as a resounding crash that sounded almost like thunder erupted from the test room and echoed down the hall. Janus pushed her companions to the ground and slammed the door shut before hitting the deck herself. She covered her head and waited, hearing and feeling everything that was happening in the room.

After long minutes, Janus stood and tapped Barker on the back. The blonde looked up and rose as well, followed by Cobb and Donahue. Janus opened the door and stepped back as black smoke billowed out. When the air cleared they started down the hall, taking in the charred walls and door that had been blown off its hinges by the explosion.

Donahue kicked the door and stuck her head into the room. A low whistle sounded. "Wow, and I thought this would be safe!" Their machine was blackened and falling apart, and the entire room was pulverized. She looked up at the ceiling, saw a large dent, and shook her head. "If we keep on like this, we'll do the Ebokras' work for them."

Janus stepped back and shook her head. "I do not know what 'appened."

"Don't sweat it, no harm done. At least we know that isn't the answer." Donahue started back toward Engineering. "I have another idea I want to work on. I could use your help, Cobb."

Barker looked up at Janus's face as the engineer and doctor left. She placed her hand on Janus's arm and gave a slight tug. "Come on, you look wiped. When was the last time you slept?"

Janus opened her mouth to speak.

"And I mean not in the medical bay."

The taller woman remained guiltily silent.

"That's what I thought. Come on."

* ~ * ~ * ~ * ~ *

"We're docking."

"Roger that, Tryst." Karton's voice came through the com. "Be careful."

Patrik stood and grabbed a supply pack, and waited patiently while Tryst finished the docking procedures. They had timed the disappearance of the sections of the *Versai* so precisely that they knew they had exactly fifteen minutes and forty-five seconds until the docking bays were in phase with everything else. If they missed that window, it would be another fifteen minutes and forty-five seconds until they could attempt to leave.

The door inched open and, side-by-side, they stepped onto the *Versai*. Tryst gazed around and analyzed the ship. "Not a lot of damage here caused by a fire fight. It's almost like the ship is being eaten alive."

"Just for my peace of mind, we'll be okay when we move from a section of the ship that is out of phase to a section that is normal, right?"

"We should be fine."

Patrik nodded and looked around nervously. "Yes, but see, there's my problem. You said 'should'. Can't you just say 'Of course, Patrik, no doubt about it'?"

Tryst moved to the large door with Patrik trailing. "I could, but then I'd be lying."

It wasn't long before they turned a corner to come face to face with the business end of a plasma gun. "Whoa!" Tryst raised her hands and out of the corner of her eye saw Patrik hastily do the same.

The man on the other end of the gun had a hard, suspicious face and was wearing the Jopus Prime uniform. "What are you doing here? Who are you?"

"Quip'lee sent us," Tryst piped up. *Not exactly the truth, but close enough.*

The man shook his head. "Quip wouldn't, it's too big of a risk. And I've never seen you around Jopus."

Tryst sighed and tilted her head in Patrik's direction. "No, you haven't seen me, but *he's* a friend of Quip's."

This caused the gunbearer to turn all his attention to Patrik, who threw a distinct "thanks a lot" look in Tryst's direction. "We are here to help. And you're right, Quip didn't send us. I asked him to but when he said no, I came myself."

"You're lying. No one would disobey Quip's direct orders. And why would you come looking for us?" The man peered at this friend of Quip's, deciding that he did look vaguely familiar but didn't know why.

"We're looking for Janus, she's a good friend of all of ours."

"Janus?"

"Yes."

The man slowly lowered his plasma gun and nodded. "Okay, come on." He turned and started to walk away, fully expecting them to follow.

Tryst threw a glance at Patrik, who raised an eyebrow and shrugged. They quickly moved to catch up to the form seen moving through the dimly lit halls. After a few twists and turns, they walked onto the bridge and stopped as their guide reported to the captain. They exchanged a few brief words before the captain nodded, patted the man on the shoulder, and started over to the two uneasily shifting newcomers.

He smiled, showing off very pointed and sharp fang teeth, and held out his hand. "Greetings. I hear you are looking for Janus."

Tryst took the lead and answered, "We are. Do you know what happened to the *Avenger*?"

The captain shook his head sadly. "I regret to say that I do not. This whole thing went bad right from the beginning and we all got split up. We can't send any messages either. My ship, as you can see, is not in the best of shape."

"We might be able to help you out of here."

"Really?"

"Yes. We discovered that any technology that doesn't reach a certain level of energy output isn't attacked by this...infection. Do you have propulsion?"

"Minimal."

"Focus on that, and then you can just drift out of Sector Eight. In the meantime, I think it would be prudent to search for some way to kill this thing."

"Ah, I think I can help you there. We haven't been able to stop it entirely, as I'm sure you have guessed, but we have been able to slow it down. Maybe you'll be able to build on what we've discovered and find a way to stop it altogether. Please, this way."

The captain led them off the bridge and into what looked like Engineering. "We discovered it quite by accident. One of our engineers was trying to fix our cooling system to keep our engines from exploding when a line ruptured right in his face. Everyone was more concerned with getting him to sick bay than the ruptured line, so when someone did try to stop the leaking coolant, she realized that all the consoles that had been sprayed were now up and running. She wanted to be sure, so she fixed the line and waited, and sure enough, after about five or six minutes, the consoles crashed again. Ever since, we've been going around spraying the ship, but we don't have enough man power, so the infection just moves and grows in a different area."

Patrik pursed his lips. "Is your engineer all right?"

The captain smiled. "Yes, he's fine."

Tryst cocked her head and gazed at the previously ruptured cooling line. "What do you use for a coolant?"

"It's a synthetic substance that was only developed about six years ago. They call it Xeratium."

Patrik shook his head. "Never heard of it."

"Me either."

The captain smiled again. "I'm not surprised. Jopus Prime wasn't too keen on trading it until they were certain of all its uses and consequences. At the moment it's only in ships as a coolant, but they've been testing it for several other applications."

"So," Tryst stepped forward and ran her hand along the wall, "do you think that all the ships are infected?"

"I would bet on it. But I think we got it the worst because we were caught in weapons fire from the Ebokras. It didn't do any damage; I think they deliberately coated my ship with this thing. The other ships will be infested slowly. Judging from what I've seen here, it'll start with technology failure then begin eating away at the ship's hull, and finally the crew."

Patrik looked up, wide-eyed. "The crew?"

The captain nodded solemnly. "I've had eight die already, but our doctor has managed to mix Xeratium into a medicine that slows it down. If we don't get out of here soon, though, I'm afraid we'll all die."

"Tryst," Patrik gulped audibly, "we have to find the *Avenger*. They don't have Xeratium; they don't have a chance."

Tryst sucked in a breath and blew it out between her teeth. "What if we go back to Jopus Prime and get more Xeratium from Quip? Then we'll be able to get you guys out of here and look for the *Avenger*."

The captain nodded. "That would work well, and I would be indebted to you for saving my crew."

"Would it be quicker if we sent Karton and stayed to help repair the *Versai* and fight the infection?"

Tryst nodded. "It would. Do you think we can get a message to Karton? The last one we sent was pretty full of static."

The captain shook his head. "I'm sorry. Our communications relay is completely inoperative and I had power diverted to life support and structural integrity."

Tryst and Patrik locked eyes, the same phrase forming on their lips. "The shuttle!"

Patrik checked the time. "Two minutes."

Tryst pushed on his shoulder. "Go, go!"

He took off running down the hall and towards the docking bay as fast as his legs would carry him. *Two minutes.* Patrik stumbled around the corner and lunged into the shuttle, seeing he had one minute left. He tapped his controls and confirmed both his and Tryst's suspicion. The shuttle needed to be out of the *Versai* for a message to be sent.

Patrik started frantically entering in commands as his watch clicked down to forty-five seconds. He needed to get the shuttle off, needed to send this message. The *Avenger* might not be able to wait much longer for help. Patrik finally engaged the engine and maneuvered out of the docking bay just as the walls around him shimmered into nothingness.

He slumped in his chair and sighed in relief before keying the com system. "Karton, do you read me?"

"Yes, Patrik, I've got you."

"Listen carefully. We need you to go back to Jopus Prime and ask Quip for a large supply of a compound called Xeratium. It's used for cooling systems in their ships. Tell him we need it to stop an infection and save the *Avenger* and all the other ships."

"I've got that, Patrik. You and Tryst take care."

"We will. And Karton?"

"Yes, my boy?"

"Hurry."

Chapter 11

Barker rolled over, then froze as her body bumped up against something very large, very warm, and very alive. She kept her eyes closed, remembering that she had taken Janus somewhere she could sleep – the blonde's own quarters. And she remembered how, after only a few minutes of trying valiantly to stay awake, she had carefully crawled in next to her friend.

This close, Barker could hear the regular thumping of Janus's heart along with her gentle breathing, smell the scent that was so uniquely Janus that Barker couldn't even put a name to it, and feel the living warmth emanating from Janus's body. Even though it was relaxed in sleep, it still maintained tension and awareness as manifested by a slight twitching of Janus's muscles.

Barker finally opened her eyes and blinked to clear the lingering fog of sleep from her brain. She lay still so as to not wake her friend, wanting to take advantage of this one moment when she could study Janus without being under that intense blue regard. She looked first at Janus's face – all sharp planes and angles, the skin a deep brown which caused the platinum markings to stand out even more distinctly. Barker spent a moment looking at them, taking in the bright colour that she guessed was in some way indicative of Janus's health. The brighter they were, the healthier Janus was.

Barker continued her inspection, her eyes following along the exposed skin of Janus's arms and tracing the patterns there. While she was studying Janus's hand, Barker had a sudden awareness that if she were to look up, she would be met with very open and alert blue eyes. She tested her theory, and sure enough – Janus was looking back at her, her face as inscrutable as ever. The blonde smiled as she rested her chin on her wrist. "Hey."

"'Ello."

"Good sleep?"

"Aye."

"Good. May I check your wound?"

When Janus nodded her consent and lay still, Barker pulled back the cover and very carefully pushed up the hem of her friend's shirt. Barker gently ran her fingers over the thin red line and shook her head. "Incredible," she whispered and then allowed her eyes to stray and focus on the platinum designs.

They appeared to run down Janus's sides and branch out over the top of each of her ribs. Barker traced one with her fingertip and watched as her friend's breathing changed slightly – not much, but enough to cause her to raise an eyebrow in mild surprise. Barker glanced up at Janus who was studying the ceiling, seemingly oblivious to anything else until her expression suddenly changed from one of puzzlement to mild concern and then alarm. "What? What is it?" Barker asked.

Janus reached down and latched onto the blonde's arm, and gently pulled Barker up to lie beside her. "What do ya see?"

Barker obediently turned her eyes upward and noted the yellow streaks, along with the usual texture of the ceiling that she had spent many sleepless nights gazing up at. "I...I don't see anything out of the ordinary."

"Do not look at the yellow, try and see beyond it – not just yer ceiling, but the metal it is made of." *Come on, Barker,* Janus thought. *Ya can do this.*

Barker squinted, trying very hard to do as Janus told her but not really understanding what she was looking for. With all the yellow lines, it was hard to even see or remember what her ceiling usually looked like. She continued to gaze at it and was finally able to filter out the yellow infection and see the metal ceiling. And still she looked and stared and scrutinized until the grainy texture of the metal came into sharp relief and she was able to detect lines, a spider web of lines in the metal that weren't supposed to be there.

Janus watched Barker's face carefully and when recognition appeared on the blonde's face, she asked gently, "Do ya see it?"

"I think so...yes. Little black lines...cracks, almost, in the metal."

"Aye. Those are not supposed ta be there."

Confusion showed on Barker's face. "So, there's something wrong with the ship?"

"Somethin' wrong with the hull." Janus sat up and removed herself from the bed, taking a moment to luxuriate in a long stretch. "It will breach if somethin' is not done."

"Harrison and the bridge must know–"

Janus shook her head. "No. They are only micro-fractures now; with the sensors damaged, the bridge might not see them until they grow."

Barker stayed in the bed, staring at Janus's back as she pulled on her boots and left the room. *Micro-fractures?* She tilted her head back to stare at the ceiling, now clearly seeing the encroaching black lines. *Micro-fractures?* She flopped onto her back and considered for a moment how she could possibly see tiny micro-fractures. After another moment, she leapt out of bed, tugged on her shoes, and pounded down the hall after Janus's striding form. Barker caught up, latched on to Janus's arm, and pulled the taller woman to a stop.

Janus simply raised an eyebrow and waited for the small blonde to speak. It didn't take long.

"Micro-fractures? How on Earth can I see micro-fractures!"

"Ya can not, on Earth." Janus proceeded toward the bridge.

Barker followed with quick steps and again pulled Janus to a stop. "Hold on there, bucko! I go to bed with you, I'm perfectly normal. All of a sudden, I wake up able to see microscopic cracks in the hull, and all you can say is 'not on Earth'. I don't think so! I want a straight answer, Janus."

"Ya did not go ta bed perfectly normal."

Green eyes blinked several times in silence before Barker said eloquently, "Huh?"

Janus waved her hand in a gesture that encompassed the ship and the few crew members who were walking by and giving the two women a wide berth.

Barker gazed around, not having any idea what Janus was talking about until she looked back at her friend and took in the obvious difference. *The streaks.* "So you did this?"

"I did not do anythin' except make ya able ta see a threat. Anythin' else that 'appened was a side effect that I did not expect." She again attempted to resume her course to the bridge and was again halted by the blonde now attached to her arm.

"Side effects? What other side effects are there going to be!"

"I do not know."

"Well then, take it away!"

"I will not until this is over."

"Why?"

Janus turned to face Barker head on and stared into her eyes. "Because if somethin' 'appens ta me, ya will not survive if ya can not see 'em. Trust me." Janus continued on her way to the bridge and this time was unimpeded.

Barker remained rooted to the spot, her eyes flickering frantically around the ship, her face slack.

~~*~*~*

"What do you mean the hull is breaching!"

"That is exactly what I mean," Janus confirmed.

"Our sensors haven't picked up anything like that."

"Yer sensors are no good in 'ere! I can see the breaches, and if ya do not start ta fix 'em now, it will be too late when ya do decide ta listen ta me."

Harrison threw up her hands. "Fine. I'll dispatch one team now and you can show them where you saw the first breach. If it's actually there, then I'll send out more teams to fix them all." Harrison spoke to someone through the com, then looked up and nodded. "An engineering team is waiting for you out in the corridor."

The two men followed Janus to Barker's quarters. They started analyzing the ceiling with their little machines, hemming and hawing for long moments without doing anything. Finally one engineer turned to her and shook his head. "We can't detect anything here."

Janus sighed and rubbed her forehead, stepped forward and held out her hand. The technician hastily deposited his machine into her palm and stepped back as she studied it. It didn't take long for Janus to conclude that the device was worthless and wouldn't pick up any breach, no matter how large it was. "Fix it."

"What?"

Janus pointed up at the ceiling, tracing an area with her fingers. "'Ere. Do what ya would ta fix a breach."

The tech looked skeptical but stepped forward and began the standard repair procedure. When he finished, he had a decidedly perplexed look on his face as he scratched his head in confusion. His partner came forward and peered over his shoulder. "What is it?"

"This says that I actually fixed a breach, but I don't know–"

"Yer other machine is not workin', just like the rest of the ship."

Both of them looked at her and then at each other. They silently came to a decision and looked back at her simultaneously. "Okay, I believe you. I don't want to risk a massive breach so we'll tell Harrison that it's real, but you'll have to show us where to make the repairs."

"Aye. Barker can 'elp too."

"Barker?" they asked in unison.

"Aye. She can see 'em."

~~*~*~*

Melvin Kodiac looked up as someone thumped down next to him and sighed. He waited a moment as Barker arranged herself with her elbows planted on the tabletop before daring to ask the question that had been literally making him itch since he had heard the news. "I hear you were hunting out micro-fractures in the hull this morning...with your eyes."

Green eyes glared up at him from between a few wisps of blonde hair before Barker returned to staring morosely at the table.

Undaunted, he continued. "What was up with that?"

"I dunno," she mumbled.

"You don't know?"

Barker blew out a quick breath and dropped her head onto the table. "I asked Janus; she doesn't know, so I don't."

Kodiac opened his mouth and raised a finger, paused and considered exactly what he wanted to say. "But it is because of something Janus did, right?"

"Yes."

"And she can't tell you why you can suddenly see microfractures?"

"No. She wanted me to see the infection in the ship – that's all."

"So aren't you just a little, teeny tiny bit worried about what else might happen?"

"She says she can undo it."

"And you believe her?"

Barker's head shot up as she stared at him. "Of course I do!"

Kodiac looked skeptical.

"Janus has never lied to me."

"That you know of. Be reasonable, Barker. All she did was touch you and all of a sudden you can see these yellow things and then tiny cracks in our hull. Aren't you just a little concerned about what else might happen, what long-term effect it will have on you? Or what her agenda is?"

"Agenda! Agenda! Let me tell you one thing I know, Kodiac: if anyone on this ship has an agenda, it sure as *hell* isn't Janus!" She stood angrily, but paused as he reached out and grasped her arm.

"I'm just worried about you, Barker, about what could happen. Don't you want to get rid of those?"

He was pointing at her eyes and she was reminded of the silver markings she now wore displayed on her skin. "I can take care of myself, I don't need you to worry about me."

She left then, her mind mulling over what Kodiac had said. She had initially wanted to be back to her very normal and very human self as soon as possible. As she had become used to her increased visual acuity and gotten over the shock of the incredible new range of things she could see, she had gotten to like it. If she was experiencing even a fraction of what Janus did every moment of every day, Barker could only begin to imagine the whole other world that her friend lived in. It had to be, at times, overwhelming.

Barker privately admitted that she was more than a little curious as to what new developments might arise from the changes Janus had made to her human biology. She needed to get a few facts, and although Omelian'par was the best person she could think of to go to, Cobb was the only doctor readily available. She directed her steps toward the medical bay.

* ~ * ~ * ~ * ~ *

Karton disembarked as soon as the ship was docked at Jopus Prime, his steps purposeful. Quip'lee looked up in surprise as the older man walked into his office unannounced and took up an authoritative stance in front of his desk.

"I need large quantities of a substance called Xeratium."

Quip's eyebrow crept upward as he processed Karton's request. "Nothing like getting to the point, huh?"

"Now."

Quip raised his hands and nodded. "Just hold on a minute. Mind telling me what you need it for? It is still an experimental substance, you know."

"We found the *Versai*. It was badly damaged and suffering the effects of some kind of infection that has spread through all of Sector Eight. The captain of the *Versai* discovered that Xeratium stops the infection, so we need as much as we can get to help them and eventually the *Avenger*."

"You realize that I can't just authorize–"

Karton slammed his fist on Quip's desk, startling the man into silence. "They do not have time for this! You are the military commander of all of Jopus. You must trust me when I tell you that we do not have time to go through normal channels."

"Karton, I understand–"

"You do not! If they do not get the Xeratium soon, then the hulls of their ships will be eaten through, along with the flesh and bone of the crew members. You will give us what we need or by God, Quip, I'll take it from you."

Quip nodded slowly and stood, gesturing Karton to follow. "Come." He led the bearded man through the many corridors of Jopus Prime and finally stopped at one of the more out-of-the-way cargo bays. Quip keyed in the entrance code and waved his arm in a sweeping gesture to encompass the entire room. "This is all Xeratium. Take as much as you think you need. Load it up on those," he pointed to four transport vehicles, "and then go get my people."

Karton nodded and smiled his thanks before activating his personal com link. "Come on down, guys, and give me a hand." A few minutes passed and then a group of people walked in and started quickly loading up the crates. They were on their last trip back to the cargo bay when Karton detected two familiar faces approaching.

Warber and Evril stopped in front of Karton and grinned as hugs were exchanged all around. Warber threw a glance at the crates, his striped face crinkling as his nose detected a distinctly chemical odor coming from them. "What is going on?"

Karton started walking back toward their ship while recounting what he knew. "Janus and some other crews from Jopus Prime have gotten themselves into something of a predicament."

Evril snorted and smiled. "What else is new?"

"Hmm. So Tryst and I, along with Patrik who is a very good friend of Janus, have set out to find them and–"

"Save their asses?" Warber asked.

"Yes."

Warber and Evril exchanged a glance as the threesome stepped onto the ship. "Count us in."

Karton smiled at his old friends. "I was hoping you'd say that."

* ~ * ~ * ~ * ~ *

Tryst looked up as Patrik walked back into the room and headed directly for her. "We good?"

"Oh yeah." He crouched down next to her and watched as she finished repairing a power relay. "Karton is off on his mission."

Tryst nodded and sat back as she finished her task. "Good. The *Versai's* propulsion is almost up and running again. Soon we'll be able to just float out of Sector Eight."

Patrik ran his hand along the back of his neck and made a face at the sweat that he found there. "I'm looking forward to that. Is it me, or is it getting hot in here?"

She glanced around the room, taking in thermal readings and comparing them to previous data. "It's hot. Environmental systems went a little wacky just before you got back. We managed to keep life support up and running but..."

"But we're in serious trouble."

"Yep."

"Just great. I can only imagine what it's like over on the *Avenger*." He rubbed his tired eyes and gently probed his link with Janus. He wasn't picking up anything except mild agitation and worry, and that served to soothe his soul a bit.

"I would imagine that Janus is keeping things relatively intact over there, at least the ship."

"Yeah, but what's going to happen once that infection starts in on the crew? Janus won't be able to stop that," Patrik said.

"Hopefully we'll get to them before that happens."

Patrik let his head thump back against the wall and unzipped his jacket. "I dunno, Tryst, we still have to find the ship, and it's obviously deeper in Sector Eight than the *Versai* or we would have detected it from the shuttle." He shook his head and closed his eyes. "Even if we do drift in and try to find them, the chances of actually happening across them or–" A hand covered his mouth, effectively stopping his rambling.

"Don't think about all the 'what ifs', just think about Janus and everything she's managed to survive. You really think she's going to let something like this stop her? And the good thing about Janus is, she'll have gotten the *Avenger* to a secluded spot, meaning we look for a nebula or asteroid belt. It narrows the search area considerably."

A small smile crossed Patrik's lips as he ducked his head and acknowledged Tryst's logic. "All right, you've convinced me."

"Good." She patted his head and sat back to rest for a moment.

A blaring alarm brought them both to their feet, and soon they were running through the hall to avert yet another disaster in the making.

* ~ * ~ * ~ * ~ *

Barker hopped down from the bio bed and adjusted her shirt as Cobb walked to the main console in the medical bay. "So?"

The doctor looked up and shook her head. "No matter what changes I've found in your body, I can't detect any negative effects that would pose a threat to you. There are several things changing that I won't even claim to understand, but it all seems to be happening slowly enough that your body can adapt. It looks to me like Janus knew exactly what she was doing."

Barker pursed her lips and rubbed her face. "So I'm not going to just drop dead any time soon?"

Cobb gave a little laugh and walked over to stand beside the blonde. "If you do, it will be totally random and undetectable."

The ensign grunted and leaned against one of the bio beds. "So, how did things go for you and Donahue?"

Cobb groaned and shook her head vigorously. "Nothing good happening there. Everything we tried blew up in our faces. We finally had to stop or risk doing some really serious damage. Donahue and her team are still analyzing everything they can get their hands on and turning over ideas, but I don't think we have what we need to stop this infection."

"So we're stuck. Can't leave, can't call for help. Great."

"Mm. And I heard you and Janus were identifying potential breaches in the hull?"

"Ughh. Yes. That's another problem. If those fractures start up again," she shook her head, "I don't know if we'll be able to stop them all in time."

The ship rocked, sending them stumbling into one another. They exchanged a quick glance of concern before Barker turned and dashed out of the medical bay. She wasn't sure exactly where she was going, but she knew she needed to be there, and quickly. As she ran, she started to notice more fractures in the hull, lots of them and spreading fast. She tucked her head down and started running faster. Barker finally slid to a halt and stared in horror at the gap in the hull before a voice jarred her into action.

"Barker, come over 'ere!"

The ensign knew that voice and had no trouble in locating Janus's tall form. She moved over quickly, keeping a very cautious eye on the hole in the hull. A clear patch of space was visible, showing a few asteroids floating by so close she could almost reach out and touch them. "How are we still alive?" she yelled over the blaring claxons and panicked yells from the crew.

"The ship's emergency containment fields are still workin', but not fer much longer. I need yer 'elp!"

"What do I have to do?"

Janus reached over and tugged Barker into position in front of her, positioning the blonde's hands just below her own and on the threshold of the containment field. "Just stand like that. Do not move, not one inch."

Barker looked over her shoulder at Janus, eyes wide. "Bu...but what will that do? I–"

"Just do it!" Janus yelled and then turned her attention back to her task. She raised her arms and allowed them to hover just above the containment field, narrowing her concentration down to this one focal point, this one thing. If she managed it, it would buy the *Avenger* a little more time.

Barker watched as Janus took a familiar stance and closed her eyes. It happened very much like it had before – the strain showing on Janus's face and her markings slowly beginning to glow. The blue cloud that Barker was getting used to seeing appeared and flowed through the containment field to fill the hole in the hull.

As she watched with her newly enhanced vision, Barker saw the cloud spread not only through the breach, but into the tiny black cracks that branched off the gap. The molecules spread outward faster than she could follow, just like a raging river running down a mountain and obliterating anything in its path. It took only a few seconds before the opening started to get smaller, and Barker watched as the metal of the hull stretched and strained, devoting horrible amounts of effort to spreading over that last little bit of space to finally come together and be whole. The blonde blinked in amazement and drew her head back, staring in bewilderment at the unbroken surface in front of her. *No more hole.*

She had seen it happen, up close and personal, but still it took a moment for her mind to recover from the shock. A resounding thump brought Barker out of her stupor and she turned to see Janus crumpled on the floor. She rushed over and knelt beside her, then gently pulled Janus's head into her lap. "Are you all right?"

Janus sucked in a deep breath and made an effort to move, seemingly wanting to get up but suddenly collapsing back into Barker's arms. The attempt was too much. "Aye. Just give me a minute."

Barker stroked her friend's cheek and wiped away beads of sweat that were dripping into Janus's eyes. She looked up at where the now nonexistent hole had been, and then back down, briefly studying the silver markings that were only now losing their residual glow. "So what, exactly, did you just do?" She looked around, not seeing any of the black micro-fractures that had been making a re-appearance.

"Bought us more time."

"Time? To do what?"

Janus sat up slowly and rubbed her temples. "Ah do not know."

Barker blew out a breath and looked behind them at several of their shipmates who were lurking in the corridor. She couldn't decide exactly what emotions were showing on their faces, perhaps a mixture of concern, fear, and awe. The ensign stood and held out her hand to Janus, who grabbed it and was hauled to her feet. When Janus swayed unsteadily, Barker kept a hand on her arm and started walking them away from the gapers. She wasn't sure where she was heading, but knew that it should be anywhere but the site of the miraculous repair.

~~*~*~*

While Janus and Barker were dealing with the imminent hull breach, Rita Donahue and her team were working to restore the ship's crippled systems. "Maybe if we change this here like that... No, no...like... No, that won't work either." Donahue sat back and sighed. "We're getting nowhere."

Hans McKenna dropped his pad onto the worktable and shook his head. "You are right, Rita. We just do not know enough," he said, his German accent thick.

"Or have the right materials." She looked up at her right-hand, an engineer almost as brilliant as herself. It had been a long running joke when the crew had first assembled that the *Avenger* was toting an engineering think tank.

"The only thing I can think of is shutting down nonessential systems, since only technology with high energy outputs...well..."

"Blows up?" Hans supplied, a smile on his boyish face.

"Mhm." And what had it taken for them to figure that out? *Oh boy...* Donahue's eyes drifted around the room, taking in all the various scorch marks and hanging wires. Granted, a lot of the damage was from the relay disaster, but they had added to it in their quest for a solution.

"Um...if I could interrupt?"

They turned at the new voice and Donahue smiled up at the newcomer. "Yes, Brad. Of course."

"Well, it seems to me that..." His head jerked a little and he rubbed his eyes before continuing. "If we could find a way to..." Brad scratched his hand in annoyance, then lowered his eyes to look at it. He let out a scream and collapsed to the floor.

Donahue and Hans jumped forward, Hans grabbing the younger man's body to keep it still while Donahue pinned his furiously scratching hands. Her eyes widened as she saw the skin under his fingernails and the places it had literally peeled off his body, revealing oozing red blood and the bone beneath.

~~*~*~*

Barker and Janus were moving at a moderate pace, bypassing scurrying crew members without taking notice of them. Barker leaned closer and asked in a low voice, "Are you sure you're all right?"

Janus nodded carefully so as not to jar her pounding head. "Aye, ah just 'ave a 'eadache."

A pained scream broke through the din, causing all the personnel within earshot to stop in surprise before lurching into action. Barker guided Janus over to the wall and watched as her tall friend leaned gratefully against it. "Stay here, I'll check it out."

"But–"

"Please."

Janus lowered her head. "Aye."

Barker gazed at her friend for a long moment before another scream spurred her into action. She turned and started down the hall to Engineering.

Janus leaned against the wall and watched through bleary eyes as Barker shot down the hall. She tried to stay standing, but the effort to fight gravity in addition to her pounding head and jelly-like knees was just too much. She slid down the wall and covered her ears, trying to block out all the noise that was seeping through her rapidly eroding defenses.

~~*~*~*

Brad continued to scream and thrash, trying to reach all the unbearably itching parts on his body. Donahue looked up at her staff who were all staring in horrified shock. "Someone get Cobb!" she yelled, not hearing the thundering footsteps behind her.

Barker charged into the room and immediately sized up the situation. She hurried over to Brad, but stopped when she saw the blood staining his skin and clothing. She turned her focus to the yellow markings that covered his entire body, registering the fact that he was almost a solid yellow. The ensign fell to her knees next to Donahue and quickly grabbed Brad's legs, which were dangerously close to kicking the engineer in the head. "What happened?"

"He just started yelling and fell to the floor. I don't know why."

"I do," Barker whispered as she maintained her firm grip on the young man's legs. "We've got to get him to sick bay."

~~*~*~*

Janus could feel Barker's terror as well as the ripples in the energy that the entire situation was causing. It was very disconcerting to discover just how disturbed the ship and area around it were, just how far from normal everything was. She was just too tired, too drained after her fight with the yellow infection and repairing the ship to sustain the control that was normally second nature to her. All the sounds of the ship, the poor man's yelling from Engineering along with Barker and

Donahue's voices, Cobb's harried speech as she hurried along to Engineering, Harrison's commands from the bridge: all of it crashed and clattered on her hearing like a waterfall, serving to make her headache worse. The sound of approaching footsteps struck a cord in her memory. They were something she had made a point of storing.

Samson rounded the corner into the chaos and stopped short, seeing something he never would have expected: that alien woman – someone who had always come across as damn near invincible, untouchable –huddled in a corner, knees pulled up to her chest and covered in a very unhealthy looking sweat. When she looked up at him, her eyes were unguarded and as open as he had ever seen. Being sure to keep some distance between himself and Janus, Samson knelt and looked closer. There was something in those eyes that he recognized – an enormous amount of pain that, he was disgusted to note, made him feel a kernel of compassion. He looked over his shoulder toward Engineering where the flurry of activity was continuing and then back at Janus. "Are you okay?"

Janus lifted her head slowly to see Samson's tall form standing above her. She blinked several times and tried to focus in on his mouth. She could see it was moving and hear the words he was speaking, but she had no comprehension of what he was saying. It took a repetition from Samson before the sense of the words trickled down her awareness, and she had to blink some more before she could decide if she had heard him right. *He is asking if I am all right?* Janus couldn't wrap her mind around that, the idea of Samson caring whether she was okay. But she did know the answer to his question.

Samson watched as she stared at him, his concern growing bit by bit. Finally, her head shook ever so slightly in the negative. He cursed roundly under his breath as he stood. It took another minute of pensive consideration and wrestling with his beliefs before he bent and pulled her arm around his neck. Samson straightened, pulled Janus to her feet, and wrapped his other arm around her waist. They started moving, very slowly, while he continued to curse. "Why the hell am I doing this? I can't God damn believe this." He continued to mutter and throw the occasional look at Janus, whose eyes were closed and head lolled to the side. *Maybe*, his mind mocked, *maybe because you know she'd do the same for you.*

Shut up, his more cynical side responded, the side of him that ran in the Human Supremicist circles.

But the other part, the part that was Dion, Tina Cobb's little brother, relented. *Admit it, despite everything, you know she is a noble person with a good heart. No matter how much you want to dispute that, it's true.*

Samson growled a little, but trudged on down the corridor with his cargo.

Chapter 12

Cobb maintained her grip on Brad's wildly thrashing head as Barker, Bobby, and two other engineers positioned the young man's body on the bio bed and quickly went about restraining his arms and legs. As soon as that was done, the doctor shooed them away and started to work.

Her eyes betraying her nervousness, Barker stepped back, then jerked as a hand fell on her shoulder. She looked up into the concerned eyes of Rita Donahue and gave what she hoped was a reassuring smile before suddenly pulling away from the engineer.

Janus, I have to go check on Janus.

Barker was two steps from the door when it whooshed open to reveal Samson's grim face and Janus's limp form. A gasp escaped the ensign's lips, as seeing the two of them together was more than a little surprising. "What did you do?"

He glowered as he continued into the room. "Nothing. I found her in the hall and asked if she was all right. She said no."

"So you just thought you'd lend a hand? Out of the goodness of your heart?"

Samson threw another look at Barker as he hoisted Janus's body up onto a bio bed with an uncharacteristic gentleness. "Pretty much, yeah," he snarled, then backed off as Barker moved up to the side of the bed.

The blonde placed her hand on Janus's forehead and leaned closer as blue eyes inched open. "Janus, you have to tell me what's wrong."

Janus blinked a few times and gave a weak smile just before another of Brad's screams ripped through the medical bay. "I am fine. I 'ave ta—"

When she made a move to get up, Barker grabbed Janus's shoulder and tried to hold her down. "Hang on a minute, you are not fine. You need to rest and regain your strength."

"No, I need ta..."

Janus tried to sit up again and Barker felt the coiled power against her arm, knowing if Janus really wanted to get up there was no way she could stop her.

Another arm descended into the blonde's view, gently grasped Janus's other shoulder and pushed down. It was Samson.

Together, they managed to get Janus to lie down with only a small fuss. Barker looked around. Doctor Cobb and a number of the nurses were tied up with Brad and several other crew members who were coming in with the same symptoms. She turned her attention back to the bio bed and studied the controls that were on the side, finally deciding to raise the containment field in hopes of getting Janus a little rest.

Janus had allowed herself to be pushed back onto the bed and felt her eyes closing and mind start to drift up and away as it often did when her body required time to recuperate. Through slitted eyes, she saw the orange shield that suddenly covered her bed and through it, Barker's concerned face. She relaxed as she became aware that something was different. It took only a moment before Janus realized that all the noise from the ship that had been grating on her hearing was now blocked out, allowing her to drift away more easily.

Barker watched until Janus's eyes closed and she fell into one of her coma-like sleeps. She turned to thank Samson and was surprised to find that the man was gone. Giving a slight shrug, she headed over to Cobb to see if she could help.

Donahue tossed her head toward Janus and asked, "How is she?"

Barker shot an over-the-shoulder glance at her comatose friend before giving a small smile. "I'm not sure. She seems to be resting, but what do I know?"

Donahue grunted.

"And Brad?" Barker asked.

Donahue grimaced. "Doc's stumped, I think. Like several of the other systems on the ship, most of her machines aren't working and she can't seem to get him to stop scratching and shredding his skin." She shook her head as she rubbed her face. "It ain't pretty."

The ensign hummed in her throat as her gaze drifted around the room. Her eyes lit upon something and she latched on to the engineer's arm and started to drag the woman out of the medical bay. "Come on."

"What are we doing?"

"Trying to patch up Janus's quick save."

"Huh?"

Barker looked up from under lowered brows and managed to resurrect her sense of humor from somewhere. "Micro fractures, my dear engineer. It's all about micro-fractures."

* ~ * ~ * ~ * ~ *

A muffled scream earned Patrik a glare from Tryst who proceeded to jab him in the ribs as she removed her hand from his mouth. "That was a rat," he hissed.

"Yes, it was."

"There are not supposed to be rats on space ships!"

"Keep your voice down."

Patrik snorted and turned back to staring out the tiny slit in the wall. Things had been going fine: they were managing to keep the ship in one relatively intact piece, biding their time until Karton arrived with more Xeratium. But sometimes the universe was just against you. And that's what he felt like today. Pradonites, a species that was a wandering band of marauders who loved to scavenge for almost anything, had boarded the *Versai* in one offensive sortie. Compared to the Ebokras, the Pradonites were amateurs, though Patrick was impressed that they were capable of manuevering their ship, also infected with the sickness, enough to board and attack. Still, there was only so much the *Versai* and its crew could take, only so much time that the *Avenger* had left. Everyone on the *Versai* had been occupied with spraying down the ship, not at all concerned with who might be lurking out in space, so the entire crew had been taken by surprise.

At the onset of the Pradonite incursion, Patrik and Tryst had run, not having any weapons and believing wholeheartedly in living to fight another day. And that was why they were currently stooped in a tiny access port that was scarcely large enough for the two of them, and getting on each other's nerves.

Tryst shifted forward and peered out into the hallway through the tiny slit. Seeing that the way was clear, she reached forward. "That is it; I'm getting out of here."

Patrik grabbed her arm. "Wait, wait. Why don't we just stay here until we know they've gone?"

She pursed her lips as she turned to stare at him. "Weellll, someone will have to be at the docking bay to meet Karton or else he won't know what to do. Plus, we don't know if anyone else is still alive, so just how would we know when the Pradonites are gone?"

He thought about that for a minute and then nodded. "Okay, I'm coming with you."

"Fine. Then let's get moving; my legs are cramping up." In one smooth motion, she ripped the cover off their hideaway and dropped it to the ground with a resounding crash, totally unconcerned about the amount of noise she was making.

"Hey!" Patrik scrambled out after her. "You tell me to be quiet and then you do that?"

"Pradonites are practically deaf. I know no one is out here now, but if one had been standing right there in the hall when you screamed, it would have heard you." She started toward the docking bay, knowing that Karton was due in three and a half minutes.

"I did not scream," Patrik said as he jogged to catch up.

"That was a scream."

"Was not!"

"Was too."

"It was a sound of startled surprise."

Tryst looked at him and smiled. "It was a scream."

Patrik growled and grumbled as he followed after her.

* ~ * ~ * ~ * ~ *

As often happened, Janus was totally unaware of the amount of time that had passed or anything that was happening around her. The only thing that mattered, the only thing that registered in her mind, was the status of her mind and body as they replenished lost energy reserves and healed any injuries – physical and mental.

Omelian'par had compared it to a meditative state that some humans and other species entered into in order to relax and, as he said, "to find their center". He had also said that although the states seemed similar, no other species actually healed themselves during such times and no other species experienced the process as swiftly as she did.

Whatever it was that was happening, Janus knew that she was once again restored to an almost fully healthy condition, and her presence was probably needed elsewhere. She rose from the deep state of blissful unconsciousness slowly but at a steady rate, and was opening her eyes in a matter of minutes.

Janus gazed upward at the ceiling of the medical bay, seeing it in an orange tint before her memory kicked in and she recalled the energy barrier that Barker had erected. She squinted up at it and gazed around, looking for the mechanical means to lower it before giving a little shrug and simply tapping it with her fingers.

The energy field collapsed and Janus sat up, evaluated the room, then stood. Doctor Cobb was leaning over a patient and Janus didn't need her acute sense of smell to detect the unpleasant tang of blood that permeated the room. She walked over and assessed each of the patients, feeling her heart sink as she realized there was nothing she could do to help them.

Doctor Cobb felt someone standing behind her and turned, surprised but relieved to see Janus. "You feeling better?"

"Aye."

"Good, do you think you can do anything for this?"

Janus walked to the edge of the bed and gently placed the back of her hand along the woman's forehead. It was an engineer, the one she had saved from the explosion in the small engine room when the *Avenger* had first been attacked by the Ebokias. Janus shook her head slowly, her face revealing her despair. "No, I can not 'elp these people."

"Why not?" Cobb sounded desperate.

"It is beyond me."

"How can it be beyond you? After the things I've seen you do, you mean to tell me that you can't stop this?"

Janus jerked her head around to stare at the doctor. The yellow marks covering Cobb's skin were almost solid, signaling that she was another victim of the infection. "I do not mean the effects, I mean the cause. I can not stop that, so I can not 'eal these people." Her entire body suddenly shuddered as her eyes closed and her head tilted. An expression of great urgency and distress appeared on Janus's features before she turned and tore out of the medical bay at top speed.

Doctor Tina Cobb had no guess as to where she was going.

~~*~*~*

It appeared as if the Pradonites had left the *Versai*, at least no one could find a trace of them. The crew of the *Versai* seemed relatively intact, although Tryst felt as if something was wrong somewhere. She didn't believe that the Pradonites would just abandon such a profitable source of both machinery and people. It was rumored that they dabbled in the slave trade. Before turning back to fetch Patrik, Tryst finished giving her instructions to the newly arrived team that Karton had brought over with him. They had decided that they would leave enough people and Xeratium to purge the *Versai* of the infection while they went on ahead to find the *Avenger*, hopefully in time to save it.

As Tryst approached Patrik, she saw him jerk violently, fall back against the wall, then grab his head. He appeared to be shaking and that sent Tryst into a dead run. Visions of the people lying in the medical bay flashed through her mind, even though she and Patrik had both been given the Xeratium cure that the doctor had concocted. When she reached him, she knelt and clasped his shoulder, waiting an agonizingly long minute for some kind of response.

Finally, he raised his head and gave a sheepish little smile and shrug. "Sorry, just a…" He trailed off, uncomfortable.

Tryst blew out a silent sigh as she studied his face, clearly seeing the strain around his mouth and eyes – the tiny lines that were etched in his skin, and the reemergence of the shadows in his hazel eyes. She knew about the mental link between Patrik and Janus, he had told her the first time he had almost collapsed with the shock of a sudden blast of sheer terror. This, though, this one had been the worst so far, and seeing Patrik react so violently to Janus's usually carefully restrained emotions did nothing to settle Tryst's mind. Things were apparently degrading on the *Avenger* at a rate faster than she would have hoped.

She didn't make any comment on his situation, knowing full well how disconcerting dealing with someone else's emotions could be. "Come on, we're leaving."

Patrik got up slowly, his legs a little shaky, but the first real smile in a long time spread across his face. "Good, very good. We need to hurry."

"I know. Karton is all ready to go and we have a nice eight minute window in which to leave."

Side-by-side, they started back to the ship and boarded without incident. They were undocking and drifting out of Sector Eight before Patrik even had time to analyze the sudden feeling of heart-wrenching fear that was strong enough to make him sick to his stomach and cause the onset of a crushing headache.

* ~ * ~ * ~ * ~ *

"Could you please explain to me what we're doing?" Donahue asked as she followed a determined Barker down the corridor.

"The micro-fractures are appearing faster, and if we don't try and stay ahead of them they'll rip the ship to pieces."

"Okay, but what makes you think you can predict where they'll show up?"

Barker looked up and studied the walls for a long moment before continuing down another corridor. "I've been paying extra attention to the walls, and I'm pretty sure that right before a micro-fracture shows up..." She stopped suddenly and pointed. "Ah ha!"

"What?"

"Right here. There should be one right here in just a few seconds." Barker kept her eyes on the spot that exhibited a slight glow. She tapped Donahue's arm. "Get ready. Okay." Barker leaned forward and marked the wall with some chalk. "There. Repair that area."

Donahue raised an eyebrow, but she stepped forward and started mending the area of the hull that the blonde ensign had indicated. She looked over her shoulder as Barker fairly bounded down the hall to another spot and marked it.

"Hurry up!"

Donahue sighed and followed down the hall in Barker's wake. "I'm working as fast as I can. You know, you could fix them too, instead of just drawing on the wall!"

Barker continued to mark the areas where micro-fractures were appearing, but slowed her pace so that Donahue could keep up. She paused as she came to an intersection and looked down each corridor, trying to decide which direction would yield the most effective results. As she felt Donahue come up behind her, she turned and opened her mouth but stopped, frozen, as her eyes took in the engineer.

"What?"

Barker just continued to stare and study her.

"What! That's the exact same look Janus gets on her face right before something bad happe... Oh." Donahue looked down at herself, then back up at the ensign. "You can't be serious!"

Barker raised her eyes to look into the engineer's. "How do you feel?"

"Fine, I'm fine. There's no way I'm going to end up like everyone else in the medical bay."

"We'd better get you back."

"But what about–"

"You're more important," Barker said.

"Not if we all end up dead because the hull breaches and there's no one around to fix it! I can get back on my own."

Barker just shook her head and retraced her steps down the corridor, heading back in the direction from which they had come. She slowed a little as a feeling flitted across her awareness and then was gone – nothing she could really place, just a sensation. The ensign concentrated on feeling it again, her steps leading back to the medical bay without her conscious direction. It came again, this time sending a shiver down her spine to settle as a cold ball of anticipation in her gut. Her eyes flicked around the hallway, looking for some sign of what was wrong. She couldn't detect anything except the beginnings of new hull fractures, and started to seriously doubt her senses.

Donahue grimaced and leaned closer to Barker. "What's wrong?"

"What makes you think anything's wrong?"

"Like I said, you get the same look on your face that Janus does, and I'm having a hard time believing that all that concern you're showing is just for me."

"Something's going on, but I'm not totally sure what it is." Barker shook her head as she continued to study the area around them. "It's the strangest feeling."

~~*~*~*

"Captain!"

"What?" Harrison asked, her voice sounding strained and irritated to everyone on the bridge. It just wasn't her day. All the problems, one after the other, and now she not only had the imminent destruction of her ship to worry about, but also what amounted to the flaying of her crew. She had been down to the medical bay and it was not a pretty sight. Eleven people had already reached the critical point, and Cobb had been unable to stop the spread of the disease.

"The secondary containment doors on Deck Seven have closed, and the entire deck is about to be vented."

"What!" Harrison moved over and checked her own console, seeing that the venting process was indeed in its first stages. "How many people are on that deck?"

"I can't be absolutely sure, but since there were only supposed to be repair crews up there – somewhere between four and twelve."

"Can we get the doors open?"

"No, ma'am. They were designed to prevent exactly that."

Harrison turned in a circle and rubbed her forehead. "But they shouldn't be closed in the first place. They're activated only in the event of a hull breach, and if the containment fields go off-line. What about...what about manual override?"

"Controls for that are on Deck Eight, which is–"

"Evacuated and filled with engine coolant."

Harrison sneered as she thought about that and keyed the com. "Get a crew to Deck Seven. Try anything and everything you can think of to get those damn doors open!" She turned to her bridge crew. "Start working on getting the environmental systems fixed for Deck Eight so we can get to override. Also, try and stop the venting process."

* ~ * ~ * ~ * ~ *

Barker and Donahue were almost to the last intersection on this end of the deck, heading for the lift up to the next level, when a heavy metal door slammed shut right in their faces. The duo pulled back in surprise and stared at the door before sharing a bewildered look. "What the hell is that?"

"Secondary containment."

"Containment for what?"

Donahue jerked involuntarily and leaned heavily against the wall. "They're probably off line."

Barker looked at the engineer, concern showing clearly in her face as Donahue slowly sat with her knees pulled up to her chest and trapped her hands underneath her feet. A slight whirring sound filled the air and Barker looked all around, trying to figure out where the noise was coming from. A groan from Donahue caused the ensign to kneel and place a hand on the engineer's knee. "What?"

"The deck is getting ready to vent."

"What! How do I turn it off?"

"You can't."

"Then how do I get these doors open?"

On the verge of passing out, Donahue just shook her head and closed her eyes. Her arms were twitching at regular intervals and Barker could see the urge to scratch was overwhelming. She could also see a few strips of skin were beginning to peel off around Donahue's neck and arms.

Barker blew out a determined sigh and stood to glare at the door before delivering a healthy kick against it. The metal thrummed a little and she kicked it again and again, until her feet and legs hurt and the whirring sound was almost deafening. The ensign moved up to the tiny glass window that was set in the very thick door; she saw people standing on the other side arguing, apparently trying to decide how to get them out.

The air was getting thinner and thinner; Barker could feel it. And she knew that in a matter of moments, the entire deck would be a vacuum and absolutely everything would be sucked out into space. She looked down at Donahue and then at the walls that bracketed the engineer. An incredulous smile spread across Barker's face as she took in the small, sturdy looking hooks that were protruding from the walls.

They were like...miniature handles, and Barker wasted no time in whipping off her belt and tying it around both hooks to make a triangle, her belt being the slanted edge and the walls the other two sides. Barker moved to sit in the improvised sling, calculated the extra room she had and nodded.

She scurried to her feet and undid one side, then slid Donahue into position. Barker crawled carefully behind the engineer and rehooked the belt, satisfied that with the two of them there was no give to her makeshift seat belt. She wrapped her arms around Donahue and grabbed the belt, then tucked her head down as a rattle filled the hallway and all the air rushed out.

* ~ * ~ * ~ * ~ *

Janus pounded down the hall and stumbled as she rounded the last bend to see a crowd of people gathered in the corridor in front of a very thick door. She moved forward and looked through the little window, then felt a sense of panic when she couldn't see Barker. It took another moment before she saw two pairs of feet flying up into the air to the left of the door. Janus strained her eyes, finally seeing Barker's blonde hair.

Janus backed up and looked at the man closest to her. "What 'appen's if I break this door down?"

"Venting should stop because there will be no more containment."

Her theory confirmed, Janus backed up a few steps, took a running leap and struck the door with both feet. She landed on her back with a loud thump, but when she looked up she had the satisfaction of seeing a large dent in the metal. She stood quickly, prepared herself, and did it again with the same results. The dent grew in size, but her progress was far too slow for Janus.

* ~ * ~ * ~ * ~ *

Barker felt her body being pulled up and down the hall. She felt them both straining against her belt and spared a thought for Kodiac, who had insisted that she buy the leather belt and not the flimsy fabric one. *It really isn't that bad*, she thought. Once she got used to the noticeable lack of air, she just squeezed her eyes shut and prayed that if she died it would be swift. The ensign did not consider for even a minute why she was able to breath at all in a containment field.

A pounding seeped into the edges of her consciousness, and it took a long time before she realized that someone was trying to break the door down. She knew it was Janus, knew that if anyone could get her and Donahue out, it would be Janus. Barker focused on a feeling of panic and fear mixed with a good dose of adrenaline, far preferring it to her own sense of impending death. It seemed like an odd combination of emotions, and Barker wondered briefly where they were coming from. As a sense of lethargy swept through her body, the thought fled her mind as quickly as it had come.

~~*~*~*

A sound of aggravated frustration filled the hallway as Janus delivered another kick to the sorely abused door. Instead of backing up for another running jump, she walked up to it and bent to study the dent more closely. She squinted as she judged the metal, then drew her fist back and slammed it forward with all her body weight behind it. She did it one more time and had the satisfaction of feeling her fist go through into open space instead of the solid metal of the door. Janus stood back as air started to be sucked through the hole with a loud whistling sound. She paid it no heed as she wrapped her hand in the hole she had created, set her feet, bent her knees, and pulled.

The door creaked and groaned and protested the entire way, but Janus gave one final heave and it was ripped from its hinges. She threw it to the ground and rushed inside where she knelt before Barker and Donahue and removed the belt from its hooks. Janus checked Donahue and gently lowered her to the ground where she lay for only a moment before someone whisked her away to the medical bay.

Janus looked at Barker and her eyes widened before the blonde groaned and stirred, feebly opening her eyes for an instant before they drifted shut again. Her sense of relief almost dizzying, Janus reached forward and scooped Barker up into her arms, then moved toward the medical bay unhindered.

She carried her precious cargo over to a bed in the back of the room where it was quieter and out of the way. Janus carefully positioned the blonde, grabbed the blanket that was lying at the foot of the bed, and threw it over the ensign. When she found herself unconsciously smoothing Barker's hair back, Janus sighed a little and leaned against the bed. Her mind started to drift a little as she kept her gaze on Barker's face.

A hand on her shoulder caused her to start, and she turned to see Doctor Cobb standing there with a very tired look on her face. Janus rubbed her face and looked around the room. "'Ow long was I..."

"Not long, don't worry. How is she?"

"She is good."

"Hmm." Cobb stepped forward and her eyebrows rose in surprise. She threw a look at Janus, who shrugged. The doctor shook her head and continued checking Barker's condition, finding nothing out of the ordinary except for a few more changes in the ensign's physiology.

"'Ow is Donahue?"

"As good as can be expected. She's alive, but suffering from the infection just like everyone else in here."

Janus raked a hand through her hair and blew out an exasperated breath. She felt the doctor grasp her wrist and looked up at Cobb questioningly. The doctor's gaze dropped and Janus looked down as well, seeing that there was blood on her hand and that her knuckles were dislocated. "It is fine."

"It doesn't look fine."

"I am 'ealing. Ya do not need ta do anythin'."

"If you say so."

Janus's eyes flicked around the room before returning to Cobb's face. "Can I take 'er out a 'ere?"

"I don't see why not. She's stable."

"Aye." Janus moved to the bed and took Barker into her arms. It was a short walk to the blonde's quarters, where Janus lowered the ensign gently into bed.

Chapter 13

Barker rolled over and mumbled in her sleep, bringing her clenched fist up to rest just below her chin. It was another moment before she slowly started to emerge out of her unconscious state and her senses reasserted themselves with startling clarity. She remembered being trapped on the venting deck with a very sick Donahue clasped in her arms and that jerked her awake. She sat for a long moment, eyes wide. As she looked around, she slowly started to relax when the familiar surroundings of her quarters registered. Her gaze wandered around the room and a small smile appeared as she looked at the floor with its perpetual scattering of dirty clothes, and the small shelf filled with very old Earth novels that no one besides her had probably ever read. And she was indeed tucked into her own bed.

Barker yawned and stretched, feeling absurdly good considering her recent near-death experience. She squinted a little and tried to come up with some idea of how long she had been sleeping. She didn't have a clue. The ensign rubbed her face vigourously, trying to rid herself of the residual fogginess.

When she caught sight of her arm, she froze in startled surprise and just stared at her skin, then leapt from the bed and scrambled over to her little mirror. She examined her reflection, not seeing the sleep-mussed hair or very alert eyes, but focusing instead on the silver markings that were on her eyelids. That was where she had expected them to be, but they appeared to have spawned additional wee designs that gleefully marched their way down the bridge of her nose and onto her neck. She turned her head and saw that her ears also sported tiny versions of the silver markings, as did her hands – from the tips of her fingers to her wrists. There, they stopped.

Barker pulled up her shirt to look at her stomach, then turned to see her back. She sat hurriedly and pulled up her pant leg, but didn't find any other marks. She wasn't sure if that was good or bad or if the spreading was normal. "Ohh, Janus, you'd better have an explanation for this."

She changed into an outfit that wasn't quite so wrinkled and worn looking, then started out the door, following the innate sense that told her exactly where her tall friend was. She felt as if everyone she passed was looking at her strangely. Barker rounded a corner, then quickly poked her head back around and saw the expressions of confusion and surprise on the faces in her wake. Some of the people were even laughing. The ensign smiled at the few comments she overheard, but continued on her quest.

She found Janus standing in the hall with her hand on the wall and her eyes closed. Barker watched as she mended another micro-fracture and took the opportunity to scrutinize her friend. Janus looked good – healthy and rested, and not in danger of collapsing any time soon. Barker was relieved. She had been quite concerned about her friend and her apparent lack of stamina. Although, when she considered that Janus had pretty much been going nonstop since her original ship had been attacked, Barker figured that it had all just finally caught up to her.

Barker drew nearer as Janus finished and stepped back from the wall, giving a satisfied little nod. Before Barker was within touching distance, Janus turned, and the blonde saw a slight smile cross her features. Barker found herself smiling back before she remembered why she was there and assumed an angry look. She held out one hand and pointed to it with the other.

Janus raised an eyebrow and Barker saw her bite her lip before she grabbed the ensign's arm and started to lead them elsewhere. They ducked into a supply closet and just stood looking at one another.

"Sooo, any explanation for these little guys spreading?"

"No."

Barker nodded to herself. "Yeah, thought so. Don't get me wrong, Janus, I think they're pretty darn cute."

"Cute?"

Janus almost squeaked out the word, which caused the blonde to laugh a little. "Sure, cute. I haven't seen what all of yours look like, but I know enough to realize that mine are different."

Janus's eyebrow rose as she pulled Barker's hand up to her face and studied the designs that were located there. "'Uh."

"Huh? What does huh mean?"

Janus gave her friend a pointed look before dropping her arm and stepping back to lean against the wall. "We try not ta alter other people's physiology."

Barker tilted her head, silently asking for more information.

"It tends ta go beyond what we first intend ta change."

"You mean like this?"

"Aye."

"And that's a bad thing?"

"A lot of people do not like the idea of becomin' more like us."

"But you can still undo it, right?"

Janus hesitated for a long second, her brow wrinkling as she thought.

"Right?"

"I do not know. If ya change too much, I might not be able ta reverse it." Janus rubbed her face and sucked in a breath as she considered the problem. "Can ya tell me what 'as been 'appenin'?"

"Um, sure." Barker thought about that for a long time and finally nodded. "I can hear a lot better, I guess. And my vision, that's an obvious one. I also sort of, I mean it's like there's this...with you...and me..." The ensign looked up to see Janus looking at her, an encouraging expression on her face. "I always seem to... know...where you are, and when you're around and how to find you, like on Deck Seven. I kind of remember hearing someone trying to knock the door down, but I knew they wouldn't get through. Then I remember hearing it again, but that time I knew that it was you and that you would be able to save us. Silly, huh?" Barker gave a little laugh, feeling absurd for sharing that with Janus.

Janus shook her head. "It is not."

The blonde looked up and suddenly picked up on the tone in Janus's voice, very serious and very quiet. "Wh...what do you mean?"

Janus stepped a little closer so there were scant inches between them and looked down at Barker. "Do ya feel it now?"

"I...I'm not sure I..."

"Close yer eyes." Her voice was very quiet, just a whisper traveling past Barker's ear. "Just close 'em, and let yer mind wander."

Barker did as she was instructed and let her mind float. It was just a moment or two before it lighted irresistibly on the topic of Janus and her ever-growing feelings for the woman. It seemed to the ensign that as she thought of Janus, all her senses suddenly got kicked up a notch or ten and she could smell and hear everything that was happening in their little closet.

A feeling that was not unlike the one she had experienced on Deck Seven came to her, only this time it filled her with a sense of peace and happiness. Barker felt that perception grow around her, evolving until it exploded into an almost tangible pull between herself and the woman standing just in front of her. Barker could feel every emotion that Janus evoked in her running between them, and vice versa. She sucked in a surprised breath at the infinite, unconditional love that was running right inside her chest to wrap around her heart and blow away every doubt or second thought she had ever had, like so much dust in the wind.

She could feel tears running down her cheeks, and then a warm touch was there to wipe them away and gently cup her cheek. Barker leaned into it and opened her eyes to look up into Janus's face, seeing in those blue eyes an openness and honesty that surprised her. Barker wrapped her arms around Janus in a fierce hug and felt it returned with equal vigor. She pulled back a little and looked up again, knowing what was about to happen and not caring one bit. She wanted this, she did. It would be different this time; it would be better.

As Janus leaned down almost hesitantly, Barker stood up on her toes and they met in a kiss that caused the line of energy connecting them to surge up and fill their senses before it raced down their bodies in an electric tingle to settle, finally, in the very pit of their stomachs where something very simple, and primal, slid home for the first time in their lives.

The rightness of it all, the absolute sense of completion and happiness, almost made Barker want to break down and sob for pure joy. That, along with the need for air, caused her to pull away and slowly open her eyes. Her head tilted as she looked at Janus's face and the silver marks glowing as brightly as she had ever seen them. Barker looked down at her own hands to see the marks there shining as well. She looked up at Janus, still standing there with her eyes open and a stunned look on her face. Barker reached up and turned her friend's head so that blue eyes focused on her own. Janus looked at her for a long time before a smile spread across the planed face.

Barker hugged Janus again, squeezing with all her strength as that wonderful feeling returned, and she relished the simple pleasure of being able to hug Janus whenever she wanted. And to be hugged back. *Wow. Janus is a great hugger.*

The ship rocked suddenly, and they looked at each other with almost identical expressions of exasperation but headed purposefully out the door.

* ~ * ~ * ~ * ~ *

"Wait, wait, look right there!"
"Where?"
"There! You see that little blip?"
"No."
"You can't see that? Can you make this picture any bigger?" Patrik waited, wanting very much to tap his foot anxiously as the picture on the view screen got bigger. He stepped forward and pointed directly at the spot he was talking about. "There; you see that?"

Karton leaned a little closer and squinted as Tryst gazed speculatively at the area. They turned to look at each other and a simple nod from Tryst ended their silent conversation. "Move us in there, but be careful of all those asteroids," Karton ordered quietly as his eyes shifted from his companions.

They were all a little on edge and irritable, especially Patrik, but he seemed to have become considerably calmer in the last few minutes. He was a little bit strange, Karton would admit, but the bearded man could also see in Patrik a bravery and stalwart resistance to the cruelties of the universe which told him why Patrik and Janus had become such good friends.

The view screen showed them their incredibly slow progress through the asteroid belt, the ship running only on propulsion and very little of that. It took forever before they were upon the *Avenger*, which was floating between two large chunks of rock. Parts of the ship were missing, just as they had been with the *Versai*, except this time there seemed to be no set pattern to the changes and the *Avenger* was simply in a constant state of flux.

The internal com system crackled to life and one of the engineer's voices filled the bridge. "Whatever our fearless leaders plan to do, you'd better do it fast. It looks like the *Avenger* is on the verge of literally coming apart at the seams, and whatever has kept it together this long won't be able to keep it up. If my calculations are correct, they're about to experience a massive wave of..."

His voice died suddenly as Karton cut the com link and rolled his eyes. At the startled looks from everyone else on the bridge, he just shrugged and smiled. "He's terribly long winded, and that was all I needed to know."

Tryst eyed the *Avenger* speculatively and pursed her lips. "We have a lot of the Xeratium?"

"Yes. As much as the ship would hold."

"Load some of it into our mines and program them to detonate on impact. That should stabilize the *Avenger's* hull long enough for us to get in there and start fixing the inside."

People started scurrying about and Tryst turned. With Patrik following, she headed down to the docking bay where three shuttles were already loaded with Xeratium and volunteers, and prepared to embark. "Are we ready?" Tryst asked.

"Tryst," Karton spoke from the bridge, "the mines are away. They should impact the *Avenger* in about four minutes. Make sure you move in as soon as the docking bay materializes. You might only get one chance to board."

"I hear ya."

* ~ * ~ * ~ * ~ *

Janus leaned against the wall as the entire ship rocked again. She grabbed the back of Barker's shirt and pulled the smaller woman in front of her.

"What the hell is going on?" Barker yelled.

Janus ducked her head down right next to the blonde's ear. "The ship is comin' apart."

"Can't we do something?"

"No."

Barker felt her body relax and lean against Janus's. "So, all this time fixing the ship, it was just..."

"Delayin' the inevitable."

The ship suddenly ceased its lurching and they stilled with it, looking around in nervous anticipation. When nothing further happened, they started to make their way carefully down the corridor to the bridge. It seemed like the logical place to be.

Barker threw a glance over her shoulder at the woman striding behind her. She caught the slightly confused look on Janus's face and took another look around. "What? What is it?"

Janus cocked her head and tried to focus in on a new presence that she was detecting. The interference from the yellow infection got into everything and made it almost impossible for her to distinguish between things. "I am not sure."

Barker shook her head and kept walking. "Whatever it is, let's hope it's on our side."

They arrived on the bridge to see Harrison barking out orders that were being carried out before the captain even finished her sentence. The duo just stood and watched it all, knowing that it was pointless and nothing they could do would help.

"Captain! The hull is stabilizing! I'm getting picture on the view screen."

"Let's see."

The screen flickered halfheartedly a few times, going from a depressing blackness to a reluctant view of the asteroid belt. It was grainy, but it was their first view of the outside world in two days. "Is that a ship?"

Janus strained her eyes and looked at the entire picture, seeing the faint outline of a ship that struck a cord in her memory.

Barker looked up, hopeful. "Janus?"

"Aye." A slight smile creased her face. "It is a ship."

A floating form crossed into their field of vision, followed by two more, the sight of the shuttle craft evoking a weary cheer. Janus tugged on Barker's arm and she led the smaller woman from the bridge. "Come, we will meet 'em."

The docking bay admitted three shuttles in succession; they unloaded their passengers and cargo in record time. Patrik was one of the first off, followed by Tryst, and they quickly located Janus and Barker standing off to one side. Patrik gave a quick wave and grabbed a smaller crate before they headed over to the two women. "Do you have people who are sick?"

"Aye."

"Let's go then. This is an antidote."

Janus led the way to the medical bay, the others trailing behind in a single file. Barker slowed so Patrik was beside her and she smiled at him. "You guys have great timing."

He looked at her out of the corner of his eye, noting the silver marks on her skin and acutely aware of the feeling of happiness that he was picking up from Janus, acutely aware of the sudden jolt of sensual delight that had overwhelmed him for a brief moment on their trip through the asteroid belt. "We had pretty good motivation."

The medical bay was in chaos, which wasn't appreciably different from how it had been before the arrival of the rescuers. They each grabbed a canister of serum from the crate and moved around the room injecting the patients. Barker winced in sympathy when she came across some of the more advanced cases and looked up at Janus who was working at the bed next to her. "Is this going to help all of them?"

Janus stood back a little and looked at the man she was working on, then over at the woman beside Barker. Finally, she threw her glance around the room, her roving eyes stopping briefly on each bed before coming back to rest on Barker's face. "Aye, for most of 'em, it will be enough."

After finishing with the medical bay, all personnel who were sufficiently healthy divided into teams and proceeded through the ship, vaccinating all crew members. It didn't take long, as almost everyone knew someone who had fallen prey to the infection and they did not want to endure the same thing themselves. There were one or two people who refused to be injected with an unknown substance by someone they didn't know. Janus resolved that by grabbing the uncooperative individual and twisting their arm up behind their back. It was then a simple matter of injecting them despite their reticence.

Eventually, senior staff officers reassembled to meet with Harrison as the captain had requested. They were the only ones in the briefing room and sat at the table with relief, taking the opportunity to relax for the first time in a long while.

Harrison shifted in her chair. "So, when can I expect my ship to be up and running?"

Patrik took the lead in answering. "Judging from the progress we have already made, it should only take another hour and a half before all of the infection is out of your ship. Then it will depend on what systems you have working and how much repair work you need to do on the ones that aren't."

"We'll need to fix propulsion, and I'll have to check the subspace engines." Harrison rubbed her forehead and sighed. "And you're sure that as long as we keep our energy output below a certain level, the *Avenger* won't suffer from this infection again?"

"Yes, positive," Patrik said.

"Good. Thank you for a job well done. You all can go. Barker, can I have a word with you?"

Janus paused and looked back at the blonde, who gave her a smile and a nod. Janus inclined her head and proceeded out of the room. Barker turned her attention back to the captain and waited patiently while Harrison composed her thoughts.

"I'd like to know what happened."

"What do you mean?"

"Have you looked in the mirror lately?"

"Yes."

"Well?"

"Well, what? It really is not ship's business what's going on in my personal life. This will have no effect on me performing my duties. In fact, it will only help me."

Harrison stood and moved closer to Barker. "It's my job to take care of my crew, to know if they're in danger—"

"I'm not in any danger. I had Cobb check me out, and my body is adjusting fine. It's probably what saved my life through all this, kept me from being infected."

"I didn't mean you were in danger from the physical changes in you."

Barker looked at the captain, her brow puckering in confusion. "I'm not sure I know what you mean, Captain."

"Well, Janus is—"

"Janus? You think I'm in..." Barker stood quickly and started for the door. "Oh no, nonononono. The last thing she'd ever do is hurt me. I don't want to hear that from you again, not ever! Do you understand me, Captain?" Barker bit off her words, her green eyes flashing as her ire rose.

Harrison continued to sit on the table, her eyebrows rising higher and higher. "Fine."

After hearing that one word, Barker stepped out the door.

~~*~*~*

Janus left the briefing room but remained right outside the door, just in case. Patrik waited beside her and she felt his eyes on her. Janus let a minute or two tick by before she turned her head to gaze at him with her typical passive look.

He grinned and slapped her on the shoulder. "Good to see you again, Janus."

"Aye, ya too."

"So, what's up with Barker?"

"I changed 'er."

Patrik waited in an expectant silence before he cleared his throat. "More information, please?"

"So she could see the infection. It spread."

He nodded a little, his mind still scrambling to fill in some of the blanks. "I see. Well, I take it that sometime in the recent past she managed to muddle through her feelings for you, right?"

She looked at him and tilted her head. "Aye."

"And?"

Janus blinked at him and a smirk quirked her lips before she turned her gaze back to the door of the briefing room.

Patrik sighed and shook his head. "Listen, when she gets out of there, you two should go get some rest. You look wiped. Tryst and I and the others will help with repairs, and hopefully we'll all be home in no time."

She nodded a little to signal that she had heard him and Patrik smiled again before leaving to find something to do. Janus continued to stand there and was waiting when Barker stormed out the door and walked right into a warm body. The blonde looked up and smiled. "Come," Janus said as she grabbed Barker's hand and started to lead her away.

"Where are we going?"

"To sleep."

"Oh." Just the word triggered a large yawn. "I didn't realize how tired I am."

By the time they reached Barker's quarters, she was blinking sleepily and allowed Janus to push her into bed and remove her shoes. Barker reached out and grabbed the woman's larger hand, gave an insistent pull, and was rewarded by Janus falling into bed beside her. Barker felt her body responding to Janus's warmth as she cuddled up next to the woman. Her mind had enough time to register how nice it felt before she drifted off to sleep.

~~*~*~*

"Janus? Janus, you awake?" Patrik whispered in his friend's ear, being very careful not to wake Barker or touch his friend. He had learned long ago that the absolutely worst way to wake Janus was to shake her. The one and only time he had tried it, she had hit him across the face and broken his nose. Janus had, of course, been very apologetic, but also told him never to do it again. He never had. "Janus, wake up."

Janus rolled over very carefully, drawing her arm from around Barker and moving from her side to her back. She blinked at him a few times before clearing her throat. "'Ow long?"

"You've been asleep for four hours."

"Wha..."

She started to sit up, but Patrik placed a hand on her shoulder. "Hang on there, nothing's wrong. The world went on just fine without you. We're back at Jopus Prime."

She looked up at him and tried to comprehend exactly what he was saying. *We're back home. 'Uh.*

Patrik smiled and patted her on the shoulder. "I think you need more sleep, my friend. You still aren't up to speed. I'll leave you; I just thought you'd want to know in case you needed to see Quip or anyone."

"Aye. Thank ya, Patrik."

"No problem."

Janus settled back and looked at Barker, who had rolled over and was comfortably sprawled across her chest. It was weird and a little scary. Janus had never once in her entire life looked at her parents and imagined she would have what she saw reflected in their eyes. She had thought that it would just be her alone for the rest of her life, thought that she wanted it that way. But now, when she looked at Barker and felt that current between them surge through her awareness, Janus could hardly recall what it had been like before she had met the blonde. And that hadn't been very long ago. It was scary how things changed, how quickly you came to depend on something that had never been there before, that came into your life by pure happenstance.

Janus felt a sigh of contentment pass her lips as her eyes traced Barker's face, taking in the smooth lines of her jaw and cheekbones and nose. The face was very clean cut, with slopes and gentle rolling angles that gave Barker a soft, more youthful and enticing look. Her nose tended to crinkle up in pleasure, Janus had noted, or disgust. But that crinkle was slightly different. She had a congenial, happy look to her that made you want to smile and laugh and delight in the woman's company. But her eyes could flash in anger or indignation, and she wouldn't hesitate to defend herself, her friends, or her beliefs. Janus liked that. Barker had...spunk. That was it. Patrik had said that word once, spunk, and it fit Barker perfectly.

Eyes flickered open, blinked a few times and focused on the blue ones beneath her. And as Barker smiled, her nose did indeed crinkle up as the blonde gave a happy sigh and squeezed Janus, just because she could. "Hi."

"'Ello."

"You been up long?"

"No. Patrik was just 'ere ta tell me that we are back at Jopus Prime."

"Really?"

"Aye."

"Mph," Barker mumbled and made a point of snuggling deeper into the covers. "Does that mean we hafta get up?"

Janus looked in amusement at the head on her shoulder and smiled. "No."

"Good." Barker closed her eyes and allowed herself to lie there, absorbing the contentment that was flowing through her. She didn't remember the last time she had felt so good and wasn't sure what, exactly, was causing it. It was probably largely Janus's doing, maybe mixed in with finally being out of danger after such a long period of not knowing what was going to happen next. "Hey, Janus?"

"Aye?"

"What do you think that was all about in Sector Eight?"

Janus was silent for a time as she mulled that over with several possibilities coming to mind. She really didn't like what any of them meant and would admit to herself that there really was no way they could be sure. "It could 'ave been many things. Or it could 'ave been random."

"Random?"

"Aye. A long time ago, my people encountered the infection. It came ta our 'ome one day, just showed up. They did not know what it was or 'ow ta stop it. Many died. After a while, though, it just left and we 'ave never seen it again."

"Until now."

"Aye."

"How long ago was that?"

"Before I was born."

Barker thought about that for a minute and rose up to lean on an elbow and look at Janus. "That tells me a lot. How old are you?" Barker waited and continued to look at Janus in idle curiosity.

"Around five 'undred years." The utter silence from Barker was pretty much the reaction Janus was expecting.

The blonde just continued to lie on the bed with her eyes glued to Janus's face, not moving a single muscle. Slowly, her mouth opened, her eyes grew wide, and she dropped her head forward in an exaggerated slow nod. "Are you serious?" she asked after a period of shocked silence.

"Aye."

Barker blinked a few times and processed that, then raised her hand to gently run her fingers along Janus's cheek. The woman didn't look any older than thirty in Earth terms. "What do you mean – 'around' five hundred?"

"After the first century or two, it seems very inconsequential 'ow old ya are."

"Oh." She thought about that and suddenly realized how many people Janus must have known and watched die, and how hard that must have been. How hard it must be for her to make friends, make connections at all. "So, how old were your parents?"

Janus smiled and looked up at the ceiling. "They were...more than a millennium old, with more than half of that together."

Barker felt her eyes grow to the size of saucers. "Wow. How...how do you not get bored?"

A laugh escaped Janus's lips as she turned her gaze on Barker. "Many 'ave left ta explore places no one 'as ever been before. Many 'ave started wars and many 'ave stopped 'em."

Barker shifted onto her stomach and put her chin on Janus's chest. "So, what's considered old age?"

"My parents were middle aged. I am what Patrik calls a young adult. My father, the last time I saw 'im, 'is 'air 'ad started ta turn silver, as it does with all of us. The oldest 'ave totally silver 'air. It is a good age indicator."

Barker shook her head as best she could considering her position, and laughed a little. "Amazing. I could never imagine living that long."

"It can be overwhelmin' at times."

"I bet." Just then Barker's stomach growled in protest at being ignored for a very long time. "Guess it's time to get up?"

"Aye, so it is."

~~*~*~*

The cafeteria on Jopus Prime was as noisy and crowded as Barker had ever seen it, and she pushed her way through the crowd with single-mindedness determination. She was only just realizing how long it had been since she was able to sit down and have a real, warm meal without having to jump up and avert a new crisis.

Janus was following in the blonde's wake, content to let Barker take the lead and find a spot to sit. Her needs in the food department were far less pronounced than those of humans and most other species; she could survive for several days without food or water. Janus looked around the room at the familiar faces, glad beyond measure to finally be back in friendly territory. Over Barker's head, she spotted a hand waving in the air that she quickly identified as Warber's.

Janus reached out and grabbed Barker's shirt, effectively bringing the smaller woman to a halt. When she turned, Janus simply nodded over to the table, causing Barker to look around the room for a long moment before she too nodded and smiled and waded back into the crowd in the food line. Janus looked after her for a second, then made her way to the table, where she found not only Warber, but Evril, Tryst, and Karton as well.

Evril was the first to smile and slap Janus on the back as she sat in one of the two empty chairs. "Good to see you, Janus. You have no idea what Warber and I thought when we got here and heard that you were in trouble. Again."

"Aye." Janus turned her glance to include Tryst and Karton. "But ye managed ta solve the problem, again."

"And just in time," Karton interjected into the conversation as he looked at Janus. "Quip is sending some scout ships to look for the *Pro Re Nata* and *Torken*. Now that they know what is happening in Sector Eight, he thinks they'll be able to find the ships easily, hopefully in time to prevent them from disintegrating."

Barker's arrival interrupted further conversation as Warber and Evril studied the woman they had never seen before, and Tryst and Karton took the time to say how glad they were that she was unharmed. No one commented on the new additions to her skin.

She sat in the remaining seat and placed a tray laden with food in front of her. Barker picked up a fruit that was a lot like an apple and threw it at Janus. Janus caught it and studied the surface for a long moment before she decided on an appropriate spot and bit into the fruit with a loud crunch. Barker dug into her food with gusto and the table was silent for a time. Barker finally paused in her incursion into the food on her tray, looked up at her tablemates, and gave her face a quick wipe with the napkin on her lap. She smiled and held out a hand. "I don't believe we've met."

"No, we have not." Warber smiled toothily, exhibiting a few fangs, and held out his hand. "I am Warber; it is very good to meet you." He smiled again and the tiger stripes on his face creased into a different pattern and wrinkled his flat nose.

Barker decided it was kind of cute, then turned her attention to Evril. There was something about him and his eyes, that seemed to be a mixture of black and grey, which sent a slight shiver down her spine. She held out her hand anyway and smiled, knowing that any friend of Janus was well worth her time to get to know. Evril smiled back at her, composing his face into a more open look that dissipated her fears. "It is great to meet you, Barker. I am sure that you have a lot to tell us about your adventure."

"Well, sure, but I think you'd rather hear it from Janus."

Janus glanced up from her intent study of her apple-fruit and raised an eyebrow. Chuckles rose around the table and the woman in question returned, quite happily, to systematically eating her fruit.

Evril grinned at Barker and shook his head. "Janus is not the most descriptive storyteller. We'd all much rather hear it from you."

Barker shrugged and smiled. "Sure, but if you want the entire story you'll have to talk to Janus, too. We weren't together the entire time."

She started at the very beginning, telling of being called to man the *Avenger* and their subsequent attack by the Ebokras and running from Sector Eight, eventually ending up in the asteroid belt. Barker paused midway through the story and looked over at Janus, who was sitting very still with her almost totally eaten fruit raised halfway to her mouth and the strangest look on her face.

Everyone looked at her and then exchanged swift glances, as if intuitively understanding the situation. Barker placed her hand on Janus's wrist and waited until her friend's eyes tracked to her own. "Janus? What's up?"

"Nothin'. I just need ta do somethin'." She stood and tossed her fruit into the garbage on the way out of the cafeteria.

Karton watched Janus leave and then stood up in one smooth motion as he excused himself from the table and trailed after Janus.

Barker turned back to her audience and continued her story, knowing that if, for any reason, Janus got into trouble she would know.

Chapter 14

Normally, Janus would not have presumed to stick her nose into Patrik's business simply because she could. It was, after all, his business, and if he wanted her to meddle then he would ask, as he had before. So the only excuse Janus could come up with, as she walked down the hall to his quarters, was that there was something distinctly different about the feelings she was getting from him, and perhaps a feeling she was getting herself.

She paused outside the door to Patrik's room and a brief worry crossed Janus's mind which she immediately discarded. They had been friends for a long time, had been through a lot together, and in the long run, walking into that room would not make much of a difference in their relationship. Janus stepped through the door and looked around the room that was darker than usual; the bed was in disarray. Patrik was sitting on a chair off in one corner and glaring across the room to another corner where...

Janus turned and peered through the darkness to see Emmeline sitting there and staring back at her father with an expression just as intent and fierce as Patrik's own. Janus looked between father and daughter and leaned back, feeling as though getting in the energy that was being thrown between them was an invasion of their intense silence. She quickly reviewed her options. She doubted that Patrik and Emmeline had even noticed her entrance, so intent were they in their staring contest. She could probably leave, just take three steps backward and be in the hallway, then return to the nice safe cafeteria where Barker was likely still regaling her friends with stories and her own easy charm and humor.

Or, she could announce her presence and... And what? Either she would be told to get lost, it was none of her business, which was very likely, or she'd be asked a question that had no real answer, which was also very likely, and would get her embroiled in whatever family problem she was witnessing. Her decision came down to her willingness to get involved and the possibility of alienating two of the only people she had left in the world.

"Janus?"

Oops...guess that settles that question. "Aye, Patrik?"

"Do you think we could get your opinion on something?"

Janus felt her eyes get wide as the third scenario she had concocted in her mind slammed her in the face. "Uh..."

Not used to seeing Janus at a loss for words, Patrik turned from his defiant offspring and looked at his friend. "Well?"

"Aye, Patrik." She felt herself nodding as her mind continued to race with all the possibilities. A stirring in the corner drew their attention to Emmeline who was standing and smoothing out her shirt. She looked up at them, her eyes – a mirror of her father's – flashing, and her long dark hair – a trait of her mother's – flowing around her face. Emmeline started to the door, her adolescent body showing far more confidence and knowledge than one her age typically had.

"I won't change my mind," was the phrase they heard before the door closed behind the child and left Patrik and Janus alone in the room.

Patrik groaned and dropped his head back onto the chair, then gave a little laugh. "When I married my wife, I had no idea that we would end up with such stubborn children."

Janus felt her eyebrow creeping upward and moved over to an empty chair across from him. She felt a smile growing as she thought of Patrik's late wife and what the woman had been like. Then she laughed. "I did."

He looked up at her and grinned. "You always seemed to know everything. You even knew that we were in love before we did."

"Aye, and I was glad fer it."

Patrik sighed and looked down at his lap, and the hands that were clasped together and squeezing each other so hard his skin was turning white. "God, I miss her."

"As do I."

He looked up at that and stared at Janus for a long time before he lowered his eyes again. "Sometimes I forget that I'm not the only one who lost people, the only one who's hurting." He swallowed hard and sniffled a little. "We were on that ship for...a long time, Janus. It was home."

Janus studied him and mentally let out a sigh of relief. Patrik's emotional meltdown had been a long time coming and she was glad of it. After they had been attacked by the Ebokras, there had been no time to grieve or even think about what had happened. They had acted on instinct and fear and adrenaline – no time to consider or analyze, no time to realize just how calamitous everything had been and how close they had all come to dying. Patrik needed this, but she had to wonder what was spurring it on now.

"Do you ever think about any of them?"

Janus looked up, above Patrik's head, and looked back on all that had happened in the last days and weeks. "There are a lot of people I knew and remember, that I will always remember. I 'ave not thought about 'em in the last little while, but I did a lot when I was searchin' fer survivors on the ship." She looked back down to Patrik's face. "I miss 'em all."

Patrik rested an elbow on the table and sat in silence as he considered the situation with his daughter. "Emmeline and I...had an argument, as I'm sure you know. She won't budge and I can't decide what to do." He cleared his throat and shifted forward to plant his elbows on his knees. "You know that my wife was something of a...um, clairvoyant, right?"

"Aye."

He nodded and continued. "And that Emmeline inherited that, among other things?"

"Aye."

"Well, that's pretty much what the argument was about. She wants to pursue her gift, develop it like Troi, but I...I don't want her to."

"Why?"

Patrik sighed and rubbed his face. "You saw what Troi was like – the things she saw, sometimes she couldn't deal with it. She knew what was going to happen with the Ebokras; she knew she was going to die."

Janus shifted and pursed her lips. "Patrik, I can count on the fingers of one 'and 'ow many times she 'ad a problem with 'er gift. I do not see why ya are so set against Emmeline learnin'."

"Because she is just a child!" He slammed his hand down on the table with a resounding crack. "She doesn't have anyone to help her to learn and understand, to guide her as Troi's parents did. And I can't; I can't help her with this."

"Ya are afraid of it."

Patrik sucked in a breath and stared up at Janus's face. "Yes."

Janus tilted her head to the side and stared back at her friend as her mind whirled and finally settled on the only real answer there was. "Patrik, ya can not...ya can not put Emmeline in a box and limit who she can become. It will only make yer relationship worse." There was a long silence as Patrik digested those words and Janus considered telling him something more, hopefully to settle his mind. "Karton is clairvoyant."

Patrik's head jerked up. "You're kidding?"

"No. 'E would 'elp 'er; 'e would be more than 'appy ta 'elp." Janus studied him for a moment, noted the thoughtful look on his face and stood, knowing that she could say no more to help him or his daughter.

* ~ * ~ * ~ * ~ *

Karton was standing in the hallway leaning against the wall when Janus stepped out of Patrik's quarters. They looked at each other for a minute before Karton gestured to her with a toss of his head and started walking.

Janus followed him, her curiosity piqued. She had had little time alone with any of her friends since they had arrived, and she found herself wanting very much to know how they had fared in the intervening years since they had separated. Janus had a feeling, though, that Karton had followed her out of the cafeteria to do more than simply catch up. They stepped through the door to Karton's temporary quarters and Janus felt her heart rate pick up as Karton sat and folded his hands quite precisely in front of him. His bearded face seemed tense and Janus could sense a feeling of unease coming from the man.

"Janus," Karton said, "please have a seat."

"I think I will stand."

Karton nodded and pursed his lips. "I...I really don't know how to tell you this except to just say it." He looked up and made eye contact with his friend. "Janus, I'm dying."

The room was so silent it was deafening.

Karton continued to gaze up into Janus's still face, willing her to show some kind of reaction. He knew better than some that when Janus didn't say anything or have any visible reaction, those were the times she was feeling the most. He also knew that she tended to keep all her emotions bottled up inside, just like all members of her species. Karton did not know whether their stoicism stemmed from the fear that if they were to express themselves they would lose total control over their baser urges and tendencies towards violence, or simply a desire to appear unfeeling.

"*What?*"

The single word, uttered in a low rasp, allowed Karton to relax slightly as Janus sat down across from him with rough movements. Staring directly into her eyes, Karton leaned forward and spoke. "I'm getting old, Janus. It was bound to happen eventually." Karton was attempting to reassure her, knowing she would likely view his imminent death as being partly her fault.

The experiments carried out on them in Marson could, he supposed, be responsible, but he doubted it. He had just celebrated his eighty-seventh birthday. If anything, he credited the "Fountain of Youth" experiment with extending his life to some extent. Nowhere near as long as it had done for Tryst, Warber, and Evril, but Karton liked to think he had gotten a few extra years out of it.

Janus was in shock. She couldn't take her eyes off of Karton, nor could she wrap her mind around the concept of his mortality. She had seen more than her share of friends die in her lengthy lifetime, but for whatever reason she had never considered that she would see Karton die. She finally managed to get her jaw to open and emit some kind of sound. "I do not..." Janus stumbled to a halt as words failed her.

Karton reached out and grasped Janus's forearm to get her total attention. "Listen to me, my friend; listen closely. I have enjoyed a long and mostly happy life, which was made even better by having met you. Know that I have only ever been overjoyed to call you friend, and that thinking about our time together always raises my spirits. Dying is something we all must face eventually and, unlike the others, I am merely human."

Karton stood then and started out of the room. When he passed behind Janus, he paused and placed a ghost of a kiss on the top of her head.

~~*~*~*

Barker had finished relating her story to her avid audience and then abruptly excused herself when she felt a vague sense of upset coming from Janus. Following her instincts to the corridor outside of Karton's quarters, she saw him exit, but decided not to talk to him. She was lurking in the hall when Janus finally stepped out of the door. The ensign took note of Janus's troubled, sad expression and wasted no time in reaching her friend's side. Janus smiled briefly as Barker wrapped her arm around Janus's waist in mute comfort. Barker found the behaviour a little odd but said nothing as they walked quietly down the hall.

They were soon standing in a relatively empty corridor and looking out a window towards Jopus. Barker peered out and studied the colorful atmosphere as she sensed that Janus was gathering herself to speak.

"Karton," Janus started slowly and quietly, "'e told me that 'e is dyin'."

Barker's eyes widened and then blinked in shock as she turned to study Janus's face.

"I...I 'ave 'ad friends die before, but this seems different." Janus rubbed her face and blew out a breath. "I do not know why."

Acting on instinct, Barker wrapped her arms around Janus in a long hug. Her muffled voice rose into the air. "You love him, Janus, that's all. He's been a significant part of your life, in some ways – a mentor. It's natural to not want to lose that."

Janus's brow creased as she processed that, deciding if it was true. Karton had taught her a number of things – chiefly, how to control her anger and hatred and channel it into something useful. That had been a big help in Marson.

Not wanting to wade into murky territory, she had never categorized her feelings for any of her friends. However, when she thought about how she felt about Barker, and then compared that to her feelings for Karton and Patrik and all the others, Janus had to admit that it was very much like love. A different kind of love than that she felt for Barker, but it was love.

The ensign kept quiet and watched as Janus's focus turned internal. It always amazed her how inexperienced and very much like a child Janus was in some regards. It was fascinating to watch a very old and wise mind deal with things it had never before considered.

After another long moment, Janus looked into the blonde's eyes and managed to smile.

Barker returned the smile and turned back to the planet. Janus was still upset, she knew, but she also knew that her friend needed a break from the emotional overload. "Do you think we could go down to Jopus? I really want to see more of the planet."

"Aye."

Barker grinned and started walking to the super shuttle's direct line. It was fairly empty so there was no wait, and they were once again standing in the almost untouched environment of Jopus. The blonde looked around and sucked in a deep breath, reveling in being back on the beautiful planet. "I love it here."

"Aye, as do I."

Barker looked up at the sky, then turned to see Janus gazing around with a half-smile on her face. "How long 'til the sunset?"

Janus considered for a moment before answering. "Not too long, a few 'ours."

"Mm." Barker grabbed Janus's hand and started walking. "Come on, let's check this place out."

Janus allowed herself to be led around the terrain as Barker cooed over absolutely everything she found. It was nice to see her so relaxed and happy after everything that had happened, and Janus discovered that she was happy when she saw Barker happy.

They found themselves on a small embankment leaning against a tree and just enjoying the warmth of the sun and each other. Barker leaned back against Janus's chest, elated to be able to do so. "Hey, Janus?"

"Aye?"

"What does *wiparia* mean?"

A low humming sound vibrated against Barker's back and neck as Janus considered the question. The blonde smiled, wondering if Janus knew she made that noise when she was thinking.

"Ya 'ave a god?"

"Yes, we believe in God."

"*Wiparia* is like our version of god, except we do not believe in a supreme creator or someone who controls our fate. When we die, we believe that our spirit, our...Patrik called it soul, we believe that it continues to exist somewhere, watchin' over family and friends. We portray them as lights, large yellow and white lights that float around."

"Do they actually exist?"

"I think so. It was told that they used ta involve themselves in our lives when asked. You remember when I told ya about the yellow infection on our 'ome planet?"

"Yes."

"That was the last time *wiparia* intervened in our lives."

"Why do you think they stopped helping you out? I mean, obviously people are still praying and asking."

"Aye, but many people 'ave lost their belief. I think it is because of 'ow we are livin'. The spirits do not like the changes that 'ave occurred."

Barker thought about that and felt her brow wrinkling as she remembered something Omelian'par had said to her during their very long and enjoyable conversation in his office. "But I thought that your people were less prone to the...uh, lighter emotions?"

Janus could hear the hesitancy in the blonde's voice and looked up at the sky, trying to decide if she should reveal everything. *Probably. It would be unfair to keep her in the dark.* "Aye, we tend ta the more negative emotions when we're alive. But when we die, they say that changes and *wiparia* becomes the polar opposite."

"Oh."

"Barker..."

"Mm?"

"I...I want ta tell ya somethin'."

Barker picked up on the serious tone in Janus's voice and turned around so she could see the woman's face. "Of course, anything."

"Do ya remember when ya asked me about the marks on my skin?"

"Yes."

"And ya said somethin' about families and parents...grandparents?"

"I remember all of that."

Janus swallowed and looked at the ground. "I thought ya should know – our people are not like ya think. We...we don't 'ave families or 'omes. My people, except fer the rare time, do not fall in love and 'ave families."

"Rare exceptions? Like...your parents?"

"Aye."

"And you?"

"Aye."

Barker sat back on her heels and considered that for a moment. "Okay. Well, that's good to know, but I don't see how it has any bearing on us."

Janus looked up at the blonde and stared into her eyes, seeing the absolute truth of her words.

"How does your species continue to exist, though?" The question popped into Barker's head and she blurted it out without thinking.

"Um..." Janus cast around in her mind for the word she needed, annoyed with herself over her sudden failure with the English language. "*Ecartus*...uh..." Janus blew out a sigh and rubbed her face as she thought furiously.

At once amused and concerned, Barker looked on as Janus struggled to speak. She had never seen anything quite like it before and wondered if she was the cause. Well, not she, herself, but perhaps Janus was nervous.

"Breed." Janus finally blurted out what she thought was the correct word and waited.

"Breed...your people breed?"

"Aye."

"Hmm...not very romantic."

Janus blinked up at the blonde as she considered what Barker had said. *Romantic... Hmm, I will have to remember to ask Patrik about that.* She shook her head and smiled. "Anyway, if ya want ta know more, it would be better ta talk ta Omelian'par. 'E is much more concise."

Barker smiled as she remembered the impressive evasions the good doctor had executed during their last conversation. "Okay, but you have to tell him he can answer my questions. I was afraid he was going to hurt himself last time, he was trying so hard not to say something he shouldn't."

"Aye."

Barker settled herself back in Janus's arms, content to wait for the sunset. "Janus, would you answer my questions if I asked?"

"Aye."

* ~ * ~ * ~ *

Patrik wandered down the hall looking for Karton. He didn't know where the older man would be or even what he was going to say to Karton once he found him, but Patrik knew that Janus was right. He couldn't limit his daughter and dictate what she could and could not do or be. Not because he was afraid of what she might become, not for any reason at all. Doing so would only serve to alienate her, and that was one thing Patrik definitely did not want. She was the only blood family he had left and although he considered Janus family, it just would not do to lose his daughter. If he stubbornly held his ground, Emmeline would leave one day to learn on her own, and then who knew where she would end up.

Ah, but if only Troi were there, his beautiful wife who had told him one day a week before the Ebokras had attacked that she was going to die. He didn't want to believe her, refused to at first. But deep in his heart, Patrik had known that she was right; she was always right. And it had led to a week of being together, of indulging each other, of spending time with their children and doing some of the things they had always wanted to try.

It had been the best and worst seven days of his entire life, but Patrik took some measure of comfort in knowing that Troi had died in much the same way she lived – with no regrets. She wouldn't hide herself away and try to avoid what she had seen. Instead, she had jumped in head first with all the energy and determination that had made Patrik fall in love with her. She had laughed and yelled and almost dared Death to come and take her away, and for a brief, hopeful moment, Patrik thought that the Grim Reaper would step back in the face of this woman who was so alive and vibrant, and staring back at him with defiance.

That one moment of hope had died an instant later with Troi, as she fell to the deck of the ship under the cruel claw of an Ebokras. And despite the chaos, Patrik swore he saw her lips form that simple phrase that meant so much: I love you.

With her death, part of his world had come crashing down, but he still had his sweet children to take care of and to love. Both of them: his daughter, almost a copy of Troi in personality; and his son, in looks, with the same strong ideals of his mother. Emmeline was tucked safely away with Janus, and Anwar, at sixteen, was more than capable of fighting and did so with a passion that surprised his father.

But Troi had not foreseen the explosion that took out part of the engine room, and with it the life of their son, and so Patrik was not prepared when Janus came to him with an all-too-familiar form limp in her arms. He had cried and yelled and cursed and taken most of it out on Janus, his friend – who had been there when he met Troi, had witnessed them falling in love, and who was at their wedding, the birth of both their children and the subsequent birthdays and anniversaries. And as another part of his world came down around him, Patrik had pulled it together and resolved then and there to either walk away from it all with his daughter and the Ebokras dead, or not at all.

Then, when he thought he had lost Emmeline as well and could no longer trust his own mind as it had been playing tricks on him, Patrik had prepared himself to die there on that ship in the middle of nowhere. He would see Troi in the afterlife with both his children and they would all be together again, a family. One thing, though, had kept picking at him over and over, pulling him out of the depths of despair and urging him to live on. It had been Janus, his lifelong friend. Janus had kept him from lying down to die, from giving up when she had been hurting just as much, had lost just as much as he.

Patrik was grateful that Janus had been so persistent and he would have to remember to thank her. Sometimes, he wondered where he would be if they had never met and sometimes the answer came to him: Patrik knew that he owed his entire life and family to Janus, who had saved his life countless times – both from physical danger and his own self-destructive tendencies.

He shook himself from his recollections and looked up to see where his feet had taken him. He was standing outside Karton's assigned quarters and hesitantly raised his hand to knock. The door opened swiftly and he stuck his head in and saw Karton seated at a table, his daughter across from the old man.

Patrik felt his eyebrow creeping up, but just threw a small smile at his daughter and motioned for Karton to step outside with him.

Karton stood and exited into the corridor with Patrik. The bearded man had been anticipating this conversation, but the look on Patrik's face... Karton didn't know what to make of that.

Patrik shuffled his feet and planted his hands in his pockets. "Um...all right, obviously you're helping my daughter with her gift. And I...um...ah..." He stumbled to a halt and rubbed his face. "Thank you."

Karton inclined his head. "You are most welcome, Patrik."

Patrik nodded and looked back at his daughter, who he could just see through the open door. "How is she doing?"

"She is most talented and very powerful. I am confident that in a short while she will be able to handle her gifts all on her own."

Patrik nodded. "Good, good," he mumbled.

Karton studied the man with a small measure of amusement. *He really is lost in a vast sea of uncertainty, isn't he?* "You should not fear it, Patrik. You should help Emmeline to embrace it and use it to her advantage. Your wife, did you ever once hear her complain or say that she wished to be rid of the gift?"

Patrik gave that question the consideration it deserved, going over their life together and trying to remember. They definitely had never had a serious conversation about it. "No, not that I can recall."

"And didn't it, in the end, give you and your wife time together with your children that you otherwise would not have gotten?"

Patrik nodded as he felt tears pooling in his eyes.

Karton smiled, the gesture curiously gentle. "She may be a child, but she is wise beyond her years, and she is hurting like you. Use each other, my friend. Use each other to get through this. Talk and listen and support one another, and you will be just fine."

With tears running freely down his face, Patrik looked up at the bearded man whose quiet and bluntly stated insight reminded him a lot of Janus. "You promise?"

Karton smiled and patted Patrik on the shoulder. "I promise. Now go, talk to your child."

* ~ * ~ * ~ * ~ *

"Close yer eyes. Now just relax and let yer senses come alive."

Barker listened intently to the voice that was so close to her ear and tried to do as Janus was instructing. Hands landed on her shoulders and gave a quick rub followed by the return of that low voice.

"Ya 'ave ta relax, Barker, and not think about what yer doin'."

"Not think about it? How am I supposed to not think about it?" She turned from her position directly in front of her friend to look up at Janus's surprisingly patient and open face.

"'Ave ya ever noticed when yer tryin' ta go ta sleep 'ow empty yer mind is? 'Ow calm it is?"

Barker pursed her lips and considered that question, bringing to mind all the nights she had crawled into bed and fallen to sleep. "Not really, no."

Janus sighed and thought for a moment before she tried again. "'Ave ya ever not been able ta sleep, because ya are thinkin' too much?"

That answer was easy. "Yes."

"And 'ave ya ever tried ta consciously stop thinkin' and just...be still?"

The shorter woman's brow creased for a long moment before clearing and she nodded. "I think I know what you mean." She turned and felt Janus standing right behind her, the vista of Jopus stretched out before them as the sunset approached.

Several long minutes stretched into an eternity as the two women stilled, their forms in utter contrast as they stood so close together. The sounds of the planet rose around them – the chirping of a few birds and the ominous growl of a fiercer forest dweller. Janus felt her own senses relaxing and extending outward to soar across the planet with a sense of joy, the rising energy patterns greeting her with an easy familiarity that served to soothe her battered nerves.

It had been more taxing than she would readily admit, all the unknown people and disturbances in the world around her hammering down on her senses, relentless. Janus had devoted incredible amounts of energy to dealing with it all and analyzing for threats so she wouldn't throw some hapless engineer through a bulkhead. It had made her more susceptible to the yellow infection and energy drain, both in the physical and mental sense. And that...that had lead to her sitting helpless in the hallway of the *Avenger* to be rescued by Samson. Definitely not an experience Janus cared to repeat, so she took the time to simply rest and recharge her energy supply.

Another moment passed where her mind continued to float happily through oblivion, when her innate sense of the woman standing before her flared up from a relaxed connection to one that required her attention. Slowly, her mind came back and her eyes opened to see Barker once again facing her with the most peaceful expression on her face. Janus didn't say a word.

"Wow!" The word exited the blonde's mouth on a breath to be carried away by the wind. "I felt all that. It was incredible!"

Janus felt herself smiling as she stared at Barker's face. "I take it ya did not 'ave success?"

"No, not so much."

Janus's head tilted and a smirk transformed her face just before she ducked her head to capture Barker's lips in a soul searing kiss. She felt the blonde stand up on her toes and respond, then that small body started to relax as she felt the current between them come alive with a sudden jolt to engulf their bodies in a blanket of warmth and security.

Barker was a little surprised at first, but that lasted hardly a millisecond before she returned the kiss. She felt it happen much as it had on the *Avenger* and was once again filled with that wonderful sensation that she was coming to associate with Janus. Then, as her body relaxed, for an instant Barker felt what she imagined Janus had been talking about. Suddenly the world seemed to be totally open to her and she could detect the rasp of the fibers of Janus's shirt, the rustling of the leaves in the forest far behind them, and a predator stalking its prey.

Then Janus was pulling up and away, and the feeling was gone. Barker sighed and wrapped herself comfortably in Janus's long arms where she buried her head in the woman's shirt and breathed in deeply, remaining there for an immeasurable amount of time. "I felt it...what you were talking about."

"Aye. Now ya just need some more practice."

"Well, not right now." Barker turned and pointed up at the sky where the colours were starting to swirl about in an ever-changing pattern. "Or we'll miss it." She sat, and pulled Janus down behind her.

Janus wrapped her arms around Barker and placed her chin on the blonde's head, settling in to observe one of nature's many wonders.

Chapter 15

Quip'lee brought up another screen on his computer and looked at it for a moment before he sighed a little and changed screens again. He was supposed to be reviewing the yearly budget for the fleet, a mundane and seemingly pointless task considering the current state of affairs. He had said as much to his superiors – that where the money was being spent wouldn't matter if they didn't have a fleet left, but it seemed that all the paper pushers cared about was the damn budget and keeping the people happy and not going into debt. *As if the people would be happy if the Ebokras came and blew them into the next solar system.* The bureaucracy was frequently too much, which was why Quip stubbornly refused any other promotions no matter what they offered him. He could barely handle all the political crap at his current level.

Which, he sighed again and rubbed his face, *brings me to my next and most recent problem.* The powers that be were hopping mad at him for giving away all that Xeratium to Karton. They didn't care that it was used to save not only their own people but also allies of Jopus, all that mattered was that enormous quantities of an experimental substance were released without them knowing about it, without all the proper channels and procedures being taken, blah, blah, blah.

As a result, he was in the hot seat once again, but Quip wasn't really worried. His actions had helped to save his friends, which was something he wouldn't ever regret and besides that, he had done too much for the people of Jopus and had too many friends to be removed from his current position. All that could happen was already happening, and it bore little or no consequence for him.

Quip turned his attention to the extremely annoying blipping sound and an icon blinking in the corner of his computer. When he clicked on it, a new screen popped up, and it took him a long, silent moment before his brain caught up and registered exactly what his eyes were telling him. He stood hastily, the chair falling to the ground, and ran out of his office. On his way, he paused at his aide's desk. "Call a meeting of all officials for first thing tomorrow morning." *It is too late to get all the stuffies out of bed.* "Wake Julio and send him into my office."

"Yes, sir."

"And do you know where Janus is?"

The aide shook his head. "No sir."

Quip nodded and continued out of the room, down the corridor and into Patrik's room, all without much thought.

As the lights flicked on, Patrik shot out of bed then collapsed back onto the mattress as he saw Quip standing in the middle of the room. "For... What are... I... What?"

"Where's Janus?"

Patrik looked at the man with wide eyes before flopping onto his back in exasperation. "Where's Janus? Where's Janus! You barge in here in the middle of the night and scare me half to death to ask where Janus is?"

"Yes."

"Augh! Why should I know? Have you checked her room? Or what about Barker's?"

"Well, you two always seem to know exactly where the other is, or at least how to get them. I just figured that–"

"Quip!"

"... since this was... Yes?" He looked up at Patrik and smiled.

"What is so important?"

"We found it."

"Found what?"

A base camp."

Patrik moved his arm from where he had it thrown over his eyes to peer out at the military commander, who was standing in the middle of his room decked out in full uniform. He squinted a little as he tried to decide whether Quip had gone mad or if maybe it was him. "Are you totally nuts? Remember what happened the last time you sent people out to a supposed 'base camp'? We all almost died!"

Quip winced and nodded. "I know. That's why I thought I'd see Janus first and find out what she thinks before just...um..."

"Jumping in with both feet before looking?"

"Yes."

Patrik dropped his arms to his sides and stared plaintively up at the ceiling. "Why me? Why do I have to get woken up from one of the best sleeps in my life...all for this..." Much to the amusement of Quip'lee, he mumbled for a long minute before he stood and pulled on a pair of pants, followed by his boots.

"Patrik?"

"Yeah?"

"Don't you need a shirt?"

Patrik looked down at his bare chest, then around the room. Not seeing any clothing lying within easy reach, he turned back to Quip and shook his head in the negative. "Nope."

They headed down the dim hallways and stopped in front of Janus's assigned quarters. Patrik glared over at Quip, knowing for a fact that Janus was inside. "You didn't even consider coming here, did you? Just barged into my room, didn't you?"

Quip cleared his throat and shrugged his shoulders. "Well, you are a lot safer to wake up than Janus is."

"Augh..." Patrik shook his head and entered his friend's room with no small amount of caution. He glanced around and saw that the bed was empty, so he turned and started around a protruding corner.

"Over 'ere, Patrik."

Patrik glared over at Quip. "See, she isn't even asleep."

Quip sighed and followed the younger man around the corner where he saw Janus hanging upside down from the bar in her wall, meditating. It didn't surprise him. He had known Janus long enough to be privy to the majority of her quirks, and the ones he was just now discovering paled in comparison to Janus as a whole and very interesting person.

"Somethin' I can do for ya?"

Patrik sat down on a very soft padded chair, noting that Janus was very relaxed for once and really not wanting to be the one to ruin it for her.

Quip stepped forward and started to speak. "I believe we may have found an Ebokras base."

Janus continued to gently swing, back and forth.

"Um...I'd like you to look at what I have and give me your opinion on the whole thing."

Backward. Forward. Backward. Forward.

"Janus?" Quip was wondering if she was even listening to him.

There was a long pause before an answer came. "Aye?"

"Did you hear what I said?"

"Aye."

"So, what do you think?"

Backward. Forward. Stillness. Janus's eyes popped open. They glowed slightly in the darkness of the room and locked onto Quip's face, who shifted uneasily under her disconcerting regard. "What makes ya think it is any more real than last time?"

"It's a planet, for starters. When our sensor tracking started to look promising, we sent out a scout ship so he's enhancing our sensors. It's definitely a real planet and we're picking up life signs from the surface. We were tracking an entire squadron that was traveling together, and we're almost positive that it landed in the southeastern hemisphere of the planet."

Janus was still for another stretch of deafening silence before she nodded and dropped down to the floor with a thunk. That was all the invitation Quip needed to turn around and head toward his office, with both Janus and Patrik trailing.

Julio was sitting in one of Quip's visitor chairs when they arrived, and the young man stood hastily as he recognized both Janus and Patrik, in addition to his boss.

Quip turned his computer screen around and pointed at it. "Take a look for yourself," he said to Janus. She did, spending several minutes going over the data that was scrolling across the screen.

"All right, now what?"

Quip sat and cleared his throat. "You both remember Julio."

They turned to the young man, who smiled nervously and ran a hand through his thick black hair. Patrik studied him and took note: human, very nervous, with dark skin and – if he remembered correctly – a thick accent. Probably from Spainsha, a planet not that far away and populated sparsely with people all very much like Julio.

"He's one of our best strategists and has been working on just this kind of situation since the beginning. Julio?"

The aide nodded and cleared his throat nervously, wiping a bead of sweat off his cheek. "You see, the best thing in a situation like this is a small group. Go in, do what you hafta, and get out, no causalities, hopefully. Skilled people who know what they're doing. No more than five or six. You'd have to be in the group, Janus."

Patrik, who had been listening intently, leaned forward. "Just what would we have to do?"

"Um, well, that all depends. As you saw in the data, there is significant atmospheric interference. At the moment we can't tell what is on the planet – a big base, scattered colonies, a cave system infested with Ebokras. But I imagine you'll ultimately be blowing something up since, you know, that seems to best way to kill almost anything." Julio shifted and wiped his brow again, then sent a pathetically pleading look over at Quip, who nodded. He sighed in relief and scurried out of the room.

Patrik watched him go and smiled. "Not the most social guy, huh?"

"No, but he is very, very good at what he does."

Janus was staring at the floor, going over her options. She looked up into Quip's eyes. "I choose the team; I do whatever I need ta and not 'ave ta worry about ya or anyone else when I get back. Ya supply me with what I need, no questions, no 'esitation."

"Just wh... Janus, I can't..." Quip spluttered and searched for words, then closed his eyes and nodded. "If that's what it takes to end this war, fine."

Janus's eyes remained on Quip's face. "I will start tomorrow." She turned and disappeared from the room, almost as if she had never been there in the first place.

Lips pursed, Patrik looked at Quip for a long moment before he too stood and left the room with a tiny shake of his head.

Quip watched with an almost bewildered expression, wondering why the room had suddenly gotten so cold.

* ~ * ~ * ~ * ~ *

Barker stuck her head around the door frame and squinted into the room, very aware of the time but knowing she wouldn't be able to get to sleep if she didn't at least check. The medical bay on the *Avenger* was still and quiet, and she could see Tina Cobb bent over something on one of the tables.

The ensign headed quietly into the room, noting that very few of the beds were still occupied. Once she was standing directly behind the doctor, Barker cleared her throat gently and was surprised when Cobb still jumped in surprise. "Hey, didn't mean to startle you."

Cobb looked over her shoulder and sighed before she turned around on her stool. "No, it's all right. I was due for a break anyway." She ran speculative, knowing eyes over Barker's form and nodded. "You seem all right. How are things?"

Barker couldn't keep the large smile from blossoming on her features. "Great. I'm great; everything's wonderful. What about you? And the others?"

Cobb raised an eyebrow at Barker's enthusiasm but held her tongue. "All things considered, I'm pretty darn good. As you can see, almost everyone has been released with a clean bill of health. These are some of the more serious cases, but I'm pretty certain they'll recover eventually. Donahue is resting in her quarters and has been ordered to take a few days off, per the captain. But she's going to be fine."

The blonde let out a sigh of relief and rubbed her face. "Good. I was really worried about her."

"Mm." The answer was distracted as the doctor's attention was on the silver designs marking various parts of the ensign's anatomy. "I thought you would have gotten Janus to get rid of those by now."

"What?" Barker looked at the doctor, confused, and then her face cleared when she looked down at her hands. "Oh. Well, I had thought of it but...um, well I really like...it."

Cobb continued to look at the ensign, waiting, sensing that perhaps Barker had a lot more to say and was just itching to tell someone.

"We have kind of...um...well, you see...I'm..." Barker tilted her head as she struggled to say the words.

"You're falling for Janus."

The blonde swallowed her embarrassment and looked up into Cobb's eyes. "I'm pretty sure that the falling has already happened." She laughed self-consciously and ran a hand through her hair. "I'm starting to think the falling happened as soon as I saw her."

"And Janus?"

"Feels the same."

"You're sure?"

"Yes."

"Has she said anything?"

"No."

"Then how–"

"Trust me, I know. It's just complicated."

Cobb pursed her lips and smiled. "Try me."

"I feel...when Janus..." Barker blew out a breath that ruffled her bangs. "I feel what she feels."

The doctor was silent for a long time before she blinked a little. "Oh."

Barker shook her head. "You know what? Never mind. You think it sounds crazy; hell, you're probably like Harrison and think I'm in danger from her or something. I don't know why I'm here." Her mind whirling, she turned to go. *What am I getting myself into? Everyone thinks I'm nuts, Kodiac probably would too.*

The thought of her friend made Barker realize how long it had been since she had seen him. She made a mental note to stop by his quarters first thing in the morning.

"Barker, wait." Cobb stood and grabbed her arm, then pulled the blonde around. "Please, I'm sorry. I wasn't thinking any such thing; it just surprised me a little. It'll surprise anyone here, because Janus is so different and unlike anything we've seen before. But I think she's a pretty awesome friend to have; I just need a minute to get used to it, is all."

Barker dropped her chin to her chest and blew out a sigh. "You're right. I'm sorry, too. Just, with the captain on my back about Janus, I'm a little on edge, and I felt I needed to tell someone before I just exploded."

Cobb smiled and pulled Barker over to the more comfortable chairs by her desk. "Well, I do have a husband, and we are friends. Feel free to spill your guts, I'd love to hear it all."

With a relieved smile, the ensign took the indicated seat and allowed herself to be prodded into a description of her connection with Janus.

* ~ * ~ * ~ * ~ *

The next morning Jopus Prime was filled with a tense expectation, the only sign that something was different. Except, of course, for the almost constant flow of people in and out of Quip'lee's office.

It started with a meeting of all the officials of Jopus: war ministers, politicians, and the leaders of the scientific community. Some of them squabbled over who should go on the mission, while others clustered around data and studied it from every possible angle.

Quip ended most of the discussion by stating that the entire operation already had a very capable leader who was going to be assembling a team, and that he had no control whatsoever over who would go on the mission. Suddenly the recipient of seemingly endless questions, concerns, and outright bribes that made her wonder about the morality of some of the people she was dealing with, Janus gave Quip a threatening look.

Being inundated with volunteers led to Janus almost breaking a few arms until Barker quietly came in and suggested that Janus conduct her "interviews" with a closed door policy: only one person at a time, and only if their desire to help was legitimate and they had specific skills to offer. Since Janus had already begun picking people the night before, Barker's suggestion allowed her to easily go about filling the remaining two slots.

Early in the afternoon, Barker decided to poke her head into Janus's temporary office and see how she was doing. "So, how'd it go?" she asked, taking a seat across from Janus.

"I 'ave filled one spot, but I am not sure about t'other."

"Why?"

"Five people is not a lot when doin' somethin' like this. There are three people who would be a lot of 'elp ta 'ave, and I can not decide."

"Why don't you come out with me and take a break for a little bit?"

"Aye." With a little frown, Janus stood and poked at the pile of junk on her desk, which caused Barker to chuckle. Janus looked up and raised an eyebrow.

"I'm sorry. You just look like it's going to bite you or something."

Janus sighed and gave everything one last poke before stepping around the desk. "I can not understand 'ow so few people can generate so much...stuff."

Barker stood and wrapped her hands around Janus's arm, then led the taller woman out into the hall. "I never figured that one out myself. It just happens."

"I do not like clutter."

"Not any clutter at all?"

Janus looked down at the blonde head that was bobbing next to her shoulder and scowled. "What do ya mean?"

Barker looked up with a smirk and twinkling eyes. "Oh, there are different kinds of clutter. First, there's useful clutter – that's stuff you use all the time and know exactly where everything is in a big, unorganized pile. Then there's messy clutter – that's just junk that you've thrown into a corner in your room 'cause you don't know where to put it. And then there's–" Her explanation stopped abruptly as Janus clapped a hand over her mouth. Barker looked up, green eyes wide and innocent.

"Ya are enjoyin' this?" Janus felt the smile grow under her hand and pulled it away to hear the little blonde's reply.

Barker grinned up at Janus and nodded. "Oh yes. Culture gaps are always sooo much fun to work around."

Janus pursed her lips and considered. "I think this is much more than a culture gap." She paused and nodded. "Messy clutter. I do not like messy clutter." Janus glanced down to see Barker looking up with the cutest little smile on her face.

"I'll keep that in mind."

"Aye, ya better."

They spent another hour or two of gentle teasing and not much else before Janus reluctantly pulled herself away from Barker and started back to her little office. She wasn't that crazy about the whole thing. Janus was, and always had been, a person of action. Tell her where to go, what to do, and she would comply with no small measure of enjoyment. She had neither the patience nor the inclination to lead a group of people on any kind of mission. She didn't have much of a head for politics and the elaborate dances that took place in that world, finding the entire thing boring and mindless. Janus was very much like her mother in that way, who tolerated her father's responsibilities with a gracious smile before escaping to do her own thing.

Janus found herself wanting very much to be with Barker, talking and getting to know the woman, who often surprised Janus with little rambling speeches much like the one on clutter. And Janus found herself not only enjoying those and listening to Barker talk, but was greatly looking forward to an opportunity to return the favour.

Almost to the door of her office, Janus sighed when she heard her name called. She turned, mildly surprised to see Samson slinking down the hall toward her.

"I hear you're selecting the people to go on this...mission."

"Aye."

"I want to go."

Janus cocked her head and studied his face. "Why?"

He sighed and looked all around – the walls, ceiling, his boots, anywhere but her face. "I'm a soldier and I'm used to doing this kind of thing. But I can also strategize and follow orders." He glanced up at the faint snort he heard, then looked back down at his boots. "I...I can help you. I want to help you."

"I do not understand ya."

Samson straightened up and looked directly into her eyes. "Whatever you may think of me, there is one thing that will never change – I like who and what I am, and the way things are for me back home on Earth. I really like that. And I really hate to see humans killed by these things. I'm not stupid. I know that the best chance everyone in the universe has is assembled here, on Jopus Prime. Maybe I'm even looking at our best chance." He shook his head and cleared his throat. "This is the front line of defense. If it fails, there isn't any hope for anyone else, including Earth."

Janus continued to study his face as the silence lengthened. Samson embodied several qualities that her other three candidates had divided among them, and the survival of one's species was very good motivation. But, she didn't really trust him. "Listen ta me. I will take ya, but if ya do one thing I do not like, if ya disobey one order I give ya, ya will not be comin' back. Understand?"

He ducked his head in acknowledgment, then turned on his heel and stalked off down the hall.

~~*~*~*

"Janus, can I have a minute of your time?"

She looked up at Evril – who was only a step or two away from her – and nodded. "Aye."

He smiled and waved her over. "Excellent. Come this way, please. I've been working on the Ebokras problem ever since...well, ever since they surfaced. I was making good progress for a long while, but hit a roadblock because I didn't have any genetic material. Ever since we all joined forces here, I've had plenty, and I started up my research again." They stepped through a door and into Evril's lab.

"Quip was kind enough to supply me with everything I needed and so..." Evril turned and gestured to the area in front of them, a long, narrow hall that had, at the farthest end, a life-sized blob that didn't look like anything Janus had ever seen. Closest to them was a table covered with numerous devices and little capsules. Evril grinned. "I know exactly what you're thinking and that," he pointed down the hall at the blob, "is a genetic duplicate of an Ebokras. As effective as having the real thing, except this one won't run at you and try to kill you."

"It does not look like an Ebokras," Janus murmured.

Evril rolled his eyes. "Always the practical one... That doesn't matter. Anyway, I've been thinking about you and everyone else out there fighting these guys with plasma guns loaded with pesticide. And then I started to think, 'Hey, what if they run out of pesticide or the plasma guns fail?' 'Cause they do, ya know, more often than regular guns. So I started to think–"

"Evril."

"...and this... Yes?" He came to a rambling stop and looked up with a smile.

Janus raised an eyebrow and he nodded. "Right, right. Get to the point. Well...um...watch." He turned to the table and scooped up a sleek looking gun, loaded a capsule, and then went over to stand next to Janus. He grinned and faced the blob, took careful aim, and fired.

Her interest piqued, Janus watched, raising her eyebrow when nothing happened.

Evril's lips twisted into an unhappy little snarl and before he could draw breath to reply, the room was doused with a thick coating of slime, courtesy of the exploded blob. He laughed happily and removed a glob of goo from his face as he turned to look at Janus, who was also brushing off her face.

She turned a speculative eye down the hall, seeing the splatter on the walls and that the pseudo Ebokras was not the slightest bit intact. "Can ya make it 'appen faster?"

"Hmm." Evril cleaned out his ear and ran his other hand through his hair as he went back over to the table. He swept his arm along the surface to remove the very large clumps of Ekokras gore. He studied his pad for a long moment then looked back up at Janus. "Can I get back to you?"

"Aye. Just make sure any changes ya make do not ruin what ya 'ave already accomplished."

Evril grinned and nodded. "Sure, sure. Come back in a few hours. I should be done by then."

Janus rubbed her arms and shook herself vigorously before she headed into the corridor. She was almost at the door to her quarters when a familiar warm presence made itself known behind her. She turned to see Barker standing with her hand clamped over her mouth and laughing.

"What happened to you?"

Janus grumbled under her breath and pulled Barker into her room. "Evril's new weapon makes the Ebokras blow up."

The ensign fingered a piece of goo that was hanging off Janus's shoulder and looked up at her face. "So this is...what? Ebokras guts?"

"Aye."

"Very nice." She dropped the goo with a grimace. "Have you finished choosing your team?"

Janus straightened from taking off her shoes and turned to face the blonde. There was a brief silence as she studied the ensign. "Aye."

Barker turned and raised her eyebrows. "And?"

"Do ya want ta go?" Janus blurted before she could lose her nerve.

Barker opened her mouth, closed it, and finally opened it again, this time managing to form a word. "What?"

"Do ya want ta go?"

She shook her head and stared at Janus. "I heard you. Why would you take me, Janus? There are many people here who would be so much better, I don't understand."

"I...I would worry about ya, if ya stayed 'ere, and then I might make mistakes."

"But I'll put people at risk."

"Ya will not. Ya 'ave shown that ya are more than capable of takin' care of yerself, maybe even moreso now."

Barker placed her hands flat against Janus's stomach and looked up at her face with serious intent. "I don't want to be the cause of anyone's death."

"Barker," Janus ran her fingers along the designs on the blonde's face and let out a little breath, "'Arrison sent ya ta our ship. Ya saved lives on the *Avenger*, both times. And with these..." she continued to trace the markings on Barker's face, "with these ya are not...totally 'uman anymore. Ya are more than capable."

The blonde ensign's eyes closed and she dropped her forehead against Janus's chest, "You wouldn't lie to me, would you?"

"Never about somethin' as important as this."

"I don't want to take anyone's place."

Janus felt her lips curl into a smile. "I 'ad always planned the team with ya on it."

Barker sucked in a breath and wrapped her arms around Janus's waist in a hug. "Thank you."

Janus returned the hug and buried her nose in blonde hair, breathing in a scent that was all Barker. "Ya are welcome."

The ensign pulled back and smiled, wiping a lone tear from her face before she rose up on her toes to capture Janus's lips.

~~*~*~*

For their expedition, Janus commandeered the ship that Warber and his people had arrived in. It was designed as a war ship, and well equipped for what they needed to do. On the day of their departure, Janus was pacing nervously up and down the corridor outside the docking bay, reviewing everything in her head to be certain she had not forgotten anything.

Weapons? Check. Plasma guns with several crates of pesticide and Evril's new invention. He had never quite gotten the timing right, it was still several long seconds before the Ebokras would explode, but that was fine with Janus. She liked having back up for everything just in case something went wrong.

Medical supplies? Check. Including Xeratium, on the off chance that the Ebokras were somehow involved with the yellow infection and controlled how, where, and when it spread.

Several different types of gear to suit all environments, in case the planet turns out to be a jungle or an ice-planet, or totally incompatible with our physiology? Check.

Janus scowled a little and rubbed the back of her head. She hated this "being in charge" thing, way too much responsibility as far as she was concerned. She stopped pacing when she felt Barker step into the hall and make her way over.

The blonde smiled up at Janus and patted her on the arm. "Would you calm down before you give yourself a heart attack or something? I'm quite certain that you haven't forgotten anything. Besides, with Warber on the team, I suspect he's keeping track of what you have and would have told you if he thought you needed something else. We'll all be just fine. Now come with me and relax a little."

Janus smiled as she allowed herself to be led onto the ship, where she sat on the bridge and just closed her eyes, taking in the quiet of the room. They were early because Janus had wanted to do a final run through to be certain that everything was in place. Soon, she knew, her team would start to arrive and then they'd be underway.

The estimate was that it would take two days of traveling before they were within range of the planet, and then possibly an additional day before they would be able to land, depending on atmospheric conditions and any modifications they might have to make to the ship.

There were several things that had made Janus select Warber's ship. First off, he had designed it himself, and had taken into account everything any of them —"them" being herself, Karton, Tryst, and Evril – had ever said about ships and what they thought made a ship good or bad. It was sturdy and strong, able to stand up to a lot of punishment in battle but also fast and stealthy, equipped with a cloak that Janus absolutely loved.

And the ship was sleek and compact, with nothing extra or unneeded to slow it down. At the same time, the ship felt roomy enough that the crew would be able to co-exist without getting on each other's nerves. Its medical bay was also completely up-to-date, something Janus had insisted on in whatever ship they took. The Ebokras could do a lot of physical damage, and she wanted a good place to treat the wounded.

Janus blew out a breath and turned her mind to the crew. She hoped that she wouldn't regret bringing Samson along. If he was true in his intentions, however, he would be a great asset.

And Warber... Janus smirked. Of all her friends, he was the one who had immediately come to mind. Fierce and an awesome fighter, he had no scruples about doing whatever he needed to do to win a fight. If that meant sinking his teeth into an opponent's neck or poking them in the eyes, Warber would do it. That made him a good person to have along, very reliable, someone you could depend on to have your back whatever happened. He also had a compassionate, tender side, which allowed him to care for the sick and wounded and he would, therefore, also serve as their medic.

Finally, Janus had approached. He was an old friend whose past and origins were almost as unknown as Janus's own. Lucius was a native of Jopus Prime, and Janus had actually had to make several enquiries to find out if he was still alive. It had taken a little asking around and poking into some very tight social circles before Janus had finally located his house out in the middle of nowhere on Jopus, where Lucius had been staying out of the war, citing retirement. Nevertheless, Janus knew her friend well, that it was hard to keep a good fighter down. Janus was thrilled when Lucius greeted her with a smile and open arms. He had been getting twitchy, and so had accepted her invitation to join the sortie.

His was an odd style of fighting, as he preferred to use a long – almost as long as Janus's body – metal stick to fight. He was very skilled with it and threw in some very impressive body work that made Lucius two things: poetry in motion and incredibly deadly.

Janus sat up as she felt someone other than Barker step onto the deck. She turned to see Warber headed her way with his usual assured step. He collapsed into the chair next to her and grinned toothily. "I want you to know, Janus, that I haven't had this much fun in years."

Janus felt her eyebrow creep up at that. "Ya 'ave not been keepin' busy?"

"I have, I have. It's just...that's not the same as this. Being out there fighting, the danger and adrenaline; it's in my blood."

She inclined her head in acknowledgment then looked back up at him. "I know what ya mean."

"Hmm. So, did I hear right? Lucius will be joining us."

"You did, indeed." The new voice sounded from the door to the bridge and Warber turned to see him standing there, in his usual garb and serious expression, his longish blond hair pulled back off his face with a simple piece of leather which exposed his somewhat pointed ears. Other than those, he looked damn near human.

His green clothing shimmering, Lucius walked over and kneeled before Janus who sat up straighter, recognizing the implications. The first time Lucius had kneeled before her, they had argued vehemently. Janus hadn't wanted that kind of fealty, but he had looked up at her and explained it was his custom to pledge his life to the leader of whatever expedition they were embarking on, it was his honour to die for whomever was commanding him.

Luckily for all of them Janus did not die easily, which was something she was always very glad of when Lucius was around. She didn't want anyone to sacrifice themselves for her. But Janus knew arguing about it with him was pointless, so she just sat and waited, holding her tongue while he once again pledged himself to her.

The rest of the crew arrived but the bridge remained silent, all of them recognizing how important the moment was to Lucius, feeling the energy that fairly radiated off the man as he bowed his head and said a few words that none of them could catch.

Finally, he rose and stood stock still for a long moment before he relaxed and smiled. Janus allowed herself to smile back and nod at him, then she was standing and taking count. Seeing that everyone was present, she gave the order to get underway.

Warber took the helm and maneuvered his ship safely out of the docking area of Jopus Prime, locked in the course, and engaged the autopilot. It was simply a matter of time before they would all put their lives on the line to ultimately decide the fate of the universe.

Chapter 16

Barker peered around the corner and then moved to lean against the wall and watch. They had been traveling for a little more than a day and anticipation was high though tempers grew short. Janus was managing to keep everyone from killing each other while keeping her own cool. Barker could see that sometimes, sometimes all Janus really wanted to do was just throw someone through a wall, even if it was a friend.

The blonde ensign felt she was getting a much better understanding of Janus's reluctance to get involved in anything political. She didn't have the patience for all the games and the tiptoeing that everyone participated in. Instead of dancing around and trying not to hurt anyone's feelings, Janus would much rather smack a few heads together if that would solve the problem. That approach led to the current activity, which Barker was watching with great interest.

Janus and Lucius were sparring with Lucius's weapon of choice. *A big metal stick*. Barker smiled at that, thinking that most everyone would deem that weapon absolutely useless. However, she had studied Earth history and knew how useful a staff could be. And it wasn't as if Lucius was using a wooden stick that could be split in two.

It was obvious from the way that the two opponents moved that they had worked together before and were very familiar with each other's style. Janus looked to be in top form, considering that she probably hadn't used a staff in a long time, and it was almost like poetry watching the two of them weaving, ducking, and spinning about.

She shifted her eyes to Lucius, who was proving to be a very interesting character. His pointed ears reminded her irresistibly of elves and all the legends that surrounded the creatures. She had been hard pressed not to giggle when she had first met him, but she had managed. He was a soft-spoken individual with a great sense of loyalty, Barker could tell that much. There was also a nobility about him that reminded her a bit of Janus.

Barker winced as Lucius took a particularly nasty hit to his shin before following up with a swing at Janus's head. She raised her arm and caught the weapon. The look on Lucius's face was priceless, and then he smiled, stepped back, and gave a little bow, which Janus returned. He looked up and shook his head. "That really isn't fair, you know. Most people can't do that."

Janus looked back at him with a smirk. "I can." She wiggled her eyebrows at him, then turned to Barker. "Did ya enjoy the show?"

Barker grinned up at her and rubbed her nose. "You know, I did. Feel better now?"

"Aye."

"Good. Come on, let's go grab something to eat." Barker looked over Janus's shoulder at Lucius and extended the invitation. "Care to join us?"

"Yes, thank you."

The next day they all assembled on the bridge as Warber guided the ship into orbit high above the target planet. There appeared to be a heavy cloud cover and it took a moment or two of manipulation before they could get a sensor reading. "Okay, listen up, folks," Warber announced. "The planet isn't too big, and I'm getting some strange readings from the southeastern hemisphere. It looks rather tropical and shouldn't be a problem for any of us. I suggest we cloak the ship and take it in to land here," he pointed at a rough map of the planet, "in this large clearing. It's about a two-day's walk from all the activity. There is no indication of any life on this planet so we don't have to worry about bothering the locals." He looked up at Janus, who nodded her head in agreement. Warber looked around at everyone else. "Any questions?"

There were none and they wasted no time in cloaking the ship and starting their descent. There was mild turbulence, but it was negligible compared to what they had all been through before. Soon, they were in the supply room stocking up on the items they would need on the surface.

Janus studied the array of weapons available and scowled. She had always associated weapons and the like with mass destruction. She didn't like using them, much preferring to rely on herself and her abilities. After another moment of equivocating, she scooped up one of Evril's pistols and a small pouch of the bullet capsules.

No one else was having that problem, as both Samson and Warber were strapping on a small arsenal. Lucius was keeping to his staff with one back-up gun tucked into his waistband, and Barker had two of Evril's ingenious pistols. They all had small packs of supplies, everything from provisions to explosives.

When they were ready at last, Warber keyed in the code to open the bay doors and they shielded their eyes from the bright sun. As everyone filed out, taking a cautious few steps into the new environment, Janus hung back a little. It was one of the first lessons that her people had learned: when faced with a new place one has never been before, don't enter it quickly. Ease into it, just in case there were any major differences in environments that had the potential to blast you silly. Sometimes having heightened senses really sucked.

Janus cautiously stretched her awareness out across the planet, feeling Barker's warm presence and those of her team. The land was pulsing with energy and she was relieved to not pick up on anything hostile. It took another moment or two before she encountered the area Warber had mentioned, and her whole body jerked. It was that same feeling of everything being totally wrong and out of place and Janus knew, without a doubt, that the Ebokras were there.

Barker kept a close eye on Janus, not sure what to expect and not wanting to repeat what had happened on the shuttle right after they had rescued Janus and Patrik from their doomed ship. She saw Janus's hesitant movements out onto the planet and the sudden jerking of her body. Barker could almost feel her cautious probing and the shock that rolled through her body upon detecting the Ebokras. Then, finally, Janus opened her eyes and started acting more normal, going so far as to throw a wink over at the blonde woman.

Everyone had been waiting and watching as their leader went through her ritual. When Janus stepped out next to Warber, he pulled out a remote and pressed a few buttons, and they watched as the bay doors closed and their entire ship disappeared from view. It was eerie. Janus sucked in a deep breath, tasting the thickness of the air and knowing that it wouldn't be a problem for any of them.

With Janus in the front following the disturbance in the energy of the planet, they started walking, single file. Barker was directly behind Janus, and was followed by Lucius, then Samson, and finally Warber – whose animal instincts were almost as keen as Janus's own. The forest rose up around them, the tall green trees providing a canopy that kept the sun off their necks.

Barker looked up at the sky and saw that it was clear. The cloud cover they had spotted from above must have been in the upper atmosphere or something; it was a little weird. As she looked around, she felt her own senses reaching out a little, just as Janus had tried to teach her. She found that the longer she and Janus were in close proximity, the more she changed and the easier it was to utilize those changes. Barker was liking it and the extra awareness it gave her – both of the environment and Janus.

Her silver specks had not migrated further, and that was fine with her. Her face, hands, and neck seemed to be getting a few more though, filling in some pattern that only they knew of. Barker would admit to looking at her reflection in the mirror for hours, trying to see the pattern that she knew must be in them somewhere. After all, Janus's marks had a pattern to them; there was a method to their madness. Maybe she should ask the woman.

Samson gazed around the forest with alert eyes, holding his gun carefully in his hand. He had kept quiet for most of the trip, having sensed that everyone wanted it that way. He was there to help, not cause trouble, and that was truly what he intended to do. For that matter, he didn't think Janus made idle threats, and would be more than happy to either kill him or leave him behind if he disobeyed her. And he really wanted to get back to his life, of which he was rather fond.

He would hardly admit it, even to himself, but the whole situation was starting to creep him out. These aliens, these Ebokras, were not like anything the people of Earth or the United Space Coalition had encountered before. They were resilient and ruthless, not obeying any rules of war, which made them unpredictable and even more deadly. In another time, another place, he would have no qualms about allying himself with their species if it suited his needs. They were, however, bent on conquest for some reason that none of them knew. Or maybe they didn't have a reason at all. Maybe they had all just woken up one morning and decided, "Hey, let's go out and take over the universe." And if that truly was the case, it made the Ebokras even more scary. The idea that they had the resources to just decide one day to start a massive war, the size of which staggered the imagination, was baffling. It sent a cold shiver down his back.

The group was trekking through the forest in comparative silence. It had been a few hours when Janus finally slowed and halted for a rest. Barker was glad. They had been gradually going uphill and the burn in her legs was starting to get to her. She sat on a rock and looked out, seeing that they were on a small plateau that overlooked a continuous stretch of forest. Trees were still in abundance, but were a little more spread out. Barker thought that maybe Janus preferred it that way, so there weren't any tall trees that Ebokras could leap from to attack them.

Everyone sat down in a different place and pulled water and provisions out of their pack. Janus was standing edgily on the precipice, looking out with a scowl on her face. She turned to look at them and jerked her head toward the forest. "I am goin' ta scout around." Then she was gone, jumping over the side before any of them could utter a word.

Janus half slid and half walked down the steep edge of the hill they had been climbing and then loped off into the forest. She had a feeling that they were being followed and wanted to check it out. The last thing they needed was to be caught in an ambush before they were even near their target.

She took a running step and jumped up into a tree, swung on the branch a little to get momentum and then launched herself up higher. She got her balance, then gazed out into the forest and followed her senses. It didn't take Janus long to travel through the trees, and soon she was back to a spot they had only just recently passed. She dropped to the ground, checking it over carefully with experienced eyes.

Warber's tracks were distinctive, since he didn't wear shoes and had slight claws instead of toes. And Lucius, he too had boots that left an unusual pattern in the soft ground. Samson and Barker's prints were as human looking as ever and she, herself, hardly left a trace. Janus knew by the small circular dots that were just beside their own tracks, that an

Ebokras was following them.

Leaning closer, Janus smelled the ground, picking up the stench that she associated with the ooze that covered their bodies. Her brow knit as she thought about that, and she stood studying the entire area carefully. There was none of the grey coloured slime, and that was very odd indeed.

She carefully circled the area, looking up into the trees and at the leaves of every plant. But there was no telltale slick to be found. Given the apparent presence of an enemy, that didn't make sense, so she continued to look, going so far as to jump back into the trees and survey the ground from above. Janus crouched down on the branch and studied the ground, thoroughly puzzled. She blew out a peeved breath, ready to give up the hunt and return to the others. She turned and moved her hand along the branch, moving steadily out very much like a large cat. Her hand slipped suddenly, followed by the rest of her body, and Janus found herself hanging by one arm, several feet in the air. She growled a little and looked up at the branch, seeing the glob of ooze and realizing that her hand was still slipping. Not wanting to fall out of the tree, Janus reached up with her other arm, but gravity won out and she was dropping through the air and landing on her back with a hollow thud before she could even process what had happened. Janus felt the air leave her lungs and winced as the impact pounded through her body.

Janus looked at her hand and the alien ooze that covered it, and muttered a few choice words before she stood and shook herself out, glad that she didn't bruise and would be feeling fine in a few minutes. Having confirmed that the Ebokras had indeed been following in the trees solidified her decision to travel more in the open, and Janus started back, anxious to get back to the others, concerned about what kind of trouble they might have found.

~~*~*~*

Barker looked up as Warber came over and sat beside her on the large rock, looking around himself with no small amount of pleasure. He sucked in a breath and blew it out, seeming to take great satisfaction in the act. The blonde smiled at him but sat in silence, knowing from experience that waiting for other people to start a conversation could be very useful.

"What do you think so far?"

"About what?"

Warber turned his eyes on her and studied the young woman's profile as she continued to gaze out at the scenery. The silver markings had been a surprise to him, to all of them actually, when they had first met Barker. But they were not stupid, and knew well enough that Janus had found her half, as Karton called it, in this small but spirited human. They had all been glad for their friend, knowing also that Janus had been very much alone for most of her life. Patrik was a good friend, yes, but he could only offer so much. Warber was happy to know that Janus would not be alone anymore.

He reached out and gently grasped the woman's hand, bringing it closer to him. The act grabbed Barker's attention and she turned to him with questioning eyes. He smiled at her and ran a very gentle claw along the pattern. "This."

Barker blinked at him and thought about what he had said. Such a simple word, but accompanied by his gentle tracing motion it meant so much. She considered it carefully and everything the question could imply, finally deciding that Warber was talking about more than her change in physiology. She looked into his coloured eyes and saw there the human he had once been, before the people at Marson had altered his DNA, before he had mutated into the creature that sat before her. "Janus, and everything that comes with her, is the best thing that has happened to me in a very long time. I love her, and nothing is going to change that."

They stared at each other a little longer and then he smiled, showing fangs that didn't look that threatening to Barker. Warber nodded a little bit and stood, padding over to Lucius who was leaning against a rock with his staff across his lap.

Barker nodded to herself and stood as well, moving over to the area that Janus had occupied a short while ago. She looked around the planet, taking in its beauty and the peacefulness of the place. Then a feeling tickled across her neck, one with which she was becoming very familiar, and she turned to search the area, drawing her gun at the same time.

The others picked up on her behaviour and stood, spreading out on the plateau and searching every nook and cranny that could possibly hide an alien. It came out of the blue – a high pitched screech followed by a blur of grey movement that landed squarely on Samson's chest, bringing the large man to the ground.

Lucius was the closest and lurched into action, swinging his staff down and around to catch the Ebokras on its claws, which had been raised to tear Samson's chest out. He swung again, this time hitting the alien in the chest and sending it flying off Samson, who stood swiftly.

Barker stayed alert and fired at the movement in the tree line, having the satisfaction of seeing something organic explode a moment later. Warber was at her side, and soon they had formed a square, all of them back-to-back and fighting off the attack.

It was a different tactic: the Ebokras weren't swarming out at them, but were waiting in hiding to jump out and surprise them at the most inopportune time. She could hear Lucius right behind her, swinging and thwacking at anything that got into his range and issuing the odd grunt himself. Something made her turn and look up. High above them, she saw an Ebokras perched on a protruding rock, ready to jump.

Barker felt herself take aim and fire before she could even think about doing it, but the alien jumped anyway, and she saw it falling upon them with claws raised and letting out an ear-piercing screech of triumph.

Then it exploded.

Trying to rid herself of the alien ooze, Barker shook her head, all the while silently cursing Evril and his stupid time-delay weapon. She suddenly realized that she had left her back open to attack and turned sharply, to be met by a grey blob that tackled her to the ground. She watched helplessly as her gun went skittering off to the side, out of her reach. Warber saw her fall but was too busy with an alien of his own to lend a hand. Barker looked up into the Ebokras's eyes and saw malicious intent staring back at her. She squeezed her eyes shut for only a breath, but it was enough to feel the sudden surge of energy and power that rose up from around her and engulfed her entire body.

As she grew warmer, Barker opened her eyes and saw that her silver markings were glowing brightly. She blinked a few times and looked up as the Ebokras prepared to sink its claw into her neck. A strange sense of calm filled her mind as the warmth suddenly rushed down her body and exploded outward from her hands in a column of bright light, hitting the alien squarely in the chest and sending it flying backwards and into a tree.

The blonde woman lifted her head and watched as it got up and scampered back into the trees, taking all its comrades with it. Barker dropped her head to the ground and blew out a breath, feeling her pounding heart start to settle. She lifted her hands and studied them, seeing that the markings were no longer glowing brightly, but had returned to their slightly shiny, reflective state.

A body thumped down beside her and she looked up to see Warber there with a slight smile. "Interesting weapon you have there."

Barker looked up at the sky and laughed. "You're telling me." She closed her eyes and just let herself relax while the others collected themselves and ensured that no one was injured. The blonde let her senses rise up and start to drift, followed by her mind, and she soon focused in on Janus's energy that was moving in their direction very quickly, with a feeling very much like panic.

Her eyes popped open as she realized that Janus had felt her battle and had to be terrified about the possible outcome. She considered the situation and decided to just...try. Barker's eyes drifted closed again and she carefully reached out, along the line binding them together, and sent as many positive thoughts as she could.

It took a moment before she felt some of the urgency on the other end of her bond relax as Janus responded and calmed. Barker smiled and sat up. "That's pretty cool," she muttered and crawled over to her gun, retrieved it and just continued to sit. "Janus'll be back soon."

No one asked how she knew, they just nodded and continued to rest. It was only another two or three minutes before Janus appeared on the plateau, coming up at the same spot she had gone down. She looked around at the alien matter that was scattered liberally across the plateau and all over them, and just shook her head. "Ya always seem ta find trouble. They've been followin' us all day. We 'ave ta go, and stay out in the open, where we can see them if they attack."

They moved out quickly. No one had been hurt except for the odd little scratch or bruise, and they continued to make good time. Their next rest came well into the afternoon. They stopped near a small burbling creek that wound its way down a hill and into a very large sparkling lake. Janus prowled around checking the area as the others gladly washed as much of the alien matter from their skins as they could. Barker scooped up a handful of water and scrubbed at her face, going so far as to dunk her head into a deeper section of the creek. Happy to be relatively clean, she shook herself off and saw that everyone else was doing the same.

Warber jumped into the creek and was rolling around in the water trying to remove the dried bits from his matted hair. He didn't wear a shirt and had a considerable amount of hair covering his chest, back and arms, making it look more like a coat of fur than anything else. He finally stood and shook himself, spraying droplets all over the place. He sat next to Barker and leaned back, just looking out at the lake and enjoying the land. "So," he started slowly, "from what I hear, you study history."

Barker looked up at him and nodded. "I do. I like to know what has happened, what made us the way we are now."

Warber nodded and sniffled. "And do you know everything about Marson?"

Barker felt her brow knit as she wondered at the question and why he was asking now, in this place, when there were so many more important things happening. "I like to think I know everything, yes."

"Has Janus...ever spoken to you about it?"

"No."

He nodded and plucked at a bit of hair on his wrist. "We all had a rough time of it."

"How long were you there?"

His eyes squinted as he thought and Barker felt like she could see his mind going back and counting days, years. "Janus and I were in the same new group and we all kind of stuck together to survive. When they found out about her...what exactly she was, what she could do..." He shook his head and frowned. "It got worse. There were times when she should have died, when I thought she wanted to, but she never did, just kept going, even when they killed her...her mother. That was the worst..."

Barker felt a shock travel through her body. *Her mother? Janus and her mother were both in Marson.* The blonde turned her head and stared out at nothing as she thought about that, about some of the things Janus had said about the prison and the Coalition. No wonder she hated them so much.

Warber's quiet voice continued and faded back into her hearing. "...she just kind of stopped living for the longest time, stopped fighting, and let everything just happen. And then, I don't know, something changed and she was back, only filled with so much more hate and anger." He shook his head and looked down at the ground. "Janus was inspiration for the rest of us to keep going in light of...well," he chuckled a little and raised his arms, "whatever happened to us."

He finally turned to look at Barker and saw the tears that were trickling down her face. "Hey, don't cry for us, Barker. It was a long time ago and we've all more or less gotten over it. Now we use what they did to us as a tool; it's our advantage. We are unlike anyone else in the universe. I mean – look at me with my tiger DNA, not to mention that of several other animals. It gives me a lot of skills that I wouldn't have as a normal human. Hell," he laughed and smiled, "if I had never been there, I'd be dead by now." He turned and looked up at the tall form that was pacing along a ridge higher up, scowling at the ground and searching. "She blames herself for that, for extending our lives and our suffering." Warber looked back at Barker, into her watery green eyes. "But I wouldn't give it up, not all the time I've had and all the people I've met." He shook his head and looked up at Janus. "Not in a million years."

Samson finished rubbing his face clean and sat back against a rock, pulled out a hard trail bar and munched on it. He looked around and saw Barker and Warber in quiet conversation, Janus on the ridge, and Lucius skulking around in the bushes somewhere. Then he turned his attention to the lake and decided that it wasn't a bad place, except for the slight alien infestation. It was calm and reminded him a little bit of Earth and the tropics. *Hmm...the tropics.* Maybe, when they all got home he'd take a nice little vacation somewhere, just him and a nice little bungalow by the sea. He knew a good island that was relatively uninhabited. Samson nodded and smiled to himself. *Yeah...a vacation.*

Lucius headed off into the bush, checking the perimeter for any lurking enemies. There was something, a feeling in his gut, which was telling him that the rest of their day was not destined to be nice and quiet. Not yet. He doubted that the Ebokras were going to take the invasion lightly. *After all,* Lucius thought, *if people just barged into my territory, I'd defend it to the death.*

He continued moving branches aside with his staff and looked up at Janus, her form starkly visible against a rock face. He squinted and studied his friend, whom he had not seen in so long. It had been a surprise to open his door and see her standing there with that cool confidence that had at first aggravated him to no end.

When they had first met in a bar on the Higachi Cluster, he and

Janus had not gotten along. They had ended up in a drunken brawl and had fought their way out handily, together. But that had been where the togetherness had ended as their two personalities, so similar yet so different, had rubbed each other the wrong way. They had been shocked to see that their arrest had been ordered for their role in the bar fight, and had banded together out of survival.

Lucius smirked as he thought of all the ducking into dark alleys they had done to avoid the authorities on their way out of the city. Their only way off the planet, Janus's shuttle, had been sitting in a clearing which was a three day trek into the wilderness. It had been a miracle that with all the fighting they had done with each other, they had still managed to leave the planet unscathed. The two of them had managed to avoid coming to blows until they had gotten to her ship. And what followed, *that* had been a fight. A fight where Lucius learned that Janus had been holding back in the bar, and she learned that he was quite capable of taking care of himself. Then, finally, they had managed to get along.

He stopped suddenly, a feeling alerting him to danger. Lucius turned and looked at the others, who were still lounging comfortably on the ground, perfectly safe. His eyes tracked to where Janus had moved to a far side of the ridge and was standing very close to the edge. He searched frantically for something that he knew was there. When he saw it, he burst out of the bushes and started running for the ridge, yelling at Janus. Everyone was paying attention now and they stood to see what was happening.

Janus was studying the ground and more tracks, trying to decide if there was a pattern to them. She heard Lucius and looked up, detecting the presence behind her a moment later. She turned and ducked as the alien swung for her head and she returned the attack with a punch. The alien reeled slightly, then charged her, and there was nowhere for her to go except backwards.

They fell off the ridge together and hit the ground, rolling down the hill with increasing speed. Janus tried to keep her sense of up and down as her mind scrambled to recall what was at the bottom of the hill. *A lake. Oh great* wiparia, she thought. *A lake.*

Lucius watched as they fell and started rolling down the hill to the lake. They landed in it with a splash and he changed directions quickly, pouring on the speed, joined by his crewmates.

Janus and the Ebokras bounced one last time and started falling again, hitting the water with enough force to take the breath from her lungs. She felt herself sinking, the alien still on top of her, and Janus opened her eyes to see the Ebokras staring back. She felt the sandy bottom underneath her hand, planted her feet, and pushed off with all her strength.

The expeditionary force all arrived at the shore at the same time and looked down, unable to see a thing in the dark blue water.

The alien opened its mouth, seeming to release a silent scream as it buried its claws deeply into the bottom of the lake, effectively creating a cage that kept Janus pinned down. She looked around wildly for something, anything, as her lungs started to burn with lack of oxygen. Desperate, Janus pushed on the grey chest in front of her but the Ebokras didn't budge, just looked down with those cold, knowing eyes.

If there was one thing that did not mix well with Janus's people, it was water. They could drown so easily. *Take away our oxygen in the vacuum of space, no problem. Impale us with metal or shoot us, we hardly notice. But dump us in a lake, trap us at the bottom, and we drown.*

Janus felt herself growing lightheaded as her thoughts started to mock her with their morbid, stark logic. She felt her mind detach from everything else and start to float away, but still Janus fought, twisting her body about as something kept nibbling at her. A feeling, a feeling that suddenly surged up into her mind with such fear that she was reminded of the little blonde to whom she was bonded. The thought of dying just when she had found her half gave Janus one last surge of adrenaline and she planted her hands and feet on the alien's body, used the lake bottom to brace herself, and heaved upwards. She was aware, dimly, of the constricting body surrounding her just...floating away.

All of Janus's friends and crew stared at the surface of the water in frozen shock before Lucius threw down his staff and ripped off his green cloak, then waded into the water without a second thought. Janus and the alien had hit a slight hillock which had given them height and distance, and they had plunged into the water very near the center of the small lake.

Lucius dove under as soon as he was out deep enough and started swimming down, keeping his eyes open and searching, scanning desperately for some sign of life. He swam and swam and soon he was at the bottom, but there was no sign of Janus or the Ebokras. His lungs started to burn and he planted his feet, pushing off and breaking through the surface with a gasp.

Down again and back up, without any luck. He glanced briefly at the shore where Barker was in the water up to her waist, staring at him with wide, pleading eyes. Lucius turned and looked around, just about ready to dive again when the water rippled and suddenly exploded outward. The grey body flew several feet up into the air before landing again.

Lucius looked at the spot from which the alien had come and dove down again, knowing that he would find Janus there and praying that she was still alive. He reached the bottom and ran his fingers across the deep gouges in the sand, feeling his heart sink at his failure. He turned and kept looking and then, faintly, he could see a shape. Identifying it as Janus's boot, he swam to it.

He grabbed her limp body and pushed up off the bottom, and they broke through the water together. Strong strokes moved the two of them over to the shore and the three anxious faces. Lucius carefully dragged Janus up out of the water and leaned over to wrap his arms around her chest and squeeze. He did it again and again, feeling her bones creak against the pressure. Finally, his efforts were rewarded with a splutter and cough.

Barker watched as Lucius tried to get the water out of Janus's lungs, and almost fainted with relief when Janus took a gasping breath and spat out a liberal amount of liquid. Janus shook off Lucius's grasp and rolled onto her side to cough some more.

Lucius collapsed back on the ground in relief and closed his eyes. Warber moved off and came back with two pieces of linen. Janus took one and rolled onto her back, her hand unconsciously gripping the smaller one that was at her side. They all just sat quietly on the ground as both Janus and Lucius caught their breath and dried themselves off a bit.

Samson looked up at the sky, noted the position of the sun, and said a few words to Warber before he stood and strode back up to the small circle of rocks in which they had been resting. He gathered their packs and assembled the makings of a small fire. Nightfall was coming and Warber agreed that they wouldn't be moving on any further that evening.

A short while later, Lucius and Warber joined Samson and left the two women along the lake shore. Barker watched them go and leaned over, placing her hand on Janus's cheek to be met with tired looking blue eyes. "You doing okay?"

"I 'ave been better."

Barker studied the dark face and gently smoothed her thumb along one of Janus's eyebrows, removing a few droplets of water in the process. "You scared me, Janus. I thought..."

"I scared myself." She sat up and leaned her head against the blonde one that was resting on her shoulder. "I am sorry."

Barker sniffled and laughed helplessly, feeling the relief that was flowing through her body and thinking that maybe it was making her a little lightheaded. "It wasn't your fault. Just..." she looked up and Janus met her eyes, one eyebrow slightly raised, "just don't ever...die on me. All right?" The plea was a quiet whisper and almost carried away on the wind.

"Aye, I promise," Janus responded just as softly, and allowed herself a brief moment to kiss the little blonde human who had, it seemed, saved her life. "Come, let us join the others."

Chapter 17

Quip'lee looked up as he sensed someone standing in front of his desk. It was Patrik, and he did not look at all amused. "Yes, Patrik, is there something I can do for you?"

"How come I am not going?"

"Would you be referring to the little trip out to the *Pro Re Nata?*"

"Yes! Damn it, Quip, I have just as much a right to help as everyone else."

"You do, but that's not the point, Patrik. You also have a daughter who very much needs her father. I won't send you out there and be responsible for making that child an orphan."

"You let me go before. This isn't any different."

"It is. Before it was Janus that was in trouble, and nothing would have stopped you from going. It's too dangerous, Patrik. I'm sorry."

His lip twitched a little but he didn't say a word, just turned and walked out of the room. Patrik headed down the hall without paying attention to his course and stumbled to a halt when he rounded a corner.

Tryst gazed at him with a small measure of amusement and jerked her head for him to follow. "Is something wrong?"

"No," he growled, nearly sub-vocally.

"Of course not. I hope you don't always lie this badly."

Patrik let out a cough and rubbed his face, feeling the slight stubble that he had allowed to grow in the last little while. He was itching to help, as always. Whenever Janus was around, he was never short of things to do to deplete his restless energy. He had never been so edgy before Janus had healed him, and he figured it was yet another side effect of picking up on his friend's almost constant flow of every emotion, good or bad. When Janus was away, although their mental link was weaker, he tended to get twitchy, especially if she was off on some action-packed trip that resulted in an adrenaline surge along with a collection of other emotions.

So far, nothing too serious had happened to Janus while they were apart, and he was rather hoping it stayed that way. Patrik tended to get a little hyper when he would pick up a sudden blast of fear or sadness and have no idea what had caused it. Then his imagination would start to run wild and he would be a nervous wreck until Janus returned and he saw with his own eyes that she, and anyone else with her, was fine.

"I just...I need to be doing something, anything, and Quip won't let me," he admitted.

Tryst stopped and turned to face him. Placing her hand on his shoulder, she looked intently into his eyes. "Listen, you and I, we don't really know each other – not like friends do – but I'd say we have a pretty good sense of each other."

Patrik looked up at the woman who seemed to know more of Janus than he did, and thought of everything they had gone through together when the *Avenger* had been in danger. He decided she was right. When you went through tough, deadly situations with someone, you tended to get a pretty good sense of what kind of person they were. He nodded.

"Right. Well, I'm no expert, but I really think the best place for you to be is here, with Emmeline, where you can rest and just take it easy. You and Janus have both been going pretty much nonstop, and you're only human, Patrik. You need to relax a little and take some time to let it all sink in. Go mess around in the lab with Evril, he'll be happy to have you, but take a break. You can't keep pace with Janus; believe me, I know. Sometimes even she can't keep pace with herself. Okay?"

Patrik blew out a breath and looked down at his shoes. Tryst was right, he knew it. He might not feel it all now, but it would catch up with him soon and when it did, if he were out in the field, someone's life would be put in danger. Patrik didn't want that. He nodded and headed down the hall, then paused for a moment. "Thanks," floated back to Tryst's ears before Patrik's legs started moving again and he disappeared from her sight.

Tryst turned and continued toward her original destination. They had indeed located the other ships, but the *Pro Re Nata* was in need of the most assistance. It was docked in an abandoned drift, badly damaged but intact. Scans had detected ships closing in, ships that belonged to the Ebokras. She, along with several others, had been assigned to go and protect the *Pro Re Nata* and help with repairs.

The wonderfully effective weapon designed for the previous battle was still on the ship and was fully intact, and Tryst knew that Quip was itching to test it. As long as they blew away some of the Ebokras, Tryst didn't really care if they wanted to test the weapon. She was there on Jopus Prime, taking orders from Quip, for a single and very simple reason – Janus.

Janus – who had led them out of Marson and helped them to get back on their feet, who had been on hand to assist with any problem just as soon as you asked, who was her friend and inspiration – had called. And she, Tryst, had answered that call without hesitation, along with Warber, Evril, and Karton. As far as they were concerned, Janus was the reason they were all still alive and living the lives they had. If one were to ask Janus, she would deny it, say that they had been the masters of their own fate and would have found their way without her. Janus was like that.

So Tryst had made a promise to herself: that she would be there for Janus when and if her friend ever called. No hesitation, no second thoughts, no conditions. She would just be there to back Janus up, no matter what. And Tryst had a sneaking suspicion that Warber, Evril, and Karton had made similar commitments to themselves.

There was, of course, their original agreement to be there for each other and to stop, in the future, anyone or anything that paralleled the injustice and travesty that had been Marson. But this...personal devotion...went above and beyond that, and Tryst acknowledged that fact and took pride in it. Janus deserved that kind of devotion. She was perhaps the only person Tryst had ever met who did.

~~*~*~*

Warber threw a glance over at the women who were still sprawled out beside the lake shore and then looked back up at his companions. "So, what do we think?"

Lucius moved back to his rock and planted his elbows on his knees, his long wet hair hanging over one shoulder. "I think the Ebokras know exactly whose shoulders the success of this whole thing is resting on."

Samson grunted a little and stretched out his legs. "Not a bad conclusion."

Warber looked over at the human man who had been very quiet the entire trip and yet managed to be helpful. "What do you mean?"

Samson looked up and right into Warber's eyes while he considered how to answer the question. "The Ebokras always seemed like anarchists. They just swarmed onto a ship without much obvious organization or plan. They won their battles through sheer numbers and the fact that no one knew how to stop them. But now, they've changed their tactics drastically. They're organized and know exactly what they're doing. They know what they need to do to stop us: they need to kill Janus."

"But," Warber shifted and his eyes squinted as he stared at the ground and thought about the situation, "how do they know that? Why not just kill us all?"

Lucius was the one to answer. "That's the part that makes me nervous. Why did they go after Janus specifically? Sure, she was pretty damn visible up on that ridge, but I was all alone skulking in the bushes and you guys were sitting around here looking very relaxed and like easy targets. Which begs the question, how'd they know to go after Janus? Or did they know? Was it just dumb luck that the Ebokras tackled Janus and they landed in the lake?" He shook his head a little and scowled. "I don't think so.

"If we were a typical group, the best thing they could do would be to kill us off one by one, so no one is left to do the job. But we're not a typical group. For starters, there are only five of us, each with our own strengths and weaknesses. Together we're likely to come out of this without any causalities, but apart...apart, I think only Janus would have a chance to accomplish this alone."

Warber rubbed his hands together and nodded. "And you think they know this?"

"Aye," Janus's voice broke in and she and Barker stepped into the circle of firelight, "they do."

Lucius looked up at that confident declaration and waited while the two women seated themselves before continuing the discussion. "Which raises the question, how do they know so much about us?"

Samson's eyes narrowed as his hands unconsciously worried a small branch he had picked up. "Do you think someone from Jopus Prime is working with the Ebokras?"

The group fell into silence as everyone considered that possibility, then Warber cleared his throat and shook his head. "I don't think that's very likely. Everyone has lost someone, or something, to the Ebokras. I find it hard to believe that after all the destruction they've caused, anyone would be helping them to continue."

"Aye, Warber is right."

"So where are they getting their information?" Barker asked as she gazed around at the grim faces that were partially cast in shadow from the flickering firelight. When no one answered, the young blonde looked over at Janus who simply pursed her lips and lowered her eyes.

"We should try ta get some sleep."

Lucius nodded and stood. "Janus is right. I'll take first watch."

Bodies shifted for several moments and soon Barker found herself stretched out next to Janus on the inside of a rough circle. She was glad that she wouldn't have to worry about any creeping beasties coming up and attacking her at night, and felt her hand curl around Janus's as her eyes drifted shut.

~~*~*~*

Barker felt the sun warming her face and was peripherally aware of the far off murmur of voices. She rolled onto her side and cracked one eye open to gaze around their rough campsite, locating Lucius a ways off poking at something on the ground, and Warber and Samson in quiet conversation.

Janus was, she knew, seated directly behind her, and she craned her neck up to confirm that. Her friend was sitting quietly, legs crossed and eyes closed, seemingly unaware of everything. Barker continued to watch for a few more minutes until one eye opened to peer at her, its attendant eyebrow raised, before Janus returned contentedly to her meditative state.

The young blonde sighed and sat up, leaned comfortably against a rock, and ran her hands through her hair. She indulged in a long stretch, feeling her joints crack back into place as her body mildly protested being forced to sleep on the ground.

Barker looked down at her arms, which had a light covering of dirt and other things she'd rather not consider, and stood, scooping up her pack and heading to the lake.

"Barker, wait up!"

She kept walking but slowed to allow Warber to catch up to her. He did, throwing her a toothy smile and clasping his hands behind his back.

She dropped to her knees at the shore and her eyes drifted out to the center of the lake, where they stayed for an indeterminate amount of time. Her mind kept replaying the previous night over and over again in vivid detail. Finally, she shook her head and managed to dislodge her thoughts; they were pointless at best and heartbreaking at worst.

Warber watched without seeming to, sensing the slight melancholy that Barker radiated as she started scooping up handfuls of water and washing off her arms and face. He did the same, hating the feeling of dirt when it got deeply into his fur and rubbed against his skin. She finished first and sat back, pulling a bar from her bag and munching on it while studying the surroundings. He was content to sit quietly in her presence and wait until she was prepared to return to the others.

"Did you sleep well?"

Warber looked up and nodded. "I did all right. You?"

"About the same." Barker chewed while she thought and jerked her head in the direction of the camp. "Do you know what she's doing?"

Warber threw a glance over his shoulder at Janus, who was still sitting in quiet repose, "I think...she used to, after something went bad, sit like that sometimes for hours on end. After, she was always more calm and less volatile. I think it helps her to find her balance again, her center."

Barker nodded as she considered that, remembering all the other information she had learned about Janus and her people. That they were, inherently, a very violent race of beings, and in light of that it made sense that Janus would see a need to meditate and find her center after almost dying, when her strongest and initial reaction would likely be anger and a desire to exact revenge.

A few more moments of comfortable silence passed between them before they both stood, almost in unison, and turned back toward the camp. Janus was just standing and shaking the kinks from her body as they, Lucius, and Samson walked back into the circle of rocks.

"Do we have far left to go?" was the first question Lucius asked as everyone settled quietly to hear what Janus had to say.

"We should be there in a few 'ours. Are ya all ready?"

The assembled group nodded, gathered up their bags, ensured that the camp was tidy, and fell back into the single file arrangement of the previous day's walk. Janus kept her eyes and senses on full alert, aware that they were likely to face greater resistance as they got closer the area in which the Ebokras were hiding. She very much wanted to leave with as many people as she had come with.

Lucius kept himself in full alert mode, his eyes restlessly scanning everything around them, looking for potential danger spots or areas that would allow an ambush. After the events of the previous night, he found that his pledge to protect Janus's life at all costs was in the forefront of his mind. He was used to having to jump into the fray on almost every occasion when one of his friends was in trouble. Granted, they were all capable of taking care of themselves, but in a battle where the odds were largely stacked against them, none of them would refuse a little help. It had taken a while for Lucius to accept the idea that his new friend was very close to indestructible.

Janus had been something new in his experience, something he'd had a hard time understanding and accepting, and his over-zealousness to keep his pledge to her had almost cost him his life on a number of occasions. That had led to the argument of the century, after which they had agreed, tentatively, that Lucius would not hold back on his pledge – to do so would have been like sacrilege to one of his species– but he would exercise far more caution before jumping into the middle of a situation that Janus was more than able to handle herself.

Last night had been the closest he had ever come to failing, and that thought didn't churn his guts as much as the idea that Janus had been very close to dying. He had felt it – her life slipping away, seeping through his fingers – and that had frightened him more than anything. So now he was being extra vigilant, even though he knew that there was not much that was able to rip his friend from the land of the living. Still, it didn't hurt to be cautious.

Warber settled his shoulders and sniffed the air, sorting through all the smells that came to him and deciding that there was nothing out of the ordinary. The Ebokras had a stench that he could easily detect. It was kind of like...sulfur and... His mind sorted through the various things he had smelt in his life and finally settled on one. Sewage. That was it, a mix between sulfur and sewage. *Quite unpleasant*, he thought.

But he couldn't detect any of that on the wind and was secure in the knowledge that they were, at the moment, quite alone. Of course, if the enemy were downwind, he likely wouldn't smell them, but that was what Janus was good for – all of those energy patterns and whatnot. He had once asked her how she always knew when certain people and things were around, and she had explained it in a halting, stumbling manner. It had given him a bit of a headache, as the concept was just a little too extreme for him to grasp.

Warber's eyes lifted to his friend's back and his lips quirked as he thought about Janus and Barker. That Barker – very human, with an inner spirit the likes of which was very rare. And now, with the addition of those qualities that were courtesy of Janus's biology... His mind chortled silently as he considered what he had seen of the woman. She was strong willed, noble, loyal and compassionate, with an inner strength that appeared almost as formidable as Janus's own. And she was completely in love with Janus, which he was incredibly happy to see.

Samson shook out his leg and took a step, shook his foot again and scowled. He had quite thoroughly shaken his boots out the moment he had awoken that morning, as was his habit, formed from a lifetime in the military. He had learned that when you spent very close to an entire day marching through God-knew-what kind of territory, things had a habit of getting into your boots, even if you never took them off. So Samson had started shaking his boots out every morning, as the commanding officer would not be pleased at all if he had to stop so you could sit, take off your boot, empty it, put it back on, and then start marching again.

He thought he was quite justified at being annoyed to find something had found its way into his boot, since in more than ten years, he had never had that problem. He shook his foot once more and took a step, gratified to feel that whatever had invaded his boot had shifted so that it no longer poked into the bottom of his foot. Samson grinned a little at having defeated the annoying invader, so caught up in his thoughts that he almost walked into Lucius's back.

Warber stepped up next to Janus who was leaning with her hand on a tree and looking a little paler than normal. "Are you all right?"

"Aye. I just..." She looked up at the large mountain that wasn't too far in the distance and shook her head. "Can ya not feel it?"

Warber looked over at the mountain and tested the wind, opening himself to every possible thing he could detect, coming up empty. "No."

Barker stepped forward and the wind blew her hair back off her face as the young woman stared off into the unknown. "I can."

A silence fell over the group as Janus turned and leaned against the tree, seemingly trying to catch her breath. Lucius looked at the two women and finally let his gaze settle on Janus. "Are you going to be able to keep on?"

"Aye. I just need a minute." She lowered her head and tried to overcome the horrible sick feeling that had suddenly blasted her with an intensity she had not expected. The Ebokras had always aroused such a response from her, but being so close to so many of them had apparently been too much for her normal defenses. Janus concentrated and gradually felt her normal barriers extending themselves, and the feeling receded to only a slight annoyance that sat in the back of her mind and served to remind her of the Ebokras' presence.

Janus straightened and sucked in a deep breath, nodded, and without a word started toward their destination. She was more than normally cautious, aware of the fact that the Ebokras were probably still trailing them, but with so many so close she wouldn't detect them until they were practically on top of her and the rest of the group.

It rubbed her the wrong way to know that these things had such an adverse effect on her senses. Awareness of the world as a whole or, if one so chose, only a small subset of their environment was one thing that had kept her people alive for so long. That, and their very long lives. Janus prided herself on not being totally dependent on her heightened senses for survival, but like so many of her people, she did like the sense of security that they afforded her.

The group trekked on in a tense silence, everyone aware that they were very close to entering the lion's den and that the probability that one of them would not return was rising exponentially. They took comfort in the fact that Janus had chosen the team with the express purpose of seeing that everyone left the planet alive.

Still, there was a feeling in the air – a sense of foreboding – that anyone with experience in battle would pick up on. It made their hackles rise. As they got closer and closer and the mountain loomed larger, the air fairly crackled with an energy that stood their hair on end and set their hearts pounding. They slowed to a halt and gazed upon their ultimate destination that was so very close. It was massive.

The rock face of the mountain rose hundreds of feet into the air, its black and grey colouring adding to the menace that it projected. There was a steep slope that slanted upward quite a ways to the only visible opening that was itself pitch black, and gave no indication of what lurked just beyond the threshold. The sun dipped behind the peak of the mountain and cast them all in its shadow.

Samson felt his eyes go wide and he threw a look behind him to see the mountain's shadow stretching outwards until it reached the forest that was barely visible behind them. "How are we supposed to destroy that?"

Warber was studying a little rectangle in his hand that was sending off the occasional beep. After a moment, he grunted. "Looks like there's a cave system under the mountain as well as in it, and as far as I can tell, the whole damn thing is infested with the damn creatures."

Janus studied the mountain and rubbed the back of her neck, not liking the sudden pounding headache that assaulted her. Warber's observation did not make her feel any better about the situation. Since this planet was believed to be their primary point of origin, she had expected there to be a lot of them, but she hadn't expected an entire mountain full. It raised many questions, not the least of which how they were going to finish their mission. Going into the mountain was not an option, not with the small group of people she had. They'd be killed in less than five minutes. And even though she was sure she'd last a little longer than they, she couldn't go in herself; she didn't have sufficient back-up. That left them with few options.

Her eyes drifted over the outside of the mountain, taking in dimensions and locating weak points. Maybe, if they managed to get explosives in the right place, they could bring the whole damn top of the mountain down. Maybe. Janus turned and moved off to one side to continue her study.

Barker watched her for a moment and then went back to analyzing the feeling she was getting. When she had said that she felt the Ebokras, it had been true; she had also realized that she had felt that sensation before. Just an awareness that wasn't strong enough for her to even put a name to it, but back at the edge of the forest, she had known exactly what it was.

Barker wasn't sure if it was their proximity to the mountain or if things inside her were just changing so quickly that the feeling was now noticeably stronger, but that wasn't what was puzzling her the most. There seemed to be another feeling, equally as disgusting and disturbing, but with an increased evil about it. Janus hadn't picked up on anything, though, so maybe she was just imagining it.

Lucius was studying the ground and knelt over something that caught his eye. "Warber, come here." Lucius pushed aside a bit of grass and pointed at the deep marks in the dirt. "What do you think of these?"

Warber studied them, his lips pursing, and moved a ways further, searching for and locating similar marks. He spent a few more moments looking at the ground before kneeling beside Lucius. "Looks like they go all the way up to the mountain and also back the way we came. Kind of remind me of a...a cart or something."

"Mm. Me too."

"You think the Ebokras are using carts?"

Lucius pulled on his bottom lip and looked up at Warber from under lowered brows. "No. I don't. I think someone is, though. Someone who is very much like us."

Warber shook his head, "I told you already. No signs of life. There is no way this planet is populated, and even if it once was, I doubt it still is," he jerked his head toward the mountain, "what with them here."

Janus placed her hand flat against the rock wall and immediately regretted it. Landing on her side against a very sharp rock, she let out a slight groan. Janus rolled onto her back and heard the others come charging over, Barker in the lead.

Barker had seen Janus place her hand on the rock and the instant reaction. Her entire body had shuddered before almost being pushed backward by an invisible force. She knelt next to Janus and anxiously placed a hand on her arm. "Are you all right? What the hell happened?"

Janus opened her eyes and gazed up at the concerned faces. A brief chuckle escaped before she nodded. "Aye." She sat up and shook her head, trying to dispel the images that had been conjured by touching the rock. She accepted the hand Lucius held out, gave her limbs a shake, and dusted herself off. "We should go and make camp fer the night. We will decide what ta do in the mornin'."

Hoping that they'd have a quiet night, Janus led her small band back toward a clearing on the edge of the forest that would be defensible.

* ~ * ~ * ~ * ~ *

It is a nice clearing, Samson thought. Large in size, the forest was sparse around the edges, giving ample time to spot a potential attack. There were a few fallen logs towards the center that provided the odd backrest, which Samson was more than happy to take advantage of. He had been a soldier for the majority of his life and his body was starting to resent that fact, even though he was just over thirty. He was honest enough with himself to admit that he feared what would happen when he could no longer live up to the expectations placed on people who worked in the field. He didn't think he could survive behind a desk.

Samson looked around and exhaled sharply, dismissing the troubling thoughts and focusing on the situation at hand. The mountain had been a bit of a surprise. Even he had detected the shock on Janus's face before she had turned contemplative and started to analyze the problem. At present, she was on the other end of the clearing with Barker crouched at her side, probably discussing the little incident that had occurred at the mountain. He briefly wondered what Janus could have experienced by simply touching the rock that had been powerful enough to send her to the ground. The possibilities worried him.

Barker knelt next to her friend and placed a gentle hand on her arm. Green eyes filled with concern drifted over Janus's body before she asked in a slightly hushed voice, "What happened back there?" For a long time Janus was silent, so much so that the young blonde thought she was not going to answer.

"There is somethin' else in that mountain."

The statement caused Barker to sit and lean a little closer as she recollected her own feelings. "Like what?"

A minute shake of the head was followed by a strangely chilling statement. "I do not know."

Barker's eyes drifted down from Janus's face to focus on the hands clasped tightly in her lap, a faint tremor running through them. "Are you sure you're all right?"

"Aye."

The blonde ensign waited in silence until Janus looked up and locked eyes with her. Then, she wordlessly allowed her own to drop down and stare intently at Janus's hands.

Janus clasped her hands between her knees in a useless attempt to stop them from shaking and cleared her throat. "It just...brought back some bad memories."

Her gaze was fixed on the ground, and Barker knew that they would not be discussing this one thing here. Not now, maybe not ever. In an attempt to offer the only solace she could, the blonde moved closer until their shoulders were touching and placed her own, smaller hands on top of Janus's.

It took a few agonizingly long minutes, but eventually Janus's body started to relax and accept the comfort afforded by her half. Barker watched as Janus's large tanned hands slowly became still and steady, and she felt some of her own apprehension start to dissolve.

As the others quietly moved about their camp, setting things up and arranging the site to their liking, the two women sat in a comfortable, companionable silence. Barker allowed her eyes to close in contentment, but it was short lived as her brow creased and her mind tried to identify a sudden feeling. It was different from the other sensations, but it had one thing in common with them: it carried with it a distinct sense of danger. She felt Janus's body tense into awareness and knew then that she was not imagining it.

They both stood, almost as one, and looked around the camp, seeing that the others had taken up similar states of vigilance that had been triggered by their sudden rise to attention.

Janus stretched her senses out, not detecting anything that she would associate with the Ebokras or any other kind of attacker. No, the new feeling was more natural, and foretold something much more dangerous than an ambush from a vengeful, angry enemy. It warned of something even she could not control or predict, and that was the worst kind of threat.

Before anyone could so much as breathe, the ground started to shake and rumble, throwing their world into utter chaos.

Lucius's eyes widened as the ground on which he was standing suddenly heaved upward and sent him flying through the air. He managed to keep his senses about him and execute a half-roll that saved his body from most of the painful jarring of landing on the ground. He had hardly a second to analyze what was happening before a loud splintering crack alerted him, and he turned his head to see a large tree descending on him.

Samson jerked and scrambled out of the way of the creeping crevice in the earth that was getting wider and wider as it headed directly for him. He managed to regain his feet and stumble away until he thought he was safe. Another second of seemingly breathless silence and suddenly he was falling, and there was nothing he could do to stop it.

Warber was on the very edge of the camp, furthest away from

everyone else, and darted underneath a group of fallen trees that provided him adequate shelter from anything else that had the potential to fall on him. His face slackened in shock as he watched the ground splinter, then rise and fall in an unpredictable pattern. He quickly lost track of the others, but thought he could detect the odd shout of startlement or fear.

Janus instinctively dove toward Barker and took the blonde woman to the ground, rolling them away from falling trees and flying stone. She rose to her feet and pulled Barker up beside her, then quickly studied the ground, trying to get a sense of which areas might be the most dangerous. The ground suddenly shifted and heaved and they both lost their balance, rolling off in different directions.

Barker covered her head as her body seemed to follow the dips and valleys that were now a part of the ground. She finally slid to a stop, but stayed very still as she tried to decide if it was safe to stand. A minute passed, then another, and the blonde noticed that her sudden feeling of danger had passed. She carefully removed her arms from where they had protected her head and uncurled her body, cautious of any holes that might have formed close to her position. Seeing that the ground was relatively flat and stable, she stood and looked around.

The clearing wasn't a clearing anymore. Some of the forest remained behind her, but it was mostly a collection of fallen and broken trees with several crevices and sheer rock mini-cliffs that hadn't been there just moments before. She turned to rejoin her friends, but stopped abruptly when she saw the wall that was blocking her way.

Barker tilted her head back and estimated that eight or nine feet of the ground had risen, or maybe sunk, and now stood between her and the campsite. Her eyes flicked over the craggy surface but did not find any suitable handholds. She knew Janus had to be up on the peak, which meant she needed to get up there. Her mind registered the sudden, eerie quiet that had descended upon the land. It was as if the entire planet was holding its breath in the wake of the sudden and violent destruction, perhaps to see if it was truly finished or if anything had survived.

With that thought, her mind moved to her friends and she desperately tried to remember where each had been. Warber, she knew, had been in the forest... Barker turned and looked around, not able to see him. Given his natural camouflage, however, that didn't mean very much. "Warber? Warber!"

There was a long silence and then finally, from not too far away, he replied, "Barker? That you?"

"Yeah. You all right?"

"Fine. You?"

Barker looked down at herself. She had several nasty looking scrapes along her arms and she could feel more of them on her legs, but it could have been a lot worse. "I'm okay."

"Good." His voice sounded closer and then his tiger-striped face popped out of a tree not three feet in front of her. Warber dropped to the ground and somehow found the energy to smile before studying the area with interest. His nose wrinkled a little and he held out a large hand. "What do you say we get outta this pit?"

* ~ * ~ * ~ * ~ *

As he felt his grip slipping, Samson desperately tried to find purchase on the slick rock with his feet. His fingertips were starting to cramp and his shoulders felt like they were pulling out of their sockets. The odd little rock skipped down the wall and rained dust on his bent head.

"Oh, God, I am so not ready to die." The whisper escaped his lips as his hands slipped a little more and his body dropped several inches closer to death. "Please, please, please..."

When his arms started to shake with the strain of supporting his body weight, Dion Samson resigned himself to the very real possibility that he was about to die. The thought sent a surge of fear through him the likes of which he had never before experienced, and an image of his sister, Tina Cobb, rose in his mind's eye.

He felt his cheek scrape against the rough rock and draw blood as his hands slipped even further, and then he was just hanging on by his fingertips. The thought of just...letting go rose in his mind, but he pushed it down, determined to cling to life. If he was going to meet his Maker, then he was going to hold out as long as he could – just to spite Death.

Sweat broke out on his forehead and almost everywhere else, adding to the slickness of his hands. One more slip and that was it – he'd be a dead man. Samson sucked in his last breath as he felt the rock slide beneath his fingertips, millimeter by millimeter. Just as his body was about to succumb to the force of gravity, a strong hand wrapped around his shoulder and in one gigantic heave he was lifted bodily out of the crevice and onto solid, flat ground.

As Samson impacted the ground, he felt the breath leave his lungs in a sigh that sounded like a cry of joy and relief mixed with a sob. His eyes opened and looked up at the twilight sky where the first stars were beginning to shine down upon him, and he smiled. He turned his head and saw a disheveled Janus on the ground next to him, breathing heavily. When she looked at him, Samson opened his mouth, but an unusual lump rose to his throat and made speech impossible. He decided that his face must have expressed his thoughts because there was a softening in her gaze, so slight he thought maybe he had imagined it, and then she nodded at him once before she stood and surveyed the area.

Samson allowed his head to fall back to the ground. Unless someone asked him to do something, he was happy to stay exactly where he was and just exult in filling his lungs with air. He could hear Janus's boots crunching on the gravel and an odd little grunt floated over to him from a few feet behind. When he heard it again he rolled onto his side and stood, moving cautiously over to another large drop that — to his great relief — had a bottom.

He squinted, finally identifying the moving blob that was issuing the odd human sound. It was Warber, with Barker practically hanging off his back, scaling the wall. He was only a foot or so below the rim, where he had run out of handholds. Samson anchored himself and extended his hand.

Warber's head jerked back a little as his vision was suddenly filled with flesh, but after the initial shock he grabbed the offered assistance and pulled himself and Barker to the top of the wall. Warber nodded his thanks and they all sat for a moment or two before a yell from Janus motivated them to get moving again.

She was on the far side of the camp, beyond a few minor holes and little hills that weren't much of a problem to navigate. When they arrived beside her, they found Lucius, face etched with pain, trapped under a huge tree.

"Warber, I need ya ta git over there," Janus pointed, "and give me some leverage."

Warber searched for a sturdy branch, which didn't take long to locate, then moved into the indicated position and jammed the lever under the tree. He waited until Janus started to lift, then he pushed on his stick to keep the tree from rolling back onto Lucius. It took only a moment and then Lucius was free, with an obviously broken leg.

Everyone stayed silent as Janus considered for a moment before she bent, scooped him up, and gave a brusque order. "Try and find our stuff. We need ta move, find a better place."

Lucius grimaced and found the energy to pound on Janus's shoulder. "Janus...put me down... I...aghh!" He let out a yell as he twisted the wrong way to return the glare that Janus was giving him.

"Be quiet. Ya need 'elp. Ya 'elped me, now I am 'elpin' ya."

He drew in a deep breath to dispute her, but let it out in an aggravated sigh as he realized that he really was in no position to argue.

Janus moved carefully out of what had been their clearing with Barker close behind and keeping a hand on her back. Janus didn't mind, in fact she took great comfort from the touch, knowing that Barker was all right. If they weren't in such a hostile area with so much that had to be done, Janus would have probably just wrapped the little blonde in her arms and never let go.

It was only ten minutes before Samson and Warber joined them, having found only two of their packs. Thankfully, one was Warber's, which had most of the medical supplies in it; the other was Barker's. The ensign had brought along a lot of food, as she had realized that the more she did the larger her appetite got.

Warber took the lead to search for a strategic campsite that was still intact, and managed to locate a suitable one in less than half an hour. Janus settled Lucius as Samson lit a small, smokeless fire. Warber made use of his medical supplies, as Barker focused on clearing some debris from their camp to give them all a little more comfortable sleeping area.

When Warber had completed his ministrations, Lucius scowled at his leg and pulled himself up into a more comfortable position. "What was all that?"

"Earthquake," Warber muttered, not looking up from his stitching of a nasty cut on Samson's arm.

"An earthquake?"

"Yep."

Lucius blinked and looked around at the faces of his companions. "What caused it?"

Warber was silent and leaned back after he finished stitching. He pulled out his ever present, multifunctional rectangle and opened it. "There aren't any fault lines...so, maybe mining."

"Minin'?" The question was evident in Janus's voice. No one needed to voice the question and no one could have answered it: who would be mining on a planet that was inhabited only by the Ebokras?

Chapter 18

Quip'lee entered and took his seat at the head of the table in his conference room. The assemblage looked up at him and remained silent as their military commander settled himself for the meeting.

Quip was, in title, the Totarian Commander of the Ninth Fleet of Jopus, a title that was itself fictional. There wasn't really a Ninth Fleet in the most traditional sense of the word. Quip was the supreme commander, and had the final decision on all things military; the fighting forces of the planet Jopus and its outposts were ultimately under his command.

Not only was there no Ninth Fleet, there were, in fact, only four very large fleets. For some reason lost to history, someone had decided that a title that indicated an imaginary fleet that actually encompassed *everything* would make it clear who was in charge of the military. Quip had spent a long time pondering the whole thing, and found it got more confusing the longer he thought on the subject. He preferred to view himself as the man with all the military clout who reported directly to the stuffed shirt political types.

"Report." Quip gave his order quietly and it was all the prompting that the gathered officials needed.

"Well, sir, in regards to our war with the Ebokras – we haven't suffered any significant losses and have been making steady, if very slow, progress. The...um, people...that Janus called in have proved very effective. They gave us the extra manpower and element of surprise that we needed to continue to hold our own."

With that report finished, the next started. "As far as the mission to recover the *Pro Re Nata* is concerned, the rescue ships departed on schedule yesterday evening, and at last report were in position to converge on the ship. If everything goes smoothly, they should all be back here by tomorrow morning at the latest."

In much the same manner, it continued all around the table until the last person had given their report and resumed their seat. Quip digested everything he had heard. It had not taken as long as some meetings did, because at this point in the war they were all pretty much in agreement about what should be done. After a few moments of silence, Quip nodded and gave a small smile. "Good news, everyone. Keep up the good work. Are there any questions before we conclude?"

The room fell into a brief, expectant silence and Quip's eyes drifted around the table in mild amusement. He knew they wanted to ask him something, but they were reluctant to speak up. He wondered who the nominated spokesperson was. A faint motion caught his eye, a slight jerk from a woman who was sitting at one end of the table. The man across from her scowled at her, and Quip concluded that the woman had kicked him in the shin. He waited until finally the man turned and cleared his throat before opening his mouth to speak.

"What about Janus and her group?"

Quip leaned back in his chair and steepled his fingers before him as his eyes went around the table and made brief, but meaningful contact with each individual seated there. He had expected the question and had given some consideration to his answer before the meeting had started. "That entire...situation...is completely out of my hands. They have their job to do and I'm confident that they'll do it. They'll either come back, or they won't."

Everyone turned their eyes to the tabletop and thought about his statement. Most, if not all, of the people in the room were well acquainted with Janus and what she was capable of. It was for that reason that they believed Quip's assessment of the situation. Janus would go to the ends of the universe to finish the job, if that's what it took. One by one, they slowly stood and walked out of the room to resume their daily tasks of fighting and winning the war.

Quip continued to sit at the head of the table until the room was empty, thinking about everything and nothing. His mind flashed through his relationship with Janus, which had started when he was very young, still in the academy on Jopus. She had been a very free and unrestrained spirit back then, full of restless energy and power. When he thought back on those times, his mind often called forth the word "brimstone".

It had been before Marson, perhaps two years, but he remembered it well. His species enjoyed long life, though hardly a fraction of Janus's life span, and a good memory of the events of their life. Quip often found himself wishing he had known her better then. Nevertheless, she had made an impression on him and he had never forgotten.

The next time he had seen her, he had detected the changes in her immediately. Before, she had been free of everything, all limitations, barely able to sit still. Post-Marson, there were walls in her eyes that hadn't been there before and a cautiousness with the world that almost broke his heart. It was with that realization of the changes in Janus that Quip discerned how hard her confinement had been. There were some people, even some species that you just couldn't lock up and expect them to survive; it went against their nature. Janus was one of those people.

But some things about her hadn't changed and Janus had, over time, worked her way into his heart like few people ever had. He had often worried about her, even though he knew she was more capable than most of taking care of herself. The worry sprouted more from the fact that she seemed very much alone. She had never returned to her home planet, and did not ever remain on Jopus long enough to cement any abiding friendships.

The first time she had returned with Patrik in tow and introduced him as a friend, Quip had almost fainted. It had been several years since he had last heard from her, and the shock of Janus just suddenly being there, and with a friend to boot, had been enormous. Patrik had proven to be a very likeable young man and soon held a place in his heart right next to Janus.

Quip shook off his idle musings and stood, stretching his muscles before he headed back to his office. He had things to do, a war to fight.

~~*~*~*

Emmeline possessed a power greater than Karton had anticipated, and the child would soon be beyond his ability to tutor her. She learned quickly and exhibited a control that he had not expected in one so young and with so little training. "Now take a deep breath and hold it. Let it out slowly and just relax. Let the peace fill you." Karton's low voice resonated in the air between himself and his young student who had proven to be an enjoyable pupil.

The young girl did as instructed and after several long minutes of no noise, she opened her eyes and looked up at her teacher. He was nice; she liked him. She would have much preferred being taught by her mother, but Karton was a good teacher. She felt like she was developing much better control over everything, which was good. Her mother had always said how important being in control was; so had her brother.

Emmeline frowned at the memory and felt her eyes tear up. She missed them both so much, but it was a little better now that she and her father had talked about it. He was starting to act more like the father she remembered, but Emmeline knew, the same way she knew lots of things, that he would never, ever be the same.

That made her sad, because her father deserved to be happy. She knew how much he missed her mother and Anwar, and that sometimes he blamed himself for their deaths. She had hugged him and told him it wasn't his fault, and even though he knew she spoke the truth, it didn't help. But Janus made him happy. Janus and her father had always had a good friendship, and she knew that they would for a long, long time.

Her brow creased and she shook her head at the influx of thoughts that were sometimes overwhelming. Emmeline knew she was young and had a knowledge far greater than her years, and sometimes it was confusing. Sometimes she felt like an ancient adult in a child's body, a child of eleven years with the collective understanding of almost all the people and things that would be.

Almost all people... A grin broke out across her face. Janus wasn't like most people. She hardly ever picked up a stray thought or feeling or flash of something that would happen from her father's friend, and Emmeline liked that very much. It was refreshing, and one of the reasons she so enjoyed being with Janus.

"My dear child, what are you thinking about?"

Karton's voice broke into her thoughts, which she shook off to focus on him. "Nothing."

A small smile made Karton's beard twitch as Emmeline smirked. "That was not a 'nothing' look."

"Nothing important." Her eyes studied his face and she cocked her head, trying to decide if she should ask him.

"Go ahead, my dear."

Emmeline dropped her eyes and studied the tabletop, tracing an idle pattern with her fingertip. "Do you know what's going to happen after?"

Karton's eyes narrowed as he detected more than idle curiosity behind her question. "Do you mean after the war is over?" When Emmeline nodded, he asked, "Right after the war is over?"

She looked up into his eyes and shrugged. "Sure."

He ducked his head. "I do."

"Me too." There was a silence until Emmeline swallowed hard and then finally whispered, "What about later?"

Karton leaned forward to hear her better, and then shook his head. "No. My sight does not extend that far. Do you know?"

Emmeline hesitated and finally breathed out her next word so very quietly. "Yes."

He waited a beat or two but when nothing else was forthcoming, he leaned even closer and replied, just as softly, "Do you want to tell me? Whatever it is, it can't be that bad, my dear."

She looked up then, right into his eyes which were so very close, and he saw in stark detail the burden that this knowledge was for her.

"It is."

"Tell me."

* ~ * ~ * ~ * ~ *

Janus's gaze drifted around the clearing, not really focusing on any one thing. Her mind was otherwise occupied with trying to decide what their course of action would be. Things had changed drastically. With Lucius out of commission and most of their supplies gone, she admitted to herself that the chances of them succeeding in their mission were slim.

She wasn't used to relying on other people to carry out portions of her missions, but Janus knew that she would not be able to complete this one on her own. Therefore, sending the rest of her team back to the safety of the ship was out of the question. Janus's eyes swept over to the small blonde who was curled up in sleep no more than a hand's breadth away. Even had she wanted to go in alone, she was pretty certain that Barker wouldn't allow it.

Janus blew out a breath as once again her mind stalled in the same spot. *What options are left?* She looked up at the lightening sky and knew that soon Warber and Samson would wake, and then Barker, once the sounds of movement drifted into her sleeping mind. And then they'd all look to her for a solution, their next move; she didn't have anything to tell them.

Warber and Samson got up and started moving around as Janus continued to sit and dissect every scenario that her mind constructed. Eventually, Barker stirred and stretched her body, making cute little morning sounds that caused Janus to smile a little bit. Lucius let out a grumble as well and situated himself on the ground, finding the energy to throw a disdainful look at his badly broken leg.

Janus was aware of the moment when they were all settled and waiting for her to join them, so she refocused her thoughts and turned to face them. "I am not sure what ta do now." She knew that honesty was the best way to start off; maybe they'd be able to see something she couldn't. "We do not 'ave our supplies and we are short of personnel, and there is more goin' on 'ere than any of us know."

"I guess we can't really just pack up and leave, huh?"

The semi-joking comment came from Barker and everyone acknowledged, privately at least, that they would very much like to do just that – go home and be done with the whole thing. At the same time, they all realized that the threat needed to be eliminated before anyone else lost their lives or got hurt.

Warber looked up at the sky and scratched his neck. "I guess we don't know what else is in that mountain?" The ensuing silence gave him all the answer he needed.

"And we have no real way of finding out," Samson chimed in, as he kicked at the ground. "Going in there without any intel would be suicide."

"Aye."

Lucius fingered the staff that was stretched out beside him and thought about the earthquake that had disrupted their peaceful night. "What about this mining thing? It must be a massive operation to have caused what happened last night. Is there any way we can find out where they're working and...I don't know..." His thought process reached a dead end.

Warber's eyebrow crept up as his mind started working over that idea. He reached over to one of their two remaining bags and checked inside. The explosives remaining were limited in amount, but there was enough to cause significant damage if they were used in the right places. He looked up at Janus to see that she had been following the same line of thinking and was starting to formulate a plan.

Barker looked between the two of them and then threw a glance at Samson to see that he was as baffled as she was. "What? What is it?"

Janus looked over at her and a small smile shaped her lips. "The mine shafts. They 'ave ta originate under the mountain and extend far ta cause an earthquake. It would depend on 'ow long they 'ave been minin', but if we could find the weak points we might be able ta...." Janus stopped speaking and opened her mouth a few times, seemingly searching for the correct words.

"Open a massive sinkhole, basically."

As Warber finished the explanation, Barker blinked in some surprise as her mind started to provide vivid pictures of the damage that would result. "And if that happened, everything inside the mountain would be killed?"

"Aye. 'T'would be like another earthquake, except with a whole mountain fallin' on yer 'ead."

"Huh." The sound escaped Samson, who leaned back on his braced arms and considered the situation, ultimately approving with a slight nod of his head.

Janus called up what she remembered of the mountain and began to pose potential flaws in the plan. It was not likely that the land directly underneath the mountain was so unstable that simply blowing out the supports for the mine shafts would cause the whole thing to come down. But, if she could give the explosives a little help...maybe they could be successful. She nodded, then froze as her senses detected a presence that was steadily making its way towards them. Janus looked up and her eyes locked onto one area, staring in a mixture of surprise and disbelief.

Everyone else picked up on her sudden alertness and started looking around, reflexively reaching for weapons. Barker looked up at Janus and tried to figure out what she could be sensing that was causing the emotions Barker was picking up on. She was fairly sure that whatever it was wasn't out to hurt them, because there was no sense of danger around her friend. It was more like a curious, half hopeful and half incredulous expression that Barker was certain no one else could even distinguish from Janus's normal stoic indifference.

Janus stood slowly but remained where she was, and soon they all could hear a quiet rustling that bespoke of people approaching, people who walked on two legs and were definitely not Ebokras. It was another set of long, almost breathless seconds before the branches of a tree parted and a shadow fell into their camp, followed by a group of four people. A group that stopped uncertainly on the very edge of the clearing and stared at Janus, who herself was staring back, mouth slightly open and such shock on her face that it was obvious to everyone.

A group that Samson looked at in some surprise as he noted the telltale platinum tracings that marked the newcomers as members of

Janus's species.

Barker's eyes widened as she stood and glanced back and forth between Janus and the small group. The man standing in the lead had a small smile on his face that was growing steadily with each second that passed. Green eyes drifted over to see a similar thing happening on Janus's face.

"Gregor." Janus breathed the name out quietly and then moved forward. The two almost collided in a hug that lasted much longer than anyone would have expected before they pulled back with full-blown smiles on their faces. Janus jerked her head and moved back to her spot, followed by Gregor and his followers. "What are ya doin' 'ere?"

"Looking for you." Gregor's eyes studied everyone else in the clearing, pausing a little longer on the blonde woman who bore the unmistakable markings of his species. He felt his eyebrows creep upward as he tested the space between the blonde and his friend. He briefly lost his concentration as he was hit by the shock of Janus having found her half.

Gregor shook his head clear and rubbed his face as he recaptured his train of thought. "That little speech of yours back home riled the people up Janus, mostly the young ones and those who were the staunchest supporters of your father. And your brother. Nulas pulled himself together and challenged Taykio."

Janus gave him a pointed look and Gregor chuckled. "So I had to kick him into action, but he did act. It took a while to settle things and then Nulas contacted Quip, who told us where you were and that he thought you might need a hand."

Barker wondered where Quip would have gotten that impression before her mind landed on the obvious answer. Patrik. He was at Jopus Prime and she knew that both she and Janus had been throwing off some pretty strong emotions since their arrival on the mining planet. Unbidden, an image of a lake rose in Barker's mind and she pushed it down with savage determination. She decided that it was natural for Patrick to pick up on their distress and then report to Quip that he thought Janus might be in serious trouble.

"Ah am glad ya are 'ere."

"Does that mean you have a plan?"

"Aye." Janus turned and looked at Warber who was crouched next to the injured Lucius. "Ya stay 'ere and take care of Lucius. The rest a ya, follow me." Janus stood, scooped up the pack that held their explosives, and started out of the clearing. Everyone else scrambled up and filed out after Janus, who trekked them directly to the mountain without stopping.

Gregor gazed up at the monstrosity, his head tipping way back, and then turned a skeptical eye to his friend. "So?"

Janus squinted and was quiet a moment before she turned and threw the bag at Samson. "Set those where Warber told ya."

The man nodded and sped off, pulling out the little rectangle that Warber had given to him before leaving. It showed him the exact coordinates at which to set the explosives.

Janus turned back to Gregor and motioned him closer. "Ya all 'ave ta spread out 'round this side of the mountain in a semi-circle. We are goin' ta take the top right off."

Gregor's eyes widened as he realized exactly what Janus was thinking of doing, and then he nodded and barked out a few quick orders to the people he had brought with him. They moved off quickly, sensing as Janus did, that the attack needed to be initiated as quickly as possible. There was a rumbling beneath the surface of the planet that was getting ready to explode into violent action by the Ebokras.

It was only ten minutes later when Samson jogged back into sight and stopped, his feet shifting nervously as Janus and the others prepared themselves. Barker slipped up next to him and they shared a brief look before returning their attention to the little group of platinum people, who were all standing with their heads lowered, looking relaxed.

As if the whole thing was choreographed, Gregor raised his arms slowly, then the woman standing to his left did the same. Around the line it went until Janus raised her arms up to the sky.

Barker felt her eyebrow creep up as her mind supplied pictures of ritual sacrifices and whatnot that had been carried out in Earth's early history. That's exactly what it looked like to her.

The familiar blue cloud started to take shape around Janus's hands, growing in size and the colour darkening until it was bigger than Barker ever remembered seeing before. A cloud was also forming around the hands of Janus's friends, each in a different colour. Gregor's was a bright red, and the others had green, yellow, and orange. Each cloud got bigger and bigger until their very edges touched one other, small tendrils swirling together in an odd dance.

Their faces tilted up to the sky, necks stretched, and Barker caught the slight arc of energy that started to jump up and out of their fingertips. With each passing second, the tendrils of energy grew larger and longer until they remained visible depictions of their power and extended out into the sky to travel up through the colourful clouds.

As she caught a feeling from Janus that was her cue, Barker elbowed the entranced Samson. "Now!"

It took only a second before the man responded and pressed the button on the small rectangle that detonated the explosives he had planted.

As the sounds of the explosions pierced the air, the energy surged upward from the extended hands, up and up until it impacted upon the very peak of the mountain with a thundering roar that pounded against Barker's eardrums.

The air became charged with electricity, the hair on her arms and neck standing on end, her skin tingling with the feel of it. The blonde watched as the mountain shuddered and then collapsed in on itself, the sides and top falling as the energy created by Janus and her people bombarded the rock which was far too weak to stand up under such an assault.

Suddenly the ground shifted and rumbled as more of the mountain fell. One side rippled and then succumbed to gravity, the boulders thundering down the steep rock face and buffeting the ground with enough force to send vibrations up Barker's legs. Her eyes widened as she realized that things seemed to be getting out of control, and then she was on the ground, a warm and gasping body crouched over hers, hot breath streaming past her ear.

She closed her eyes and tried to curl up into a small, protective ball, concentrating fiercely on that connection between her and Janus, praying that she wouldn't feel any fear or pain. An eternity passed with her there on the ground, Samson above her, until a silence fell and the world stopped shaking.

He moved slowly and carefully as he unwrapped himself from around the ensign, and Barker could feel the sun on her back as she untucked her body and rolled onto her back. She gazed around, seeing a scattering of smaller sized rocks around them and larger boulders closer to what had been the mountain. Her eyes stopped there and stared. It was completely gone, leaving just a mound of granite monoliths that she didn't think would even reach as high as her shoulders. That was all that was left.

"Good God," Samson breathed out as he too took in the area.

Barker glanced at him and assessed the spattering of cuts and bruises that he had taken in her place. Before she could comment, she registered that something was missing and she surged upward. Janus, Gregor, and the other three Platinum People were nowhere to be seen. "Janus!" She started picking her way through the maze of rocks, following the unmistakable tug that linked her to Janus.

Samson followed and almost ran into her back as Barker stopped suddenly. He looked over her head and saw the woman he had at first hated and despised, and now found himself grudgingly liking, sitting on the ground with hardly a speck of dust on her. As he hung back and kept watch, Barker ran forward and slid on her knees.

Barker placed a hesitant hand on Janus's leg, her eyes on the quiet, composed face. Janus was seated in her classic meditation pose, looking for all the world like she wasn't even in her own skin. The blonde bit her lip and made a simple choice as she took up the same position and wrapped her hand around Janus's wrist. She closed her eyes and concentrated, trying to do exactly as Janus had taught her. It was hard to release her mind and let it float away, but slowly a sense of detachment grew in her body and before Barker knew it, her mind was racing across a world that was at once strange and familiar.

She found Janus easily there in that world and reassured herself that her tall friend was indeed all right. Then they were racing back to their bodies as a sudden sense of urgency from Janus's body called their minds back.

Barker felt a rush work its way through her body, which jerked as her eyes popped open and a small gasp left her mouth. "Whoa!" The blonde ensign had hardly a second to process her feelings or the experience she had just had before Janus was surging up to her feet and studying her surroundings with more than normal attentiveness.

Samson picked up on it and looked around nervously as he fingered his gun. "What? What is it?"

"We 'ave ta get out a 'ere."

Barker managed to regain her feet as well and looked around. "What about..."

Just then Gregor's head popped up over the top of a rock and his body followed. The other three appeared as well and all converged on Janus in a matter of seconds. They knew as well as Janus, that it was time to leave.

Samson took one look at their faces and executed a swift about-face, starting back to the clearing at a slow trot. Warber stood up as he heard them come barging through the underbrush and lent a hand down to Lucius. Everything was packed and ready to go in the event that they needed to make a quick exit. It sounded like they did.

Janus hardly stopped as they slid into the clearing, just headed forward, picked up Lucius, and started out of the clearing again at a run. Lucius didn't protest, just wrapped his arms around her neck and held on as they started flying across the terrain.

It seemed like hours before Janus slowed and finally stopped, set her cargo down carefully and looked around. Barker fell gratefully to the ground and tried to catch her breath.

"What is going on?" Warber finally asked as Janus sat and relaxed a little, seemingly confident that they were safe. "Did it work?"

"Aye, it worked. We did not get 'em all and those left are comin'."

"Wonderful."

Samson let out a breath and looked back the way they had come. "We can't outrun them back to the ship."

"No, we will 'ave ta fight."

Gregor ran his hands through his hair and shook out his legs. "I think the point is to minimize the amount of fighting we must do. Right?"

"Aye."

He nodded and studied the ground. "There are still a large number of them, but compared to how many there were before..."

"We're in good shape?" Lucius ventured as he carefully situated his leg.

"Yes." It was true. From the sense of disturbance he had first gotten, Gregor knew that they had probably been looking at several million Ebokras that inhabited the mountain. Compared with the sensation he got now when he probed the area, he would estimate that only a few hundred thousand remained. Considerable progress had been made.

"Gregor, where is yer ship?"

He looked up at his friend and jerked his head back the way they had come. "Pretty far that way."

"Ya will come with us."

Gregor nodded and smiled. He had missed Janus all the time that she had been gone and it felt good, felt right, to be back with her doing this together, even if there were several other people involved as well. They all seemed pretty nice. He couldn't quite contain his curiosity about Barker and Janus; he really wanted to know how they had first met and what Janus thought about the whole thing. It was obvious that they had both embraced the connection between them or else it would not be so strong. He studied it with his sixth sense and smiled as he realized how strong their bond was. It rivaled that of Janus's parents.

Barker sat down next to Warber, who was fiddling with his little rectangle once again. "Whatcha doing?"

He looked up and smiled, shifting so that she had a better view of his instrument. "I'm checking to see what kind of damage they did. See here?" He pointed at a long network of snaking tunnels. "These are the mine shafts. And this is where the mountain was. This was before Janus and the others did...what they did." He pressed a button and the screen flickered briefly before popping up again. "Now, these mine shafts collapsed here, which set off a reaction..." Warber traced the lines all the way back to the mountain and showed Barker how most of them had collapsed entirely. "Without the support structure and with the little push Janus gave it, the mountain... Well, you saw what happened."

Barker nodded, then looked up as Janus stood and picked up Lucius.

"We 'ave ta go."

Without much fuss, everyone organized themselves and resumed their hike back to the ship at a much more sedate pace. They were still walking very quickly, but as far as Barker was concerned, it was better than running.

Lucius looked around from his comfortable perch in her arms and grinned, just a little bit. "I could walk, Janus."

Blue eyes looked down at him and an eyebrow quirked briefly before she returned her attention to her surroundings.

Lucius let out a sigh and settled himself for the trip back.

Barker found herself walking next to Samson and was a little surprised that it didn't bother her as much as it previously would have. He was not a bad guy when he wasn't snarling on about aliens and how evil they were, yadda, yadda, yadda. She wondered how much longer his mellowing would last.

Gregor looked around and then jogged up to the front where Janus was leading the way. He only had to look at her to communicate his thoughts and received a slight nod in return. "How much further?"

Janus looked up at the sky and judged how long they had been on the move and how much of that time they had spent running. "Ah think only a little bit more."

He nodded and shifted his shoulders, not at all liking the feeling he was picking up. Something was brewing. "Good."

Janus stopped suddenly and Gregor plowed into her. He quickly moved aside and looked around as the sudden rise of a disturbance grated on his senses. Janus set Lucius down to lean against a tree and motioned to Gregor, who took up a defensive stance.

Everyone else was in a state of similar alertness, not needing to be told that they were about to be attacked. There was a stillness, a silence in the forest that smacked of something not being quite right.

It happened suddenly, a quick explosion from the bushes as grey bodies bounded outward with deadly intent. They didn't make a sound, not letting out their signature screech, and the observation sent a slight chill down Warber's back as he engaged his first enemy.

Janus felt a grim determination fill her as she fought, realizing that the Ebokras had changed tactics yet again. They were bounding in and out of the clearing in rapid succession, taking quick slashes at them that were meant to either disable or kill. It seemed that they had learned from previous encounters and were no longer sticking around to be slaughtered. Despite that, the Ebokras were losing. Guns were far superior to the Ebokras' style of close quarter fighting.

The situation striking a false chord with her, something made Janus turn and take a quick survey of her friends. There had to be something else going on, there had to be. If there wasn't, why the drastic change in tactics, why had they been able to take the mountain down so easily? Not one alien had emerged from the mountain to try and stop them from blowing the mines and Janus wondered why. Was there something else that the Ebokras were after?

A ripple in the energy alerted her and Janus ducked sharply as an Ebokras swung, its eyes wild and its movements erratic. Janus planted her balance foot and delivered a kick that broke its neck. She turned and saw that Gregor was aware of the disturbance as well, she could see it in his face, but he was also thoroughly engaged.

A weight on her back sent her to the ground and her head impacted painfully on a rock. Janus's eyes searched wildly and she yelled out a warning to the others as she sensed the descent of a claw toward her back. Her body fought without any conscious direction from her mind. Janus rolled onto her back, was lifted again and smashed back down on the ground. Her vision blurred and darkened, and as the disturbance in the energy grew, she knew it was too late.

It built with violent intensity and the world fairly thrummed with tension as the ground started to shake and rumble again.

Lucius's eyes widened as the tree he was propped against started to vibrate, sending leaves down on his head.

Samson swore colourfully as an alien knocked him to the ground and leaned heavily on his chest, staring down with oddly triumphant eyes.

Warber let out a feral growl and jumped, only to be plucked out of midair by an Ebokras whose claws raked painfully down his arms and chest.

As she backed away from an attacker, Barker tripped. She spent one fleeting moment looking for Janus, finally locating her on the ground, seemingly unconscious and at the mercy of a crouching Ebokras.

The earth trembled and the air roared and darkened, as the world fell out from beneath them.

Chapter 19

He groaned and rolled over onto his back, opening his eyes and blinking a few times when all that registered in his vision was inky blackness. He took in another deep breath and coughed as his lungs were filled with the smell of rock dust along with the stench that he associated with the Ebokras. That's when Samson decided he wasn't dead. No pleasant afterlife he could think of would have the Ebokras, and there were far worse things in the world that he imagined would inhabit his Hell.

With that decided, he sat up and tried to take stock of his situation. Looking up and not detecting the slightest bit of light, he figured he had to be pretty deep underground. He gingerly moved his limbs, glad to find nothing broken, then winced as his head expressed its discomfort.

Samson moved his hands along the stony ground and pulled back suddenly when he encountered a slimy ooze. "Ewww..." Disgusted, he shook his hand in an effort to remove the substance. Soft breathing attracted his attention and he froze, different scenarios running through his mind. When he didn't detect any other sound, he stood carefully, quietly, and continued to listen, walking very slowly toward the noise. Sounds of shuffling set his heart to beating faster and Samson reached about him, desperately seeking something he could use as a weapon. There was something there, he knew he wasn't imagining it. Closer and closer he crept, until finally he ran into something that jerked and screamed.

"AHH!"

Two voices yelled in tandem and there was a brief, pregnant pause, as those voices were recognized.

"Samson?"

"Barker?"

There was a dual sigh of relief and Samson reached out a hand to feel his way forward again. "Where are you?" A hand gripped his wrist and then the blonde was just there, in front of him, the outline of her face barely visible.

"Hi."

She was smiling; Samson could hear it in her voice. He cleared his throat to respond. "Hi."

"Dark in here, huh?"

"Um...yeah."

She sniffled and rubbed her nose as she looked around, trying to ascertain where they were. "I don't suppose you have a—"

"You think I carry a flashlight with me every minute of every day?" Samson could feel her looking up at him as his hand went to one of his side pockets and pulled out a very small cylinder, which he flipped on and shone in her face. "Well, I do." He grinned and then turned the light on their surroundings.

It was a long tunnel with irregular walls but a fairly smooth floor, and a very solid looking roof. Which raised the question, if they had fallen down, how had they gotten into this particular tunnel? And where were the others?

"So," he turned to face the blonde beside him, "which way do you want to go?"

Barker's eyes flicked briefly between their two choices and she shrugged, then pointed in the direction they were facing.

* ~ * ~ * ~ * ~ *

Slowly and fuzzily, Lucius became conscious, and realized that he couldn't be in a worse position. He was on his back with his lower back and legs propped at a very odd angle on a large pile of rocks. His left arm was trapped between two sturdy looking rocks, and he couldn't move at all. Because his arm was stuck, he couldn't lift his upper body to try and move his legs; because his broken leg was sending painful jolts down his entire body, he couldn't get enough leverage to try and remove the rocks from around his arm.

He shifted a little, trying to dislodge the pointy stone that was pressing into his spine, then looked up at the dimly seen ceiling of his new little prison. "Well, you've really done it this time, huh?"

The walls were silent.

"How do you plan to get yourself out of this mess?"

Again there was no answer and his eyes flicked about, not seeing anything within reach that would be of use to him. He sighed and turned his mind back to the problem. After several long minutes in which he listened to the odd, irregular pattering of small stones falling from somewhere, he sighed again and pursed his lips. "Guess there's always the old fashioned way." He took in a large breath, held it for a brief second, and let it out in a bellowing, "Help!"

* ~ * ~ * ~ * ~ *

Barker squinted as she gently probed her link to Janus; it felt extremely subdued. It wasn't that there was nothing there, there was. It was just a very faint...trickle, as if something was interfering with whatever made it work. She was a little worried because, other than that weak sensation, she wasn't feeling much of anything. Normally, when Janus was just sitting around and didn't have cause to feel anything extreme, Barker received a sensation of peaceful warmth that curled up inside her and made her feel absolutely wonderful. That wasn't happening. What she was getting seemed to be a simple acknowledgment that Janus was out there somewhere, alive, but nothing else.

Barker pursed her lips as she thought that over, a little perplexed over exactly what her mind was telling her. She shook her head and rubbed the back of her neck, wondering if maybe she had smacked her head on a rock and that had scrambled her brain. She was aware that Samson was walking beside her, probably giving her odd looks, and she shifted her eyes up to him to confirm her supposition. His eyes skittered away immediately as he gently cleared his throat and shifted his shoulders.

The blonde woman sighed and, tired of the silence and rhythmic scuffling of their boots, said the first thing that popped into her mind. "So, what's your favorite colour?"

Samson threw her a look before refocusing on their path and scratching his ear. "Um...green." He glanced at her again out of the corner of his eye. "You?"

"Purple...or maybe blue." A smile creased her face as she nodded. "Yeah, blue."

"Mm." He grunted and kicked a stone.

"Favorite animal?"

There was a silence before his gruff voice replied, "Eagle."

"I like cougars."

Samson just nodded this time and they walked on in a heavy silence. When the next question came, he stopped, spun toward his companion, and just stared at her with his brow wrinkled in confusion.

Barker looked right back at him and shrugged. "We don't have anything else to do. Might as well get to know each other. Right?" She could see him chewing on his lip a little before he gave a small, hesitant nod, and turned again to continue walking.

She smiled and sniffled, thinking briefly before another question floated up into the air. "What do you think about..."

~~*~*~*

As his last desperate yell echoed off the walls, Lucius closed his eyes and took in a few gasping breaths. He had no idea how long he had been lying there, yelling, he just knew that his throat was getting hoarse and painful jolts were traveling the entire length of his body. He prepared himself to holler again, but paused as the sound of footsteps reached his ears. Lucius strained his eyes and twisted his head, attempting to see who was coming. "Who's there?"

There was no answer, just the continued sounds of someone approaching.

"Hello?"

Lucius turned his head as far as he could, but finally gave up and relaxed his body to wait for his potential savior. A head finally popped into his vision and a sigh of relief escaped him. "Gregor! Am I ever glad to see you."

The man smiled a little and crouched down to start removing the rocks from Lucius's arm. It took barely a minute before Gregor was helping Lucius to balance on his uninjured leg and gently work the kinks from his body.

"You all right?"

"Yeah, yeah, I'm fine now. Thanks." Lucius looked up at Gregor, his face hard to see in the darkness, and leaned a little closer to see a large cut gracing the side of his platinum marked jaw. "Hey, how come that hasn't healed?"

Gregor wrapped one of Lucius's arms around his neck and started walking slowly and carefully. "There seems to be a slight problem with that down here."

"Why?"

Gregor's eyes flicked about the tunnel and he opened his mouth to answer but stopped suddenly, his body frozen into rigid alertness. Lucius looked around and then ahead of them as the very slim beam of a light became visible. It got closer and closer and soon revealed to them Barker and Samson, who smiled and broke into a slight jog.

"Hey," Barker reached them first and threw a concerned glance at them, "we heard some yelling."

"Um, that was me. I was stuck."

Barker blinked and her eyes shifted to Gregor briefly. "Are you both all right?"

They nodded.

Samson surveyed the tunnel and blew out a breath. "Which way do you all want to go now? There isn't much in the direction we came from."

Before anyone could answer, pounding footsteps were followed by a yell. "Gregor! Gregor!"

They all turned and watched as the woman Gregor had brought with him came stumbling to a halt behind them, breathing hard. "You all have to come. Rijas is trapped; he's in bad shape." Then she was gone.

Gregor handed Lucius off to Barker and took off at a slow jog as the other three started walking slowly in deference to Lucius's broken leg. They had gone hardly ten paces when Samson blew out an annoyed breath, handed the flashlight to Barker, and picked Lucius up.

"Hey!" Lucius squawked, which earned him a glare from Samson.

They caught up with Gregor and the woman in a matter of minutes to see them frantically moving rocks by hand. Samson set Lucius down and he and Barker helped. It seemed like several never-ending hours of digging passed before Gregor finally, finally, removed the last stone, which resulted in a small tunnel through which the trapped Rijas could escape.

Exhausted, the group collapsed and sat in silence. Barker leaned back and studied the rock dust that covered her liberally along with several fresh cuts from the sharp rocks. She shook her head as her mind reviewed the entire trip that would probably end up being one of the most convoluted missions in the history of Jopus Prime. But those sometimes ended up being the best kind of mission.

Poor Rijas. It looked to Barker like he had been almost crushed by the rocks, and both Gregor and the woman were crouched over him with grave concern.

After a few minutes, Gregor came over and sat beside them. "We decided that Rijas and Corrin will stay here while we go look for Janus and Warber."

Barker leaned forward and planted her elbows on her crossed knees. "Why aren't you guys dipping into your usual bag of tricks?"

Gregor stared at her for a long moment before he lowered his eyes and his brow scrunched. "What do you feel right now, in connection with Janus?"

Barker knew exactly what he meant, and had a feeling that he knew exactly what her answer would be. "Not much, just a very small awareness."

Gregor nodded. "Whatever is interfering with you and Janus is doing the same with us. We can't heal down here or do any of our...um...usual bag of tricks."

Samson shook his head as he tried to follow the vague conversation that he didn't understand at all.

Lucius reached out and placed a hand on Gregor's arm. When the man turned to look at him, Lucius lowered his eyes to his broken leg and stumbled through his question. "Um...could you still...are you able to... uh..."

It didn't take much for Gregor to catch on and he nodded. "I could, but you know we don't usually, unless it's something serious..."

Lucius quickly nodded. "I know. But I want to help; I need to help."

Gregor ducked his head and placed his hands above Lucius's broken leg. In hardly a second, he was leaning back. "Okay."

"That's it?"

"Yes. It wasn't a very serious injury and didn't take much energy to heal. Rijas, on the other hand, requires much more than I can tap into now."

Lucius stood very carefully and tested his limb, finding it as good as new. He laughed a little. "Thank you, Gregor."

Gregor didn't answer, just turned to look one last time at Rijas before starting out of the tunnel in a new direction with everyone following.

Barker picked her way carefully around some rocks and chewed on her lip. She hoped they would find Janus and Warber soon. The longer they were missing, the more her gut twisted with a sense of unsettlement. She wondered where they could be.

* ~ * ~ * ~ * ~ *

The rocking motion was what trickled into her brain first, a very faint rocking motion that for a brief moment made Janus think she was on a boat of some kind. Then came the chanting, low rhythmic chanting that grated on her hearing in a most unpleasant way. Finally, she became aware of two things at once: that she was lying on her stomach and that her back hurt, a lot.

Slowly, her mind cleared and she remembered the attack by the Ebokras — that one had been above her, one she had been unable to stop, and that it had dug its very long claw into her back. Then she had fallen, and the entire world had winked into darkness.

Janus allowed her eyes to drift open slowly and they flicked about, taking in her surroundings quickly and without moving the rest of her body thus confirming what she had sensed with her eyes closed. She was on some kind of litter that was being carried by...she couldn't really see who. They were moving through long rock tunnels and the light of sputtering torches threw the walls into flickering shadows that danced oddly and took strange forms that would fuel almost anyone's imaginings.

She turned her head and raised it slightly, managing to get a glimpse of another litter that was just behind and to her left. Squinting a little, she identified Warber stretched out on it, still unconscious. He was hurt, that much Janus knew. She could smell the blood, blood that wasn't her own. Acting on instinct, her body moved upward and toward him to see if he was all right. She had barely risen an inch off the litter when a hand descended on her back, pushing her down with unrelenting strength. Janus fought back and soon more hands were there, pushing on her, and then something tightened across her upper back, something that restricted her movement and kept her tied in place. Janus's breathing became more rapid as she started to lose control and soon she couldn't move at all.

As her body continued to struggle against its bonds in the name of self-preservation, a dark memory rose from the depths of her mind. In Marson, it had been the common practice to take them into the lab and strap them quite firmly to a table. The absolute lack of control over oneself was something that would make anyone almost crazy after an extended amount of time. And then, then the doctor would come in, whistling his jaunty little tune that was off key. He would clatter about for a long while, still whistling, and finally would arrive beside you with a little tray on wheels that held a variety of tools. Then he would cut into you, wherever he felt like it, sometimes with the intent of doing some experiment but often just because he felt like exploring. His victims got nothing for the pain, nothing to sedate them. He relished making his patients scream out in abject terror and agony, and Janus had found herself on his table often. She had only ever yelled out twice.

As those times in prison rose to the forefront of Janus's mind, she kept pulling at the bonds that held her in place and her breathing got louder and raspier. She could feel the skin along her wrists starting to tear and the trickle of blood as it ran down her arms. In the back of her mind, she knew that she was making it worse, that whatever was holding her in place was designed very well and was using her own strength against her.

She didn't care. She wanted out. Immediately.

Warber came to slowly and opened his eyes, taking a good long look at the people who were carrying him. They were short and furry, and had long pointed ears with a darker tuft of fur on the tips. Their cheeks were round and pudgy and came together at their mouth, which was a small, yellow beak.

He blinked and carefully looked around, getting a glimpse of Janus on another litter. He squinted as he saw her struggling, her eyes wild. His hearing returned with a sudden rush of sound that brought her harsh breathing to his ears. When he caught sight of her hand straining against being tied in place, he knew immediately what was causing his friend's reaction. Warber watched as Janus suddenly tensed and one of the furry things placed something on her back. Then it shook up a small bottle of some kind, popped off the top, and poured it down her back.

Janus froze as something cold and slightly wet was placed on her back, just below her neck. She could hear a splashing sound and then liquid was poured down her back to seep into the wound that was there. She heard the hissing first, the hissing sound that occurs when acid burns through something, and then the sizzling followed by the blinding, white hot pain of a million knives slicing into her back at once. She screamed.

Jaw and fists clenched, Warber's ears reverberated with the sound of her yell, the likes of which he had not heard in a long, long time. He continued to watch as she passed out from the agony, and then they were moving again. Warber stayed very still and kept his eyes closed, hoping that maybe they'd leave him alone. He could feel the deep gouges on his chest and arms from the Eborkas' claws and concentrated on that pain as they continued down the tunnel, their pace set by the annoying chanting.

* ~ * ~ * ~ * ~ *

Gregor paused at yet another fork in the tunnel and threw a look over his shoulder at the people behind him, silently polling them for their opinion. He received several responses, ranging from a shrug to fingers pointing in both possible directions. Gregor sighed and picked one.

"This is ridiculous. We could wander around in here for days and not find them," Samson carped.

"We don't have any other choice," Lucius responded as he continued to study a powdery substance on the wall that he had already noticed several times during their trek. He and Samson almost plowed into Barker's back as she had stopped walking and stood looking straight ahead with a peculiar look on her face. Gregor was in a similar stance.

"What is it?"

"Shh." Barker held up her hand to silence them and crept forward, straining her eyes to see into the blackness. There was something there; Gregor sensed it, too.

Slowly, a patch of the darkness shifted, resolving into a small, furry form that pattered toward them, an odd chittering sound issuing from its beak. It stopped a foot in front of Gregor, looked up at him with large golden coloured eyes, and then hopped forward to clasp his hand. The creature turned and started back the way it had come with Gregor in tow, who looked over his shoulder and shrugged helplessly. Barker started moving after them and almost screamed when another little creature popped out of the shadows and took her hand. Two more followed and latched onto Samson and Lucius. The only clothing they wore were little vests of varying colours with two buttons on them that were not fastened.

The furry little things led them through winding tunnels in silence, and it wasn't long before they were all standing in a large chamber that was well lit and appeared to have only the one entrance. The creatures chittered to one another before one moved off into the wall and disappeared. They proceeded in single file until the last remaining creature pointed at the wall and tugged on Gregor's hand.

As they moved closer, Barker shone the flashlight on the wall and revealed a small crevice, close to the ground, which might just barely permit Samson's broad shoulders to pass. They shared speculative looks before the furry thing chittered at them, sounding agitated. Barker sighed and got onto her stomach, then wriggled slowly and carefully through the opening. She emerged on the other side to find their other guides waiting there, sitting on the ground with small legs crossed and hands clasped. *Interesting little creatures*, she decided.

Lucius came out of the crevice next, followed by Gregor and then finally Samson, who was now covered liberally with dust and dirt and a few fresh scrapes. The last little furry thing popped through the small opening and led them down a long, wide hall that showed evidence of frequent use. Curiosity piqued, they followed, and stood stunned as they finally reached their destination. It was an enormous cavern that had small dwellings built into the walls, stretching from the ground all the way up the rocky walls. There were other buildings on the ground that were larger, and Barker supposed they were for common usage.

"It is good to see that our home still inspires awe."

They started at the deep, rough voice and turned to see yet another one of the furry denizens standing before them, this one with greying fur and a posture that was slightly hunched.

"Who are you people?"

The elder ducked his head to answer. "We call ourselves Zaire."

"Are our friends here?"

"They are. One of them is not in the best of conditions."

Barker felt her heartbeat race at his declaration as her eyes flicked desperately around the cavern, searching for some sign of Janus or Warber. "Why? What happened?"

The elder turned to her and looked up with his large round eyes. "You were fighting the Scourge were you not?"

"If you mean the Ebokras, then yes, we were."

"We are very aware of the Scourge and learned of the ambush they had planned for you. We intervened, hoping to help you avoid it altogether, but we were too late. The best we could do was get you to safety. The two who were badly hurt, we brought back here with us."

Gregor shook his head and rubbed his neck. "So, you're fighting the Ebokras? That's why you helped us?"

"Yes."

"Why do you fight them?" The question came from Samson who looked typically skeptical.

The elder changed his focus and Barker swore she saw his beak somehow smile.

"Why do *you*?" There was a brief silence before the elder spoke again, "To understand us, you must know our past."

"So tell us," Barker said.

"I think you would like to see your friends first. Come."

* ~ * ~ * ~ * ~ *

Karton paused outside Quip's door and took a deep breath before knocking and entering. He sat down very precisely and folded his hands. "We may have a major problem."

The seriousness in the man's voice attracted all of Quip's attention and he closed down his computer screen and turned to face Karton. "What is it?"

"You are aware of Emmeline's gift?"

"Yes, of course."

Karton nodded and continued. "The other day she shared something she had seen with me. It deals with after the war, at least a year There will be a sickness, a plague that quickly becomes pandemic."

"Okay. What does this have to do with what's happening right now?"

Karton shifted in his seat and cleared his throat. "She said she saw flashes of faces, specifically Janus, Barker, Lucius, and Samson, plus a few others she couldn't identify. That's the exact group that's out there now."

"And?"

"I guided Emmeline through a meditative state that allowed her to reexamine her vision slowly and talk to me at the same time. We learned that on their way back from their mission, they will fly through a nebula that contains an asteroid belt. There they will pick up some kind of virus or disease, or whatever you want to call it, and all of them will become carriers. It will spread unabated, and in a year people will begin to die." Karton finished explaining what they knew and counted under his breath, waiting for the explosion he knew was about to occur.

"Why did you wait so damn long to tell me all this!"

Quip's yell was loud enough to make the walls vibrate and Karton waited patiently for Quip to be quiet before he answered. "You have to understand. When we see things, it usually isn't so that we can change the event; it is so we can prepare ourselves for what is to come. More often than not, trying to change the course of what is to be only makes things worse. When Emmeline told me, once I had all the information, I spent a long time meditating on the matter. I came to the conclusion it was best to tell you."

Quip took a few deep breaths to calm himself and closed his eyes to try and get the vision of strangling Karton out of his mind. There were already so many problems to worry about; this was absolutely the last thing he needed on his plate. "What do you think we should do?"

"I think you should send an interceptor ship or two over to the planet they're on to prevent them from entering any and all nebulae."

"I don't have anyone available." Quip thought about the ships that were docked on Jopus Prime, knowing that if they were in port, they probably were unable to fly.

"Come on, Quip, you have an entire planet's resources; there must be someone!"

Quip shook his head. "I..."

"Sir?" His aide was standing at the door looking uncertain. "There's a communication for you on channel three."

Quip turned and flipped on his computer, calling up channel three and almost grinning at who he saw there. "Captain Lang. I trust you're in good shape?"

The captain of the *Pro Re Nata* grinned and gave a small salute.

"Yes, sir. Tryst and her people have done a wonderful job getting us all cleaned up and working again."

"So your ship would stand up under another mission right away? Nothing too serious, mind you."

"Yes, sir, I believe it would. There are only minor repairs left to be made, and we can probably do those en route."

"Excellent." He looked up at Karton briefly before returning his attention to the captain. "Here's what you need to do..."

* ~ * ~ * ~ * ~ *

The elder led them around the corner where they saw Warber perched on a small cot with a scowl etched firmly on his face as he tried to fend off a little creature that was pulling insistently on his arm with the intent of bandaging it. He saw them and swiftly stood. "Where's Janus?"

Lucius's eyebrow crept up; he considered that to be an odd thing for Warber to ask. "We haven't seen her yet."

The elder poked his head out from around Samson's leg to look at the difficult patient. *Though not as difficult as the other one.* "You are concerned for your friend?"

Warber looked around for a moment, trying to locate the voice that had spoken to him, and finally saw the furry head. "Yes, I want to see her. Now."

"Very well, this way." He started walking and Warber wasted no time in following.

Barker ran two steps to catch up and looked up at his angry face. "What is it?"

He looked down at her and debated briefly, not wanting to say anything that might upset Barker or possibly set her off. He didn't know if these little creatures were friends or enemies, but it looked like they intended to help. What he had seen happen to Janus rubbed him the wrong way, but he readily admitted that he could have interpreted the entire situation inaccurately. Janus had been pretty...well, not lucid.

They stepped inside one of the larger huts. It was very warm and people were scattered throughout, all of them participating in the strange chanting. The elder led them into a smaller room off the main hall that just barely managed to accommodate them all. Samson hung back in the main anteway.

Janus was stretched out on her stomach on a small cot like the one Warber had recently occupied. The back of her shirt was ripped open, which displayed a large gash that started just below her neck and ended around her lower back.

Barker gasped and kneeled beside Janus, looking closer and seeing flesh that appeared as if it had been burned. "What did you do?" she whispered as she reached out a hesitant hand. Janus was sweating, but her breathing sounded normal and her face appeared peaceful.

"Yes, what did you do?" Warber echoed, his voice containing much more menace than the blonde's.

The elder took his place on a small wooden chair and settled himself to sit for a long time. "Before you jump to any conclusions, let me explain. Many days before any of you arrived on this planet, we heard news that the Scourge had in its possession a new kind of poison that they intended to put in our water supply. Some of our patrols had already fallen victim to it because the Scourge doused their claws in the vile stuff and so it got into their wounds. We were unable to save their lives as it acted quickly, with horrifying results.

"When we found you both and were bringing you back here to safety, it came to our attention that your friend here had the poison in her wound. We were surprised that she had not already died and sent someone ahead for our healer who had been searching for a way to at least slow down the action of the poison.

"She awoke and started moving around, which was going to spread the venom more quickly. You see how close that is to the spine."

It was indeed very close, with a portion of white bone actually visible in spots.

"So we tried to hold her still, but she is very strong, as I'm sure you know. Since there was no one present who could communicate with her, they had to resort to restraining her, which only seemed to make things worse. It was the only thing we thought to do that would keep her from inflicting serious and possibly irreversible damage to herself.

"The healer arrived soon after with the only potential way of slowing the poison – to burn it out with a substance that is abundant around here. That is what we did."

Barker felt tears pooling in her eyes as she studied Janus closer, seeing the bruises around her wrists and tears in her skin. This close, she could feel some of the anguish that was radiating from Janus and it made her stomach churn.

Warber clenched his jaw as he mulled that over, finally deciding that it sounded like the truth. "Did it work?"

The elder was silent for long, long moments before he released a sigh and shook his head. "We do not know. Your friend is very resilient, as evidenced by the fact that she was still alive when we found her. As close as that wound is to a vital area, if it had been one of us, we would have perished immediately. So, the antidote might have helped or it might just be her, doing it all herself."

Lucius grimaced as the chanting continued and finally had to ask, "What is with the bad singing?"

The elder's head cocked and his beak opened. "It is part of our healing method. We believe it helps to put the soul at ease. There is nothing more we can do for your friend. If she is to survive, it will be her own doing."

He stood then and padded over to the door, where he paused briefly. "I have matters I must see to. If you wish to see me, all you need to do is go to the main hall. Anyone there will know you want me. You should all rest now; it is late. You can use the cots in the main hall. Tomorrow at breakfast, if you wish, I will share our history with you."

Everyone filed out except for Barker, who remained kneeling beside Janus. She put her head down on the cot, her hand unconsciously finding and clasping the larger one beside her. Barker didn't even realize when she fell asleep and found herself drifting off to a place Janus often visited. It was just like she remembered from when they had taken the mountain down. The colours were vibrant, and the whole place seemed safe. She easily followed the river of warmth and was soon wrapped up in strong, warm arms and looking into blue eyes that were open to her alone. "Are you all right?"

"Aye. I will be fine."

"Are you sure? Janus you look so..." Barker stopped talking as her practical mind reared its head and pointed out how ridiculous the situation seemed. She deliberately pushed down those thoughts because she knew this was real, that she was speaking to Janus's mind or essence, or whatever was there with her. Lips descended on her own and Barker found herself forgetting all about what was wrong with Janus, all about her concerns that they wouldn't survive the cosmic chaos they had landed themselves in. It was just the two of them there, together, like it should be, and in that instant everything, the entire world, was simply perfect.

* ~ * ~ * ~ * ~ *

Barker was vaguely aware of someone shaking her and it seemed odd, since as far as she knew she was lying on a bed with Janus curled up behind her and gentle breath warming the back of her neck. The shaking became more insistent, and slowly her world of contentment dissolved and she became aware of a pain in her neck and the warm clasp on her hand. Barker's eyes drifted open and she realized that she was on the floor with her head on Janus's cot, and the two of them were holding hands.

She looked up to see Lucius above her and she stretched herself out slowly, feeling oddly rested despite her position. Barker carefully removed her hand from Janus's and stood, rotating her neck and hearing something pop into place.

"Are you all right?"

Barker looked at him, confused. "Yeah, why wouldn't I be?"

"I just... Last night you were so sad, and you spent the entire night in here. I was...worried."

Barker looked down at Janus and smiled. "She's going to be fine. And I slept very well, thank you."

Lucius still looked concerned, but Barker ignored him and stepped into the main hall where everyone else was up and ready to go. Just as Lucius stepped back into the room, the elder entered from outside and motioned them to follow. They were led across the way into another large building that had tables set up in neat rows all along the walls. He led them to one near the front of the room and motioned them all to sit. "How is our patient doing today?"

Everyone looked to Barker, who grinned and nodded. "She's going to be okay."

The elder didn't question her certainty, simply nodded and once again gave the impression of smiling. "I'm glad to hear that."

When their food came, they spent a time eating before the elder put down his spoon and clasped his hands before him. Everyone else was done and listening intently.

"Our history is not a short one. It starts many thousands of years ago, in the time of my great grandfather's great grandfather. We Zaire were a simple farming people of the land. We took only what we needed and it treated us well in return. Then people came from the sky, the Others, in great ships and with machines the likes of which we had not seen nor experienced before.

"They claimed that they had come in peace, looking for a better way to live. We did not protest, we took them at face value, for we also had no experience of any people from other planets. And it did work for a time – Zaire and the Others coexisted peacefully.

"But then they discovered something they called a mineral. It was in great supply everywhere, and for some reason that they did not share, the Others placed great importance on this 'mineral'. We could not understand what was so important about this thing that they found in rocks, for Zaire had never considered such things.

"The Others started to mine their mineral and we did not protest. But as it became evident how dangerous their mining was, they took us and used us to mine their mineral. Zaire became a people of bondage, but that was not the worst. No, the worst was still to come.

"Slowly, our people started to change. First, our children became more violent and short tempered, and then the newborns started to look...different. We did not know what was happening or why, just that something was wrong. The mutations continued through the generations. Now we know it was because of their mineral. The long term exposure was hurting us." He took a deep breath. "Then, the first of the Scourge was born." The pain at his statement was visible on his face.

A perceptible shock ran around the table as the avid listeners realized what they had just learned: the origin of the Ebokras. No one dared to interrupt the elder with so much as a question of verification.

"We did not call them that at first. They were our friends, our brethren, and they helped what was left of Zaire – the people who had immunity or built up resistance – to overthrow the Others. Finally, when they realized they could not win, the Others left and once again Zaire became a farming people of the land, coexisting with the Scourge.

"There were distinct barriers, though. They stayed on their side of the mountain and we on ours. We did not interact, other than to trade. They continued to mine the mineral themselves, and slowly Zaire became aware of the change in them. They were growing more and more violent and hateful, and after the passing of a few generations, they began to attack us.

"We were no match for them; that is when the Scourge was truly born. That is when they became what they are now, what you have come to know. And Zaire became a people of the shadows, of myth, living in abandoned mine shafts, the very shafts our ancestors mined and suffered in, died in."

The elder turned his eyes to Samson and stared at him for a long, penetrating moment. "Now you know why we fight, for we are their forefathers, their creators, and the destruction they wreak rests solely on our shoulders."

Chapter 20

As everyone else melted away to do something or other, Gregor walked out of the dining hall beside the elder. He looked around the cavern and then bent his head to the small Zaire beside him. "So, this mineral...where is it?"

The elder looked up at Gregor and blinked his large, round yellow eyes. "All around you. It is in every speck of dust and every rock, but only concentrated enough to see in certain areas. Did you see the white powder in the rocks on your way here?"

Gregor cast his mind back. He had been more concerned about Janus and Warber than the rock, but he did remember Lucius taking an interest in the walls and the white veins that traveled through the rock in twisting patterns. "Yes."

"That is the mineral." The elder paused as another...person, Gregor supposed, ran up to them chittering away and sounding very agitated. The elder listened and responded, and after a few moments the person left at a run. The elder turned to look up at Gregor and his beak wiggled a moment before he spoke. "You must excuse me, we have a problem. Please, tell your friends that you are all welcome to stay as long as you need, and that when you are ready we will take you through the tunnels to your ship."

Gregor inclined his head and graced the furry little man with a smile. "Thank you."

The elder simply nodded before he turned and scurried off, all the while chittering out orders in what Gregor supposed was their version of yelling. He smiled as he continued his relaxed walk.

~~*~*~*

Barker headed back to the hut that housed Janus, her curiosity about these Zaire fully engaged but her concern for Janus far greater. She sat next to the cot, noting that nothing much had changed except that the long gash in Janus's back appeared to be not quite as deep or angry looking. The young blonde leaned against the cot and clasped Janus's fingers, comforting both herself and her injured friend. She knew Janus would be fine, there was no doubt about that, but Barker was still worried about how slowly Janus was healing and the fact that she had really been put through the wringer of late.

A small sigh escaped her as her eyes tracked idly along Janus's face, following the lines of her nose and jaw. She supposed, though, that if anyone were going to be the target of the Ebokras, then it should be Janus. She wasn't easy to kill, and although it made Barker's heart clench to see Janus hurt, the ensign knew it would be worse to see a friend die. It helped ease her worry to know that if she really wanted or needed to, she could technically be with Janus in a place that was so real, so vivid, that it was almost...almost like having the actual, physical person standing in front of her.

Barker couldn't wrap her practical mind around the concept or even begin to understand exactly what it was. She just knew that when she was there she felt an incredible sense of peace and happiness, a contentment that had been missing from her life for a long time but had started to come back when she had met Janus and allowed her feelings free rein.

She put her face down on the pillow and gave a small sigh of happiness as she closed her eyes briefly and took a breath that filled her lungs with a scent that would always, always mean Janus. The blonde leaned forward and placed a gentle kiss on Janus's head and then allowed herself to speak the phrase that had not yet passed her lips when Janus was present. "I love you." She breathed it past Janus's ear and then sat back and clasped the strong hand, fully prepared to wait until her friend awakened.

~~*~*

Patrik wandered down the hall of Jopus Prime, whistling a tune that had popped into his head. He was bored and he would admit it to anyone who would listen. His daughter was once again in session with Karton, the two of them spending more time together than Patrik thought necessary. He wasn't sure, but he thought that maybe something had happened, that one of them had seen something...disturbing. But he knew from being married to Troi that he shouldn't ask, that the likelihood of getting an answer was slim to nil. So, he had resigned himself to walking around until he got some brilliant idea about what to do with himself. Two steps past a doorway, he paused and then backed up and turned to look in.

It was one of the shuttle repair bays, and a familiar form was crouched on the floor by a fighter. Kodiac. Patrik hadn't seen him around in days. He walked into the room, clearing his throat softly to get the man's attention.

Kodiac stood and smiled when he saw Patrik standing there uncertainly with his hands in his pockets. "Patrik, what are you doing here?"

"Nothing much. I'm bored, actually. Haven't seen you around in a while."

Kodiac nodded and wiped his hands on his pants. "Yeah, I know. I told Quip of my intention to stick around and make Jopus Prime my home. He was pleased, but then I had to tell Harrison."

Patrik's eyes widened as his eyebrows rose. He had no idea that Kodiac was thinking of staying on Jopus.

Kodiac laughed at the expression on Patrik's face. "Yeah. That's kind of what Harrison looked like right before she started yelling at me."

"And?"

"And when it comes right down to it, she doesn't have much say in the matter. Just asked me if I knew what I was doing et cetera."

"And do you know?"

Kodiac looked into Patrik's hazel eyes, all traces of humor gone from his face. "Yes. I've made many friends in such a short amount of time, I'm happier here than I ever was at home. I really don't have any family back on Earth, so I think this is the best place for me to get on with my life."

Patrik nodded and a smile creased his lips. "As long as it isn't something you'll regret."

"I won't. So, anyway, after that, Quip put me with a regular squad from Jopus Prime to get everyone else used to me, and we've been away on missions. I've always just missed catching up with Barker. She left me a note about this mission or whatever she was going on with Janus and a few others. It was pretty lengthy." He paused and looked up at the man standing in front of him. "Any idea when they'll be back?"

Patrik shook his head and shrugged. "Janus said she had no idea. But I think if we don't hear anything soon, I'll start worrying." He did not share the feelings he had been picking up from Janus, which had ranged from the normal hum of activity to an aching terror the likes of which he had never experience via his friend.

He wondered what had happened to evoke such feelings in Janus, and the only answer his mind could supply was that something had happened to Barker.

Patrik knew that no one ever felt just one thing. It was never just pure fear or happiness, there was always something else, something smaller, in the background make-up of those emotions. When he was sensing Janus, it was usually a quietly seething anger and sadness, but this time it had been a general joy in life and friendly warmth, not like his friend at all, and therefore perhaps coming from someone else. From Barker. It made him wonder if maybe, instead of something happening to Barker, something had happened to Janus. Since Janus and Barker were so strongly connected, it seemed likely that Barker could experience an emotion that was strong enough for him to feel through Janus.

He groaned and rubbed his head as his thoughts got more convoluted. It was sometimes difficult enough with just him and Janus in his head, the last thing he needed to sort through was a third person's emotions. Regardless, Patrik had gone to Quip and reported that he thought the team was in big trouble.

Patrik set aside his thoughts as he heard his name and looked up at Kodiac whose brow was creased above the decidedly worried expression on his face. Patrik smiled sheepishly. "Sorry. I kind of got lost in my thoughts there."

"Yeah, I noticed. They looked pretty deep. Everything okay?"

Patrik drew a deep breath and blew it out in a sigh that ruffled the front of his hair. He met Kodiac's eyes. "I hope so."

~~*~*~*

Janus stirred and it brought Barker out of the light half-doze in which she had been floating. The blonde straightened and stretched out her neck as Janus's eyes slowly fluttered open, closed again, and then finally stayed open to meet her own. "'Ey."

Barker leaned forward and grinned. "Hey yourself. How are you feeling?"

Janus shifted and moved as if to sit up, but a light hand on her shoulder stopped her attempt. Janus raised an eyebrow in question.

"Just...stay still for a little longer, please?" Barker risked a glance at Janus's back, where her skin was still a livid, angry red and the large gash was still deep enough that sections of her spine were visible. "I don't want you hurting yourself more, all right?"

"Aye." Janus settled herself and her eyes simply stared up at the blonde, a small smile quirking her lips. "What 'as 'appened 'ere?"

Clearing her throat and settling herself more comfortably, Barker considered where to start. Finally, she just dove it at the beginning: her waking up in the dark tunnel with Samson, meeting up with the others, and finally being brought to their present location. She saw Janus's face shift from idle listening to attentive interest as her story shifted focus to the Zaire and their history. A little jolt ran through Janus when Barker related what the elder had said about the Scourge and their origin. Barker watched as Janus's eyes went quietly introspective for a long stretch of minutes until she finally looked up.

They didn't say anything, but Barker leaned a little closer and whispered quietly, "Are you sure you're all right? Warber said..." Her mind finished what she refused to say aloud: *that you were pretty bad there, for a while.*

Janus's mind shifted back to waking up and seeing all those little furry creatures and hearing their chanting, to feeling restraints come down on her back and arms, and the terror of the memory tore at her with a vengeance and caused her body to shake. But this time, her mind focused on Barker's very real and warm presence, and the almost tangible threads between them that were wrapping around her heart and pushing the horror of those years in her life back into their deep, dark cell and closing the door, at least temporarily.

Gregor walked in on them like that, with their arms wrapped around each other in a hug that looked absolutely perfect. They apparently didn't hear him and were far too engrossed in their own feelings to sense him. He took the minute to just look at them both, seeing the glow that paid testament to the very real, very strong connection between them. It was so bright and so obvious that Gregor felt as though he might be blinded if he didn't look away.

A kernel of awe blossomed in him as he compared what he was seeing to what he remembered of Janus's parents, and acknowledged that this was far stronger. Barlas and Maynus, Janus's father and mother, had been the strongest pairing that they had seen on their planet in centuries. Everyone, even the greatest skeptics, had been inspired and amazed by what even a blind man would have been able to see and feel just by being around them.

Gregor had to wonder just how strong Janus and Barker's connection would become over time. As they pulled apart, he stepped back out of the room and out of sight, counted to five under his breath, and walked back into the room.

The two women looked up at him and smiled in greeting.

"How are you, Janus?"

"I am fine."

Gregor nodded. "Good. Listen, I think we need to leave soon."

"Why?" Barker asked as she pulled her legs up to her chest. "What's wrong?"

"I don't know anything for sure, but I was with the elder and another person came up and said something. Everyone out there is running around pretty panicked."

Just then the patter of tiny, furred feet reached them and a yell from Warber summoned the rest of them into the main room. Janus carefully considered her back and sat up very slowly, satisfied to feel the pull of muscle along the cut. It was almost done healing.

Gregor pulled off his jacket and tossed it to Barker who nodded her thanks and carefully helped Janus to put it on. Not only would it help to keep the wound relatively clean, but Janus's shirt had been shredded almost to the point where it could no longer be called a shirt.

Janus carefully maneuvered her arms into the jacket and stood, walking gingerly to join the elder and their friends. The elder blinked and nodded at Janus. "I am pleased to see you are doing well. You all must leave. We will take you through the tunnels to your ship, but we must go now."

"What's going on?" Gregor asked.

"We just received word that the Scourge is mounting an attack against us. They believe we had a hand in taking down their mountain. We cannot hold them off, so we will die. It is best that you escape so that you may ultimately stop them."

A beeping broke the tension and everyone looked around in confusion before Warber finally pulled out his little rectangle and flipped it open, his brow furrowed. "Tryst?"

The woman on the screen grinned up at Warber. "How are you guys doing, Warber?"

"Um..." He looked around and shook his head. "All right, I guess. What the heck are you doing here?"

"Quip sent us. We're to ensure that you don't fly through any nebulae or asteroid belts on the way home. We got a little concerned, though, when we saw all the activity of the Ebokras."

Janus peered over Warber's shoulder at her friend, "Are ya 'ere with someone?"

"Yep. Captain Lang and the *Pro Re Nata*."

"'Ave ya been back ta Jopus Prime?"

"Nooo."

Janus felt her eyebrow inch up and a reckless grin shaped her lips as she turned to face the elder. "'Ow attached are ya ta this planet?"

The elder blinked owlishly and gave a tiny little shrug.

* ~ * ~ * ~ * ~ *

Janus was attempting to bend over and tie up her boots, but was finding the act incredibly difficult due to the wound on her back. As she tried again, a little growl issued from her throat.

Barker stepped into the room and moved quietly over to the frustrated woman, placing a placating hand on her head before kneeling and securing the worn, black leather boots.

Warber entered a moment later but stayed near to the door, waiting for Janus to speak. She had asked to see him.

"Warber, I want ya ta take Samson and go get Rijas and Corrin. I spoke ta the elder and someone will lead ya there. Come back 'ere as fast as possible."

"All right, Janus."

He ducked out the door and they heard his footsteps fade. Barker sat back on her heels and gave Janus's calf a little pat, then something else occurred to her. "Janus?"

"Aye."

"What about the third person who came here with Gregor? What happened to him?"

Janus was silent for a long moment and then drew in a deep breath. "'E is dead."

"How do you know?"

The dark-haired woman chewed on her lip for a few seconds of silence and wrinkled her nose. "I spoke ta 'im."

Barker blinked a few times as her mind scrambled around that statement, trying to make some sense of it. "You mean...in that place that..." She trailed off uncertainly, feeling totally out of her element.

"Aye. We call that place *vorash*."

Gregor, who had been standing outside the door listening, moved around the corner and into the room. Janus looked up and met his eyes and they shared a moment of understanding that only two people of her race could. To Barker, it was a frozen moment of time as the air between them rippled and vibrated with energy and then Gregor was gone again, as silently and quickly as he had appeared.

"What was that about?"

"Gregor is goin' ta find 'is body, ta bring it back."

Barker looked to the door and then back at Janus. "Isn't that kind of risky right now? We don't know where he is, and with the Ebokras about to attack—" Barker's objection ended abruptly when Janus placed a gentle finger on her lips.

"My people take death very seriously. It is one thing that everyone respects, along with the rituals that accompany it. No one of our people would dare defile what it means ta us, and it is Gregor's responsibility ta find 'im and bring 'im back." *So important that you never showed up for your parents' ceremonies, right.* Janus's mind mocked her with the jibe, and Janus accepted that out of her entire life, out of more than five centuries of living, missing both of their ceremonies was her greatest regret.

She shook off her thoughts and stood, offered her hand to Barker, and then proceeded into the main hall where everyone was waiting in tense silence. They had made the arrangements with Tryst and the elder was gathering his people.

It seemed like hours before Warber and Samson returned with Rijas and Corrin in tow. Then the elder ducked into the room and announced that all of the Zaire were ready. That left only Gregor to rejoin them. Janus waited as long as she dared, but when the ground started to shake and rumble and the roof started dropping little stones and particles of dust on them, she gave the order to move out.

The Zaire started out first, weaving through the tunnels to Warber's ship up on the surface. "What are they doing?" Barker asked as they assisted a family through the tunnel opening and into the main mine shafts.

Janus looked up at the ceiling that was shaking ominously. "They must 'ave some kind of...explosives or somethin'."

"Yeah, well," Barker ducked as a rock fell dangerously close to her, "we'd better hurry up because I'm not too fond of the idea of getting stuck in a cave in."

"Aye."

There was still no sign of Gregor. Samson had gone ahead with the first group of Zaire in case the Ebokras were swarming through the tunnels as well. Warber and Lucius were in the middle with Rijas and Corrin, which left Janus and Barker to act as the rear guard. Janus surveyed the area and saw that there were only about a dozen of the furred people left. "Come on, 'urry up!"

The last of the Zaire scurried through the opening and Janus ushered Barker through as another large piece of the roof started to fall. Janus managed to wriggle through just before they heard the resounding crash as a support beam came down, along with a ton of rock.

The two women came out the other side fully intact, if a little dusty, and they proceeded at a moderately slow jog. Janus felt the motion of it pulling on her back, but the pain was minimal and she easily blocked it from her mind. She could see they were catching up to Warber and Lucius, whose progress had been stopped by a blockade of rocks. Janus felt her heart sink.

Barker went over to help move the stony barrier and Janus hung back to watch their rear. She could hear them working frantically amid the increased sounds of explosions from above. The Ebokras were shifting their bombing, which meant they either knew someone had escaped or they simply weren't taking any chances. Still, she didn't like the fact that the enemy seemed to know exactly where the tunnels were.

It was another few minutes before Warber yelled the "all clear" and they started moving again, running a little faster, with more urgency. They were approaching another junction and Janus could easily see that the support beams were about to collapse. She stopped on one side and counted silently as the Zaire ran through. She was short four.

Janus turned and saw a family running desperately, stumbling along, two small children hanging on to their parents' arms. She turned back to the junction and saw the supports start to quiver. "Barker!" she yelled, and once she had the blonde's attention, looked back at the family.

Janus moved into the junction and braced her arms against the support beam as the ensign ran back and scooped the children up in her arms. Janus felt the weight shifting and settling against her arms, then the strain as her muscles took on the load. Barker went through and put the kids down, shot one worried glance at Janus's face, and then went back to retrieve the parents.

Janus blew out an unsteady breath as the rocks shifted again, and she felt the burden all the way down to shoulder joints that were starting to burn and itch. Rocks began to fall and she threw a fleeting look at her half. "Barker!" Janus yelled again as she felt her feet slip a little and the beam shift, pushing her body back into the rock wall which did nothing to help the wound on her back. She almost yelled out at the pain, felt sweat beading on her forehead as her arms started to shake. Her eyes were closed tight as her mind chanted over and over again: *I am not goin' ta drop this, I am not goin' ta drop this...*

She risked a glance at Barker, seeing that the woman's pathway was being impeded by the odd falling boulder. Janus sucked in a breath and continued her mantra, which faltered as the rocks shifted one last time.

Then someone was there, pushing against her and taking the weight from her arms. Janus cracked her eyes open to see Gregor's tense face, and she gladly stepped out of the junction and leaned against the wall. A few seconds later, Barker was through, into the next section and setting the parents down as Gregor heaved off against the rocks and stepped out of the crossway, watching them fall and quite effectively block the tunnel.

Gregor sat down and carefully ordered the limbs of the body he had haphazardly placed on the ground in his desperate attempt to relieve Janus's burden. He ran a shaking hand across his face, then gave a slight smile.

Janus nodded and straightened. "We must go. It is not safe 'ere."

As if to punctuate her point, the ceiling rumbled, and they started off again. It was easy going and soon the remaining Zaire started chittering and pointing at a small, almost invisible tunnel. They led the way through and after minutes of pitch blackness, Barker was relieved to see sunlight at the other end. They emerged just outside the clearing in which Warber had landed his ship and they all moved quickly toward it.

It was uncloaked and waiting for them, and they filed on gratefully. Warber was already at the helm and took off as soon as Janus signaled that everyone was safely on board. As they zoomed up toward the stratosphere, Lucius looked out the window and saw a mob of Ebokras scurrying around on the surface in a mad frenzy. He blew out a relieved breath and slid down the wall.

~~*~*~*

Tryst tapped the screen as it beeped. She nodded and then queued up a channel with Lang. "All right, Captain, you have a go."

Captain Lang nodded grimly and gave the order to his tactical officer, who acknowledged and pressed a few controls. They waited and counted under their breath, and soon Warber's ship was beside theirs, poised in space to bear witness to the impending event.

Lang reached twenty and then, before their eyes, the planet started to vibrate and collapse into itself, which was followed by an explosion that reflected back on their faces, casting them in shadows, and caused a shock wave that just barely reached their ships.

There was a long, intense silence, in which even the stars held their breath as the universe shifted and rearranged itself in the wake of the massive destruction.

Lang swallowed and cleared his throat. "Let's go home."

~~*~*~*

Barker dabbed at a wicked gash that snaked along her forearm, wincing slightly at the sting of the disinfectant. She blew out a breath and looked around the small but functional medical bay on Warber's ship. They were all assembled there, each of them on their own bed and tending to their various cuts and scrapes, some serious and some not. She was surprised to note that Samson probably had it the worst, as he was sitting with his shirt off and contorting his upper body to reach his more severe injuries.

Perched on the bed beside her, Janus was lightly kicking the bed with her legs, once again in peak physical condition. Once they had gotten out of the tunnels, it hadn't taken long for her body to absorb the energy necessary to heal. In fact, when they had gotten to the medical bay and Janus had pulled off the jacket that Gregor had loaned her, Barker had seen Janus's skin stretching itself to close the very thin line that was all that was left of her grievous wound. It was eerie in a way, but she was glad to see that Janus was in full working order. Rijas was now also walking around, looking much like he had when he had first arrived on the planet. The ensign spared a brief wishful thought that with the appearance of her own silver coloured markings, she had also inherited the capacity for almost instantaneous healing.

They had shuttled some of the Zaire over to the other ships, Warber's being unable to accommodate the entire population for the voyage back to Jopus. They were understandably worried about what the future held for them. The final outcome remained to be seen over the next few weeks, but with the destruction of the Ebokras' home planet and ultimately the very origin of their species, it seemed that the war with the Ebokras could be coming to an end very soon.

Barker knew Quip'lee and the forces of Jopus Prime had been making strides against the Ebokras, and with the entrance of Janus's people into the war, she had a sense that the tide would be turning very rapidly. That left a few things weighing on her mind, chiefly – what would happen next.

She had absolutely no inclination to return to Earth under Captain Harrison and had no reason to doubt that Quip would welcome her to Jopus Prime with open arms. That wasn't what was causing her concern. What was bothering her was her relationship with Janus. They were thoroughly involved, she knew that much. What she didn't know was what Janus would do next and how she figured into it, if at all. As she understood it, Janus's shipboard home for the last decade or so had been destroyed by the Ebokras. All Barker knew was that she and Janus would need to have a conversation in the very near future.

Barker was shaken from her thoughts by a warm hand on her arm that tugged gently but insistently. She looked up into blue eyes that stared back with a sure knowledge.

"Come. Ya look beat."

She followed Janus and soon found herself in a snug little room where she luxuriated in the sight of a very soft, very clean bed. She looked down at herself and decided that a shower was a must. It wasn't long before she was clean and prepared to climb into the inviting bed. Janus joined her a few minutes later, and Barker happily wrapped herself around the long body and planted a soft kiss on Janus's lips before she allowed herself to be carried off into sleep.

~~*~*~*

Quip'lee shuffled his feet as he stood anxiously in the hallway waiting for the ships to dock. He had been surprised and then indescribably happy when he got word that Tryst and Captain Lang on the *Pro Re Nata*, and Warber's ship were all inbound with everyone accounted for. They were also bringing a few extra guests.

While he was overjoyed that Janus and the others had returned safely, he felt a twinge of shame upon acknowledging that he was just as anxious to hear what had happened, whether they had been successful in destroying the home base of their foe. He suspected they had because the other forces had begun to win their battles more easily, with far fewer reinforcements coming to the aid of the Ebokras. With help from Janus's people, they had quite literally sent the enemy running into the next star system. The Ebokras were in retreat, and victory was so close Quip could taste it.

At last the hatch opened and Tryst stepped out first, followed by numerous small, furry creatures that stumbled by with odd chittering sounds that Quip could not interpret. Next came Captain Lang, who gave Quip a tired smile and promised that a full report would be on his desk the next morning. Finally, Janus and her team came out, followed by more of the furry creatures.

Janus greeted Quip with a firm handshake and an oddly satisfied smile. That told him everything he needed to know. "You did it."

"Aye. These are Zaire, friends. We need ta find a new 'ome for them; they were the indigenous people of the planet."

"No problem. I think I might have a place in mind. Is there anyone here I can talk to?" Quip asked.

"I believe that would be me."

Quip looked around and then down to see the elder looking up at him with large yellow eyes. "All right then. We'll provide any assistance we can in finding your people a suitable place to live. In the meantime, there are rooms here in which you can stay." Quip signaled a young woman, who trotted over. "Nemia will show you."

The woman smiled and led the odd little creature down the hall with the rest of the Zaire following.

Quip looked at Janus and pursed his lips. "I trust you didn't detour through any nebulae?"

"We did not."

"Good, good. I want you all to be checked out by Omelian'par, and then we'll have a debriefing later this afternoon."

"Aye."

He nodded and spared a smile for Barker, who was standing at Janus's shoulder, before he turned and headed back to his office.

The examination in Omelian'par's office was relatively simple as no one had anything serious to worry about. He ran extensive scans to detect any viruses that they might have picked up as foreseen by Emmeline. They were clean.

After they had been cleared, Barker suggested a trip to the cafeteria. She was looking forward to sitting down and enjoying a good meal.

"Ya go. I want ta see Patrik."

"Sure, Janus. I'll meet you there."

"Aye."

Janus located her friend in his quarters and was greeted with a large grin and a brief but heartfelt hug. He stepped back and just stared at her for a long time before sitting at the table and motioning her to do the same. "So, how about you tell me what happened that sent me such strong negative vibes that I got anxious enough to go to Quip with my concerns."

She ducked her head for a minute, seemingly gathering her thoughts, and to his surprise, started relating the tale from the beginning. Patrik listened with rapt attention, aware that she was, as usual, leaving out details, but managing to follow the narrative. He felt his heart clench painfully in his chest when Janus reached the part about her near-drowning in the lake; he could hear the strain in her voice. Getting that close to death wasn't something that Janus and her people typically had to deal with, and he had an idea of how traumatic it could be. The aftermath of the earthquake sent his heart pounding, as did that last sinkhole that had opened and sucked them all into the world of the furry little people who called themselves the Zaire.

"Wait, wait." He held up a hand and looked incredulously at Janus. "You mean to tell me that those...bastards we've been fighting actually came from some sweet, cute little farming people?"

"Aye."

Patrik blinked a few times and nibbled his lip. "Well, they always say it's the short ones who are vicious." He glanced up to see Janus looking at him with a raised eyebrow and he dropped his eyes, chuckling. "Sorry. Continue."

Quietly, haltingly, Janus wrapped up her story, relating how Tryst had contacted them, and that Captain Lang of the *Pro Re Nata* still had aboard his ship the experimental weapon that had been given to him for the original attack on the Ebokran mothership. It had never been used and had still been, amazingly enough, intact and ready to be fired when they'd needed it the most.

Patrik sat back and blew out a breath as he envisioned the destruction of an entire planet. "Whoa!" He rubbed his face and just absorbed everything Janus had told him. "So, the Ebokras are gone?"

Janus pursed her lips and mulled that over. "I think so. That was their planet, their 'ome. What created them no longer exists. With time," she nodded and sat back in her chair, "I believe they will cease to exist."

The silence stretched between them as the minutes ticked by, both of them comfortable. At length, Janus leaned forward and placed her elbows on the table. "What is it?"

He looked up in surprise, then remembered who he was sitting with. He had never been able to keep anything serious from Janus for long. "I've been talking with Emmeline. We've decided that...after this war is over...we want to go to Earth, maybe see if we really do have family there."

Janus blinked as her mind recollected the information that Barker and Kodiac had uncovered: that her people had taken a select few from Earth to colonize other planets, and that the family name Patrik had been on the list. And that Doctor Tina Cobb from the *USC Avenger* had confirmed Patrik's connection through DNA sampling. She tilted her head and smiled. "I think that would be good for ya both."

"What about you? And Barker?"

Her eyes flicked around the room and Janus sighed. It was something she had considered, however briefly. "I can not stay 'ere much longer. I need ta move around, be places, do things. I will talk ta Barker, see what she wants. Perhaps we will...go places tagether."

Patrik thought it was a vague answer, but that was the norm for his friend. He was happy that Janus at least planned to speak to Barker and make it a joint decision. Patrik felt confident that the blonde ensign wouldn't have a problem setting out in a ship with Janus.

Epilogue

"All right, next issue on the table: Zaire." Quip looked at the people assembled around his conference table and shook his head at what had happened to the small furry race. They had just finished relating their story, and Quip couldn't get some of the images their narrative had created out of his head.

Gregor was the first to speak. "There is a planet near our own that is uninhabited. It has plentiful resources, good farmland, and the Zaire wouldn't have to worry about unexpected visitors. No one would bother them if they wished it that way. If they wanted to have contact with others, we would be more than happy to trade with them." He smiled as he finished and turned to look at the elder who was perched on a chair and looking at them all with large, unblinking, yellow eyes.

Finally, he nodded, and his beak once again gave the impression of smiling.

Quip clapped his hands together and stood. "Wonderful. We'll start getting you folks over there in a couple of days if everything calms down. Dismissed." The assemblage stood and filed out of the room.

Janus paused in the hall with Barker until Gregor stepped out. "Are ya goin' 'ome soon?"

They started to walk slowly down the hall as Gregor considered the question, then replied, "I think we will stick around here for a little longer, just to make sure everything works out for Quip, then we'll probably head home. Nulas will be in need of some good advice by then, I think." Gregor grinned.

"Aye."

He stopped and turned to face them both, his eyes flickering between them. "What about you two?"

Janus looked down at Barker who stared back up at Janus, then their eyes shifted as one to focus on Gregor's face. They shrugged in tandem.

Gregor started laughing and slapped Janus on the shoulder, nodded at Barker, and then turned and walked away down the hall.

The two women stood in silence for a long time, just watching him. Barker finally turned to look at the woman standing beside her and raised an eyebrow. "He has a point, you know. We don't have any idea what we're going to do." The blonde felt her heart race as she opened herself to the possibility that Janus would leave her.

Janus seemed to be contemplating the hallway and then turned her head and stated quietly, "I was 'opin' that ya would come with me."

Barker felt herself blink a few times as her mind, which had been prepared for the worst, scrambled around in an attempt to absorb the simple statement. A warm hand on her cheek didn't help her thought process and so she found herself just gazing up into blue eyes that were so close. "Oh," she heard herself whisper.

"Barker?"

Janus's voice was deep and rumbled all the way down her spine. It made her shiver. Another hand landed on her stomach and standing that close, so in contact with Janus, the threads that tied them together were pulled taut, transmitting an endless floodtide of emotion, of love.

Barker closed her eyes and her head flopped forward onto Janus's chest as she wrapped her arms around the taller woman's waist. "All right...I get the picture," she mumbled as Janus returned the hug, which was warm and all encompassing. The ensign pulled back and looked up with a smile. "You're dangerous when you don't say anything, you know that?"

Janus simply smirked and ducked her head, capturing her half's lips in a kiss full of promise.

~~*~*~*

Captain Harrison of the *USC Avenger* looked around her office with a degree of satisfaction. It had been a week since Janus and her team had destroyed the Ebokras' home planet and the war had gone from being a vicious bloodbath to a few minor skirmishes every few days. Which Quip'lee and the forces of Jopus Prime could handle quite well on their own. The *Avenger* was in good shape, as was her crew. She had lost four people, and only three of those to the actual war. It was time to go home, back to Earth. They had been missing for more than a month and Harrison could only imagine what the people back there thought.

Kodiac had taken her unawares with his declaration that he was staying behind, and that had caused her to lose her temper. But being honest, Harrison admitted to herself that she was surprised no other crew members had made the same decision. She knew how addictive Jopus Prime was, how peaceful and serene. How fast you could fall in love with it. Harrison was happy that no one else had decided to stay, since it usually didn't look good for a captain to lose half her crew, even if it wasn't in combat.

Maybe, maybe she'd come back one day to visit. Quip'lee had said that they would always be welcome, and despite the unpleasantness that stemmed from the fact that she was Coalition, she had been able to relax there. Perhaps she would be able to wipe out some of the Coalition's bad reputation in that quadrant, and maybe that would one day lead to Earth opening new trade routes to these obviously well developed planets.

Captain Harrison felt her brow pucker as her door indicated that someone was requesting permission to enter. "Come." She sat down on the corner of her desk when Barker stepped through the hatchway. Harrison knew instantly what was coming when the ensign stopped and shuffled her feet uncertainly.

"I'm not going back with you."

Harrison sat as still as a statue. Ensign Barker had always been a fine addition to the crew and had served well. Although Harrison by no means considered their relationship to be a friendship, she had always felt that there was a mutual respect between them. Which had started to slip as soon as they had met Janus.

Janus. She was the real issue. Harrison hadn't liked the woman from the start, and it had been painfully apparent that Barker had been fascinated by her. The captain stared at the uneasily shifting woman and finally, realizing she was making Barker uncomfortable, cleared her throat and stood. "All right."

Barker's eyes widened as she stopped fidgeting and looked at her now former captain. "That's it? Just, all right?"

Harrison nodded. "I've already done this with Kodiac and I blew up at him." She paused and wrestled with herself before continuing. "You're staying because of Janus, aren't you?"

Barker's head tilted as she considered her answer, "Partly. I was thinking about it before Janus and I got involved. She was the deciding factor." The blonde ensign looked into Harrison's eyes. "It was the easiest decision of my life."

Harrison accepted that and stepped forward, her hand extended.

Barker clasped it and nodded. She turned to go but stopped as Harrison spoke.

"Is she out there?"

"Yes."

"Could you ask her to come in, please?"

Barker nodded and stepped out of the office. A few seconds later, Janus's unmistakable form slipped through the door and stood easily in front of the captain.

Harrison took in a deep breath and rubbed the back of her neck. "Listen, I know we haven't had the best relationship. I jumped to conclusions and said some things I...probably shouldn't have. But you still helped to save my life and the lives of my crew, and for that I am grateful." Harrison stepped closer and held out her forearm, which Janus grasped, and held, for a long time. The captain looked up into those vivid eyes and smiled. "Take care of her."

Janus allowed herself a grin and she ducked her head. "Aye, Captain." Then, she was gone.

* ~ * ~ * ~ * ~ *

Barker stuffed the last item into her duffle bag and looked around the small room that had been her home on the *Avenger* for six years. Despite knowing in her heart that going with Janus and facing whatever was out there was the best thing for her, she felt a pang of melancholy. This single choice had the capacity to change her life in ways that she couldn't even begin to imagine. The blonde looked down at her hands and gently traced the silver designs there, a slight smile creasing her face. Just look at what knowing Janus had already done for her. She wasn't even sure if a doctor would still classify her as human.

The soon to be ex-ensign took one last look around her room and nodded, hoisted her bag onto her shoulder, and stepped out through the whooshing door and into the still hallway. She was almost to the airlock when the echo of footsteps caused her to turn, and she smiled when she spotted Kodiac moving towards her. "Hey, bud."

He grinned as they fell into step. "Hey. I see you've got yourself packed up."

"Yep. All my worldly possessions." She looked at the little box he was carrying and raised an eyebrow. "I thought you already had your stuff?"

"Oh, these are just little trinkets and things that I got a sudden urge to keep."

"Hmm." They continued to walk in comfortable silence until they entered the halls of Jopus Prime where they stopped and turned to look out a window at the *Avenger* that was making final preparations to leave. Most, if not all, of the crew were on board and they were likely carrying out last minute checks to ensure that the large ship would make it home without any problems.

Barker's thoughts drifted...to Rita Donahue, the friendly, brilliant engineer whose life she had saved, and Tina Cobb who had always been a friend and someone she felt comfortable talking to. She felt tears in her eyes and then two warm and very solid arms wrapped around her from behind and she knew, without even thinking about it, that it was Janus. And then a low voice whispered in her ear.

"Ya know ya can always go back."

She turned to look up at the planed face above her and smiled. "Only for a visit. I know where I belong." She patted the strong arms encircling her and felt a squeeze of acknowledgment. Barker felt Janus's chin rest on her shoulder, and then movement out of the corner of her eye caused her to turn slightly. Samson was standing there, a bag at his feet, looking at them with no small degree of uncertainty. Janus turned as well and Barker took a step away as she sensed that he wasn't there to say anything to her.

The two former adversaries just looked at each other for a long, long moment and then Samson ducked his head briefly and extended his arm, which Janus looked at and then clasped. He met her eyes then and a small smile quirked the corner of his mouth. Janus seemed to understand, they seemed to understand each other, and she nodded and released his arm.

He crouched to pick up his bag and turned to board the ship, paused and looked at Barker, nodded once, and then continued on his way. She watched him go with a wrinkled brow and turned back to the window, Janus behind her. Barker looked up at Janus's face as the taller woman continued to gaze out the window with a small smile. "What was that all about?"

"'E was just sayin' good-bye."

Barker's eyes flicked to the ship and then back up to Janus. "Oookkay." She supposed it was one of those things that she wouldn't ever understand. But Janus had and Samson...well, he was Samson. Barker put a cap on her thoughts and watched as the *Avenger* pulled away from Jopus Prime and zoomed off into the distance, disappearing into subspace in no time at all. She released a sigh and turned to face Janus. "So, when are we leaving?"

"Whenever ya are ready."

"All right. I'm ready." They were going with Gregor and the Zaire to see them settled into their new home and after that, she supposed, they would just play it by ear. Barker turned to Kodiac and stepped forward to be wrapped up in a huge hug and have the breath squeezed from her lungs. "I'll miss you, bud."

"Me too, Barker. But you're going to do great things. I know it."

She pulled back and smiled up into his face and patted his cheek. "That's just your imagination." She grinned, then turned suddenly serious. "Stay safe, you hear me?"

"I will, Barker. I promise."

"Good."

Kodiac threw a brief glance behind his friend to where Janus was waiting, leaning casually against the wall, then put his hands on Barker's shoulders and leaned a little closer. "I told you, didn't I? About your crush?" He grinned as she chuckled and punched him in the arm.

"You did." Barker turned to look at Janus. Turning back to Kodiac, she smiled and looked him in the eye. "But it's so much more than a crush."

"I know, my friend. And if I may say – love suits you both."

Janus watched as Barker spoke with Kodiac and felt a little surge of worry. She couldn't help wondering if it was right to take Barker from everything she knew...everyone she knew. Janus sighed as her heart tapped her mind on the shoulder and quite practically pointed out that Barker had made the decision herself, with little prodding from Janus aside from the initial invitation. She turned as she spotted Tryst approaching and spared a smile for her friend. "Tryst."

"Hey. You guys leaving soon?"

"Aye."

"Yeah, us too. We're all leaving together, but amazingly enough, Quip managed to extract trade promises from all of us."

Janus laughed at the look of befuddlement on Tryst's face. "'E is a politician."

Tryst grunted and scowled. "Must be his way of keeping us all in touch. Although I wouldn't mind seeing everyone more often. It gets a little lonely sometimes where we are. I know that Karton and Warber feel the same."

"And Evril?"

Tryst smiled and snorted. "He's Evril. Would rather be in a lab than around people. But he agreed, too." She nodded and smiled.

Janus shifted her focus as she saw Barker approaching with Kodiac in tow. Tryst turned to the blonde and extended a hand, which Barker shook with a smile. "Barker," Tryst said, "it was very nice to meet you. And you'd better keep on eye on this one." She jerked her head at Janus. "She has a habit of finding trouble."

Barked smiled. "I will, don't worry."

Tryst smiled back and turned to Janus. "And you, don't be a stranger."

"I will not. Take care." Janus pulled Tryst into a brief hug, which the startled woman returned after a moment of surprise.

"I'll see you around, Janus."

"Aye."

Tryst turned then and left at a leisurely pace that took her quickly out of sight.

As Janus turned back toward her, Barker smiled. "I'm ready now."

Kodiac nodded at Janus. "It was interesting meeting you. Make sure you both stop by regularly."

"Aye." She returned his nod and then the two women started down the hall to a further docking bay where Gregor was waiting with the Zaire. They were taking one of Quip's ships which would drop them all off on the planet. Gregor had made arrangements with Nulas for a ship to be waiting to take him, Rijas, and Corrin back home.

Something occurred to Barker. "Janus?"

"Aye?"

"How are we going to get off the planet?"

For an answer, Janus only smiled.

* ~ * ~ * ~ * ~ *

The planet was large and had more than a modest supply of resources that would help the Zaire to get back on their feet. Janus, Barker, and the elder were standing on a grassy hill overlooking the valley in which the small beings had chosen to start their settlement.

"It is wonderful. My people and I thank you," the elder said as he turned to Janus and Barker.

Janus knelt so they were face to face, "Ya will be safe 'ere, ta live 'ow ya choose. If ya 'ave any problems, my people will always be there ta 'elp."

The elder ducked his head and released a low chitter of gratitude before looking up again to meet Janus's eyes. His gaze flicked between Janus and Barker and he placed his hand over his heart. "We thank you. It is because of you both, and the others, of course, that the Zaire are once again a people of the land. We no longer have to hide among the shadows in fear; you all have delivered us. For this, you will most assuredly be remembered as an event of eminence in our long history. I believe we will call you The Restorers." He nodded and smiled. "Yes, that is quite appropriate."

Janus looked up at Barker, who was smiling though there were tears in her eyes. Janus turned back to the elder and ducked her head. "Thank ya."

He extended his hand, which Janus gingerly grasped with her fingertips as she was met with very serious and wise yellow eyes. "It is us who should thank you. You have done this great thing for us, as you have done for many others, as you will continue to do." He looked up at Barker who was kneeling beside Janus and he smiled. "Together...together you are destined for amazing things." The elder fell silent and just looked at them both with knowing eyes before he released Janus's hand and pattered down the hill to join his people.

Barker let out the breath she had been holding and turned her head to look at Janus. They stared at each other in silence for a long minute before Janus stood and pulled Barker to her feet. Hand in hand, the two descended the hill toward the clearing where Gregor awaited them, according to Janus's instructions.

When they stepped through the trees, Barker stopped and just stared. In front of them was a sleek, medium sized ship, the side of which was emblazoned with the distinctive diamond design that was etched into both her and Janus's skin. A grin on his face, Gregor was standing next to the hatch beside another man, who seemed oddly familiar.

The second man strode forward and stopped in front of Janus, who was numb with amazement.

"Nulas."

Barker felt her eyebrow creep up. *Janus's brother.*

Nulas smiled. "Janus. I had to see you before you went off. And this..." He turned to look at the ship. "I know it isn't what you had in mind, but Father wanted you to have it. In fact, by law it is yours."

Janus blinked at the vessel that had been her father's, that she remembered traveling on as a small child and also as she got older. Not only was it well equipped, but it was built for the family of a diplomat family, and only the family of a diplomat – which meant one person could easily crew it by themselves. She and Barker wouldn't have a problem.

She took in the diamond design on the sides and knew that it would help to keep bandits away. Even though her people had become quite insular, her father had done some very good work and was both feared and respected for the power he commanded. The symbol of his lineage would not have faded from the memories of the people.

Finally she looked back to Nulas, who was watching her with a hopeful smile. "Thank you, Nulas."

They fell into a long hug that went on forever. When the siblings separated, Nulas had a few tears in his eyes, which he quickly wiped away as he cleared his throat and smiled again. "Do you think you will ever come home?"

"I do not know. If ya need me, though, I will come."

He nodded and turned to look at Barker. As the two women had entered the clearing, it had been obvious to Nulas that they were bonded and it had, he was surprised to admit, made him feel good...and maybe a little bit envious. "You have found your half."

Janus grinned and motioned Barker over. "I 'ave." Barker trotted up and Janus wrapped her arm around the blonde's shoulders. "Barker, this is my brother, Nulas."

She acknowledged the introduction with a smile and extended her hand, which he shook with a return smile. "It's very nice to meet you, Nulas."

"And you." Gregor cleared his throat, and Nulas turned to his adjutant, who made a hand signal. "I hate to cut this short, but I need to get going. We have to speak with the Zaire, and then I must get back home. Things are still a little unstable there."

"Aye, Nulas. Ya go do what ya 'ave ta."

Janus returned Gregor's wave of farewell and watched as her brother left the clearing, then she turned to study the ship that was just as she remembered. "Come, let me show ya our new 'ome."

As they paused just outside the airlock, Barker rubbed the metal beside the door to reveal the faint but still legible writing. "Janus, what's this?"

"It is what my father named the ship...after some old stories of my people."

"*Amicus Humani Generis*. What's it mean?" She looked up at Janus, who smiled just a little and had a twinkle in her eye.

"Friend of the 'uman race." She boarded the ship and, after she got over the surprise, Barker followed.

"Are you serious?"

"Aye."

"Janus—"

Janus stepped forward and placed her fingers on Barker's moving lips. "Do not worry about the name. Ya 'ave a whole lifetime ta study its implications."

Then she replaced her fingers with her lips and Barker found herself forgetting all about the name and what it meant. Janus was right, after all: she had a lifetime; *they* had a lifetime.

And an entire universe to explore.

SB Zarben is a university student who lives in Alberta, Canada. She is a quiet, often reserved person unless in the company of close friends. SB enjoys various types of computer and video games as well as a multitude of different television programs. She loves animals, thunderstorms, and chocolate and hopes to one day travel throughout Europe.

Printed in the United States
91988LV00010B/161/A